Dilly Court

The Summer Maiden

HarperCollins*Publishers*

HarperCollins*Publishers* Ltd
1 London Bridge Street,
London SE1 9GF

www.harpercollins.co.uk

First published by HarperCollins*Publishers* 2018
1

A catalogue record for this book is available from the British Library

ISBN: 978-0-00-819963-0 (HB)
ISBN: 978-0-00-819964-7 (PB b-format)

This novel is entirely a work of fiction.
The names, characters and incidents portrayed in it are
the work of the author's imagination. Any resemblance to
actual persons, living or dead, events or localities is
entirely coincidental.

Set in Sabon Lt Std by Palimpsest Book Production Limited,
Falkirk, Stirlingshire

Printed and bound in Great Britain by
CPI Group (UK) Ltd, Croydon CR0 4YY

MIX
Paper from
responsible sources
FSC™ C007454

This book is produced from independently certified FSC™ paper
to ensure responsible forest management.

For more information visit: **www.harpercollins.co.uk/green**

The Summer Maiden

Dilly Court is a *Sunday Times* bestselling author of over thirty novels. She grew up in North East London and began her career in television, writing scripts for commercials. She is married with two grown-up children and four grand-children, and now lives in Dorset on the beautiful Jurassic Coast with her husband.

To find out more about Dilly, please visit her Facebook page, or sign up to Dilly's newsletter at www.dillycourt.com

f /DillyCourtAuthor

For Lottie Atchison,
my second great-niece, with love

Chapter One

Wapping, London, Summer 1873

Caroline Manning stood a little apart from the rest of the mourners who were preparing to walk away from her father's grave. The interment was over, the last words of farewell to a good man had been said, and his widow, Esther, had dropped a crimson rose onto the coffin. Her face was hidden behind the dark veil of widow's weeds, but Caroline sensed that her mother was crying. Tears stung her own eyes, but she was determined to be brave. She had loved her father dearly, but she knew that Papa would have wanted her to support the rest of the family and help her mother through the trauma of such a great loss. Max and James, her younger brothers, had been away at boarding school when their father had fallen ill and died, and Esther had travelled to

Rugby with Sadie, her friend and companion, to bring them home. The boys had been brave throughout the interment, but Jimmy had broken down and sobbed when the first handful of earth fell on the coffin, and he was clinging to their mother, who was now weeping openly. Caroline could see that fourteen-year-old Max was struggling and she placed her arm around his shoulders.

'Papa didn't suffer, Max. He just slipped away, so Mama told me.'

Max dashed his hand across his eyes. 'Yes, that's what she said, but I'm going to miss him.'

'We all are.' Caroline gave him a comforting hug. 'We'd best follow the others, Max. We have to get the train back to London.'

'We're going now, Carrie, dear.' Esther braced her slender shoulders and led Jimmy away from the yawning chasm of Jack Manning's last resting place.

'I won't be long.'

'The train will be here soon,' Sadie said firmly. 'Come on, Carrie, love. Best foot forward.'

'I said I won't be long.' Caroline could not help a note of impatience creeping into her voice. She had so far kept herself composed, but she was in danger of losing the cast-iron self-control that had helped her to get through the carriage ride from their home in Finsbury Circus to Waterloo Bridge Station, and the journey on the Necropolis Railway to Brookwood Cemetery. Mama had her standards and would not travel any other way than first class, even though Aunt Sadie was quite happy to use the omnibus and had even braved the Metropolitan Railway, which ran underground.

'Come with me, Max. We'll let Carrie have a minute to herself.' Sadie beckoned to Max and he allowed her to take him by the hand, something that he would never have done normally.

At any other time Caroline might have smiled to see her usually strong-willed brother acting so meekly, but this was not a normal day. Sadie was no relation, but she had been with the family ever since Caroline could remember, and had become a surrogate aunt with an enduring place in their affections.

The distant sound of a train's whistle jolted Caroline back to the present and she raised the tea rose to her lips, inhaling the delicate perfume before allowing it to flutter through the air, landing on the coffin with a gentle thud. Papa had loved tea roses and she had picked several from the garden with the morning dew still upon them, choosing the biggest and the best to bring with her on Papa's last, sad journey. She wiped her eyes and took a deep breath, raising her face to the cloudless azure sky. She wondered if Papa and her two baby brothers, who had been taken by whooping cough, were looking down on her, but that was childish and, at seventeen years old, she knew better.

She picked up her black silk skirts and trudged across the scorched grass as she followed her family to the station platform. It was a fiery June day and the ground beneath her feet was baked hard. The return train journey promised to be hot and sticky and less than cheerful, and she had a sudden urge to cry out that it was not fair. Papa had been in his mid-forties when he contracted pneumonia during a business trip to the Continent. Her last sight of him had been when she had waved him off, thinking that he would return soon with news of a profitable deal. Caroline bit the inside of her lip to prevent herself from bursting into tears as she caught up with her mother, Sadie and the boys.

'Are you all right?' Sadie whispered.

'Yes, of course.' It was a lie, but Caroline held her head high as she took her mother's mittened hand in hers. 'We'll be home soon, Mama.'

'Home.' Esther's voice was harsh and thick with tears. 'There is no future for me without Jack. My heart is broken and buried with him in that cold grave.'

Sadie sighed and shook her head. 'It's a sad time, but you'll feel better when you've had a cup of tea and something to eat.'

'Stop being so cheerful,' Esther said wearily. 'Leave me alone.' She broke away from Caroline's restraining hand and marched towards the station platform.

'When Mama cries it makes me sad, too,' Jimmy said, sniffing.

'It's all right to cry, Jimmy.' Max slapped his brother on the shoulder. 'Just don't let them see you're sad when we go back to school.'

'Come on, boys,' Sadie said briskly. 'We'd better get a move on, or we'll be left behind.' She quickened her pace, the others falling into step beside her.

The rest of the mourners, most of whom were employees of the Manning and Chapman Shipping Company, travelled second class, but Esther and the family had a first-class carriage to themselves.

'If only your Uncle George were here.' Esther leaned back in her seat. 'I don't know if he received the cable I sent to the agent in New York, as there was no reply.'

'He'll be as upset as you are, Essie.' Sadie turned her head away to stare out of the window. 'It seems your family are only happy when they are sailing the seven seas.'

'*Our* family.' Esther took off her gloves and laid them on the seat beside her. 'How many times do I have to stress that you're as important to me as if we were related by blood?'

'I know you believe that, Essie, but that doesn't make it true.' Sadie shot her a sideways glance. 'Jack wouldn't want you to wear yourself out with grief. He was a good man, and you're a strong woman. You've seen hard times and you'll come through this, as always.'

'Yes, but I'm allowed to mourn in my own way.' Esther brushed a tear from her cheek and her lips trembled ominously. 'Besides which, I thought that Alice might have taken the trouble to attend the funeral.'

'You know she sent her apologies,' Sadie said

sternly. 'Sir Henry is taking part in an important debate in the Commons, and Lady Bearwood wanted to be there to support him.'

'I know. I'm being unreasonable. It's all too much. If Jack had remained in London he would still be alive today.'

Caroline glanced anxiously at her brothers, but Jimmy had fallen asleep in the corner seat and Max was gazing out of the window, seemingly in a world of his own. She moved closer to Sadie, lowering her voice to a whisper. 'What's going on, Aunt Sadie? I know that Mama is heartbroken, but there's more, isn't there? I'm not a child; I need to know.'

Sadie inclined her head so that the brims of their black bonnets were almost touching. 'It's business, Carrie. I don't know the ins and outs, but the loss of the *Mary Louise* was a blow, and between you and me, I don't think it was insured.'

'That was nearly a year ago,' Caroline said, frowning.

'That's right. All were lost as well as the cargo.'

'I'm grieving, but I'm not deaf.' Esther folded back her veil. Even in her tear-stained and emotional state, she was still a handsome woman. At thirty-nine she had kept her figure and her skin was smooth with only a few laughter lines crinkling the corners of her hazel eyes, and the hint of silver in her dark hair did nothing to detract from her good looks. 'If you have questions, ask me, Caroline. Don't mutter behind my back.'

Sadie leaned over to pat Esther's clasped hands. 'I'm sorry, but you shouldn't bottle it all up, Essie. We're here to help you, and Carrie and the boys have lost their pa.'

Esther's eyes swam with unshed tears. 'I know, and I'm trying to keep the worst from them. As if it isn't bad enough to lose the husband and father that we love, it seems inevitable that we will lose our home as well.'

'Surely it can't be that bad, Mama?' Caroline said dazedly. 'We've always been well off.'

'What happened to the fortune that you brought home from the goldfields in Australia?' Sadie asked, frowning. 'You must still have your investments, and the business seemed to be going well.'

'That's all you know.' Esther's full lips tightened into a pencil-thin line. 'Jack did his best to keep it from us, and I've only just discovered the true state of affairs. My brother must have known that the business was in a bad way when he sailed off for the Americas, but he didn't think to confide in me. It was only when I went to the office and demanded to see the books that I discovered the parlous state of our finances. George should have said something before he went away.'

'That's not fair, Essie,' Sadie protested angrily. 'George was only doing his job. When he's offloaded the cargo he'll find another one to bring home, doubling the profit. You know as well as I do that that's how it goes in business.'

Esther held up her hand, tears seeping between her closed eyelids. 'Please, that's enough. I don't want to hear any more. Just leave me alone. My head is pounding.'

Caroline sat back in her seat, staring out of the window at the sun-drenched fields and hedgerows as they flashed past. Dog roses, buttercups and dandelions made bright splashes of colour against the dark green of hawthorn leaves and the pale gold of ripening cornfields. Cows grazed on patches of grass beneath shady trees and woolly white sheep clustered together on the hillsides. It was all so serene and peaceful, but Caroline had a feeling that they were heading for trouble at home, and without the solid backing of her father the future loomed before her engraved with a huge question mark.

The house in Finsbury Circus was an impressive five-storey building fronted with iron railings and a columned portico. The servants, who had been allowed to attend the funeral, had gone on ahead to ensure that everything was ready for the mourners when they arrived home. A liveried footman hurried down the steps to open the carriage door, and Ingram, the butler, stood in the doorway, waiting to usher the family and friends into the vast cathedral-like entrance hall.

Caroline drew Max aside. 'Take Jimmy to the schoolroom and I'll send up some food. This is going to be deadly dull.'

Max nodded. 'Thanks, Carrie. I'm starving, so don't forget.' He turned to his brother and whispered something in Jimmy's ear that brought a smile to his sad eyes.

Caroline watched her brothers take the stairs two at a time. They were young and resilient, and would have to return to Rugby School very soon, where they would continue their education, but it was Mama who concerned her the most. At the moment Esther appeared pale but calm, and in control of her emotions as she greeted her guests. Caroline and Sadie stood at her side, acknowledging the hesitant commiserations, awkward silences and set smiles as friends and acquaintances filed past. Housemaids relieved the visitors of hats, parasols and tightly furled umbrellas, while Ingram directed them to the Chinese Room where refreshments had been laid out on sparkling-white tablecloths. Caroline had checked everything before they left for Brookwood, and she had personally supervised the flower arrangements, refusing to stick to the convention of funereal white lilies by the addition of bowls spilling over with tea roses and honeysuckle from the garden. She drew one of the maids aside and gave her instructions to take two generous plates of food upstairs to the schoolroom. Satisfied that her brothers would be looked after, Caroline went to join her mother and Sadie.

'It will soon be over,' Sadie said in a whisper.

'That's what I'm afraid of,' Esther answered in an

undertone. 'Reality will set in, but I'm not sure how I can face life without Jack.'

Caroline squeezed her mother's cold hand. 'We'll help you, Mama. There's nothing so bad that we can't overcome it if we're together.'

Esther's lips quivered into a semblance of a smile. 'Thank you, darling girl. I know I can rely on you.' She looked up at the sound of hurrying footsteps and her smile broadened. 'Alice, you came.'

Caroline turned to see Lady Alice Bearwood, dressed in the latest Paris fashion. Her pert bonnet was decorated with silk roses and satin bows, and the frilled skirts of her gown were drawn back into a large bustle. She exuded an aroma of expensive French perfume as she embraced Caroline before turning to give Esther a hug.

'My dear Essie, I am so sorry I wasn't able to attend the funeral, but I had to support Bearwood, and I must say he addressed the House in the most impressive manner.' She held Esther at arm's length, gazing into her face. 'Can you forgive me?'

'Of course. I understand how important Sir Henry is now.'

Despite her mother's brave smile, Caroline knew that she was close to breaking point, and she squeezed her hand. 'It's been a difficult day, Aunt Alice.'

'I know, and I would have attended the funeral had I been able. Your father was a good man and will be much missed.'

Caroline looked over her shoulder, frowning. 'Is Cordelia with you, Aunt?'

'No, I'm afraid not. She was at a ball last evening and she was still in bed when I left. I didn't want to disturb her beauty sleep.' Alice smiled and shook her head. 'The season is quite exhausting, and Cordelia is much in demand.'

'Essie, you should rest now.' Sadie stepped forward, acknowledging Alice with a curt nod of her head. 'It's been a trying morning, Lady Alice.'

Esther opened her mouth to reply, but Alice slipped her arm around her friend's shoulders. 'Nonsense, Sadie. Essie will survive this terrible blow, but what she really needs is company and something to take her mind off things.'

'Thank you, Alice, but I'm quite capable of speaking up for myself. I will do my duty. These people have come to pay their respects to Jack and I owe it to them to show my gratitude. It must be done.' Esther started towards the Chinese Room, pausing to look over her shoulder. 'I'm afraid I can't face taking the boys back to school, Carrie. You will have to travel to Rugby with them.'

'I will, Mama. We'll leave first thing in the morning.'

'I'd like you to go with her, Sadie,' Esther said firmly. 'They have only a short time before the term ends, and maybe you could persuade the headmaster to allow them to return home with you. I could simply keep them away, but that would be bad form.'

She continued across the hall to join the rest of the mourners with Alice at her side.

Caroline stopped outside the Chinese Room, barring Sadie's way. 'Just one thing, Aunt. I don't think we should wear black tomorrow.'

'Why ever not? It's the custom, Carrie. We must observe the niceties.'

'Well, I wasn't suggesting you should wear your beloved red boots,' Caroline said, chuckling. 'I remember how you used to sport them on every occasion possible.'

Sadie pursed her lips. 'I was younger then. I wouldn't dream of doing such a thing now.'

'You were more fun then, Aunt. Anyway, that's not what I'm saying. I just think it's hard enough for the boys without us looking like a pair of carrion crows. I'll wear my grey poplin, and you have a pretty lavender silk, if I remember rightly. We can change back into mourning when we return home.'

'I think you're right, Carrie,' Sadie said slowly. 'Lavender silk it shall be. Now we'd better go and support your poor mother. She's being very brave, but I'm afraid she might find it all too much.'

Next day at Rugby School, the headmaster's study smelled of old books, beeswax polish and ink. Dust motes danced and twirled in the rays of sunlight streaming through the tall windows, and the sound of the school bell being rung enthusiastically by an overzealous pupil signalled the end of morning lessons. The boys had been spirited away by Matron as soon as they had arrived, and Caroline had asked to see the headmaster, but she had been told that he was too busy to see anyone. In the end she had had to demand to see him and they had been granted a brief interview.

He had listened sympathetically, although, with the boys' best interests in mind, he had said he was reluctant to grant Caroline's request for her brothers to be released early from their studies. She had stood her ground, insisting that it was their mother's wish to have her sons with her at such a difficult time. It was a short battle of wills and Caroline thought she had been winning the conversation when the headmaster was called away on urgent business. She stood by the smoke-blackened fireplace, anxiously awaiting his return while Sadie paced the floor.

'What's keeping him?' Sadie glared angrily at the clock on the mantelshelf. 'I'll be very cross if we've spent three hours on the train only to be fobbed off by some jumped-up pedagogue.'

Despite her anxiety, Caroline could not repress a chuckle. 'That's a big word, Aunt Sadie.'

Sadie tossed her head. 'Just because I didn't have much education it doesn't mean that I'm ignorant, Miss Caroline.'

'Don't get on your high horse. I remember when you used to pull faces at my governess behind her back, and you used to sneak food into the nursery when Max and I were sent to bed without any supper for being naughty.'

Sadie pursed her lips, but her eyes were smiling. 'Don't remind me. I shouldn't have gone behind your parents' backs, but I thought they were a bit too strict with you at times.'

'And we loved you for standing up for us.' Caroline was suddenly alert. 'Someone's coming.' She clasped her hands tightly, hardly daring to breathe as the door opened.

'Good afternoon, ladies.' A tall man entered the room, his black gown billowing round him, and he had to bend his head in order to prevent his mortarboard from catching on the lintel. He closed the door, turning to them with a rueful smile. 'That is the disadvantage of being too tall.'

'Maybe it's the fault of the doorway being too low,' Sadie said, smiling.

Caroline glanced at her in surprise. Was it possible that her spinster aunt, who always obeyed the rules of etiquette, was flirting with this gangly, copper-haired teacher?

'I should introduce myself.' He looked from one to the other, his smile broadening. 'My name is Laurence Bromley, and I have the pleasure of teaching both Max and James. The headmaster asked me to fetch the boys, but I wanted to speak to you first.'

'I am Miss Sadie Dixon, and this is Miss Caroline Manning, the boys' sister.' Sadie's cheeks were

suspiciously pink as she made the necessary introductions, and Mr Bromley was smiling foolishly.

'Is anything wrong?' Caroline demanded. 'Why do
you need to speak to me? I simply want to take my
brothers home before the end of term. Our mother
needs to have them with her at this sad time.'

'Yes, so I was told, but the Head is unlikely to
give his consent, and he's very strict about this sort
of thing. They're in the anteroom waiting to say
goodbye.'

'That isn't good enough,' Caroline said firmly. 'It
would be better if I had the Head's permission, but
I should warn you that I intend to take them home,
regardless.'

'In your position, I would do the same thing. I'll
show them in.' He ushered the boys into the room
and left, closing the door softly behind him.

'I'm the man of the house now,' Max said in a
choked voice. 'I want to go home and take care of
you and Mama.'

Jimmy nodded, forcing a smile. 'And I'll do my
best to cheer Mama up.'

Caroline dropped a kiss on his curly head. 'I know
you will, Jimmy. It will be lovely having both of you
at home for a while longer.'

'Mr Bromley is leaving today,' Max said eagerly.
'He's a good chap, Carrie. All the boys like him, but
he's had some rows with the Head.'

Sadie eyed him curiously. 'Mr Bromley doesn't
give the impression of being a difficult man.'

'Well, it's none of our business.' Caroline patted James on the back. 'If you're feeling better we'll get going. I told the cabby to wait for us.'

'What about our trunks and tuck boxes?' Max said frowning. 'If I know the fellows in my dorm they'll take what's left, although there's not much.'

'I'm sure we've got enough food at home to satisfy your appetite.' Sadie ruffled his hair, but he moved away, gazing anxiously at his reflection in the glass-fronted bookcase and smoothing his dark-blond curls.

'I'm too old for that sort of treatment, Aunt Sadie. I'm grown up now.'

'I used to say much the same when I was your age,' Sadie said with a rueful smile. 'That was a long time ago.'

'You're not so very old,' James said quickly.

'I'm the most senior member of the family present, so I think we should do as your sister says, and make a move.'

James opened his mouth as if to comment, but at that moment the door opened to admit Laurence Bromley. He was not smiling.

'I'm sorry, Miss Manning, but the Head is adamant that the boys should remain in school until the end of term.'

'Really? That is unfortunate.' Caroline grabbed James by the hand. 'We're leaving now whether the headmaster likes it or not. He can't prevent me from taking my brothers home and, to be honest, I doubt very much whether they will return. Perhaps you would be kind enough to ensure that their belongings are sent on by carrier.' She pushed past him, with James clinging to her hand. 'Come along, Sadie.'

'Miss Manning, please wait a moment . . .'

Caroline ignored his protest and quickened her pace. A vision of her mother's tear-stained face was enough to spur her on. She was taking her brothers home.

Chapter Two

Emotional scenes greeted the boys on their return home to find the household in deep mourning. Curtains remained drawn, mirrors were covered and Esther had ordered all clocks to be stopped at the moment of her husband's passing. Caroline grieved for her father, but she was more concerned for the living, and after a week of existing in a state of permanent gloom she managed to persuade her mother to allow daylight into the house. She was not bothered by the lack of mirrors, but stopping the clocks was another matter, and eventually Esther agreed that they should be restarted, except for the one in her bedchamber, where the gilt hands would point for ever to the moment when her heart was broken.

Caroline did her best to look after James, and although Max stoutly refused to admit that he was in need of emotional support, she knew that he, too, was suffering the loss of a much-loved parent. Their mother seemed to have drifted into a half-world where she was present in body, but her thoughts were far away.

And then there were the bills. Tradesmen began to knock on the door demanding payment. Ingram sent them on their way, but that did not stop the stream of documents that arrived daily, demanding large sums of money, which shocked Caroline to the core. In her seventeen years of life she had never needed to worry about whether she could afford a new gown or a pair of shoes, let alone how they were going to pay for the food they ate, the coal that heated the house and the candles that lit their rooms. Suddenly these problems became very real.

'What are we going to do, Aunt Sadie?' Caroline rushed into the dining room one morning, waving a sheaf of demands for payment under Sadie's nose. 'Mama seems to think that our housekeeper deals with the tradesmen's accounts, but when I spoke to Mrs Hayes she told me that she had always passed them on to Papa.'

'It's obvious that we're in desperate need of funds.' Sadie rose from the table. 'I think perhaps a visit to the office would be in order. We can't involve your mama, not yet anyway.'

Caroline nodded emphatically. 'I agree. I just wish I knew more about the business. Mama would never discuss such things with me.'

'I need to have a word with Ezra Parkinson, although I've never had much faith in him as a manager.' Sadie glanced at her reflection in one of the gilt-framed wall mirrors, patting a stray strand of hair into place. 'I always hoped that I would run the office one day, because I started working there when I was even younger than Max, but it wasn't to be.'

'Why wasn't it, Aunt Sadie? That doesn't seem right.'

'After they were married your parents built the company, working side by side until you were born, and by that time they could afford to pay a manager and take on more clerks, and I wasn't needed any more. It's a man's world, Carrie. We just have to accept it as a fact.'

'I'm not so sure about that,' Caroline said, smiling. 'But we need to sort this out, Aunt. I'm coming with you.'

'All right, but don't say anything to your mother. There's no need to bother her with this.'

'Give me five minutes to fetch my bonnet and reticule and we'll go now, before Mama is up and about.'

'It's little wonder that she sleeps until noon,' Sadie said, sighing. 'I hear her walking about her room well into the early hours.'

'That means you don't get much sleep either.'

'I've always been like that, but your mother is wearing herself out. I worry about her.'

'When we've been to the office I intend to call on Aunt Alice. She is the only person who might be able to help Mama.'

The hansom cab dropped them off outside the company office, which was situated in Wapping High Street. Caroline had known Ezra Parkinson since she was a small child. Even then she had realised that there was a certain amount of ill-feeling between her aunt and Ezra. He was always very courteous and obliging, but now she was older she felt that he was a little too familiar, and it was obvious that he had little time for women. The smile that curved his lips never quite reached the dark depths of his hooded eyes, and his obsequious manner barely masked an undercurrent of contempt.

Sadie marched into the outer office and came to a sudden halt. 'Where is everyone?' she demanded, gazing at the empty desks.

'It's too early for luncheon,' Caroline said, frowning. 'Mr Masters, the head clerk, was always sitting behind the counter when I used to visit Papa.'

Sadie rang the hand bell and its peal echoed mockingly around the empty room.

Caroline opened the door to the inner office. 'Anyone there?' she called. 'Mr Parkinson, it's me, Caroline Manning.'

'Really, this is too bad. Even in the old days we would never leave the office unattended.' Sadie pushed past her. 'Parkinson. Are you there?'

A door at the back of the building opened and Parkinson emerged, carrying a brown leather bag. 'Miss Dixon and Miss Manning. I wasn't expecting to see you here today.'

'What's going on, Parkinson?' Sadie demanded angrily. 'Where is Masters? And why is there no one on the front desk?'

'Times are hard, miss.' Parkinson edged past them. 'If you'll excuse me, I have a business appointment.'

Caroline barred his way. 'That's not good enough, Mr Parkinson. It looks to me as if you're leaving and you don't intend to return.'

'Even the rats desert a sinking ship, miss. I'm not vermin, but I know when the business is about to go bankrupt.'

With surprising strength, Sadie grabbed him by the shoulders and propelled him into the front office. She gave him a gentle shove, catching him off balance so that he sat down heavily on the nearest chair. 'Now then, you'd better explain before I send Miss Caroline down to the Dock Police and have you arrested. I wouldn't be surprised if you'd emptied the safe and the company's money is in that bag.'

'That's slander, Miss Dixon. I could have you up before the beak for that.'

'Not if it's true, and judging by your demeanour, I think I might have hit the nail on the head.'

Caroline went to the door. 'Shall I call a constable, Aunt?'

'Let him speak first.' Sadie leaned against the desk,

folding her arms across her chest. 'We're listening, Mr Parkinson.'

'You'll find out sooner or later anyway.' Parkinson put the bag down by his feet. 'The business has been floundering for months, ever since the loss of the *Mary Louise*.'

'But surely we were insured with Lloyd's?' Caroline stared at him, frowning. 'Weren't we?'

'We could not afford the premium for such an old vessel, Miss Manning. It was a total loss and that, together with the expensive refit on your uncle's ship, simply added to our difficulties.'

'There's something very wrong here, Parkinson,' Sadie said angrily. 'You need to give a full account of your dealings to Mr George.'

'The paddle steamers we owned were sold at the beginning of the year, and I don't know when Mr George will return, but whenever it is it's too late to save the company, Miss Dixon. I'm getting out before the bailiffs arrive.'

'It can't be as bad as that.' Caroline looked from one to the other. 'We own the house in Finsbury Circus. Mama is a wealthy woman.'

Parkinson shrugged. 'Tell that to your creditors.'

'Aunt Sadie?' Caroline crossed the floor to stand beside her aunt. 'Tell him that the house must be worth a great deal of money. Tell him.'

'You're right, of course, Carrie, dear, but I'm afraid it's rented. Your father wanted the world to see how successful he'd been and he insisted on moving to

Finsbury Circus, even though your mama was happy living in the Captain's House.'

Caroline stared at her in a state of shock. The safe and secure world of her childhood had been swept away with a few ill-chosen words. 'I remember living in that old house, and I loved it, but then we moved to Finsbury Circus. I thought we owned our home.'

Sadie laid her hand on Caroline's shoulder, her eyes moist with unshed tears. 'I'm sorry, my dear. This must be a terrible shock, but things are not always what they seem.'

Parkinson clutched his hands to his breast in mock horror. 'Poor child, my heart aches for you.'

Caroline rounded on him. 'Hold your tongue, you horrid man. This isn't a laughing matter.'

'Indeed it ain't, for you, anyway. I'm saving meself, Miss High and Mighty. Take my tip and find yourself a rich husband before the news gets out.'

'Shut up, Parkinson,' Sadie said wearily, sinking down into a chair. 'At least we still own the Captain's House. Thankfully, whether out of sentiment or for a more practical reason, Jack rented it out.'

Parkinson curled his lip, reminding Caroline of a snarling cur. 'Then the bailiffs will seize it first.'

'I hate to disappoint you,' Sadie said smugly. 'But Jack had the forethought to put it in my name. I own the Captain's House – it was to be my dowry.'

'I remember that it had a lovely friendly atmosphere and a wonderful view of the river.' Caroline closed her eyes, trying to envision her room at the top of the old house. 'Pa's housekeeper told me that the captain who had built the house still kept watch over it, and sometimes I could smell tobacco smoke in my room, but I wasn't afraid. If it was a ghost, it was a friendly one.'

'Your mother loved the place, and I think she would have been content to live there for ever, but Jack wanted only the best for his family.' Sadie sighed and turned her head away. 'Life was simpler then, and we were all much younger. Anything seemed possible.'

'This is all very interesting, Miss Dixon,' Parkinson said sarcastically, 'but the creditors haven't been paid for weeks. The firm is facing bankruptcy and the sooner you realise that the better.'

'I find that hard to believe.' Sadie faced him angrily. 'I think you've mismanaged the business, and now you're running away.'

'If Mr Manning hadn't died he would have been held to account, but I don't intend to take the blame for the collapse of the company. I've got an interview with one of our competitors this very afternoon. I want that job and I need to get out of here before all this becomes public.'

'But there must be something left,' Caroline said slowly. 'Uncle George will make things right when he returns.'

Parkinson leaned over to open a drawer and produced a ledger, which he slammed down on the desk. 'Study this, ladies. It lists all the ingoings and outgoings, the profits and the losses, of which there are many. The *Esther Manning* should have docked three days ago, but I reckon Mr George has seen the light and has decided to stay away. Maybe he'll start up a business of his own in the Americas. That's what I'd do if I were him.'

'No, that's so unfair.' Caroline struggled to speak as her throat tightened and she had to force back tears. 'Uncle George wouldn't do such a thing.'

'Of course not,' Sadie added angrily. 'You're the villain here, Parkinson. Did you pay off the clerks and have you taken your wages from the money in the safe?'

'It was ours by rights.' Parkinson opened a second drawer and took out a bundle of documents, tossing them onto Sadie's lap. 'Unpaid accounts. I'm sick of being dunned by angry suppliers of everything from coal to caulking. Sort that out, if you can, but maybe you'll believe me when you see how much the company owes.' He snatched up his bag, opened it and tipped the contents onto the desk. An apple, a red spotted handkerchief, a tobacco pouch and a pipe spilled onto the grimy wooden surface, which had once been polished to a conker shine. 'That's all I'm taking from here, miss. It's true I paid the clerks because they all have families to feed, and I took my wages, too, but not a penny more.' He stowed his belongings away and rose to his feet. 'Now, I'm going. Call a constable, if you wish, but

I ain't done nothing wrong. You'd best face up to the fact that it's over. You're like the rest of us now. You'll have to work to earn your daily bread.' He stormed out of the office, slamming the door behind him.

'Do you think he was telling the truth?' Caroline asked anxiously. 'Surely it can't be as bad as he says.'

'I think I'd better study the books,' Sadie said slowly. 'It's a while since I worked here, but I don't suppose the system has changed very much.' She handed the documents to Caroline. 'Look through these and see what you make of them, Carrie. I can't do it all.'

Caroline smoothed the crumpled papers. 'At least I can do something useful. Maybe we'll discover something that he's missed.'

'Maybe.' Sadie shook her head. 'It doesn't look good so far, but at least the Captain's House is safe. Your ma knows all about it, Carrie. When the *Mary Louise* was lost your pa must have known that things weren't going too well. He changed his will and left the house to me in case the worst happened, and it looks as though it has.'

'Why didn't he leave it to me or to Max?'

'I know it must seem odd to you, love. But your ma and I go back a long way. We had such adventures you can hardly believe, and I helped them to build the business until it was a genuine rival to the Colville Shipping Company. Jack knew that he could trust me, and that I would never let his family down.'

Sadie took a hanky from her pocket and blew her nose. 'Come on, love. We've got work to do.'

After two hours the desk was littered with papers and Sadie had discarded her mourning bonnet and black lace mittens. Strands of fair hair were tucked behind her ears and there was a smudge of ink on the tip of her nose. Caroline reached over to retrieve a particularly large bill for engine oil and placed it on top of the pile.

'These are all genuine, as far as I can see, and none of the accounts seem to have been settled. It looks as though Parkinson was telling the truth.'

Sadie closed the ledger and laid it on the desk. 'I'm afraid so, Carrie. Our only hope is for your uncle to return with enough money to satisfy at least some of the creditors, but even a quick glance at the accounts shows that we would need a small miracle to keep the company from insolvency.'

'Papa must have known about the state of things,' Caroline said slowly. 'Why did he allow it to happen?'

'Only he could answer that, but I do know that Jack blamed the Colvilles for taking away our trade, and I know he went to see Phineas Colville before he went to Germany. He seemed to be more cheerful afterwards, but his mood changed suddenly and he became very withdrawn. Anyway, whatever went on then, it's up to us to try to salvage what we can.'

Caroline rose to her feet and went to the window.

The sun was shining and the River Thames reflected the azure sky, but the heat of midsummer had brought misery to those in the city. Flies swarmed over the detritus in the gutter and the tangled mess of horse dung and straw, which carpeted the cobbled streets. The stench from sewers and uncollected night soil filtered through gaps in the door, and just yards from the window, she could see stick-thin, bare-footed children openly begging. A small gang of bigger and bolder boys were stalking an unwary pedestrian like a pack of hungry wolf cubs, no doubt intent on picking the gentleman's pockets for anything from a handkerchief to a wallet or a fat purse. It would be easy to condemn them as young villains, but, despite her sheltered upbringing, Caroline understood that terrible poverty existed, although so far it had not touched her life. She turned to Sadie with a sudden feeling of dread.

'What will happen to us if Uncle George doesn't return soon?'

Sadie reached for her bonnet and rammed it on her head, tying the ribbons without attempting to check her appearance in the small, fly-spotted mirror that was perched on the mantelshelf next to the black slate clock. 'Heaven help us, Carrie. That's all I can say.' She pulled on her mittens and picked up her reticule. 'But one thing is for certain – we must not tell your mama.'

'She'll have to know some time,' Carrie said,

frowning. 'Unless I can persuade her to go and stay with Aunt Alice.'

'They were quite close at one time.'

'Then I know what I must do. Have we enough money for the cab fare to Bearwood House?'

A wry smile wiped away Sadie's worried frown. 'We are not quite destitute. The cab can drop me off at home and take you on to Piccadilly. I think it might be better if you approach Lady Alice on your own.'

Cordelia was in the drawing room at Bearwood House, seated on the floor with her skirts billowing around her like the petals of a flower, and the Aubusson carpet was scattered with swatches of material. She looked up and smiled.

'Caroline, this is a lovely surprise. You're just in time to help me choose between silk, lace and muslin, and I'm at a loss to decide what colour will suit me best.'

Caroline felt a sudden surge of impatience – the loss of a beloved parent had turned her whole world upside down, and all Cordelia Bearwood could think of was her next ball gown. But Cordelia's smile was sunny and she was not to know of the catastrophic events that had overtaken the Manning family. Caroline took a deep breath and forced her lips into a smile.

'I need to talk to your mama, Delia. Is she at home?'

'What's the matter?' Cordelia scrambled to her feet. Taking Caroline by the hand she led her to the sofa and pressed her down onto the silk damask. 'My dear, you're white as a sheet. Are you ill?'

'I'm quite well, Delia. But I must see Lady Alice. It really is quite urgent.'

'I'll go and find her. Wait here, I'll be as quick as I can.' Cordelia hurried to the door, pausing to glance over her shoulder. 'You aren't going to faint, or anything stupid, are you?'

'I'm made of stronger stuff, and I'm sorry if I've alarmed you, but Lady Alice will know what to do.'

'Wait there – don't move.' With a flurry of muslin skirts and lace-frilled petticoats, Cordelia hurried from the room.

Caroline sat very still, gazing around the luxuriously appointed room with a stifled sigh. Until today she had taken this standard of living for granted, but, for the first time, she was looking at the expensive hand-painted wallpaper and the priceless oil paintings with a new eye. She ran her fingers over the peach-coloured damask, so delicate to the touch that it felt like caressing a baby's smooth skin. Each piece of furniture had been matched perfectly with its neighbour. The pier table standing between two tall windows, draped with peach damask curtains, was set below a pier glass in which she could see herself reflected. She dropped her gaze, clasping her hands tightly in her lap as the hard truth dawned upon her – this would most probably be the last time she might visit Bearwood House on equal terms with her hosts.

She jumped as the door opened to admit Lady Alice, followed by her daughter, and Caroline rose to her feet, dropping a curtsey.

'Good heavens!' Alice stared at her in dismay. 'Whatever is the matter, Carrie? Delia said that you were upset, but you look distraught. Sit down and tell me what's happened.'

Haltingly at first, Caroline explained her predicament, and then the words came tumbling out. 'I can't tell, Mama. She's broken-hearted as it is, and to lose Papa and our home would be a terrible blow.'

Alice patted her on the shoulder. 'Your mama is made of stronger stuff than you realise, Carrie. If you'd seen how she coped during our long sea voyages, when I was laid low with *mal de mer*, and how she rose to the challenge of living in the Australian goldfields, you would know that she can cope with almost anything.'

'Except the loss of my father,' Caroline said sadly. 'Even if Uncle George were to return today, I doubt if we could save our home. He might be able to persuade our creditors to allow him time to pay off the company's debts, but according to Sadie they are enormous.'

'When is your uncle's ship due in, Carrie?'

'It's overdue. No one knows where she is.'

'That's worrying.' Alice rose to her feet. 'Ring the

bell, Delia. I'll order my carriage and we'll go to Finsbury Circus. I think, in the circumstances, that it might be best if I break the news to Essie.'

Caroline stood up, eyeing her with a worried frown. 'What will you say to her?'

'Don't worry, my dear. I know how to handle your mama. We've been friends for twenty years and we've been through a lot together. I'm going down to Devonshire – I plan to spend a few weeks at Daumerle – and I'll suggest that she accompanies me. In fact, I'll insist upon it.'

'That's very kind of you, but what about my brothers? They're supposed to be in school.'

'I'll talk it over with Essie, but it sounds as if they will have to leave Rugby. Maybe they would like to spend some time with us in Devonshire, and you are more than welcome, also, Carrie.'

Cordelia put her head on one side, eyeing Caroline with a worried frown. 'You poor girl. I wish now that I hadn't accepted the invitation to spend the rest of the summer at Fairleigh Hall with Euphemia's family, which means that I won't be able to join you. I suppose I could cancel the arrangement.'

'No, please don't do that on my account,' Caroline said hastily. 'I want to stay in London. There must be something I can do to keep the company going until Uncle George returns.'

'But where will you stay?' Alice demanded. 'You're not thinking clearly. I know it's been a shock—' She broke off as the door opened to admit a neatly dressed parlour maid. 'Send for my carriage, Franklin, and tell Merrifield to bring me my bonnet and shawl. She'll know which one I need.'

'Shall I come with you, Mama?' Cordelia asked anxiously. 'I'll postpone my appointment with the dressmaker.'

'There's no need,' Caroline said. 'I'll go with your mama, Delia. This is my problem, not yours.'

Esther was in no state to gainsay her wilful friend. Lady Alice Bearwood was a force to be reckoned with, and within an hour of her arrival at the house in Finsbury Circus she had almost managed to convince Esther that a trip to the country would be beneficial to her health. Not only that, but she skilfully created the impression that she was in desperate need of companionship.

'You always loved Daumerle, Essie,' Alice said gently. 'We could visit my cousin Freddie at Starcross Abbey. You always got on so well with him.'

'I'm not very good company at the moment, Alice. Perhaps another time.'

'But that is why you need something to divert you, Mama.' Caroline slipped her arm around her mother's slender shoulders. 'A good rest and country air will revive your spirits.'

'Yes, indeed,' Alice said firmly. 'Moping around is going to make matters worse. I know how you must be grieving for Jack, we all miss him, but he wouldn't want you to be unhappy.'

Caroline could see that her mother was weakening. 'Aunt Alice is right. A few weeks in the country will make all the difference.'

'But I can't abandon the boys. They need me to be strong for them.'

'They're not babies now, Mama. I can look after Max and Jimmy.'

'You heard your daughter,' Alice said briskly. 'Come to Devonshire with me and it will be like old times. You can send for the boys when you're feeling stronger.'

'It would be nice to get away from London for a while. It's so hot and airless in midsummer, and it would be lovely to see Freddie again.' A faint smile curved Esther's lips. 'I often think about our days in the goldfields. It was hard leaving Pa and our friends when we returned home.'

'Do you regret parting from Raven?'

Esther shrugged and turned away. 'It wasn't my choice, but had I stayed I wouldn't have met Jack – he was the love of my life.'

'If you say so, my dear.' Alice held out her hand. 'You need a change of scene, Essie. If you've no objections, we'll leave for Devonshire first thing in the morning.'

It was with a feeling of relief that Caroline waved goodbye to her mother who, despite her continued protests, was ensconced in the luxury of the Bearwoods' carriage as it set off for Waterloo Bridge

Station. Merrifield, Alice's maid, followed with a mountain of luggage piled into the barouche.

'We did it,' Sadie said triumphantly as she crossed the entrance hall, heading for the morning room. 'Your mama will be well cared for, Carrie, so don't worry.'

'At least we managed to keep the worst from her,' Caroline said, sighing. 'But she'll have to know sooner or later.'

'Your father's death has hit her hard, but she's a strong woman and she'll recover, eventually.'

'She really loved my pa.'

'I know, and as I grew up I used to envy her. But I'm well and truly on the shelf, and, at my age, there's little chance of finding a love like that.'

Caroline eyed her curiously. 'You're not old, Aunt Sadie.'

'I'm nearly thirty-two, Carrie. Far too old to be romantic, or even hopeful. Anyway, I think it's time you called me Sadie. It would stop me feeling like a spinster aunt.' Sadie opened the door to the morning parlour and went to sit by the window, gazing out at the busy street. 'You would think that among all those people there might be one man, just one, who would take pity on an old maid.'

'Don't belittle yourself, Sadie,' Caroline said with a wry smile as she took a seat by the fireplace. 'You're a wonderful person and you've been more like a big sister to me. We're in this mess together, like it or not. I think it reflects badly on all the men in London that not one of them has seen you for what you are.'

Sadie glanced at her, pulling a face. 'I was abandoned as a baby. I don't suppose you know that, Carrie. It's not something I care to talk about, but I was raised in the Foundling Hospital and sent into service when I was twelve. That's how I met your mother. If it weren't for Essie I would still be a servant, at the beck and call of others.'

'I didn't know, but it doesn't matter to me. I love you as if you were my aunt.'

Sadie's pale blue eyes filled with tears and she turned her head away. 'Thank you. That means a lot to me.'

'We still have to decide what to do,' Caroline said thoughtfully. 'And there's Max and Jimmy. I'll have to break it to them that Mama has gone down to Devonshire for a while, but there's no question of them returning to school because there isn't the money to pay their fees.'

'Where are they now? They should be here.'

'I gave the under footman some money to take them to the Zoological Gardens. Max was keen to see the reptile house and Jimmy wanted to visit the aquarium. It's been such a sad homecoming for them, so I thought it would be a diversion.'

'Quite right,' Sadie said, nodding. 'But we have to face facts. Parkinson was right and the business is all but bankrupt. If your uncle returns in the next few days with a profitable cargo we might be able to hold off our creditors, but that seems more and more unlikely.'

'I went through the papers in Papa's desk, and the rent on this house is paid quarterly. It's due in a week's time, and we're almost completely out of funds.'

'Jack obviously kept the state of the company's finances a secret from Esther. It's more serious than I thought . . .' Sadie's voice trailed off as she leaned forward to peer out of the window.

'What can you see?'

'I thought I saw a familiar face, but I must have been mistaken. We'll sort something out. Don't worry.'

'There's someone hammering on the front door.' Caroline stood up, reaching for the bell pull. 'Why isn't anyone answering? Where are the servants?'

'I've a nasty feeling that they're having a meeting below stairs,' Sadie said slowly. 'Mrs Hayes muttered something about it when I saw her earlier this morning, although I didn't take much notice at the time.'

'I suppose I'd better go.' Caroline hurried from the room. The visitor was getting impatient and continued to rap on the door. She opened it, staring at the visitor in surprise.

Chapter Three

'Miss Manning?' The man snatched off his bowler hat, allowing a shock of carroty hair to fall over his eyes. 'I didn't expect you to come to the door.'

He looked vaguely familiar, but she could not place him. 'I'm sorry. You seem to know me, but I'm afraid I can't return the compliment, sir. Who are you?'

'Laurence Bromley. We met at Rugby School.'

'Of course. Yes, I remember you now.' Caroline hesitated, wondering whether to invite him in or not. 'You were about to leave your employment on the day we arrived.'

'Yes, that's right.'

'Then you haven't come to take my brothers back to school . . .'

'No, that's not the case, Miss Manning.'

She stood aside. 'You'd better come in, but I have to tell you that the boys won't be returning to Rugby.'

'I'm sorry to hear that. It's an excellent school.'

'But you didn't find it to your liking.'

'There were personal differences between myself and the headmaster.'

'So why are you here today, Mr Bromley?'

'I was in the area and I was concerned for the boys' welfare.'

Ingram had appeared from the depths of the house, but Caroline had no intention of discussing family matters in front of the butler. 'You'd better come with me, Mr Bromley.' She beckoned to the butler. 'We'll have coffee in the morning parlour, and some of Cook's seed cake, too.'

Ingram cleared his throat, standing stiffly to attention. 'I'm afraid that won't be possible, Miss Caroline.'

She turned to him, eyebrows raised. 'What did you say?'

'The talk in the servants' hall is that we are all to lose our positions, Miss Caroline.'

'Perhaps I should come back another time,' Laurence said in a low voice.

'No, you're here now.' Caroline turned to Ingram, keeping calm with difficulty. 'We'll sort this out later.'

'Cook is packing her bags as we speak. She's been offered another position and has decided to accept it.'

'This is obviously a bad time,' Laurence said hastily. 'I should go.'

'No. You came here to enquire about my brothers,

and I appreciate your concern.' Caroline turned to Ingram. 'I'm sure that someone in the kitchen could make a pot of coffee or some tea. I'd be obliged if you would see to it, please, Ingram.'

'Of course, Miss Caroline.' Ingram walked off stiffly as if performing a slow march.

'Miss Dixon is in the morning parlour,' Caroline said, making an effort to sound casual, although her mind was racing. The news of their financial problems had obviously travelled fast, and she needed time to think. 'Come with me, Mr Bromley.' She crossed the entrance hall and ushered him into the parlour. 'Sadie, we have a visitor.'

Sadie rose to her feet, a faint blush colouring her cheeks. 'Mr Bromley, I thought I recognised you. I saw you striding along the pavement, looking very purposeful. What brings you to London?'

'Please take a seat,' Caroline said, remembering her manners.

He pulled up a chair and sat down. 'I knew where Max and James lived, and I was passing, so I thought I would call, but it seems that I picked a bad time.'

'The servants have heard of our financial difficulties, Sadie. Apparently Cook is leaving and it looks as if the others might follow.' Caroline turned to Bromley. He seemed to be a sensible man and there was no point pretending that all was well. 'My father's untimely death has left us in some money problems, Mr Bromley. My brothers couldn't return to Rugby, even if they wanted to.'

'I'm sorry.'

'Why are you in London, Mr Bromley?' Sadie fixed him with a steady look. 'Have you found employment here?'

'As a matter of fact I've decided to branch out on my own.'

'Do you mean to open a school?' Sadie's eyes shone with enthusiasm. 'What a splendid idea.'

'Not exactly. I was thinking more of taking on a few pupils to start with, providing I can find suitable accommodation. I'm not a wealthy man, so I would have to start in a small way, but one day I would like to have my own establishment where I could tutor bright boys, and even a few girls.'

'How progressive of you.' Caroline met his candid gaze with a smile of approval. 'I think that the mothers of future generations should be well educated, but not many people would agree with me.'

'I do, and I hope to do something about it.'

'What sort of premises had you in mind, Mr Bromley?' Sadie asked eagerly. 'Would it need to be very large?'

'Not at the beginning. I could only take two or three pupils at a time, so a single room would suffice. But enough about me, you have problems of your own. It was Max and James who were my concern.'

'One of the servants has taken them to the Zoological Gardens,' Caroline said hastily. 'They are grieving for Papa, as you will understand, and I know that they should be furthering their education, but I'm afraid that looks very unlikely at the moment.'

'Maybe not.' Sadie focused her attention on Laurence. 'Are you a good teacher?'

'I would hope so, Miss Dixon.'

'And you need to find a suitable premises?'

'That's so.'

'I think we might be able to help you, and you in turn could help us by tutoring Max and James, but I need to talk it over with Caroline before I make any suggestions.'

Caroline stared at her, mystified. 'I've no idea what you're talking about.'

'Maybe I should call again, when you've had time to discuss matters.' Bromley pushed back his chair and stood up. 'I should go now.'

'Come this time tomorrow,' Sadie said firmly. 'I'll see you out, Mr Bromley.' She rose to her feet and hustled him out of the room, returning minutes later with a satisfied smile on her face. 'Well, what do you think, Carrie?'

'I'm completely in the dark.'

'As I told that wretch Parkinson, the Captain's House is mine.' Sadie reached out to clasp Caroline's hand. 'Although your father's will has to go to Probate, and, under the present circumstances I think it ought to have come to you.'

'I don't agree. If Papa wanted you to have the house then that's how it should be. He couldn't have foreseen the future.'

'What's mine is yours, Carrie. We can live there together.'

'Are you suggesting we should all move to Wapping? What would Mama say to that?'

'She's not going to have much choice. Unless your uncle returns very soon we'll lose this place and have nowhere else to go other than the Captain's House. It's not huge, but Mr Bromley could use one of the rooms to tutor pupils, including Max and James.'

'But we know nothing about him, Sadie.'

'That's easy, we'll just ask the boys what they think. I have a feeling that it would work well, and really, what choice do we have? We could never raise the amount it costs to keep them at boarding school.'

'I'm not giving up so easily.' Caroline gazed round the room. 'I've never thought about it before, but some of the ornaments and paintings that my parents collected must have a value. Mama took all her jewellery, I know because I saw her packing it, but there are the silver candlesticks and salvers – they must be worth quite a lot of money.'

'Are you hoping to pay the rent from such a sale?'

'Why not? If I can just keep everything together until Uncle George returns I'm sure we'll be all right.'

'I wish I could be as optimistic, but you're right to try.'

'If the worst happens, I suppose we'll have to move to the Captain's House.'

'At least we would have a roof over our heads.'

'I don't think that Mama would want to live in Wapping now.'

'She grew up in Limehouse. I don't suppose you've ever ventured into that rough area, but it's nothing like Finsbury Circus. As a child Essie worked the river with your grandfather, and they were very poor.'

'Nevertheless, I'll do everything I can to save our home.'

'You'd better start by finding another cook,' Sadie said drily. 'Would you like me to go below stairs and see what I can do?'

'Yes, please do, and I'll go through the house and sort out items we can sell. I'll make a placard to tie to the railings outside, advertising the sale. What do you think, Sadie?'

'It might work, Carrie. It's worth a try.'

Caroline spent the rest of the day going from room to room, picking out the objects that she thought had the highest value and arranging them in the dining room. Ingram was stiff with disapproval and made his feelings perfectly clear without saying a word. She ignored him and went ahead, enlisting help from Max and James when they returned from their trip to the zoo. They were bubbling with enthusiasm and James had decided that he wanted to be an explorer like Dr Livingstone and bring back rare species for the Zoological Gardens. Max was more interested in the sale of their property, but was very relieved to find that Caroline had not touched anything in his room.

That evening they made a large placard advertising the sale, taking turns in painting the letters with Indian ink. They took it outside and Max hung it over the railings for all to see, and straight away it attracted the attention of passers-by. Caroline stood back, eyeing it critically.

'I think that should do the trick.'

'It's just as well that Mama went to Devonshire,' Max said, grinning. 'She wouldn't have allowed this.'

'I can't see any alternative. The rent is due in a few days' time and there's a huge pile of unpaid bills.' Caroline glanced over her shoulder to see the butler standing at the top of the steps, clutching a portmanteau in his gloved hand. 'Are you going somewhere, Ingram?'

'This is public humiliation, Miss Caroline. I'm going to stay with my sister in Highgate while I seek another position. I've left my address in the house-keeper's office, but I think you'll find that Mrs Hayes will be the next to leave. We can't afford to work for nothing.'

'How long is it since you were paid?' Caroline stared at him in surprise.

'Too long, Miss Caroline. If you come into funds you can send the money to me, not that I'm pinning my hopes on such an outcome.' He marched down the steps and walked off, swinging a large black umbrella with a horse's-head handle.

'That belonged to Papa,' Max said angrily. 'Shall I go and get it from him, Carrie?'

She laid her hand on his arm. 'No, let him keep it. I'm truly sorry that I can't pay him what he's owed, but I'll tell you this – I will get the money somehow, and I'll recompense the servants and the creditors, even if it takes for ever.'

Max shrugged and raised his eyebrows. 'Good luck with that, Carrie.'

She gazed at her younger brother as if seeing him for the first time. 'You've grown so tall, Max. Soon I'll have to look up to you.'

'If I was older I'd go out and earn my living and you wouldn't have to worry about money.'

'We'll look after each other,' Caroline said, smiling. 'Let's go inside and see what Sadie has prepared for our supper. She tells me that she learned to cook when she was even younger than you.' Caroline linked arms with her brother and they mounted the steps together. She glanced over her shoulder before entering the house and was pleased to note the growing number of people who stopped to read the sign posted on the railings outside. Tomorrow would be a good day – she had a feeling in her bones. They would make enough money to stave off disaster and enable them to sit it out until their uncle's ship returned to London.

Next morning crowds of people flooded into the house. Caroline had opened the door and was almost knocked over in the stampede. Luckily she had placed Max and James in the middle of the entrance hall with Sadie on duty in the dining room. The house had been eerily quiet as, following Ingram's example, most of the servants had walked out. Mrs Hayes had departed that morning, leaving a couple of kitchen maids, who had nowhere else to go. Caroline had set them simple tasks and Sadie had prepared a stew, which was simmering on the hob in readiness for their meal later in the day.

'Not that way,' Caroline cried anxiously as a well-dressed couple headed for the staircase. 'The items for sale are in the dining room. Please follow the others.'

Glaring at her, the pair retraced their steps and fell in line behind the queue that was already stretching out onto the pavement. Caroline was still directing the prospective purchasers when James pushed his way through the crowd to whisper in her ear.

'Aunt Sadie says you're to come to the dining room. She can't manage on her own.'

Caroline nodded. 'All right, but you must stand here.'

'I don't know what to do.'

She patted her brother's curly head. 'Just make sure they go straight to the dining room and don't allow anyone to go upstairs or into any of the other rooms.'

James glanced at the crowds. 'I'll try, Carrie.'

'Good boy. I'll be back as soon as I can.' Caroline hurried towards the dining room, threading her way through the lines of people, some of whom were pushing and shoving as if expecting to snatch a bargain. She found Sadie besieged by customers eager to purchase an ornament, a vase or silk cushion. Others had armfuls of Esther's best porcelain dinner service, and a large lady in purple had two silver candelabras clutched to her ample bosom. Sadie appeared to be arguing with a gentleman whose raised voice and flushed cheeks indicated a state of extreme agitation.

'But that is an outrageous price. I could go to the potteries and purchase an item like this for half the price.'

'Then I suggest you buy a ticket at the railway station and travel north, sir.' Sadie snatched the vase from him, holding it high above her head. 'Any offers over one guinea for this eighteenth-century Sèvres vase?'

Caroline stepped aside as the bidding began and the vase finally sold for double the asking price. 'Well done, Sadie.'

Sadie smiled and turned back to the customers who were clamouring for her attention. Caroline began taking money and soon her apron pocket was filled with coins, including several golden guineas, and finally all the items she had chosen were sold. But the crowd refused to disperse and within minutes they were swarming over the house like a colony of worker ants. Caroline raced up the stairs after them and, having persuaded them to go back down, she positioned herself at the bottom of the staircase, refusing to allow anyone to pass. The mood seemed to change and frustrated buyers began to vent their anger on anyone who would listen. James was in tears and Max was threatening to punch the next person who accosted him. Sadie had her hands full in the dining room and Caroline was beginning to panic. She was about to rush outside and look for a constable to restore the peace when a group of tradesmen burst into the house, led by two burly officials.

'What is the meaning of this?' Caroline demanded. She managed to keep her voice steady even though her knees were trembling.

The tallest and broadest of the two leaders stepped forward. 'This is an illegal sale.'

Caroline tossed her head. 'I don't know what you mean. This is private property, so kindly leave.'

He waved a sheet of paper under her nose. 'This is a court order, miss, and these gentlemen are owed a great deal of money. I want to see Mr Manning.'

'My father is dead.' Caroline's voice broke on a sob.

'I can't help that, miss. Who is in charge of the household?'

Caroline took a deep breath. She was not going to let these men witness her heartbreak. 'I don't know exactly. I suppose it's me now that Mama has gone to Devonshire, but if that's all you're worried about I can settle some or maybe all of those debts from the sale of our things.'

'An unauthorised sale, miss. My colleague and I are here to enforce the law.'

There was nothing Caroline could do other than stand back and watch the bailiffs at work. They stripped the house of everything that had any value, leaving nothing but an echoing shell as they carried out the last piece of furniture.

Caroline put her arms around James, who was openly weeping, and she gave him a hug. 'It's only furniture and stuff, Jimmy. We're still together, that's the most important thing.'

Max braced his shoulders, holding his head high. 'I'll get a job, Carrie. I'm fourteen and I'm strong. I can work in the docks or on the river like Grandpa used to, before he went to sea.'

Sadie patted him on the back. 'Good boy, Max. It's a setback but it's not the end of the world. I know what it's like to be poor, but I'm still here to tell the tale.'

'That's right,' Caroline added, forcing a smile. 'At least we've still got a roof over our heads. Let's go to the kitchen and see if they've left the stew that Sadie made for us. I'm hungry, I don't know about you boys.' She gave James her hanky. 'Chin up, Jimmy. We've got each other – that's all that matters now.'

'The kitchen maids have gone,' Sadie said in a low voice as they made their way to the green baize door that led to the world below stairs. 'I gave them enough money to pay for a couple of nights in temporary lodgings and food to keep them going while they look for work.'

'I didn't think the bailiffs would take the money we made in the sale, but they did.'

Sadie put her hand in her pocket and pulled out a silk purse. 'Not all of it. I managed to hide this from them.'

Caroline took it from her and weighed it in her hand. 'That's nice and heavy. We'll count it out when we've eaten.'

'That's if they've left us anything to eat.' Sadie strode on, catching up with Max and James, who were about to open the baize door. 'Come on, Carrie. Best foot forward.'

The kitchen, which was normally a bustling hive of activity, was deserted. The fire in the range had died down to a few feebly glowing embers but, to Caroline's intense relief, the stew was untouched and still hot enough to make a comforting meal. There was bread in the crock and butter on the marble slab in the larder. The bailiffs had left the table and chairs, and the crockery and cutlery used by the servants was untouched, although the battery of copper pans had been taken, leaving only the old blackened saucepans and the kettle. They ate bowlfuls of stew, and mopped up the remainder with chunks of bread. Sadie managed to get the fire going again and they finished off with cups of tea, leaving Max and James to explore the house to see what else, if anything, the bailiffs had left.

'I don't think they can take our beds,' Sadie said, spooning sugar into her tea.

Caroline nodded. 'I hope not, but we don't have much choice now. I don't suppose we've got enough money to pay the rent.' She produced the purse and tipped the contents onto the table. They began counting the coins, placing them in neat piles.

'Four pounds ten and sevenpence ha'penny.' Sadie shook her head. 'That's not nearly enough, and even if it were, we still have to eat.'

'I suppose we could send the boys down to Devonshire,' Caroline said thoughtfully, 'but it would only be a temporary arrangement, and if Mama finds out what's happened she'll want to come home.'

'She's better off with Lady Alice, for the time being anyway.' Sadie replaced the coins in the purse. 'I suggest we pack up what's left and move to Wapping tomorrow. I don't see much point in remaining here, do you?'

Caroline sighed and shook her head. 'We'll be evicted soon anyway. I agree, we have to move on. I'll tell the boys.'

'Tell us what?' Max rushed into the kitchen. 'Never mind that now – look who I found wandering round the empty rooms!'

Caroline twisted round on her chair to see Laurence Bromley standing in the doorway, his hat clutched in his hand and an apologetic smile on his open features.

'I'm sorry to interrupt, especially as you've obviously had a very bad day.'

Sadie rose to her feet. 'Take a seat, Mr Bromley. The tea is still hot. Would you like a cup?'

'Thank you. That would be nice.' He pulled up a chair and sat down next to Caroline. 'I hope I'm not intruding.'

'Not at all. I dare say it will soon be public knowledge that the Manning family are all but bankrupt.' Caroline turned her head away. She was close to tears, and sympathy was almost harder to take than the brutal treatment from the bailiffs and the triumphant taunts of the tradesmen.

'I am truly sorry. If there's anything I can do to help, please say so.'

'It's good to see you here, sir,' Max said earnestly. 'Have you found a new position?'

'I still have to find a suitable premises so that I can tutor two or three boys to begin with.'

James clattered into the kitchen, puffing and panting. 'I've run all the way from the top of the house,' he said breathlessly. 'It's creepy up there without the servants, but they've left us our beds and I still have my cricket bat. I was afraid they'd take it.'

'At least that's something.' Caroline had her

emotions under control and she turned to Laurence with a faint smile. 'It was good of you to come but, as you see, we can't afford to hire you as the boys' tutor.'

'But we could offer you a room free from rent in return for tuition,' Sadie said hastily. 'We're moving to my house in Wapping tomorrow. It's large enough for all of us and, if you were agreeable, you could live rent free in return for tutoring the boys. You could take on more students, if you so wished. I'm sure there's room.'

Laurence glanced from one to the other. 'Don't think I'm prying, but what would Mrs Manning have to say about such an arrangement? I take it that she is not at home.'

'Mama went to the country for her health and it's Sadie's house. She has the final say.' Caroline sent a warning glance to Sadie. She did not want to admit that her mother was so overcome with grief that she was finding it almost impossible to cope, very much like the poor Queen, who was still in deep mourning for her beloved Albert.

'What do you say, Mr Bromley?' Sadie asked eagerly.

He hesitated, stirring his tea and staring into the swirling liquid. 'It's a generous offer, but I'm not sure whether it would be proper for me to take lodgings in a house occupied by two single ladies.'

'But we'd be there, too, sir.' Max straddled a chair as if he were riding a pony. 'It would be fun, Mr Bromley. Jimmy and I would be very good students.'

A smile replaced Laurence's frown, making him look quite boyish. 'I know you would. You were always top of the class, but . . .'

'Why don't you come with us tomorrow and take a look at the premises?' Caroline suggested shyly. She could see that Sadie was keen on the arrangement and it would solve at least one of their problems, even if it created another. But perhaps things were different in Wapping – maybe the locals would turn a blind eye to the fact of their unconventional arrangement – and it would be only until Mama returned to London. If she were in residence then it would be perfectly respectable, but for now it seemed best to leave her in ignorance of the situation. The knowledge that she had lost all her worldly goods as well as her beloved husband might be too much for her to bear.

'Please say yes, sir.' James tugged at his tutor's sleeve. 'I'd like to live by the river and I really don't want to go away to school. I miss my family and some of the other boys are very mean.'

Laurence patted his hand. 'I know that, James. Bullying is despicable in all its forms, but still exists, despite our efforts to stamp it out.'

'Does that mean you're considering Aunt Sadie's proposition, sir?' Max asked urgently.

'Let me consider your aunt's generous offer overnight,' Laurence said, smiling. 'I could offer my services in helping with your move tomorrow, and

that would give me a chance to view the accommodation and consider whether or not it's suitable.'

'Are you sure about this, Sadie?' Caroline asked
urgently as the door closed on Bromley. 'We don't
know anything about this man.'

Sadie shrugged and a smile curved her lips. 'I
know all I need to know. The boys like him and I
can't see Essie sending Jimmy to a ragged school,
and Max would have to find a job. What sort of
future would either of the boys have in that case?'

'But we'll be talked about.'

'Carrie, dear, the gossips will be chattering their
heads off anyway. What choice do we have?'

'He might refuse.'

'He might. And what would we do then?'

Chapter Four

The Captain's House on Black Lion Wharf was wedged between a warehouse and a ship's chandler. The odd assortment of buildings, some of them on wooden stilts driven into the mud, seemed to have been thrown together in a random fashion, but even before they climbed the steps to the front door, Caroline had a feeling of coming home.

Sadie took a key from her reticule and unlocked the door. 'I still feel bad about this, Carrie. The house should be yours.'

'No, it shouldn't. If Papa wanted you to have it then that's how it must be. I'm not beaten yet, Sadie. I'll get us out of this mess, if it's the last thing I ever do.' Caroline followed Sadie into the oak-panelled entrance hall. The musty smell made her wrinkle her nose and a cobweb hanging from the ceiling brushed against her cheek. The floor was thick with dried mud and the carapaces of dead cockroaches.

'I hope the rest of the house is cleaner than this,' Sadie said crossly.

'Hurry up there.' Max pushed in behind them. 'Let us in, Carrie.'

James slipped past her. 'It's creepy, but I think I might like living here. I want a bedroom that over-looks the river so that I can watch the boats.'

'I expect that can be arranged.' Caroline moved on, opening doors and peering into the empty rooms. The front parlour looked as though it might be comfortable enough, but it needed a thorough clean, and the dining room was positively filthy. Someone must have owned at least one dog, judging by the muddy paw prints on the floorboards and the smell of damp fur that lingered in the air. The dining room was situated at the back of the house and there were steep steps down to the basement kitchen.

'I spent many a happy hour in here,' Sadie said, smiling. 'The smell of baking filled the whole house.'

'It stinks now.' James held his nose. 'I think some-thing died in one of the cupboards.'

Max stuck his head round the door. 'Mr Bromley wants to know where to put the luggage, Carrie.'

She turned with a start. 'Of course. I'm coming, Max.' She turned to Sadie. 'I suppose we'd best start cleaning in here. It looks so dismal and it does smell awful.'

Max opened a cupboard and a cloud of flies

erupted, buzzing angrily. 'I don't know what it is, but it's something that's gone off,' he said, grimacing.

'Throw it out for the seagulls.' Sadie rolled up her sleeves. 'James, go outside and see if there's any coal in the yard, or anything we can use to get the fire going. We'll need lots of hot water.'

Caroline hurried from the kitchen. The house was a disappointment and it did not live up to her fond childhood memories. It was probably damp, definitely dirty and the stench from the muddy foreshore at low tide was disgusting.

She found Laurence standing in the hall amid a pile of baggage. 'Thank you, Mr Bromley. It was kind of you to help us.'

He shook his head. 'I'm just sorry to see you in such a sorry plight, Miss Manning.'

'We'll be fine,' Caroline said with more conviction than she was feeling. 'When the old place is cleaned up, I'm sure it will be like home.' She glanced out of the open door. 'I hope the carter brings the kitchen table and chairs soon, or we'll have nothing to sit on. The beds are on another wagon.'

He stared at her, frowning. 'My present lodgings leave a lot to be desired and I need somewhere more permanent. I'd like to accept your offer, if you'll have me.'

'Do you really want to live in a place like this, Mr Bromley? If you wish to take students I think the families would expect better accommodation.'

He smiled and shrugged. 'You obviously haven't

seen some of these so-called educational establish-
ments, Miss Manning. I don't include my old school
in this, but some children are simply unwanted and
sent away with little thought as to their material
comforts. Many of them remain at these places even
in the holidays.'

'That's awful.'

'Awful but true. Might I take a look at the rooms
upstairs?'

'Certainly. In fact, we'll go together. I haven't had
time to inspect them.'

Caroline led the way up a narrow staircase. The
rooms were in desperate need of a good clean, but
when they reached her old room in the attic Caroline
could not resist going out on the balcony. It was
close to midday and the heat was intense. The river
itself seemed to seethe and boil with the turbulence
created by large and small craft, and the constant
tidal surge as it met the water flowing to the sea.

'How wonderful.' Caroline shielded her eyes
against the bright sunlight. 'I could stand here all
day just watching the traffic on the river.'

'I hope you don't think I'm being impertinent,'
Laurence began cautiously, 'but I know that the late
Mr Manning owned a shipping company. Might I
ask what happened?'

Caroline turned to face him. There was nothing
to be gained by keeping the truth from him: it would
be public knowledge soon. 'When my father died he
left nothing but debts. We have only one remaining

vessel and that is so overdue that I'm beginning to fear the worst.'

'I'm so sorry. This must be very painful for you.'

'It is, of course, I loved my father very much, but it's even harder for my mother. He was her whole life and she's gone to the country to recover.'

'But hopefully matters will improve when your ship returns to port?'

'Yes, but it will be too late to save our home. All I can do is hope and pray that Uncle George returns safely.'

'Once again, I am very sorry to hear about your problems, but I have enough money saved to pay rent, and it would make me feel better if you will accept it. If you will allow me the use of two rooms – one for myself, and the other for use as a school-room – I would still be prepared to tutor your brothers free of charge until you are in a position to pay for their education.'

'But you need a proper income, Mr Bromley. Unless, of course, you are a gentleman of means.'

His laughter echoed round the empty attic. 'If I were a man of independent means I would not have spent ten years trying to force knowledge into the heads of boys, most of whom were only interested in kicking a ball around a field or riding to hounds. I could advertise for day students and see how that goes, but that would be up to you and Miss Dixon.'

'I can't see any objection,' Caroline said thoughtfully. 'I'll check with Sadie, but in the meantime we'd better try to make this old house habitable again.' She was about to leave the room when she paused, sniffing the air. 'I can smell tobacco smoke. I used to believe in ghosts, but I'm not so sure now. Maybe the carter has arrived, although I didn't hear anyone call out.' She descended the stairs as quickly as her long skirts would allow, and was met by Max in the entrance hall.

'You're in a hurry, Carrie,' he said, chuckling. 'Where's the fire?'

'I thought perhaps the carter was here.'

'No, not yet. I've been looking out of the window and I'd have seen his van.'

'It's just that I thought I smelled pipe smoke.'

'Maybe it was the captain's ghost.' Max nodded and winked. 'Aunt Sadie told me about the old man who haunts the house. When you smell smoke he's here and he's happy, but if he doesn't approve of what's going on he goes round slamming doors and rattling windows.'

'I know the story, but don't tell Jimmy or he'll be awake all night.'

'Don't worry about him – he's tougher than you think. Anyway, Jim knows all about the captain. We're planning to sit up all night and see if he materialises.'

'Never mind that now. I need you to give a hand to clean this place up before our furniture arrives.' Caroline reached for a broom that someone had left propped up against the wall and she thrust it into her brother's hand. 'You start sweeping and I'll fetch a dustpan and brush. The floors need a good scrub but we'll have to wait for Sadie to get the fire going so that we can heat some water.'

Max tossed the broom from one hand to the other. 'I think I'd rather be at school than doing house-work.'

'I've got news for you, young man.' Laurence descended the stairs with a purposeful look on his face. 'You are at school and this is your first lesson.' He took the broom from Max. 'This is how you sweep a floor. I'll make a start and you can take over.'

Caroline flashed him a grateful smile. 'Thank you, Mr Bromley.'

He paused, leaning on the broom handle. 'I think you could call me Laurence, as we're going to be living in the same house.'

'Really?' Max looked from one to the other. 'Are you really moving in with us, sir?'

Laurence nodded and resumed the task of sweeping up the debris left by the last tenants. 'I am indeed, and we begin lessons as soon as we've got this place ship-shape.'

It took more than a few days to get the Captain's House habitable, but everyone did their bit, even James, who was delegated to keep the fire going in the range. Despite his initial reluctance to take on such menial tasks, he made a good attempt at chopping kindling in the back yard, and kept the scuttle filled with coal. Sadie took over the kitchen with a determination to revive her culinary skills that was impressive, and soon the house was filled with the aroma of baking bread and savoury stews. When she was satisfied that the rooms were spotlessly clean Caroline spent her time making them as homelike as possible, but the money Sadie had saved from the sale in Finsbury Circus was dwindling away at an alarming rate. She scoured the second-hand shops and used what little money they had to purchase a sofa, even though it had seen better days. The upholstery was worn and threadbare and the horsehair stuffing protruded in places, but a couple of well-placed stitches soon put that right. She bought two armchairs in a similar state, but despite the sagging seats they were surprisingly comfortable. A rag rug added a touch of colour to the front parlour and a fly-spotted mirror hung over the mantelshelf made the room look slightly larger. Curtains had been left in all the rooms, mainly, she discovered, because they were lacy with moth holes, but they would have to do. Altogether, Caroline was satisfied that she could do no more.

Laurence's rent money was used for the purchase of food, candles and coal, but by the end of the first week it was becoming even more apparent that they were in desperate need of an outside income. Despite the fact that Caroline checked every day, there was still no news of her uncle's ship, and the office remained closed, but she refused to believe that anything untoward had happened to him or his vessel. The loss of her father had left a raw place in her heart, and, although she kept a cheerful face for her brothers' sake, she was still very much in the first stages of grief.

The city simmered in the summer heat, but there was always a breeze this close to the river, and Caroline was beginning to understand why her parents loved the restless spirit of the Thames with its ever-changing moods and colours. In the evenings, when peace descended upon the house, Caroline often chose to sit on the balcony, enjoying the sunset. The scent of tobacco smoke wafted around her, but even though she had started to believe in him, she was not scared of the old captain, and she often spoke out loud, telling him how grateful she was for the shelter his house afforded them. She was certain that he understood, but it was a feeling rather than anything tangible. Even so, she was sure that he appreciated their efforts to take care of his old home. Whether he was real or imagined, she felt that he understood and sympathised with the recent tragedy in her family, and that gave her the courage to take each day as it came.

She spent more and more evenings in her favourite place, and at low tide she could see her brothers exploring the foreshore, searching for anything of value that had popped out of the thick black mud and might fetch a few pennies in the market. They looked for all the world like the other mudlarks who spent their waking hours searching for anything the ebb tide might have uncovered. There were scuffles when territories were breached, but Max and James had learned how to defend themselves in a hard school, and it was a relief to know that they could hold their own in the harsh outside world.

Sadie and Laurence seemed to be getting on very well – so well, in fact, that Caroline felt that she was witnessing a burgeoning romance. Her aunt and the schoolmaster were ideally suited, and nothing would make her happier than to see Sadie married with children of her own, but that thought only served to make Caroline feel lonely and the loss of her old life even more painful. She was no longer Miss Manning of Finsbury Circus, the daughter of a shipping magnate, with servants at her beck and call. She was, in reality, homeless and living on the charity of a woman who, although much loved, was not related to her by blood. As the days went by the uncertainty as to the fate of her uncle and his ship hung over the household in a black nimbus cloud. Money was tight and there was only one answer . . .

Caroline went downstairs and found Sadie and Laurence in the parlour, seated on either side of the empty grate.

'I must find work.' Caroline said with a determined set to her jaw.

Sadie put down her teacup. 'What do you mean, Carrie?'

'It's quite simple. We are desperate for money and we can't live off the rent that Laurence pays us.'

Laurence leaned forward in his chair. 'I've put an advertisement in *The Times*, Caroline. I can take day boys, or even a couple of boarders. Sadie and I were discussing it before you joined us.'

'But that won't keep all of us, and you can't be expected to pay us rent and teach my brothers for nothing.'

'They're bright boys,' Laurence said, smiling. 'I'm sure I could get both of them into Oxford or Cambridge.'

'Even so, you can't support all of us.'

Sadie's smooth brow creased into a frown. 'If we're to become a school of sorts I would be happy to look after the pupils. Mrs Cooper's teaching is coming back to me gradually and I'm getting the hang of that black-leaded beast of a range.'

'But that leaves me with no place in this house,' Caroline said sadly. 'I was brought up to be a lady, even though my parents came from humble backgrounds, but I'm not like Cordelia Bearwood.'

A dry chuckle escaped Sadie's lips. 'I would hope not. Lovely as she is, Cordelia has been spoiled to death by her doting parents.'

'Just wait and see what response I get from my advertisement,' Laurence said softly. 'I'm grateful for the opportunity to start my school, and, if I'm successful, I hope one day to have my own establishment.'

'And you will, Laurence. I'm sure of it.' Sadie's pale blue eyes glowed with pride and a delicate flush coloured her cheeks.

Caroline stared at her aunt as if seeing her for the first time. The ever-practical, reliable friend of her childhood had been transformed into a radiant young woman. Was it possible to fall in love so quickly? Caroline could not answer that question, but it seemed to have happened before her eyes and she could only be glad that Sadie had at last found someone worthy of her.

'I think I'll go to my room and read for a while,' Caroline said, yawning. 'Do you mind seeing to the boys, Sadie?'

'Of course not,' Sadie said smiling happily. 'If Laurence goes ahead with fee-paying boarders I'll need the practice mothering small boys. I think it would be a wonderful thing to do.'

Laurence rose to his feet. 'I wouldn't do anything that you didn't feel was right, Caroline.'

'I think it's a splendid idea. You two could manage it beautifully.' She escaped from the room, but instead of going upstairs she let herself out through the front door and negotiated the steps down to the wharf.

Despite the noxious odours from the factory chimneys and the gasworks, it was a beautiful evening – the sort of warm, feathery dusk that seemed to wrap itself around a body like a silk shawl. The sun was a fiery golden ball plummeting below the horizon, leaving the sky streaked with blood-red and purple bruise-like clouds. The river boiled like molten copper and the smelly mud had a silvery sheen. It was a night for lovers, but that thought made her feel even lonelier than before.

A shriek from the foreshore made her turn with a start and, looking down from the wharf, she could see her brothers being attacked by a gang of ragged youths. She made for the nearest watermen's stairs and raced down them, risking a fall, but her feet barely touched the slimy treads, and she landed on the shingle with a dull thud.

'Stop that,' she cried angrily. 'Leave those boys alone, you bullies.' More fearful for her brothers than for herself, she raced over the stones and broken spars, waving her fists at the youths, who turned to stare at her. But their surprised expressions were replaced by surly grins and the tallest of them advanced on Caroline with his ham-like fists raised.

'Leave us be, lady. You'll come off worst.'

Max took a running jump and landed on the boy's back. 'Run for it, Carrie.'

She stood her ground. 'I will not. I'm not afraid of you big louts. Leave my brothers alone.'

James had his arms pinned behind his back and his captor was laughing wildly. 'Shall I break his arms, Crusher?'

The tall youth shook his head. 'Nah. Let's have some fun with the toffs first. Let's show 'em how us Wapping boys treat them as venture into these parts.'

'Why don't you take on someone your own size?'
A cultured voice rang out behind them, causing the
gang to take several steps backwards as a tall figure
emerged from the shadow of the wharf. 'Let the
boys go and if you touch the young lady you'll have
me to deal with.'

Caroline leaped forward to grab James by the
hand, dragging him free from the boy who had
momentarily released his grip.

The leader of the gang shook Max off as if he
were an annoying insect, but his attitude changed
subtly. 'We was only larking around, guv.'

'Get away from here before I thrash each one of
you.' The man grabbed Max by the collar and
marched him across the muddy foreshore to join
Caroline and James. 'Are you hurt, young lady?'

Caroline shook her head. 'No, sir. I don't know
how to thank you . . .'

'No need for that. Just keep away from here. This
isn't a playground.'

His patronising tone annoyed Caroline, despite
her intense feeling of relief. Even in the fading light
it was obvious that their rescuer was a gentleman.
His frock coat was well cut and his checked trousers
gave him a slightly dandified appearance. He was
clean-shaven, but the brim of his silky top hat cast
a shadow on his upper face and she could not see
his eyes.

'My brothers are new to this area of London, sir,'
Caroline said with as much dignity as she could

muster, considering the fact that her slippers were sinking into the cold mud and her silk skirts were wet and probably ruined.

'Then I suggest you take them home and don't venture out after sunset. This is a rough area.' He tipped his hat and marched off in the direction of the stone steps.

'Are you going to let him talk to you like that?' Max demanded crossly. 'That fellow treated you like an idiot, Carrie.'

'Maybe I was a fool for bringing you boys here,' Caroline said ruefully. 'I've no idea who that person is, but he did us a favour, and we should follow him as quickly as possible. Those louts might return if they think he's gone.'

James dashed his hand across his eyes. 'I was scared, Carrie. I don't think I like it here.'

She tightened her grasp on his hand and started walking towards the stone steps. 'We'll get used to it, Jimmy. We just need to learn how to cope with living in such a different place. After all, our parents once lived here and they survived.' She held her free hand out to Max. 'We're in this together, and we just have to make the best of it.'

'I could have thrashed the one called Crusher.' Despite his brave words, Max held her hand as they crossed the mud, making their way to the steps.

Later, when her brothers were in bed, Caroline sat on the window seat in her bedchamber, sipping a mug of cocoa as she gazed out into the moonlit night. Lights from passing river traffic bobbed and danced above the water like tiny fireflies, and the streetlamps cast golden pools on the cobblestones, but the deep shadows held menace and fights broke out as drunks spilled out of the pubs. Blood mingled with the detritus in the gutters and the sound of police whistles and the thunder of booted feet added to the cacophony of hooters from steamships. Caroline finished her cocoa and drew the curtains before climbing into bed. She might never know the identity of the gentleman who had come to their aid, but one thing was certain – tomorrow she would start looking for paid employment. Her life of luxury and leisure had ended and it was time she started earning her living.

Next morning, at breakfast, Laurence was allowing his tea to get cold while he studied a copy of *The Times*. With his steel-rimmed reading spectacles perched on the end of his nose he looked every inch a scholar, but his brow was wrinkled in a frown and he did not seem too happy. Caroline had finished her slice of toast, thinly spread with butter, and was sipping her tea in an attempt to make it last until she could have a proper look at the newspaper. She had been attempting to read the 'Positions Vacant' column over Laurence's shoulder, but it was almost impossible as he kept moving his head and obscuring her view.

'Where are those boys?' Sadie demanded as she filled the sink with water from the kettle. 'Max should be helping with the washing up. It's his turn today.'

'They're not used to rising early when they're on holiday,' Caroline said hastily. She had not mentioned the scuffle on the foreshore the previous evening, and she did not intend to tell Laurence or Sadie. The boys, she hoped, had learned their lesson.

'But they're not on holiday,' Sadie said firmly. 'They'll be starting their lessons again as soon as Laurence has unpacked his books.'

Laurence looked up at the mention of his name, peering at Sadie over the rim of his spectacles. 'I'm sorry, I didn't hear what you said.'

'I was speaking about the boys beginning their studies with you,' Sadie said patiently. 'The sooner the better, in my opinion.' She refilled the kettle from the pump at the sink and replaced it on the hob. 'Is there anything of interest in the paper?'

Laurence shook his head. 'No, not today, but there's always tomorrow.'

'Might I borrow the newspaper?' Caroline asked, holding out her hand. 'I like to keep abreast with what's going on in the world.'

Laurence handed it to her with a gentle smile, but Sadie chortled with laughter.

'That's the first I've heard of it, Carrie. Don't take too long because I want you to go to market and buy some vegetables and a beef bone. I'm afraid it will be soup again for supper.'

'Yes, of course. I'll go as soon as I've got the boys out of bed.' Caroline left the kitchen without giving Sadie a chance to think of anything else that she might want, and hurried upstairs to wake her brothers. When she was satisfied that they intended to get up and dress themselves, she took the newspaper to her room and sat down to study the 'Positions Vacant' column. Her attention was caught by the name 'Colville', which she had often heard spoken when her parents were discussing business matters over breakfast or dinner – Colville Shipping Company, her father's bitter rival, was part of the reason for Manning and Chapman's dire financial straits. She memorised the advertisement and the address, selected a straw bonnet adorned with scarlet rosebuds and ribbons, slipped on her lace shawl and prepared for battle.

Chapter Five

The Colville residence was situated in a beautiful Georgian terrace at the pier head. After a long hot walk along Wapping High Street, past wharfs, warehouses, numerous pubs and cheap lodging houses, Caroline could not help but be impressed by the comparatively tranquil setting. But she quickly realised that it was an illusion, cleverly created by green lawns and the grouping of tall trees. The houses themselves overlooked the busy entrance to Wapping Basin and the river was crowded with vessels of all shapes and kinds. The peace was shattered by the noise from the docks: the sound of flapping sails, the drumming of great paddle wheels as the steamers ploughed through the water, and the shouts of seamen, stevedores and dock workers. But dirt, noise and bustle meant money. Caroline had imagined that the Colville family would be very well situated, and now she was certain. Some of their profits had been gained at the expense of her father's company and had probably contributed to its downfall. Leaving her wicker shopping basket beneath the splendid portico, she knocked on the door and after a short wait it was opened by a trim parlour maid.

'I've come about the advertisement in *The Times*,' Caroline said with as much confidence as she could muster.

'You should put your application in writing, miss. I doubt if the mistress will see you otherwise.'

Caroline was not going to be put off so easily. 'I've been offered a position with a titled family,' she said, lying valiantly. 'But this situation interests me. I would like to speak to your mistress before I accept the other one.'

The maid cocked her head on one side, eyeing Caroline suspiciously, but she was obviously impressed. 'Wait there and I'll see if Mrs Colville is at home.'

'It's very hot out here. Might I wait inside?' Caroline stepped over the threshold before the maid had a chance to close the door.

'Very well, but stay there. Don't move.' The maid hurried off with the white ribbons on her frilled mobcap flying out behind her like pennants.

Catching sight of her flushed cheeks and slightly dishevelled appeared in one of the large wall mirrors, Caroline tucked stray strands of dark hair behind her ears. People were always telling her that she resembled her mother, and it was true that she had inherited her mother's large hazel eyes, luxuriant dark hair and clear skin, but Caroline could never see the likeness herself. She straightened her bonnet and wiped a smut from the tip of her nose, hoping that Mrs Colville would not notice the smear on her white lace gloves. The jaunty headwear gave her a pert appearance, and she was wondering whether it had been a wise choice when the maid reappeared.

'The mistress will spare you five minutes. Come this way.' She marched off, leaving Caroline to follow her.

She had a vague impression of glacial elegance as she hurried after the maidservant. The walls and the paintwork were stark white, unrelieved by touches of colour, and gilt-framed mirrors reflected the sunlight that flooded through the tall windows, creating square patterns on the highly polished floorboards. Caroline had worked out her speech but when she was ushered into a large, airy parlour overlooking the river, she was momentarily lost for words. If the entrance hall was ice-white, the parlour was the cool blue of a winter sky. The chairs and sofa were upholstered in pale grey velvet, and a similar material had been used for the curtains. After the dust and heat outside, the coolness of the room was matched by the frigid reception of the elderly woman, who was seated on a throne-like chair with an embroidery hoop on her lap.

'You may go, Gilroy,' she said in clipped tones.

The maid bobbed a curtsey and backed out of the room as if in the presence of royalty. Caroline eyed Mrs Colville warily. The advertisement had been brief to the point of terseness and had merely required an educated woman to act as companion to a young lady: no more, no less. It had intrigued Caroline almost as much as the name Colville. She had a score to settle with that family. Had it not been for their cut-throat business tactics her dear papa might still be alive.

'Well, what have you to say for yourself? Your five minutes is ticking away.' Mrs Colville fixed Caroline with a steely gaze, her hooded eyelids barely concealing her disapproval.

'I came in answer to your advertisement,' Caroline said firmly. 'I think I would be ideally suited to the position.'

'You do, do you? And what gives you that idea?'

'I'm well educated, and I know how to conduct myself, Mrs Colville.'

'What is your name?'

Caroline hesitated. The name Manning was well known in Wapping, especially by those connected with shipping. 'Caroline Manley.'

'You look very young. I was hoping for an older woman.'

'I'm seventeen, ma'am. But I'm mature for my age.'

'Hmm.' Mrs Colville raised a lorgnette to her eyes. 'My granddaughter is of a similar age, but I would not consider you to be a suitable chaperone. You may leave now.'

Caroline stared at her, shocked and surprised by this cavalier treatment. 'That's not fair, Mrs Colville. You haven't given me a chance to prove my worth. Might I not meet your granddaughter? Surely it's important that she has a companion she likes.'

'You have a lot to say for yourself for someone so young.' The lorgnette was raised again and Mrs Colville was silent for a few seconds. 'Very well. I'm a fair woman. Ring the bell and I'll send for Maria. But don't think this means that you have the position.'

Caroline tugged at the bell pull. 'I understand perfectly.'

'You're well spoken, I'll give you that, and you have the air of a lady, even if you are wearing that ridiculous bonnet. I cannot abide bright colours and in particular I hate scarlet.'

'I have more bonnets.'

'Then why do you want to work? Why are you not at home with your family, where any well-brought-up young girl should be until she is married?'

'My father is dead.' Caroline did not need to put on the tremor in her voice. She dashed tears away with her gloved hand. 'My mother is unwell, and my family have fallen on hard times. But I don't want pity. I need to pay my way and that is why this job is important to me.'

'You speak eloquently. Why didn't you accept the

position with the titled lady, or is she a figment of your imagination?'

'The person in question is Lady Bearwood, who is a friend of Mama's.' Caroline had not intended to flaunt her connection with the late Earl of Dawlish's daughter, but she was desperate. 'I am prepared to work hard and do my best.'

Mrs Colville's eyes narrowed. 'I would expect at least one reference.'

'Of course.' Caroline hoped she sounded confident, but it might be difficult with Lady Alice away in Devonshire, and with Cordelia staying with friends somewhere in the country.

An awkward silence filled the room, broken only by the steady ticking of the marble clock on the mantelshelf. Caroline did not like to sit down without being invited to do so, and Mrs Colville seemed to have forgotten her presence, as she picked up her embroidery hoop and concentrated on the intricate design, her needle stabbing the cloth as if it were her worst enemy. Caroline stood by the fireplace, wishing that Mrs Colville's granddaughter would hurry up and make an appearance.

Minutes later the door opened and a tall, dark-haired young woman entered the room. 'You wanted to see me, Grandmama?' Her voice was little more than a whisper.

'What kept you, Maria? We've been waiting for a good five minutes.'

'I'm sorry, Grandmama.'

'Don't hover, girl. You know how it annoys me.'

'I'm sorry, Grandmama.' Maria Colville slumped down on the nearest chair, head bent, staring down at her tightly folded hands.

'Stop apologising, you know it irritates me.' Mrs Colville threw her embroidery hoop at her grand-daughter, narrowly missing her head as it floated harmlessly to the floor. 'For goodness' sake sit up straight, Maria. Don't slouch.'

By this time Caroline was heartily sorry for Maria, and would have protested at the unfairness of this treatment, but she realised that anything she said might make matters worse, and she held her tongue.

'Miss Manley has applied for the position I adver-tised in *The Times*, Maria. If I were to employ her she would be your constant companion, and chap-erone. I would expect her to teach you a few social graces, of which you, alas, have none. You are twenty, and it's high time you were married and off my hands.' Mrs Colville turned her fierce gaze on Caroline. 'As she is at present I can't imagine any man taking her on, even with a sizeable dowry. Can you dance, Miss Manley?'

Caroline recoiled, the question taking her by surprise. 'Yes, of course I can.'

'Don't take that attitude with me, miss. I asked a civil question and I only expect a yes or a no. Maria does not know her left foot from her right. She has no sense of rhythm and no idea of style. She has as much charm and elegance as that poker in the fireplace, and if I take you into my household I expect you to turn her in a beautiful swan. Are you familiar with the Danish fellow's story about the ugly duckling?'

'Yes, ma'am.'

'Then that is what you must do. Maria is the ugly duckling and you are Mr Andersen, the storyteller. That is, if I decide to employ you.'

Caroline stifled the urge to tell Mrs Colville exactly what she thought of her, and she wished with all her heart that she could give the poor downtrodden granddaughter a comforting hug. Even though Maria's dark head was bent and her thin shoulders hunched, Caroline could see tears glistening on her eyelashes. The thought of working for such a termagant as Mrs Colville, one of the architects of Jack Manning's financial disaster, was against everything that Caroline stood for – but Maria was another matter. If ever anyone needed a champion it was the ungainly girl, who was sobbing quietly.

Later, walking homeward with her basket clutched in her hand, Caroline went over the interview in her mind. In the end, when Mrs Colville had seemed to tire of humiliating her own flesh and blood, she had mentioned an allowance, which was adequate, although not overgenerous. However, Caroline would be required to live in and everything, including her clothes, would be provided by her employer. These, Caroline assumed, would be plain and dowdy, causing her to merge with her background. Mrs Colville's strategy to marry off an unwanted relative was blindingly obvious. She needed someone to bring the best out of her granddaughter, but that person must not take the attention away from Maria. Caroline was so deep in thought that she almost forgot why she had been sent out in the first place, but luckily she remembered in time and she explored the back streets until she came upon a butcher's shop and a costermonger selling fruit and vegetables.

When she reached home she found Sadie in the kitchen.

'You took your time,' Sadie said, examining the contents of the wicker basket. 'Not bad, but I hope you weren't cheated. Street vendors are up to all sorts of tricks, like putting foreign coins in with the change and adding a farthing or two if they think they can get away with it.'

Caroline handed over what was left of the money that Sadie had given her. 'I had to walk miles before I found a butcher's shop, and then another where I might buy the rest of the things on your list.'

'Well, you're home now. The boys are having their first lesson with Laurence, so let's hope he gets some replies to his advertisement soon. I'd go out to work myself, but there's nothing much I can do. It might end up that I have to take in washing. At least there's a decent copper in the outhouse.'

'It won't come to that. I think I have found myself a suitable position.'

'What?' Sadie dropped the basket on the table and sat down, staring at Caroline open-mouthed. 'But what can you do? You've been brought up to be a young lady. What will Essie say?'

'Mama won't know, and anyway, it's a perfectly respectable job with a wealthy family. I just need a character reference, and it's mine.'

'Where is this job and what is it? Why didn't you tell me you were going to do this?'

'I didn't tell you because I knew you'd try to stop me.'

'I need to know exactly where you're going and I want to know more about this family.'

'You won't like it, but it's the Colvilles.'

'*What?*' Sadie's voice rose to a screech and she clutched her hand to her bosom, breathing heavily. 'You know they were partly responsible for the collapse of your father's business. How could you be so insensitive? You'll break your mother's heart.'

'I'll be paid fifteen pounds a year.'

'That seems a bit mean.'

'I'll get a uniform of sorts and all my meals. I'll be off your hands, Sadie. It will give you and Laurence a chance to build up the school, and maybe then I can return.'

'But the boys will miss you.'

'And I'll miss them, but I won't be far away and I'll get time off. We're struggling, Sadie. Admit it.'

Sadie bowed her head. 'We are, it's true, but I keep hoping that George will bring his ship home safely with a profitable cargo. We don't know anything to the contrary.'

'When he returns I'll be happy to quit. Anyway, I haven't got the job yet. I need a reference so I'm going to visit Bearwood House.'

'I thought they were all away.'

'Yes, but they have headed writing paper. I know Aunt Alice would give me a glowing reference if I asked for one, so I'll have no qualms about writing one for myself.'

'That's forgery, Carrie.'

'Have you got any better ideas?'

Taking a cab to Piccadilly was sheer extravagance, but Caroline knew that Mrs Colville was not a patient woman, and any delay in obtaining a reference might jeopardise her chances of securing the position as Maria's companion. There had been nothing more suitable in the advertisement column of *The Times*, and without qualifications of any kind it was always going to be difficult to find work.

Caroline alighted outside Bearwood House, paid the cabby, marched up to the front entrance with an outward show of confidence and rapped on the door. Of course the family were away from home, but when John, the head footman, reminded her of the fact she pretended that it had slipped her mind. She convinced him it was necessary for her to leave a note for Miss Cordelia. Perhaps it was her winning smile that won him over, but he accepted her explanation and showed her into the morning parlour.

Caroline glanced at the rosewood escritoire situated beneath the window.

'I'll need pen and paper, please, John. And would you ask the housekeeper to unlock the desk?'

He bowed and left the room, leaving Caroline to pace the floor. Her aunt's formidable housekeeper had been with the family for as long as she could remember, and both she and Cordelia were slightly scared of the woman with her birdlike eyes and straight black eyebrows that gave her a permanent frown.

John returned minutes later carrying a bunch of keys. 'Mrs Crowe begs your pardon, Miss Manning, but, at present, she is occupied elsewhere.' He handed the keys to Caroline and she tried not to look too pleased.

'Thank you, John. I'll ring for you when I'm done.'

After trying several of the smaller keys she eventually found the right one and sat down at the desk to dash off a quick note to Cordelia, explaining the situation as briefly as possible. Then, taking a sheet of headed paper and writing in her best copperplate, she gave herself a glowing reference. When it came to signing the document she hesitated, pen poised. Forgery was a serious crime, but she managed to convince herself that Aunt Alice would understand why she had to resort to such desperate measures, and she signed the reference with a flourish. She folded the two letters, placing them in envelope blanks, and used her aunt's personal seal to make an imprint on the melted sealing wax. It was done: for good or ill, she now had a reference that would almost certainly convince Mrs Colville that she was the right person for the position. She stood up and reached for the bell pull.

With her reference clasped in her hand, Caroline waited in the entrance hall of Pier House while Gilroy scurried off to announce her arrival. It was cool indoors, especially when compared with the blistering heat of midday, which turned milk sour and made tempers flare. Caroline was hot and slightly dishevelled, and she wished that she had not hurried quite so much in her efforts to return to the house before the position was granted to someone else. Her fingers twitched nervously and she longed to undo the top buttons of her bodice to allow herself to breathe more freely, but she had a feeling that Mrs Colville's eagle eyes would notice a stray hair, let alone a button undone for the sake of comfort. She looked up with a start at the sound of footsteps on the stairs.

Maria Colville came to a sudden halt. 'Oh, you came back, Miss Manley. I didn't think you would.'

'Why was that, Miss Colville?'

Colour flooded Maria's pale cheeks. 'My grand-mother can be intimidating.'

'I'm made of sterner stuff than to be scared of an

old lady,' Caroline said firmly. 'You should stand up to her.'

Maria's blue eyes widened in horror. 'I couldn't do that. You don't understand.'

'Possibly not, but I'm willing to listen.'

Gilroy reappeared before Maria had a chance to respond. 'Mrs Colville will see you now.' She bobbed a curtsey and scuttled off in the direction of the drawing room.

'Good luck,' Maria whispered. 'I hope you get the job, Miss Manley.'

Caroline answered her with a smile and hurried off after Gilroy, who seemed to do everything at a run.

As she entered the drawing room her eyes had to adjust to the dim light as the curtains had been partially closed, adding to the general greyness. Sunlight fought its way through the gaps, collapsing in narrow stripes on the floor as if giving up the struggle to survive. Caroline had much the same feeling as she stood in front of Mrs Colville while she scanned the reference. After what seemed like an interminable wait, Mrs Colville looked up and nodded.

'Satisfactory.'

'Does that mean I have the job?'

'I'm considering you seriously, but there will be other applicants. You may go. Leave your address with Gilroy and I'll let you know within the next few days.'

Disappointed but still hopeful, Caroline left the room and almost bumped into Maria, who was hovering outside.

'Well?' she whispered. 'When do you start?'

'I have to wait in case there are others more suitable for the position.'

Maria's lips trembled and her eyes filled with tears. 'I was afraid of that. I don't want a middle-aged widow bossing me about, or an ageing spinster who's forgotten what it's like to be young.' Her voice rose an octave and she clamped her hand over her mouth. 'I'm sorry. It's not your problem, Miss Manley.'

'I would love to help you, but it's up to your grandmother. She wanted me to leave my address with your maid, so that I can be contacted should she decide to employ me.'

'I don't trust Gilroy. She sneaks to Grandmama behind my back. I know she does because I get punished for the slightest thing.'

'Punished?' Caroline stared at her in astonishment. 'But you're a grown woman, Maria Colville, not a child.'

'You don't understand,' Maria said in a low voice. 'I've brought disgrace on the family and Grandmama cannot forgive me.' She took a deep breath, holding up her hand as Caroline was about to speak. 'I'm sorry. I shouldn't have said that, but if you give me your address I'll make sure that Grandmama has it to hand.' She turned with a start at the sound of someone hammering on the front door. 'That might be Phin. He's the only one who can stand up to our grandmother.' She raced across the marble-tiled floor to wrench the door open, leaving Gilroy coming to a halt, open-mouthed.

The tall well-dressed man who marched into the house looked startlingly familiar. He took off his top hat and handed it to Gilroy together with his gloves and cane.

'Phin, I need your help.' Maria grabbed him by the hand. 'Please speak to Grandmama. Tell her that Miss Manley is the best person for the job.'

'What is the matter, Maria? Why the panic?'

Caroline did not recognise the tall stranger by his looks, although he was undoubtedly handsome in a cold classical way, with fair hair waved back from a high forehead, straight features and a firm chin, but his voice was unforgettable. He was the man who had intervened when the mudlarks were attacking her brothers on the foreshore.

'Miss Manley has answered Grandmama's advertisement in the newspaper, Phin. She's supplied a good reference but Grandmama is waiting to see if anyone else applies for the position.'

Caroline stood very still, saying nothing and hoping he would not remember her, but he was staring at her with a puzzled frown.

'That seems eminently sensible to me,' he said slowly. 'Do I know you, Miss Manley?'

Caroline shook her head. 'No, sir.'

His slate-grey eyes rested on her for an uncomfortable heartbeat and then he turned away. 'I don't know why you're making a fuss, Maria. Allow Grandmama to do her best for you.'

'Oh, please, do something. I really like Miss Manley, and I don't want just anybody watching over me all the time.'

'Do you really think that Grandmama would take any notice of what I said, Maria?'

'Yes, I do. Please, Phin. I'll never ask you for anything again if you just go into the drawing room and put in a good word for Miss Manley.'

He shot a sideways glance at Caroline, hesitated and then nodded. 'All right. I can see that I won't get any peace until you get your own way.' He patted Maria on the shoulder and strolled off in the direction of the drawing room.

'You may go, Gilroy,' Maria said, turning to the maid, who had been standing to attention, staring into space, but obviously taking in every word that had been said. 'Miss Manley isn't leaving just yet.'

Gilroy curtseyed briefly and hurried off.

'This will be all round the servants' quarters the moment she reaches the kitchen,' Maria said, sighing. 'They spy on me constantly, Miss Manley. Everything I do is reported to Grandmama in detail. Sometimes I feel like a prisoner in my own home.'

'That's very sad,' Caroline said sympathetically. 'Are you sure they aren't simply taking care of you?'

'Does your idea of taking care of someone include

beatings, being locked in your room and fed on bread and water for days?'

Horrified, Caroline shook her head. 'Certainly not.'

'Then let's hope that Phineas can persuade Grandmama to take you on.'

'At least you have a caring brother,' Caroline said, grasping at anything that might bring a smile to Maria's sad face.

'Phin? He's not my brother, he's my cousin.'

'Oh, I see.'

'No, I don't think you do, Miss Manley. It's not as simple as that.'

'I don't understand.'

'My birth caused a scandal that has never been forgotten. My mother did something for which I have to atone, even if it takes the rest of my life.'

'Good heavens!' Caroline gazed at her, wondering what Maria's mother might have done that would lead to such a dire statement. 'Surely not.'

Maria opened her mouth to answer but was prevented from speaking by the sound of footsteps. Caroline turned her head to see Phineas Colville advancing on them, and she experienced a sudden and violent feeling of dislike. The man was arrogant and authoritarian. Surely he could see how his young cousin was suffering, and yet he did nothing to help her. The Colville family had a lot to answer for, and whatever the outcome of her interview she could not and would not leave Maria to endure such treatment.

'Rest easy, Maria,' Phineas said calmly. 'I've convinced Grandmama that it would be sensible to give Miss Manley a month's trial, starting tomorrow.' He headed for the graceful curving staircase, taking two steps at a time with the ease of an athlete.

'Thank you, Phin.' Maria clapped her hands, her eyes shining with delight. 'I couldn't be more pleased.'

'I'd better go home and pack my things,' Caroline said dazedly. She had not expected that Phineas would put in a good word for her, but then he had no idea of her true identity. She wondered if he would have acted so generously had he known that she was Jack Manning's daughter.

'I can't wait for you to move in.' Maria followed Caroline to the door. 'You can't imagine what this means to me. I've never had a close friend and I truly hope we will get on well together.'

Caroline turned to her with a wry smile. 'I'm being paid to look after your best interests, Maria, but I would do so anyway,' she added hastily, noting the sudden downturn of Maria's mouth and the look of hurt in her eyes. 'We will be like sisters, I promise you.'

'Oh, I do hope so.' Maria opened the front door. 'You will come early, won't you? Maybe we could go for a little walk. I'm not allowed out alone and I have to wait for Grandmama to take me in the barouche.'

'I'm sure that could be arranged.' Acting on impulse, Caroline leaned over to brush Maria's thin cheek with a kiss. 'We'll do well together, Maria. I'll see you in the morning.'

Caroline walked away, but when she glanced over her shoulder she could see Maria standing in the doorway, waving a hanky like a child saying goodbye to a loved one. She raised her hand in acknowledgement and hurried on. It was a relief to know she had employment, but as she walked back to the Captain's House Caroline wondered if she had done the right thing in accepting the first situation that had come along. Throwing her lot in with the family whose business practices had all but bankrupted the Mannings might not be such a good idea after all. But Maria's plight had touched her heart and she simply could not walk away and leave her in that beautiful but cold and austere setting. It seemed cruel and unjust to blame Maria for whatever it was that her mother had done to upset her family. Maria Colville was in desperate need of a champion, and now she had one.

Chapter Six

Caroline's first day in Pier House was not what she might have wished. Maria gave her a warm welcome, but Mrs Colville was as frosty as ever and spent a good fifteen minutes going through all the things that Caroline was not allowed to do. Having laid down the law in no uncertain terms, she rang for Gilroy and Caroline was taken below stairs to the housekeeper's office.

Mrs Bury was a little less friendly than her mistress, and Gilroy had been downright rude. Caroline stood in front of the housekeeper, hands folded demurely in front of her, but the sudden change in her status was becoming more obvious with every passing minute. A short while ago she had been Miss Caroline Manning, daughter of a wealthy ship-owner and had had servants running round after her – now she was neither part of the family nor was she a servant.

'You will be responsible only to Mrs Colville, but I assume that she will have told you that already.' Mrs Bury looked Caroline up and down with a sceptical twist to her thin lips. 'I will introduce you to the servants, and then I will show you your room.' She rose from behind her desk with a rustle of starched petticoats. 'Follow me, Miss Manley.'

Caroline had rarely ventured below stairs when living in Finsbury Circus, but she was familiar with the general layout of pantries, still rooms, boot rooms and kitchens. Mrs Bury allowed her a cursory glance into each area, ending up in the kitchen where Cook was busy preparing luncheon. Through the open door Caroline could see a young skivvy, who was standing on an upturned wooden box in order to reach the sink as she struggled to cope with the never-ending supply of dirty pots and pans. The smell of washing soda and grease wafted out in damp steamy clouds, but Mrs Bury hurried Caroline out of the kitchen and led her down a long dark corridor to a cupboard containing uniforms. She brought out a faded grey poplin gown with white collar and cuffs.

'Mrs Colville wants you to wear this, although in my experience ladies' companions usually wear their own clothes. This was last worn by Miss Maria's governess and it's quite serviceable, although it might be a bit large for you.'

'I would prefer to wear my own clothes,' Caroline said firmly. 'As you say, Mrs Bury, it's not the custom for a lady's companion to wear a uniform, let alone one that has seen better days. I will tell Mrs Colville so.'

A fleeting look of admiration crossed Mrs Bury's face. 'Very well, Miss Manley. I'm sure you would like to see your room. Gilroy has taken your luggage upstairs for you.'

Mrs Bury took the back stairs, which were steep and narrow, winding their way through the house in a discreet manner to enable the servants to do their work without disrupting the lives of the family. Caroline's room was on the third floor at the side of the building overlooking the entrance to Wapping Basin. It was small and crowded with unmatched furniture, but the single bed looked reasonably comfortable and the room was spotlessly clean.

'Luncheon is at noon,' Mrs Bury said as she prepared to leave. 'You will take your meals in the dining room, of course.'

The door closed on her, leaving Caroline to unpack her valise. She was just putting the last of her clothes in a deal chest of drawers when there was a knock on the door.

'Come in.' Caroline knew it was Maria even before she burst into the room.

'I'm sorry they put you in here,' Maria said breathlessly. 'I wanted Mrs Bury to give you the room next to mine, but she said that you were to be put in here, and I suspect that was Grandmama's doing.'

'It's perfectly fine,' Caroline said, closing the top

drawer. 'I'm done now, so what would you like to do, Maria? Shall we go for a walk?'

Maria's cheeks paled. 'I can't – I mean I have to ask Grandmama first.'

'Well, go and ask her, or shall I do it for you?'

'I have to wait until she sends for me. She doesn't like it if I do otherwise.'

Caroline stared at her, hardly able to believe her ears. 'But she's your flesh and blood. She's not the Queen of England.'

'You'd think she was sometimes. I think Her Majesty would be easier to approach. Anyway, it's half-past eleven and we have to be at table on the dot of midday.'

'I suppose that's another of your grandmother's rules.'

'Yes, of course. We have to be punctual for meals.'

'Does your cousin obey the rules at all times?'

A slow smile curved Maria's lips. 'Phin does as he pleases because he's a man, and he's also the head of Colville Shipping. I expect you've heard of us.'

'Oh, yes. Everyone has heard of Colville Shipping.'

'Phin was quite young when Grandpapa passed away, leaving him in sole charge of the business,' Maria said proudly.

'Does your cousin live here?'

'He stays sometimes to keep Grandmama happy, but he has a house in Princes Square.' Maria lowered her voice in a conspiratorial whisper. 'Grandmama doesn't know about it.'

'Doesn't she wonder where he goes when he's not here?'

'He lets her think that he's away on business, and she doesn't think to question him. Phin is her darling and I'm just an embarrassment.'

Caroline patted the bed. 'Sit down, Maria, and tell me why your grandmother treats you this way. I really need to know or I might not be able to help you.'

'Well, it's a sad story really. My mother was only fifteen when she fell in love with someone. I don't know who he was, or why he couldn't marry her. Maybe he was already married – I don't know – but I was born out of wedlock and my mama was sent away. I've never met her, but I have a picture of her.' Maria tugged at a gold chain hanging around her neck and drew out a gold locket, which she flicked open to reveal the portrait of a young girl.

'That could be you,' Caroline said slowly. 'She is very pretty, Maria. Just like you.'

'I'm not pretty. Grandmama always said I was behind the door when looks were given out. I'm very plain.'

'Indeed you are not,' Caroline said angrily. 'Your grandmama is a cruel woman. She should have taken care of her daughter, and she should have been kind to you.'

'But my birth disgraced the Colville family,' Maria protested tearfully. 'My mother was only sixteen when I was born, and I'm living proof of her wickedness.'

'Nonsense. It's not wicked to give love freely, even if it is ill-advised. Where was the father in all this? Why didn't he stand up to Mrs Colville and spirit your mother away and marry her?'

'I'll probably never discover the truth. I wish I could meet my mother and get to know her, but that's impossible.'

'Have you told your cousin Phineas how you feel?'

'Phin is quite sympathetic, but he told me that I should forget about her.'

'And you can't do that.'

'No, of course not.' Maria reached out to grasp Caroline's hands. 'I knew that you would understand. My dearest wish is to find my mother, but there's no chance of that when I am never allowed to go anywhere unaccompanied.'

'And you have no idea where she is?' Caroline gave Maria's fingers a gentle squeeze and withdrew her hands. 'She might be living abroad.'

'That's true.' Maria's eyes filled with tears. 'I'm never going to find her, am I?'

'Don't say that. There must be a way. After all, she'll still be a relatively young woman. She must be somewhere, and I'll do everything I can to help you.' Caroline jumped to her feet at the sound of a bell clanging somewhere in the depths of the house. 'What was that?'

'That's the first bell for luncheon. We have five minutes to tidy ourselves and go down to the dining room.'

Caroline stifled a chuckle. 'A five-minute bell – that's ridiculous. This isn't the army.'

'I wouldn't know about that, but Grandmama is very fussy about punctuality. There is always a bell five minutes before each meal, and that means there's no excuse to be late.'

'I see. I'll try to remember that.' Caroline glanced at her reflection in the dressing-table mirror. 'Am I presentable enough to grace the dining table, Maria?'

'It's no laughing matter. Grandmama takes it very seriously.' Maria rose from the bed and peered in the mirror, patting her already immaculate dark hair into place.

'So what happens if you are late?'

'No food,' she said tersely. 'I get sent to my room and I have to remain there until the bell for the next meal. We'd better hurry.'

The midday meal was eaten in silence and, to Caroline's intense relief, it was over quickly. Mrs Colville favoured small helpings of plain food, which left Caroline feeling almost as hungry as when she had taken her seat at the vast dining table. Maria sat with her head bowed and picked at her meal, earning a stern rebuke from her grandmother, and a sympathetic smile from Caroline.

'Don't encourage her, Miss Manley.' Mrs Colville rose from her seat. 'Maria will sit there until she has finished her meal. Good food is not to be wasted.'

Caroline had eaten the tasteless sago pudding in an attempt to stave off pangs of hunger, but it was obvious that Maria was struggling. Caroline was about to protest, but the steely look in Mrs Colville's eye was enough to convince her that she would only make matters worse.

'I am retiring to the drawing room, Maria,' Mrs Colville said coldly. 'Gilroy will clear the table in five minutes and I expect her to find a clean plate.' She swept out of the dining room, leaving the maid standing guard by the door.

'I can't eat it,' Maria whispered. 'I'll be sick if I do.'

'It's not so bad.' Caroline hoped she sounded more convincing than she was feeling. 'Sprinkle some sugar on it.'

Maria shook her head. 'Nanny Robbins used to say that sago pudding was good for me and that there were thousands of starving children in London who would be grateful for such a treat, but she kept a jar of raspberry jam hidden in one of the cupboards and she allowed me to have some to make the dish more palatable.'

Caroline glanced at Gilroy's set expression and she had a feeling that anything they said would be repeated to Mrs Colville. She snatched Maria's spoon and shovelled the rest of the dessert into her mouth, gulping it down with difficulty as it was cold and glutinous. She stood up, waving the empty plate in front of Gilroy. 'It's all gone. You can tell tales to your mistress if you like, but I'm taking Miss Maria out for a walk in the sunshine.'

Maria rose hastily from the table. 'I'll fetch my bonnet and parasol.' She scuttled past Gilroy as if afraid that the affronted servant might try to prevent her leaving.

Caroline fixed the maid with a hard stare as she left the room. Whatever happened, she would not allow the servants to bully Maria – it was bad enough having to stand by and watch the poor girl being browbeaten by someone who was supposed to love and care for her.

Minutes later they were walking beneath the trees on the pier head.

'I feel quite guilty,' Maria said shyly. 'I should have asked Grandmama's permission.'

'Nonsense. You're not a prisoner and we're only going for a short walk on a sunny afternoon. I told Gilroy to inform Mrs Colville where we were going, that should be quite sufficient. You aren't a child, Maria.'

'I know, but Grandmama is accustomed to ruling my life.'

'Then it's high time she learned that you are grown up, and in a year or so you'll reach your majority.'

'She plans to have me married off before then.'

Caroline came to a halt beneath a London plane tree. 'Has she selected your future husband?'

'I don't know, but I hope not.'

'You'll have to stand firm. She can't force you to marry someone you neither know nor like.'

'You don't know her as I do, Caroline. Grandmama has a will of iron.'

'I can be very stubborn, too. I'm on your side now, Maria. We'll stand up to her together.'

Maria came to a sudden halt as they emerged on to Wapping High Street. 'Look, there's our office building. Shall we pay Phin a surprise visit? He'll be astounded to see me out and about.'

'I don't see why not.' Caroline had not intended to visit Colville Shipping Company so soon, but now the opportunity had arisen she did not intend to turn it down. What could be more innocent than Miss Maria Colville paying a social call on her cousin, who just happened to be the head of the company?

The first person Caroline saw when she entered the building was none other than Sidney Masters. Bold as brass, he was seated behind the reception desk, but his bland smile froze when he recognised her and he stumbled to his feet.

'Miss er . . .'

'Miss Manley,' Caroline said hastily. 'I know you, Mr Masters. You used to work for the Mannings.'

He licked his lips, giving her an owl-like stare. 'Yes, Miss Man—'

'Manley,' Caroline said firmly. 'I am Miss Manley, Miss Colville's companion, and she would like to see Mr Colville.'

Masters swallowed convulsively. His face was a picture of consternation and confusion. 'Miss Manley,' he repeated dully. 'But, I thought . . .'

Caroline moved closer, leaning over the desk. 'Does Mr Colville know that you accepted money from Parkinson that he'd taken without permission from his employer?' she said in a low voice. 'I think he might be very interested to learn the facts.'

'No, miss. It were Parkinson who opened the safe, not me. Don't say anything, please. I can't afford to lose this job.'

'Just keep what you know to yourself and I will return the compliment. Please inform Mr Colville that we're here.'

'Yes, Miss Manley.' Masters stood up and backed away as if in the presence of royalty. Caroline turned to Maria, who was gazing round the remarkable entrance hall with its carved oak panelling hung with paintings of sailing ships, screw steamers and the latest ship of the line. 'This is all very impressive. You must be proud of your cousin for building up the business to what it is today.'

Maria gave her a curious look. 'You sound as if you know something about shipping.'

'I grew up close to the river, and I love ships,' Caroline said casually. 'We're a maritime nation, after all.'

'I wish I knew more about the business. Not that I'd be much use because I am quite a dunce when it comes to learning, but I'm sure there must be some way in which I could contribute.'

'I'm sure there is.' Caroline turned to see Phineas Colville striding across the polished floor. 'Your cousin is coming.'

Maria spun round and her pretty face lit up with pleasure as she hurried forward, holding out her hands. 'Phin. Thank you for seeing us. I was afraid you might be too busy.'

His taut expression lightened just a little. 'What are you doing here, Maria? This is no place for you.' He glanced at Caroline. 'I suppose this is your doing, Miss Manley. If you intend to interfere in my family's affairs I should warn you that it won't meet with my grandmother's approval.'

'Phin! That's not fair.' Maria's voice shook with emotion. 'I wanted to see the office. It had nothing to do with Caroline.'

'But I imagine it was Miss Manley who brought you out in the heat of the day. You know you have a delicate constitution, Maria. I'm surprised that Grandmama allowed it.'

'She didn't,' Maria said with an impish smile. 'We escaped, Phin. And I'm not delicate. Grandmama keeps me hidden away because she's ashamed of me.'

Phineas shot a wary look in Masters' direction, but the clerk had his head bent over a pile of correspondence. 'Come into the office, Maria. This is not the place to discuss family matters.' He turned to

Caroline, a frown creasing his brow. 'You'd better come, too.'

Caroline bit back a sharp retort. Phineas Colville was just as arrogant and disagreeable as she had thought at their first meeting, but she might learn something to her advantage. If there was the slightest chance of saving even a small part of Manning and Chapman she would be prepared to do anything within reason. She followed them across the vast, cathedral-like hall to an office that was twice as big as the front parlour in the Captain's House, and furnished with an eye to quality as well as comfort and utility.

'This is a lovely office,' Maria said enthusiastically. 'Why have I never been here before, Phin?'

A wry smile curved his lips. 'I didn't know you were interested in the business, and I doubt if Grandmama would approve of a young woman venturing into a man's world.'

Stung by his patronising attitude, Caroline glared at him. 'I heard that there was a very able lady running your main competitor, Mr Colville.'

'So able that the business is now bankrupt and closed down.'

'I believe that was caused by the sudden demise of her husband, sir.'

He turned to give her a searching look. 'You seem to know a lot about the shipping industry, Miss Manley.'

'I've lived close to the river all my life.'

'But this sort of business is not the usual subject of conversation in polite circles, or so I've been led to believe.'

'Then my upbringing must have been lacking in social graces, sir. My father believed that girls should be educated to the same standard as boys, and that women have much to contribute outside the home as well as within its four walls.'

'A radical view, certainly.' He turned away, concentrating his attention on Maria. 'Now you've seen my office, what do you think? Perhaps I should have some embroidered cushions or a few vases of flowers.'

'That would make it much more comfortable,' Maria said, smiling. 'It is a very masculine room, Phin. Perhaps a couple of pictures on the wall would make it a little more cheerful.'

It was obvious to Caroline that Phineas was merely humouring his cousin and she suspected that he was laughing inwardly, although he maintained a straight face. She picked up a copy of *Lloyd's List* and searched for the name of her uncle's ship, the *Esther Manning*, but it was not amongst the expected arrivals. On the other hand there was no bad news, and that gave her cause for hope. What had befallen the vessel was anybody's guess, but she felt a huge wave of relief and she could not wait to share it with Sadie and the boys. A sudden feeling of homesickness almost sucked the breath from her body, and she was beginning to regret her rash decision to accept the position at the Colvilles' establishment. It had been taken for the best of reasons and the worst of reasons, and perhaps she should have given it more thought. Now she was embroiled in Maria's troubles and they far exceeded her own. Even if she wanted to walk out on the Colville family she knew that she could not. Maria's sad story had touched her heart, and she could not simply abandon her.

'So where exactly does your interest in shipping lie, Miss Manley?'

Caroline looked up with a start to find Phineas watching her with a calculating expression on his classic features, as cold and impervious as those of a marble statue.

'I suppose it's the thought of being able to travel abroad that appeals to me,' she said evasively. It was obvious that in his mind all women were scatter-brains, but that suited her purpose as it deflected attention from herself, leaving her free to observe him and the workings of his company.

His eyes narrowed and, for a moment, Caroline thought he was going to question her further, but he turned his attention to his cousin. 'Well, you've seen me in my office. Does that satisfy your curiosity, Maria?'

'A little,' she said with a nervous giggle. 'But I would like to see over one of your ships, Phin. If it isn't too much trouble.'

'That could be arranged, but I doubt if Grandmama would approve.'

'Need she know?' Caroline asked casually. 'It sounds like a very interesting outing.'

'An outing?' Phin's lips curved in a cynical smile. 'I wouldn't call it that, but maybe the reality of life at sea would dispel some of the romantic notions you young ladies harbour.'

'Oh, Phin! You do say such cutting things,' Maria said, sighing. 'I would love to see over one of your ships, and I agree with Caroline. There is no reason to tell Grandmama anything that might upset her.'

'Very well. I'll arrange it for tomorrow afternoon, but I won't go behind Grandmama's back – she must be told. However, it just so happens that the *Colville Star* is in port and I intended to inspect her anyway. You may accompany me, if you wish.'

Maria clapped her hands. 'I do, Phin. I can't wait.'

'What about you, Miss Manley?' Phin asked silkily. 'Does the prospect please you also?'

Caroline met his amused gaze with a steady look. 'It will be interesting, but might I suggest that you broach the subject to Mrs Colville as you seem to be the only person who might be able to influence her?'

'Yes, please do so,' Maria added eagerly. 'You know that you can wrap Grandmama around your little finger.'

What Phineas said to his grandmother remained a mystery, but his powers of persuasion had never been in doubt. After luncheon next day, suitably dressed for the occasion in cool cotton-print gowns, lace mittens and straw bonnets, Maria and Caroline were driven to the docks in the Colvilles' landau. The *Colville Star* was similar in size to the *Esther Manning*, and Phineas introduced Maria and Caroline to the captain, who was a great deal younger than she had expected. She had met a few of her father's seagoing officers, and most of the captains had been middle-aged men with years of experience in ship handling. But, as she studied his craggy, weathered features, Caroline realised this man, who could not be a day older than thirty, had seen more of the world than many people twice his age. The corners of his intensely blue eyes were crinkled, as if he had spent most of his life gazing out to sea. He was polite but careful in his dealings with Phineas, and for that she could not blame him. One step placed wrongly might mean instant dismissal to an ordinary member of staff, but Caroline had a feeling that this man was too valuable to dismiss on a whim. Phineas was treating him with more respect than she had previously noted when he was speaking to his subordinates, while Maria seemed to have been struck dumb, and was gazing at the young captain wide-eyed with admiration.

Phineas glanced round the deck with a nod of approval. 'Everything seems to be in excellent order, Captain Barnaby. I'll have a word with you later, but perhaps you would be kind enough to show

Miss Colville around. My cousin is eager to learn more about our business and this seems a good place to start.'

Captain Barnaby's cheeks flushed beneath his tan and he cleared his throat. 'Of course, sir.' He glanced at Caroline, his sandy eyebrows raised in a mute question.

'I will escort Miss Manley,' Phineas said firmly. 'She has also expressed an interest in the shipping industry and I am curious to learn her opinion.'

'Aren't you coming with us, Caroline?' Maria asked anxiously.

'Apparently not, but we'll be close behind you.'

'Indeed we will.' Phineas proffered his arm to Caroline. 'A quick tour of the ship will suffice, Captain. Lead on.'

'Why did you do that?' Caroline demanded when Maria and the captain were out of earshot. 'You know how nervous she is.'

'No harm will come to her on board a Colville ship. Captain Barnaby is a staid young fellow and certainly no ladies' man. But the truth is I wanted a private word with you and I knew that this was my best chance.'

Caroline withdrew her hand from his arm. 'Really? I can't think what you might have to say to me that can't be said in front of Maria.'

'I want to know what your business is with my family, Miss Manley.'

'I don't know what you mean, sir.'

'I think you do. We met once briefly on the fore-shore. You were with two young boys, who were being threatened by a pack of mudlarks. What is your reason for obtaining such a menial position, when you are obviously well educated and used to better things in life? Who are you, Miss Manley?'

Chapter Seven

'I am your cousin's companion, Mr Colville.'

'That's no answer.'

Caroline met his steely gaze without blinking. Two could play at his game and she was in complete command of her emotions. Iced water seemed to run in her veins as she remembered how her father's business had suffered due to this man's cutthroat business tactics. 'Mrs Colville was satisfied with my credentials, sir. I see no reason to go through them again with you.'

His eyebrows snapped together and his eyes narrowed, but to her surprise he threw back his head and laughed. '*Touché*, Miss Manley. You have me there, but I will discover the truth, sooner or later.'

'All you need to know about me is that I am genuinely fond of Maria, and I will do my best to look after her.' Caroline pressed home her advantage. 'Now, may we continue in our tour of the ship?'

It was not until they reached the cool interior of Pier House that Caroline realised how close she had come to being discovered. Phineas Colville might have appeared to concede a win to her, but she had a feeling that he would not stop until he knew her true identity, and that would almost certainly mean instant dismissal. It was not the loss of earnings that worried her – even after such a short time in her company, Caroline felt responsible for Maria, and she could not simply abandon her new friend. There was something about her that touched Caroline to the core, and with every passing minute spent in Pier House Caroline's dislike for Mrs Colville had burgeoned mushroom-like.

'Wasn't that splendid?' Maria said enthusiastically.

'I'm not sure what you're talking about.' Caroline dragged herself back to the present.

'Everything. Surely you felt it as much as I did? I mean, it's the first time I've ever been on board a ship and I thought it was wonderful – so romantic. Can you imagine starry evenings leaning over the railings, gazing at the moonlit sea?'

'Perhaps, but I can also imagine stormy waters lashing the deck, and hours and hours with nothing to do.'

'But wasn't he handsome?' Maria stepped into the entrance hall, giving the maid a beaming smile. 'Thank you, Gilroy. Isn't it a beautiful day?'

Gilroy stared at her blankly, saying nothing.

Caroline followed Maria into the house, catching up with her at the foot of the stairs. 'I'm not sure I know who you mean.'

'Why, the captain, of course. He was so good-looking and so nice. He showed me round the ship and made me feel really important. He listened to what I had to say and he didn't contradict me once.'

'Oh, the captain.' Caroline nodded. 'Yes, he was very nice.'

'But I'll never see him again. That's so sad.' Maria ascended the stairs, trailing her mittened hand on the banister.

'I don't see why not,' Caroline said hastily. 'If you really like him, why not ask Phineas to invite him to dine one evening while the ship is in port?'

Maria came to a halt, turning her head to give Caroline a searching look. 'Do you think I could?'

'There's no harm in asking. He can only say yes or no.'

'I'll ask him tonight, but not in front of Grandmama. I'll just tidy up and I'll meet you in the morning parlour in a few minutes. We can have a lovely chat.' Maria picked up her skirts and raced up the remaining stairs, leaving Caroline to follow more slowly.

She had a suspicion that all Maria wanted to do was to rhapsodise about the captain, but it was a pleasure to see her suddenly coming to life. However, if this was first love, it might be unrequited or, even worse, it might meet with such strong opposition that it had no chance to blossom. Caroline went to her room and sat on the bed for a few moments before making herself ready to go downstairs. She had come close to telling Phineas her real name, if only to see the shock and chagrin on his face, but even though she had managed to hold her tongue it was only a matter of time before he discovered that she was Jack Manning's daughter.

Minutes later, Caroline was about to make her way to the morning parlour when someone rapped on the front door. She hesitated, waiting for Gilroy to make an appearance, but there was no sign of her and the knocking grew more insistent. Caroline crossed the hall and opened the door to find Captain Barnaby standing on the step, clutching a parasol in his hand.

'Captain Barnaby.'

'This was left in the saloon,' he said with an apologetic smile. 'I think it might belong to you or to Miss Colville.'

'It's not mine.' Caroline stepped aside, holding the door wide open. 'Do come in, Captain. I'm sure that Maria would wish to thank you in person.'

'I don't want to intrude.'

'It was good of you to come all this way.' She ushered him in with a wave of her hand.

'I'll just pay my respects to Miss Colville,' he said, taking off his peaked cap and tucking it beneath his arm.

'We were both very impressed with your ship,' Caroline said over her shoulder as she led the way to the morning room. As she had hoped, Maria was already there and she leaped to her feet.

'Captain Barnaby has returned your parasol. Wasn't that kind, Maria?'

Seemingly at a loss for words, Maria nodded, holding out her hand to take the delicate lace sunshade.

Caroline turned to Barnaby. 'Perhaps you would like to stay and take some refreshment, Captain?'

'Yes, that would be lovely.' Maria came to life and tugged at the bell pull. 'Please take a seat, Captain.'

He looked round for somewhere to sit and perched on the nearest chair, still clutching his hat. 'That's very kind of you, Miss Colville.'

'Maria,' she said shyly.

'Theodore, but my friends call me Theo.'

Maria smiled dreamily. 'I think Theodore is a very nice name.'

Caroline realised that she had been forgotten. 'I don't know what's happened to Gilroy,' she said hastily. 'I'll go and find out.'

'Thank you, Caroline.' Maria gave her a bright smile. 'Tea and cake would be lovely.'

In the kitchen, Cook had fallen asleep in a rocking chair by the range, her mobcap having fallen over one eye and her large bosom rising and falling rhythmically.

The scullery was empty and there was no sign of the kitchen maids, but the smell of tobacco smoke led Caroline out into the back yard where she found Gilroy, leaning against the wall with a cigarette between her lips. She jumped at the sight of Caroline, tossing the dog end onto the cobblestones and grinding it under the heel of her boot.

'It's for me nerves, miss. I've heard that smoking is good for all sorts of conditions.'

'Don't worry, Gilroy. I don't care if you smoke a clay pipe. Would you make up a tray of tea for three and bring it to the morning parlour? And some cake or biscuits would be good, too.'

'You won't split on me, will you, miss?'

'I won't say a word, as long as you promise to stop telling tales on Miss Maria.'

Gilroy's eyes widened and her lips trembled. 'Cross me heart and hope to die, miss.'

'That won't be necessary, just leave Miss Maria alone in the future.' Satisfied that Gilroy understood, Caroline left her and made her way slowly back to the morning parlour, where she found Maria and Theo deep in conversation. She went to sit by the window, satisfied that at least something good had come out of their venture that day. Even so, she had a feeling that Phineas was not the sort of man to let matters lie, and he would not be satisfied until he had discovered her secret. She must be very careful what she said in his presence.

The conversation between Maria and the captain

did not falter, even when Gilroy arrived with a tray laden with refreshments, but the tea cooled in the dainty bone-china cups and the cake was left untouched. Caroline was content to merge into the background and she gazed out of the window, allowing her mind to stray to inevitable thoughts of her family. She missed her mother more than she would have thought possible, and she could only hope that time would heal the wounds left by widowhood. Leaving her brothers in Sadie's care had been painful, but at least they were not far away, and she made up her mind to visit them next morning whether or not she had permission from Mrs Colville.

Eventually, after an hour, Theo Barnaby glanced at his pocket watch and stood up. 'I really must leave now. I've taken up too much of your time.'

'Oh, no. Don't say that, Theo.' Maria rose to her feet, her eyes shining and her cheeks flushed. 'I've enjoyed our talk.'

He turned to Caroline with a disarming smile. 'Thank you for the tea, Miss Manley. I must go, but I hope we meet again soon.'

'You must come to dinner,' Maria said eagerly. 'Are you free tomorrow evening?'

'I think perhaps you ought to check with Mrs Colville before making a firm arrangement,' Caroline said hastily. 'And Mr Colville might have a prior appointment. I'm sure he would want to join the party.'

'Of course.' Theo bowed and backed towards the doorway. 'I'll wait to hear from you.'

'I'll see you out.' Maria followed him from the room.

Caroline sat down again. It seemed that both Maria and the captain were love struck, but she had a feeling that Maria was going to come up against strong opposition from her grandmother, and probably from Phineas himself. It was unlikely that Mrs Colville would consider a comparatively penniless sea captain to be a good match for her granddaughter, even allowing for the fact that the poor girl had to bear the stigma of illegitimacy.

But when Maria bounced into the room she could not have looked happier. 'Isn't he wonderful, Caroline?'

'He's very nice,' Caroline said carefully.

'Don't you like him?'

'I didn't say that, Maria. Captain Barnaby seems to be a very personable man, and you've obviously made a deep impression on him.'

'Do you really think so?'

'I do, but please be careful. You hardly know him, and you seem to have led a very sheltered existence.'

'I don't think anyone would match Theo. He's so handsome and charming, and he listened to me, Caroline. He was interested in what I had to say.'

'And he'll be sailing off somewhere within the week,' Caroline said pointedly. 'What then?'

'Don't be so mean. I know he'll have to leave soon, but he'll return and I'll be waiting for him.'

'You can't know that for certain. Your grand-mother intends to introduce you to other young men, and you might find one that you like even more.'

'Whose side are you on?' Maria demanded. 'I thought you would understand.'

'I just don't want him to break your heart.'

'He won't. Theo is an honourable man. I feel as if I've known him all my life.'

Caroline realised then that nothing she could say would make the slightest bit of difference. Maria was in love and beyond reason.

It had been a long, hot and tiring day, and the early evening was muggy and overcast with a hint of sulphurous yellow in the sky and the threat of a storm to come. Caroline was ready at the sound of the first dinner bell and seated at table before the second and final peal. Maria was in her place, nervously pleating her white linen table napkin as they waited for Mrs Colville to join them.

'I hope that Phin is dining at home tonight,' Maria said in a low voice. 'I want him to be present when I ask Grandmama to invite Theo to dinner.'

'Why not wait a day or two, Maria? Get to know the captain a little better.'

'I know all I want to know.' Maria's jawline hardened and her brow creased in a frown. 'Please don't say anything that might make Grandmama take against him.'

'Of course not.' Caroline glanced over her shoulder as the door opened to admit Mrs Colville and Phineas.

Gilroy hurried forward to pull up a chair and Mrs Colville took her seat at the head of the table. 'I hope you aren't going to be fussy about your food this evening, Maria.'

Maria shook her head, subsiding into silence with a hunted look.

'I signed the contract with the Dutch company today, Grandmama.' Phineas shook out his napkin and laid it on his lap. 'It should prove very lucrative.'

Mrs Colville took a small portion, then waved aside the soup tureen that Gilroy proffered. 'It's too hot for soup. I thought Cook understood that.'

'It smells delicious.' Phineas ladled a generous helping into his bowl.

'Not for me.' Maria held her hand over her dish.

'What did I say about fussy girls?' Mrs Colville snapped. 'You'll go to your room without dinner if you persist in being finicky, Maria.'

Maria's bottom lip trembled, but she took a small amount from the tureen. Caroline kept a wary eye on Gilroy when it came to her turn – an apparent accident involving hot soup would be both embarrassing and painful. She steadied the serving dish with one hand, making it impossible for Gilroy to snatch it away at the last moment, and helped herself to a generous portion.

Mrs Colville broke a bread roll into tiny pieces

and popped one into her mouth. 'How are things at the office, Phineas? I suppose it must be easier to boost trade without Manning and Chapman competing for every contract?'

Caroline winced as she burned her tongue on the hot soup.

'What's the matter, Miss Manley?' Phineas gave her a searching look.

'It's rather hot, but very tasty.'

'We have an excellent cook,' Phineas said equably. 'As to the business, Grandmama, everything is going as it should be, but I take no pleasure in watching another company go to the wall.'

'You should rejoice in their downfall. Colvilles have always ruled the river.' Mrs Colville pushed her plate away. 'The soup is too salty. I'll have a word with Cook tomorrow.'

Maria cleared her throat nervously. 'May I say something, Grandmama?'

There was a moment of silence as everyone turned to look at her.

'This should be interesting,' Phineas said with a hint of a smile. 'Speak up then, Maria.'

'I would like to invite Captain Barnaby to dinner, Grandmama. He was kind enough to show me around the *Colville Star* this afternoon.'

Caroline closed her eyes. She could feel Mrs Colville's wrathful glance searing her skin.

'What?' The word exploded from Mrs Colville's lips. 'You've been consorting with a common seafarer? What were you doing, Miss Manley? I entrusted Maria to your care.'

'I escorted the girls, Grandmama,' Phineas said calmly. 'I took them on board ship for a brief visit, but Maria seems to have developed a schoolgirl infatuation with one of my captains.'

'How did this happen?' Mrs Colville demanded angrily. 'Has he taken advantage of her youth and inexperience?'

'No, Grandmama,' Maria cried passionately. 'He was a perfect gentleman, and he called today to return my parasol, which I left on board by mistake.'

'He's been to this house?'

'Yes, Grandmama. I'm sorry. I didn't know it would upset you.'

'You're just like your mother. I can see history repeating itself.'

'That's not fair, Mrs Colville,' Caroline protested angrily. 'I was there all the time, apart from the few minutes when I went to the kitchen to order tea.'

'You left them alone? You have a lot to answer for, young lady. I don't pay you to abandon your charge when it suits you.'

'No one came when I rang the bell, Grandmama,' Maria said boldly.

'There's no excuse. The servants would have come had you waited.' Mrs Colville pointed a shaking finger at Caroline. 'You are to blame for what occurred, Miss Manley.'

'Nothing happened, Grandmama. The captain and

I were just talking. He's a very nice gentleman and I wanted you to meet him.'

'I've heard excuses like that from your mother, and she burdened me with you. Go to your room, Maria. I can't bear the sight of you.'

'That is so unfair.' Maria scrambled to her feet and ran from the room, sobbing.

'That was cruel, even for you, ma'am.' Caroline threw down her napkin and stood up. 'How can you treat your own flesh and blood in such a way?'

'Sit down, Miss Manley. I won't be spoken to like that.'

'Perhaps it's time someone stood up to you, Mrs Colville. You are a cold-hearted bully. I've only been in this house for a couple of days, but I've seen enough.'

'Phineas, are you going to allow this young woman to insult me like this?'

'I think you owe my grandmother an apology,' Phineas said sternly.

Caroline faced him, controlling her temper with difficulty. 'I won't apologise for telling the truth. I can't imagine what that poor girl has suffered during her lifetime, but I am not going to stand by and condone such cruelty.'

'You won't have to. You're dismissed.' Mrs Colville's eyes narrowed to slits and she bared her teeth in a snarl. 'Don't expect to get a reference from me.'

'Is that really necessary, Grandmama?' Phineas

pushed his plate away. 'This has got completely out of hand. Barnaby is a decent enough fellow, and the girls were in my care on board the ship. In fact, Maria showed a great deal of interest in the running of the company as a whole, which might not be such a bad thing as she will understand better why you have arranged such an advantageous match for her.'

'Be quiet, Phineas. *Pas devant les domestiques.* Anyway, Maria knows nothing of it at the moment.'

'I know what you're saying, ma'am. I speak French quite fluently.' Caroline looked from one to the other. 'What have you arranged for Maria?'

'It's none of your business.' Mrs Colville pointed to the door. 'You are dismissed as from this moment.'

Phineas yawned, as if bored by the argument. 'At least allow her to finish her meal, Grandmama.'

'I want her out of here, Phineas. I cannot allow anyone to flaunt my wishes.'

'Miss Manley is the one person who might be able to persuade Maria to look favourably on Featherstone's offer of marriage.'

'You're talking about me as if I weren't here,' Caroline protested. 'And if you think I would do anything to upset Maria, you're very much mistaken. I don't know who this person is, but your plans are obviously based on what is best for Colville Shipping, regardless of Maria's wishes.'

'You fool, Phineas.' Mrs Colville's face contorted with rage and a bubble of saliva trickled down her chin. 'You've ruined everything. She'll tell Maria and my whole plan will be as nothing.'

'Just listen to what I have to say, Caroline,' Phineas said quietly. 'We are not monsters, and I do care about Maria's feelings even more than I care about the business, but this union would cement relations between ourselves and Featherstone Blandish, the largest shipping company in the whole country. Together we will literally rule the waves.'

The change in his attitude did not convince Caroline of his sincerity. It seemed to her that both Phineas and his grandmother were obsessed with business and motivated entirely by selfish ambition and greed.

'I'm not interested in your excuses. All I can see is a young woman who has been browbeaten and bullied all her life and made to feel inferior because of an accident of birth. You are using her and I won't allow that to happen.'

'Get out,' Mrs Colville's voice rose to a shriek. 'It's no use reasoning with her, Phineas. I blame you for this. I wouldn't have taken this creature into my house had you not persuaded me that it would be good for Maria.'

'I have my suspicions, Grandmother. I think Miss Manley has been duping us.' Phineas fixed Caroline with an uncompromising stare. 'Who are you, Miss Manley? I don't believe the story you told me. I want the truth.'

'Do you? Well, I don't have to explain myself

because your grandmother has dismissed me, and I'm leaving. I won't stay another minute in this miserable house where money is the only god you worship. You ruin other people's lives without a twinge of conscience. Shame on you both.'

Caroline marched out of the room, intending to pack her bags and return home, but Phineas caught up with her before she had reached the stairs.

He grabbed her by the arm. 'Wait a moment. I won't allow you to upset my cousin.'

'I think you and your grandmother have done that already.' She met his steely gaze with an angry toss of her head.

'You have an answer for everything, don't you?'

'No, but I think I have your measure, Mr Colville.'

'You know nothing of me, or my business.'

'I know that you use people and walk all over them. You leave families to go bankrupt because of your greed.'

He released her, dropping his hand to his side. 'Who are you, Miss Manley? You failed to answer my question.'

'What is it to you? Do you really care that you were party to my father's sudden death? Or that my mother is broken-hearted and has lost everything, including her home and the possessions for which she and my father worked hard all their lives?'

'Manning,' he said slowly. 'You're Jack Manning's daughter?'

'Yes. I am.'

'But why all the pretence? Why didn't you come to me for help? I wouldn't have pursued the loan had I realised the difficulties in which Jack found himself.'

'What loan? I don't understand.'

'I loaned him a substantial sum to help him over the difficult time after the loss of his ship, the *Mary Louise*. It was a legal agreement and when the repayments ceased I had no choice but to pursue the matter through the courts.' Phineas eyed her curiously. 'You knew nothing of this?'

'No. I didn't.'

'Your father overstretched himself financially. He had been very successful in the past, but had failed to modernise his fleet. We were competitors, but I was also his friend.'

'I don't care what you say, you are partly to blame for his early demise. I don't call that the action of a friend. In fact, I don't believe you know the meaning of the word.'

'You've said enough.'

'I haven't even begun to tell you what I think of you and all this.' Caroline encompassed the cold splendour of the entrance hall with a sweep of her hands. 'You live in an ice palace with the ice queen herself, and that in itself is odd.'

'Enlighten me, Miss Manning. You seem very free with your opinions.'

'All right, I will. A wealthy man of a certain age, tied to his grandmother's apron strings, is someone to be pitied. Maybe, if you found the courage to stand up to Mrs Colville and tell her that you have your own house you would not have to pander to her as you do, and I call it very shabby to conspire against Maria and coerce her into a marriage of convenience.' Caroline paused for breath. She knew she had said too much, but all the pent-up anger and frustration of the past few weeks had come bubbling to the surface.

Phineas stared at her as if shocked into silence. Caroline expected an angry tirade, but he turned on his heel and walked away. She took the stairs slowly, her mind racing. There was no way she could remain in this house now, and the hardest part would be saying goodbye to Maria.

Chapter Eight

'I'm coming with you,' Maria said tearfully. 'You can't leave me here, Caroline. You're the first real friend I've had.'

'That's so sad, and I am your friend, but I can't take you away from your home.'

Maria had been lying on her bed, but she snapped into a sitting position. 'This is a house but it isn't my home. I've lived here all my life, but it hasn't been a happy time.'

'I've told you my situation.' Caroline sat on the edge of the bed, reaching out to clutch Maria's hand. 'I have no real home either. I'll go to the Captain's House, but it belongs to Sadie, and I'll have to find somewhere more permanent.'

'You and I are in the same boat, so to speak.' A faint smile lit Maria's eyes, but tears sparkled on the tips of her lashes. 'At least you have a loving mother, and you know where to find her.'

'That's true, but I can't impose on Lady Alice. I call her Aunt Alice, but she's no relation, and I'm afraid I forged the letter from Bearwood House. Your cousin would probably have me arrested and thrown in prison if he knew the extent of my deception.'

'Phin can be nice, but he's so bound up with business that I see very little of him.'

'I'm afraid I was very rude to him, Maria. He'll be glad to see the back of me, as will your grand-mother, but I really do have to leave now. I just came to say goodbye.'

Maria leaped off the bed. 'I am coming with you. I don't care if I have to sleep in the kitchen at the Captain's House.'

'When all is said and done I'm sure your grand-mother must care for you, even if she doesn't show it.'

'No, she doesn't. I'm a constant reminder of my mother's disgrace.'

'Even so, I have no money of my own and I'll have to find myself another position very soon. What would you do then?'

'If I stay they'll force me to marry that hateful old man. They think I don't know about Mr Featherstone, but I overheard them talking about it, and I'd sooner go into service than give myself to someone like him.'

'How did you discover their plans to marry you off?'

'I'm afraid I've become an eavesdropper. It's the only way I learn anything in this house, and the man they want me to marry is very wealthy, but he's more than twice my age and he's already buried one wife.'

'Is he so awful? I mean, you would have money and a big house with lots of servants, and your own carriage. You'd have a position in society, and, more importantly, you would get away from your grandmother.'

'I met him once a year ago, Caroline. He's fat and middle-aged, and he's losing his hair, although he combs what's left over his bald pate, which makes him look ridiculous. He eats like a pig and he takes snuff. Need I say more?'

'I must admit that he doesn't sound like the ideal husband.'

'And he brays like an ass when he laughs. I'd sooner throw myself into the river than marry a man like him.'

Caroline sensed that this was no idle threat. Maria was desperate and it seemed that she had good reason for refusing to consider her grandmother's choice of husband. 'You would have to work if you came with me,' Caroline said thoughtfully. 'I suppose you could try for a position as a governess or a lady's companion.'

'I might, but what I would dearly love to do is to find my mother.'

'Do you know where she is?'

Maria shook her head. 'No, not exactly.'

'What do you mean by that?'

'Nanny Robbins had been my mother's nanny and she used to tell me stories about Mama when she was growing up. I've never met my mother and yet I feel I know her. I think Nanny Robbins might know where to find her.'

'So where is your nanny now?'

'I don't know exactly, but she used to live in Bow.'

'Do you remember the name of the street?'

Maria closed her eyes. 'I visited her there once, and I can see the cottage, but that's all.'

'It's a start. Now I must go, but—'

'No.' Maria grasped Caroline's hand. 'I have to come with you. Don't leave me here on my own.'

'Are you sure about this?' Caroline glanced round the elegantly furnished room. Everything gleamed as if brand new and she would not have been surprised to see price labels attached to the expensive furniture, but she realised with a pang of sympathy that there was nothing in the room that represented Maria's personal tastes. There were no mementoes of childhood or knick-knacks that Maria might have collected over the years.

'I've never been more certain of anything. Help me to find my mother and I'll love you for ever. I know they married her off to a rich old man, but that's all.'

'All right. Pack a bag quickly and we'll wait until the house is quiet.'

'Phin usually goes to his club in the evenings, and Grandmama retires to bed early. We could get away when the servants are having their evening meal, and no one would miss us until morning.'

'Wait here for me. I'll get my things together, which won't take long, and then we'll leave.' Caroline rose to her feet and went to open the door, but she paused, turning to Maria with a worried frown. 'You must be very sure that this is what you want. If you go like this your grandmother might refuse to have anything more to do with you.'

'That's a risk I'm more than willing to take. I'll be ready and waiting.'

The long summer evening was not on their side as far as concealment went, but it was dusk when they left Pier House and they hurried across the forecourt into the relative safety of the trees. Maria had crammed a valise with clothes as well as a portmanteau, and when Caroline suggested that the weight of the baggage was going to prove a problem Maria insisted that each item she had packed was an absolute necessity. They managed to reach the High Street, but two well-dressed young ladies hefting heavy luggage were bound to cause comment. They were not short of offers of help from drunken seamen and dock workers, which they refused as politely as possible. In the end, Caroline hailed a cab and they travelled to the Captain's House in relative comfort, but they still had to manage the walk along the wharf. Caroline took turns carrying Maria's portmanteau and was finding it increasingly difficult when she spotted Max strolling towards them. She called out to him and waved. He came to a sudden halt and then broke into a run.

'Good gracious, Carrie. Why are you lugging that heavy bag, and who is this?' He added, staring at Maria with undisguised admiration.

'Maria, may I introduce my ill-mannered brother, Max,' Caroline said, chuckling. 'Max, this is Maria. She's coming to stay with us for a day or so.'

Max seized Maria's valise in one hand and took the portmanteau in the other. 'Delighted to meet you, Miss Maria. Have you got another name?'

'It's Colville,' Maria said shyly. 'It's not a popular name with your family.'

Max dropped the luggage on the ground. 'I should say not. Why have you brought the enemy home with you, Carrie?'

'Don't be silly,' Caroline said tiredly. 'Maria is a friend. She can't help being related to the Colvilles and they've treated her abominably, so be nice to her.'

Max retrieved the cases with a dissatisfied grunt. 'I don't know what the others will say.'

'They'll be on Maria's side when I tell them everything. Can you hurry a bit, Max? We're exhausted.'

Sadie and Laurence were seated round the kitchen table, drinking tea, while James stood at the sink with his shirtsleeves rolled up, washing the supper dishes.

Sadie put her cup down with a clatter. 'Caroline, I didn't expect to see you this evening.'

Max followed her into the room flexing his hands. 'That woman must have packed bricks in her luggage.'

Caroline crossed the floor to give Sadie a hug. 'It's a long story. I'll tell you everything, but first I want you to meet Maria. I've said she could stay with us for a while, until she finds work.'

Laurence rose to his feet. 'It's a pleasure to meet you, Maria.'

'You might not say that when you know who she is,' Max said, grinning. 'Is there any more tea in the pot, Sadie?'

James threw down the dishcloth and wiped his hands on the seat of his trousers. 'How do you do, Maria? Do you have another name?'

'It's Colville.' Caroline pulled up a chair and motioned Maria to sit down. 'She's suffered terribly at the hands of her family, and that's why she's here now.'

Maria hesitated, gazing at Sadie as if seeking re-assurance. 'I won't be any trouble, miss.'

'Sit down, my dear. You look exhausted.' Sadie turned to James. 'Pass me two teacups, please, Jimmy. We mustn't forget our manners – Miss Colville is a guest in our home.'

'Quite right.' Laurence gave Maria an encouraging smile. 'This is a family matter, so, if you'll excuse me, I'll leave you to discuss things amongst your-selves. Besides which, I have letters to write.'

'Don't leave on our account,' Caroline said hastily.

'I've had two replies to my advertisement in *The Times*, both of which sound quite promising. We need paying students if we're to make a go of things.' Laurence left the room without giving anyone the chance to argue, and Max threw himself down on the empty seat.

'I am the man of the house, as far as the Manning family are concerned.'

Caroline sat down next to him. 'This is Sadie's house, Max. She has the final say.'

'Of course Maria must stay with us,' Sadie said firmly. 'There's nothing to discuss as far as I'm concerned.' She took the teacups from James and filled them from the Brown Betty teapot. 'Here you are, Maria. Drink this and you'll feel better.'

'Why are you here?' James eyed Maria curiously. 'You don't look like a poor person.'

'Maybe not,' Maria said seriously, 'but I haven't got a penny to my name.'

James sat down beside her. 'Does that mean you'll help with the washing up?'

'Leave her alone, Jimmy,' Caroline said, laughing. 'Isn't it time you were in bed?'

Sadie nodded. 'Yes, it is. Upstairs, both of you. You have lessons in the morning and Laurence won't be pleased if you're too tired to concentrate.'

'It was easier at Rugby,' Max muttered as he

shooed his brother towards the door. 'Good night Carrie. I'm glad you're home.'

'Good night, Miss Maria.' James came to a halt, turning to Maria with a wide smile. 'I'll see you in the morning.'

Caroline blew them a kiss. 'I'll come up and tuck you in.'

'Oh, Carrie, we're not babies,' Max said, sighing. 'Good night.'

'I haven't finished washing up.' James eyed the sink hopefully as if it were his last chance to stay up a bit longer.

'Go to bed. I'll do it tonight.' Caroline waited until the door closed on them before turning to Sadie. 'Are you sure you don't mind if we stay for a while? This is your house.'

'And your father gave it to me. If it hadn't been for his generosity I would be homeless, Carrie. This house is as much yours as it is mine.' Sadie reached across the table to pat Maria's hand. 'And you are more than welcome, Miss Colville. If Carrie wants you to stay then it's all right by me.'

'Thank you.' Maria sniffed and fumbled in her reticule for a handkerchief. 'I'm sorry, I'm just tired and overwrought. It's been a trying day.'

'I expect you're ready for bed, but I'm afraid you'll have to share a room tonight. Why don't you take Maria upstairs, Carrie? Your old room is ready for you.' Sadie stood up and moved to the sink. 'I'll soon get this done.'

'Come with me, Maria,' Caroline said, rising to her feet. 'Max will have taken our bags upstairs.'

The attic room, where Caroline had slept as a child, was large enough for two brass bedsteads and a washstand from the servants' quarters in Finsbury Circus that the bailiffs had overlooked. Sadie had obviously been very busy and everything was spotless; the smell of carbolic soap mingled with the scent of lavender, beeswax polish and clean linen.

'It's not what you're used to,' Caroline said warily. 'You still have time to change your mind and return home, Maria. No one will notice you're missing until breakfast time tomorrow.'

Maria slumped down on the nearest bed. 'This is heaven. Everyone is being so kind to me, even though I'm a Colville. I don't deserve such special treatment, Caroline.'

'That's silly, of course you do. Anyway, you'll feel better after a good night's sleep. That's what Sadie always tells me, and it seems to work.'

Maria managed a tired smile. 'I hope she's right, but at the moment I feel a bit lost.'

'Don't worry. Tomorrow we'll make plans for the future, and perhaps we can find time to visit Bow and look for Nanny Robbins. I think you need to find your mama, and I'll do anything I can to help you.'

Maria's eyes brightened. 'Really? Would you do that for me, a complete stranger?'

'Not so much a stranger now,' Caroline said, chuckling. 'The only thing that will hold us up is lack of funds.'

Maria bent down to open her valise and pulled out a shagreen-covered box, which she opened and held out for inspection.

'Oh, my goodness.' Caroline took it from her, gazing down at the diamond solitaire ring. 'That is beautiful. Is it yours?'

'It belonged to my great-grandmother. Phin gave it to me on my birthday. He said it was meant for my mother, but Grandmama had kept it from her. He thought that was unfair and I should have it. He's not such a bad person, Caroline.'

'It does sound as though he has a conscience,' Caroline said reluctantly. 'You could get a fortune for this if you sold it, or you could pawn it with the hope of being able to redeem it when you find your mother.'

'Pawn? What does that mean?'

'You have led a sheltered life. I can see that you have a lot to learn.' Caroline snapped the box shut and gave it back to Maria. 'Get ready for bed. I'm going downstairs to help Sadie finish washing the pots and pans that Jimmy left, and then I'll be up. We have a busy day ahead of us tomorrow.'

Their first stop next day was a visit to the pawn-broker. Maria was delighted with the amount she received, but Caroline knew that it was only a fraction of what the ring was worth. However, it was a considerable sum and Maria insisted on taking a cab to Bow station.

'I remember the station,' she said eagerly as the cab made its way through the narrow streets crowded with costermongers' stalls and horse-drawn vehicles, with pedestrians risking life and limb as they ploughed their way from one side of the road to the other. 'The street where Nanny Robbins lives is quite near there, and I can remember her little house. It had roses growing round the front door and a tiny garden at the front and a larger one at the back.'

'But you don't remember the name of the road?'

Maria closed her eyes, screwing up her face as if making a huge effort to recall a fact that had been long forgotten. 'It began with a D, or was it a C? I think it was a C.'

'Perhaps you'll remember when you see the street.'

'Yes, I hope so, Caroline. I really want to see Nanny Robbins again.'

The cab pulled up outside Bow railway station. Caroline alighted first, and, having paid the cabby, she waited for Maria to get her bearings.

'This direction, I think. I know it wasn't very far from here because we walked it in less than five minutes, or so it seemed.' She started off, heading west along Bow Road. 'This is definitely the right way,' she cried triumphantly, 'and I think this is the street.' She stopped at the kerb on the edge of Coborn Road. 'I'm certain of it, Caroline.'

'Then let's see if we can find the house.' Caroline linked her hand through Maria's arm and they set off along a road lined with two-storey terraced cottages, all of which looked identical to Caroline. But Maria was like a hound scenting a trail. They were almost at the end of the street when she stopped outside one of the dwellings. 'Pink roses,' she said excitedly. 'I remember them because Nanny Robbins picked some for me and I took them home. They smelled so sweet and whenever I smell a similar rose it reminds me of her.' She opened the gate and hurried up the path to rap on the door.

Caroline waited, hoping that it was the correct address and that Nanny Robbins had not moved away, but the door opened and a loud shriek from Maria was followed by hugs and tears as she embraced her former nanny.

'Come inside, my dear girl.' Nanny Robbins ushered Maria into the house. 'You are welcome, too,' she said, beckoning to Caroline. 'Any friend of Maria's must find favour with me. Do come in and close the door – the smell from the gasworks is rather pungent today. It's always worse in the summer months.'

Minutes later Caroline and Maria were seated in the small front parlour with Nanny Robbins.

'I'll make a pot of tea, but first I want to hear all

your news, Maria, my love.' Nanny Robbins put her head on one side, eyeing her with a worried frown. 'You're very thin and pale, Maria. Are you eating properly?'

Maria nodded and smiled. 'I am quite well, Nanny. But I've left home and I want to find my mother. I think you might be able to help me.'

'Left home?' Nanny Robbins tossed her head and a lock of snow-white hair escaped from her mobcap, falling over her lined forehead only to be ruthlessly pushed back into place. 'If you can call it a home. That woman, your grandmother, has a lot to answer for. I didn't want to leave you to her tender mercies, but I had no choice in the matter.'

'It broke my heart when you left. I cried for days, but I knew you weren't coming back. My life was so dreary until Caroline appeared, and then everything changed.'

Nanny Robbins turned to Caroline. 'And who are you, my dear?'

'My name is Caroline Manning . . .'

'The Manning and Chapman Shipping Company? I might have guessed.'

'I don't understand,' Caroline said impatiently. 'There must be hundreds of Mannings in London alone.'

'Of course, but I remember your papa when he was a young man. He was very good-looking and most charming. I can see a definite resemblance.'

'He died,' Caroline said with a break in her voice.

'He lost a lot of money and the Colvilles put pressure on him to repay a loan. I think that hastened his end.'

Nanny Robbins fixed Caroline with a penetrating stare. 'I'm sorry to hear that, but might I ask how you came to be involved with the family you say treated your father so harshly?'

'My mother was broken-hearted when Papa died and she went to stay with a friend in the country. Then the bailiffs came in and took virtually everything we owned and I had to find work. I answered an advertisement for a paid companion, and that's how I met Maria. I saw how she was being treated by her grandmother and her cousin and I was appalled.'

Nanny Robbins raised herself from her chair. 'I'll go and make some tea,' she said abruptly. 'This is all very upsetting.'

Maria jumped up. 'Let me help you, Nanny.'

'No, dear. Sit down and entertain your friend. The kettle was almost on the boil when you knocked on the door, so I'll only be a few moments, and I need to think about what you've told me.' She hurried from the room, leaving the door ajar.

'I think she knows something,' Maria said in a whisper. 'I know when Nanny is being secretive, although I can't think what she could be hiding from me.'

'I'm sure we'll soon find out.'

'She won't allow me to help her.' Maria grasped

Caroline's hands and dragged her to her feet. 'Please, go and talk to her. She'll confide in you.'

Caroline could see that Maria was in earnest and she did not argue. She found Nanny Robbins in the small kitchen overlooking a sunlit garden. 'Maria thinks you might need a hand.'

'More likely she's sent you to pick my brain.' Nanny poured boiling water into the teapot and returned the kettle to the range.

'Do you know where her mother is? She is determined to find her.'

'It's twenty years since Grace was married off to a man she had only just met. Finding her might prove a disappointment.'

'Why would you say that? What is it you aren't telling us?'

Nanny opened a cupboard and took a milk jug off a marble slab. 'Everything goes off so quickly in this weather,' she said, sniffing its contents. 'But this is all right.'

'Is there something about Maria's mother that you don't wish her to know?'

Nanny Robbins concentrated on pouring the tea. 'What makes you think that?'

'Because you're evading the question. I think, whatever it is, Maria ought to know. She's not a child.'

Nanny put the teapot down on the table. 'Maria was told that her mother married a rich man, but that wasn't the whole truth.'

'Who did she marry?'

'The late Mr Colville, Maria's grandfather, had a property in the country. He arranged the match and days after Maria was born her mother was sent down to Devonshire to be married to a farmer.'

'Did you go with her?'

'I wanted to, of course, but I wasn't permitted to do so. Grace left with her father one cold November morning, and I never saw her again.'

'So you think he took her to Devonshire? That's where my mother is staying at present.'

'I've never been further than Brighton, myself.' Nanny placed the cups and saucers on a tray together with a bowl of sugar. 'Would you like to carry this for me, dear? My hands are a bit rheumaticky these days.'

Disappointed, but not wanting to press Nanny Robbins any further, Caroline took the tray into the front parlour and placed it on a highly polished walnut table.

'I'm afraid I can't offer you any cake or biscuits,' Nanny said apologetically.

Maria greeted her with a tremulous smile. 'I'm not hungry, thank you, Nanny. A cup of tea will do nicely, and then perhaps you can tell me all you know about my mother. I'm determined to find her.'

Nanny Robbins sank down on her chair. 'Are you sure about that, dear? Maybe you should leave well alone.'

'Why would that be, Nanny? She's my flesh and blood and I want to meet her.'

'I think you ought to tell Maria what you know, Miss Robbins,' Caroline said firmly. 'She can make up her own mind what she does with the information.'

'What do you know, Maria?' Nanny Robbins took a sip of her tea, but her hand shook as she replaced the cup on its saucer.

'Grandmama won't speak her name, but Phin told me that Mama had married a wealthy landowner and she lives in a big country house somewhere in the North.'

Nanny Robbins shook her head. 'That's not what I heard, dear. Your grandfather owned an estate on the edge of Dartmoor, which he sold almost immediately after he took Grace to Devonshire to marry one of his tenants.'

'She married a farmer?' Maria said, frowning.

'I think so.' Nanny Robbins placed her cup and saucer on the tray. 'I don't know any more than that.'

Caroline suspected that Nanny knew more than she was saying. 'Did he have a name?'

'It was Elias or Elisha, I can't remember which, and his surname was Quick.'

'Elias Quick.' Maria shuddered. 'I don't like the sound of him.'

'It's just a name,' Caroline said hastily. 'He might be kind and charming.'

'Whereabouts in Devon?' Maria demanded.

'I don't know exactly.' Nanny Robbins' face crinkled

with concern. 'You could go to Wolf Tor Hall – that's the house your grandfather used to own – and make enquiries, but you might be heading for a terrible disappointment, Maria.'

'I don't understand. What aren't you telling me, Nanny?'

Nanny Robbins turned to Caroline. 'Sometimes the truth hurts and it's better to remain in ignorance. If you want my advice – draw a line under the past and move on.'

Chapter Nine

The owner of Wolf Tor Hall was less than friendly and treated them with suspicion, as did many of the people in the surrounding cottages, but the landlord at the village inn was more helpful and told them how to get to Wolf Tor Farm. He provided them with sturdy ponies and Aiken, the young potboy, was assigned to them as their guide.

An unrelenting sun blazed from a sky bleached of colour by the intensity of light and the heat of midday. Dartmoor stretched before them as far as the eye could see, the tussocky grassland burned brown with only patches of green surviving where underground streams carved their way through the peat to form Wolf Tor mire.

Caroline drew her pony to a halt, shielding her eyes from the sun. 'What's that?' she asked, pointing to a stone cross on a cairn constructed from granite slabs.

Aiken followed her gaze. "'Tis Wolf Tor cross. There be lots of them there things on the moor. Some say they was built so that the monks could find their way from one abbey to the next, but I don't know. You'd have to ask the witch.' He clamped his grubby hand over his mouth. 'Forget I said that, miss.'

'The witch?' Maria had been following at a distance but she joined them now, reining in her pony with difficulty. 'Where's the witch, Aiken?'

He shook his curly head. 'Just a name some gives her, miss. Don't take it serious, not if she's a friend of yours.'

'I think he means the woman who lives at Wolf Tor Farm.' Caroline fixed Aiken with a stern look. 'Is that right?'

'Yes, miss. Like I says, it do mean nothing. Just talk, you understand.'

'I can't wait to meet this lady.' Caroline wiped beads of sweat from her brow. 'How far is it now, Aiken?'

'Over yonder.' Aiken clicked his tongue and encouraged his pony to walk on, leaving Caroline and Maria little alternative other than to follow.

The land rose and fell gently, and in a hollow surrounded by stunted trees and a low, dry-stone wall, Wolf Tor Farm came into view. A thin plume of smoke spiralled up into the sky and washing hung limply on a line stretched between two wooden posts. A collie burst out through the open door and flew across the vegetable patch, barking its head off.

Aiken cupped his hands around his mouth and emitted a strange sound, a cross between a halloo from the hunting field and a cry of pain, but this had the desired effect and a woman emerged from the house. She uttered a sharp command to the dog and it dropped to the ground, eyeing the intruders with suspicion.

'I should leave you here,' Aiken said nervously. 'Can you find your way back without I?'

'I think you should wait for us. This might not be the right place.' Caroline turned to Maria, who was staring wide-eyed at the unkempt creature who was hurrying towards them. She might, to someone who believed in such things, have been mistaken for a witch. Her long dark hair hung in lank strands and her skin was tanned to the colour of a walnut, but as she drew nearer, Caroline was struck by the size and shape of the woman's eyes, which were so like Maria's that there was no mistaking their relationship. Her heart sank. Could this thin, ragged creature be the mother that Maria had so longed to meet?

She dismounted, handing the reins to Aiken. 'Wait here. I don't think we'll be staying long.'

'This can't be the right place,' Maria said slowly. 'I think I might wait here while you ask directions, Caroline. That woman doesn't look very friendly and I'm afraid of the dog.'

Caroline walked slowly to the gate in the wall and waited for the woman to reach her. The dog was lying down, but it was looking at her distrustingly, and even though she was not afraid of animals, Caroline knew enough to treat the creature with respect.

She waited until the woman was close enough to hear her. 'Good morning.'

'What business have you here?'

The cultured voice came as a shock, but Caroline was wary. 'I'm sorry to intrude, ma'am, but we are seeking information and I wonder if you could help.'

'I have nothing to say.'

'I think you know why we're here,' Caroline said softly. 'I can see by your expression that you think you might know the young lady who came with me. Her name is Maria Colville.'

The woman tossed her head, a haughty action that sat oddly on someone dressed in rags, and the hand that she raised to smooth back an unruly lock of hair was work-worn and calloused. 'I've never seen her before.'

'Might I ask you name?'

'You'd better leave before my husband sees you. He doesn't like strangers.'

'I'm not surprised. If you are who I think you are then he should be ashamed of treating his wife like a common skivvy.'

'I hear him coming. Go now.'

'Grace.' A man appeared in the doorway, filling

155

it with his huge bulk. What little hair that remained on his scalp was iron grey, as were his mutton-chop whiskers and shaggy beard, but he was dressed like a country gentleman, and his well-cut tweeds were a complete contrast to the shabby garments worn by his wife. 'Come inside, woman.'

'I told you to leave. Now look what you've done.' She turned and ran towards her husband, head bowed and shoulders hunched, as if expecting a rain of blows.

Elias Quick stepped forward, giving her a shove that sent her stumbling into the house. He shook his fist at Caroline, baring yellowed teeth. 'I don't know who you are, but get on your way. We don't welcome snoopers here.' He whistled to the dog and it ran to him, ears flattened and tail between its legs. Quick booted the unfortunate animal into the house, stepped inside and slammed the door.

A shudder ran down Caroline's spine. There was no doubt in her mind that the woman was Maria's mother, but perhaps Nanny Robbins had been right. Maybe it would be best if Maria kept her romantic notions about her parentage rather than being exposed to the horrible truth. She walked slowly back to where Maria and Aiken were waiting.

'That was my mother, wasn't it?' Maria's cheeks were deathly pale and her eyes brimmed with tears. 'You don't need to lie, Caroline. I heard the brute of a man calling her Grace, and Aiken said that this farm belongs to Elias Quick.'

'We'd best be heading back, miss,' Aiken said urgently. 'I can smell rain in the air and with it will come the mist. Us don't want to get caught in Wolf Tor mire.'

'I can't leave yet, I need to speak to her.' Maria caught hold of Caroline's hand. 'I want to ask her why she abandoned me.'

'Not now,' Caroline said in a low voice. 'It's obviously a bad time.'

'But I might not get another chance.'

Aiken circled them on his restless pony. 'Look at they clouds forming to the west. It'll start to mizzle soon.'

'We're coming.' Caroline used the stone wall as a mounting block and settled herself in the saddle. 'Lead on, Aiken.' Ignoring Maria's protests she urged her pony into a trot, heading in the direction of the village.

Aiken's forecast proved correct, but thanks to his warning, they reached the inn before the going became too difficult. The cold, damp fog had swallowed up the moors with alarming speed, obliterating the sun within seconds. Aiken led the ponies off to the stable, leaving Caroline and Maria to make their way into the snug bar behind the taproom, where a fire had been lit. The landlord's wife bustled in, clucking like a mother hen when she saw their dishevelled state.

'Lord love us, what you need is a nice hot cup of tea, maybe with a tot of brandy in it to warm you up, and a bowl of my beef broth. It might be high summer, but that there mist makes it feel like winter.'

'Thank you, Mrs Brewer,' Caroline said, smiling. 'That would be lovely.'

'Shall be done dreckly, miss.' Mrs Brewer was about to leave the room when Maria called her back.

'Wait a moment, Mrs Brewer.'

'Yes, miss.'

'Do you know the people who live at Wolf Tor Farm?'

Mrs Brewer's lips pursed and her brow crinkled in a frown. 'Not exactly, miss. Will that be all?'

'Yes, thank you,' Caroline said, casting a warning look in Maria's direction, which apparently went unnoticed.

'What does that mean, Mrs Brewer?' Maria demanded. 'You must know something of the family. Everyone seems to know everyone's business round here.'

'I'm sure I keep myself to myself, miss. As to the Quicks – they don't mix with us in the village and we don't venture often to that part of the moor. 'Tis haunted, they do say.'

'Can you tell me more?' Maria said eagerly. 'What sort of ghost is it?'

'I don't hold with such pagan nonsense, miss. Now, I'd best get your hot food. We don't want you to take a chill after your soaking.' Mrs Brewer whisked out of the room without giving Maria a chance to question her further.

'It's just silly superstition.' Caroline stood up and held her damp skirts out to the heat of the fire, watching the steam billow up in front of her. 'Don't take any notice, Maria.'

'They talk of hauntings and witches as if they were an everyday occurrence. Do you think there's any truth in their tales, Caroline?'

'None at all. They're just stories made up to frighten children and gullible people.'

Maria stared at her, frowning. 'But what we saw at the farm was real enough. I think that poor woman is my mother.'

'You don't know that for certain,' Caroline said carefully, although she herself was convinced that the woman they had seen was Grace Colville.

'I feel it here.' Maria clasped her hands to her heart. 'I have to speak to her and persuade her to leave that terrible man. You saw how he treated her and the poor dog.'

Caroline shook her head. 'It's none of our business, and even if she is your mother she chose that life. She could have walked out at any time over the past twenty years, but she stayed with Elias Quick. Don't ask me why.'

'I think he keeps her a prisoner. You saw how thin and ill she looked, and her clothes were in rags. I won't rest until I've seen her again and asked her all the questions that have been bothering me all these years. You must help me, Caroline. Please say you will.'

Faced with such a heartfelt plea it was impossible to refuse. 'All right,' Caroline said grudgingly. 'But we will have to work out a strategy.'

'I don't want to waste time talking about it. Let's go tomorrow, first thing.'

'Mr Quick must leave the house at some point. Perhaps he goes to market or has business in the nearest town, which takes him away from home. We need to find that out.'

'And will you go with me?'

'Of course I will, but only if I can be sure that we won't bump into that dreadful man.'

Maria leaped to her feet and threw her arms around Caroline, giving her an enthusiastic hug. 'Thank you. I knew I could rely on you.'

Caroline ventured into the taproom early that evening, which was quiet apart from a few old men seated round the inglenook smoking clay pipes and drinking ale. Mr Brewer was behind the bar and pleased to share his local knowledge, although he was obviously curious as to why Caroline was interested in such a rural event as the local market, which he said was being held next day in Bovey Tracey. Caroline diverted his attention by asking if they could hire Aiken and the ponies again in order to see more of the countryside, and, at the mention of money, Mr Brewer's eyes lit up.

Caroline escaped from the prying eyes of the locals

and went to find Maria, who was in the snug bar gazing out of the window.

'It's arranged,' Caroline said triumphantly. 'Aiken will take us to Wolf Tor Farm tomorrow morning.'

'But what about Mr Quick?'

'It's market day in Bovey, which isn't that far from here, so Mr Brewer said. That should give us time to visit the farm and have a word with Mrs Quick.' Caroline sat down on the settle beside Maria. 'Are you sure this is what you want? Are you prepared to face the truth, either way?'

Maria nodded. 'I think so. I have to know if she's my mother. You must understand that, Caroline.'

'I do, of course. I know how much I miss my mama and she's safe and well and not too far away from here, as it happens. I thought we'd pay a call on Daumerle before we return to London.'

'I'm not sure I'll be coming with you,' Maria said hesitantly.

'Really? Why?'

'If Mrs Quick is my mother, I want to get to know her. Perhaps I can find somewhere to stay so that I can see her often.'

'Maria, you're not thinking straight. From what I've seen of Elias Quick he wouldn't be sympathetic. If he treats his wife as he does, how do you think he would behave with you?'

'I don't know. Perhaps I can persuade her to leave him and we could set up home together.'

'And live on what?' Caroline clasped Maria's

hands in hers. 'The money from pawning your ring won't last long, and you'd have to find work of some kind or you'd starve.'

'I don't know what I could do. I'm not fitted for anything, Caroline.'

'I know, and I'm in a similar situation. We just have to think things through, and if Mrs Quick is your mother, and if she wants to be free from her bullying husband, then we'll have to get her away from here as soon as possible.'

'I could take her home to Grandmama,' Maria said doubtfully.

'Do you really think she would take both of you in?'

'No, I suppose not.'

'We'll deal with each situation as it happens. Tomorrow you'll find out if this person is your mother, and then you'll have to decide what you want to do. I'll help all I can, but I can't promise a miracle.'

It had rained in the night and the ground was soft, but the sun had come up and steam rose from the damp turf as they rode to Wolf Tor Farm. The scent of wet peat and meadowsweet filled the air and the bright sulphur-yellow flowers of bog asphodel added splashes of colour to the greens and browns of Wolf Tor mire. A skylark fluttered above their heads, singing her beautiful song in an attempt to lure the intruders away from her nest, and bees buzzed in the creamy-white flower heads of the bridal wort. It was a scene of perfect peace and harmony, but Caroline realised how fast that could change on the moor, and her heart was racing as they approached the gate in the stone wall. Once again the dog raised the alarm and Caroline dismounted, handing the reins to Aiken. Maria followed suit and Caroline unlatched the gate, but the dog went down on all fours, snarling and baring his teeth, as if preparing to attack.

'Down, Bramble.' Mrs Quick stood in the doorway, brandishing a shotgun. 'Stay where you are.'

Caroline stood very still, but Maria seemed to have put fear behind her and she walked slowly towards the house. Mrs Quick raised the gun and then let it drop to her side, calling to the dog to heel.

'What do you want?' Her voice shook and even from a distance Caroline could see that the woman was deathly pale and trembling violently.

'That man called you Grace.' Maria held out her hand. 'Are you my mother?'

Caroline hurried across the vegetable patch and the overgrown area that might once have been a lawn, and she placed a protective arm around Maria's shoulders. 'You'd better answer her, Mrs Quick. Maria won't give up until she learns the truth.'

'You'd best come in.' Grace Quick glanced around as if half expecting her husband to materialise, and then she retreated into the house.

The smell of boiling onions and herbs wafted from the kitchen at the back of the building, and the hot steamy atmosphere enveloped Caroline as she followed Maria into the room. The collie threw itself down on a tattered blanket in the corner, but it kept its eyes on them as if a single word from his mistress would bring him leaping to her defence.

'You shouldn't be here.' Grace stood with her back to the black-leaded range, clasping and unclasping her hands. 'What do you want?'

'You haven't answered my question.' Maria's voice shook with emotion. 'Are you Grace Colville?'

'My name is Grace Quick. I am married to Farmer Quick.'

Caroline could see that this line of questions and answers might go on all morning and she stepped forward. 'Mrs Quick, we don't mean to intrude or to upset you, but please could you put Maria out of her misery? Was your maiden name Grace Colville? It's a simple enough question.'

Grace sank down on a wheelback chair by the range. 'I'm no longer that person. She died twenty years ago.'

Maria flung herself on her knees beside her. 'Look at me, Mama. You are my mother, I feel it in my heart. Why did you abandon me?'

'My father left me no choice, Maria. He led Elias to believe that you were the result of a youthful indiscretion, and that you survived only for a few short hours after I gave birth to you. My husband has treated me like a slave, and has thrown my past back in my face at every possible opportunity.'

Caroline stared at her in disbelief. 'But it was so many years ago, Mrs Quick. Surely he would forgive you for something that happened when you were little more than a child yourself.'

'Elias is a jealous and violent man. You wouldn't want to cross him, believe me. The peat bogs have swallowed many a person who got lost on the moor.'

Caroline pulled up a chair and sat down. 'Mrs Quick, are you saying that your husband is a murderer?'

'I'll say nothing more.' Grace clutched Maria's hands, her eyes brimming with unshed tears. 'You must go now and never come back. Do you understand?'

'But you can't send me away without a word of comfort,' Maria sobbed. 'I've dreamed of this moment ever since I can remember.'

Grace raised her hand as if to stroke Maria's bent head, but withdrew it hastily. 'Don't put words into my mouth. There's nothing for you here.' She turned to Caroline. 'Take her away, please.'

'I will, of course, but I think she deserves an answer, Mrs Quick. Your husband has gone to market. He was seen on the road to Bovey Tracey early this morning and, according to the landlord at the Wolf Tor Arms, is unlikely to return until late this evening. What are you afraid of?'

'If you knew Elias as I know him you would not

ask such a question. He's unpredictable and he could walk through that door at any moment, so go now, please. It's too late for me to be anything other than what you see now. I can't help this girl.' She tried to stand but Maria flung her arms around her mother, sobbing against her shoulder.

'You are my mother and I won't go until you tell me why you didn't fight to keep me.'

Caroline's eyes filled with tears at the sight of Maria clinging to the woman who had given birth to her and then denied her existence.

'You know nothing of my life.' Grace pushed Maria away and rose unsteadily to her feet. 'You have had everything that I couldn't give you. You're a young lady and you're a Colville – be happy with that and leave me alone.'

Maria kneeled on the flagstone floor, covering her face with her hands. 'I don't understand why you're being like this.'

'You must come with us, Grace,' Caroline said hastily. 'You can't stay here and be treated worse than that animal in the corner. We saw how brutal your husband can be.'

'He treated me like a servant from the first day he brought me here. I'm not the same person I was twenty years ago.'

'Even more reason for you to leave him, Mama.' Maria sprang to her feet. 'I won't go without you. If you stay, I stay.'

'No, you can't do that. You can't begin to imagine

what he's like. He'd enjoy taking you like a common slut, and he'd humiliate and hurt you until you lost all respect for yourself.'

Maria covered her ears with her hands. 'I won't listen to this. I can't bear to hear you talk about such things.'

'Take her away from here, miss.' Grace fixed Caroline with a pleading look. 'She has no idea what she would face if she remained, and I would suffer more because of her.'

'Then you must come with us,' Caroline said firmly. 'I haven't known Maria long, and yet I feel as if I've known her all my life. I know that she won't give up. Please reconsider.'

'Where would I go? My mother would die rather than allow me back into the family home, and I would either end up on the street or working my fingers to the bone as a skivvy.'

Maria uncovered her ears. 'I heard what you said, Mama. I'll look after you. We'll manage somehow.'

A tender smile curved Grace's lips. 'I wish with all my being that things could have been different, but I would drag you down. Go with my blessing and live a good life. Forget you ever met me.'

'I can be as stubborn as you, Mama,' Maria said gravely. 'I refuse to leave you. Take your choice, but we are not going to be parted again.'

'She's right,' Caroline added. 'Maria would never have a moment's peace if she walked away from you now, and neither would I. That man you married is a brute and he should be locked up in prison for ill-treating you.'

'I've been shut away from the world for so long that I've almost forgotten how to speak to people,' Grace said desperately. 'I would only hold you back and, even if I did agree to your mad plan, my husband would be sure to follow. We're legally wed and I belong to him, whether I like it or not.'

'I won't listen to this.' Maria rose to her feet, her small frame rigid with determination. 'Go upstairs and pack anything you want to save. We're leaving in ten minutes.'

Caroline could see that Grace was wavering. 'You'll need a mount.'

'Quick took the horse and cart. I'd have to walk and that would slow you down.'

'We'll manage somehow,' Caroline said firmly. 'Come on, Grace. This might be your only chance of escaping from this dreadful existence.'

'You're very free with your orders.' Grace stared at Caroline, her eyes narrowed. 'Who are you, anyway? I don't recall you introducing yourself to me.'

'I'm Caroline Manning, a friend.'

'Manning!' Grace's eyes widened. 'The Colvilles' rivals?'

'That was true once,' Caroline said sadly. 'But it isn't the case now.'

'You can reminisce about old times later.' Maria turned to her mother, clasping her hands and dragged her to her feet. 'Where is your room, Mama? I'll help you to pack.'

'We have to get away from here before your husband returns,' Caroline said urgently.

'He'll come after me and he'll kill me, as he's always threatened to do if I tried to escape.'

'He'll have us to deal with,' Maria said stoutly. 'Don't lose heart now, Mama.'

Caroline watched Maria guide her mother towards the narrow staircase, and, despite the gravity of the situation, she had to smile. Not so long ago it had been Maria who was scared of her own shadow, and now she was the strong one, leading her mother from the pit of despair to a better life. But now was the time for action and Caroline let herself out into the farmyard with a vague hope of finding a cart of some kind to which they could harness one of the ponies. She tried the barn, but the door swung crazily on a single hinge, shrieking in a rusty protest. Alarmed, she took a step backwards and collided with a solid male body . . .

Chapter Ten

Caroline spun round, coming face to face with Aiken. 'You fool,' she said angrily. 'You scared the life out of me.'

'Sorry, miss.' He bent down and patted the dog. 'I was outside having a smoke when this fellow must have heard you and he shot off like a bullet from a gun. So I come round to see what was up and I saw you struggling with that there door. 'Tis a ramshackle old place, to be sure.'

'Well, I'm fine, as you can see, or I will be when my heart stops pounding. I thought you were Farmer Quick, returned early from market.'

Aiken threw back his head and guffawed, a harsh sound that echoed off the buildings and caused the chickens that had been peacefully scratching and pecking for food to flutter off, cackling loudly. 'You'd know it if it was old Quick. He'd have you off your feet and in the hay as soon as look at you.'

'Do you mean he has a reputation for seducing women?'

Aiken grinned. 'That's one way of putting it, miss.'

'He is a thoroughly despicable man, and we're taking Mrs Quick with us, Aiken. I'm looking for some means of transporting her back to the village.'

Aiken's face paled beneath his tan. 'That'll raise a storm, miss. The master won't have her staying at the inn, and I wouldn't want to be in your shoes if Quick comes looking for his missis.'

'Then the sooner we get her away from here, the better.'

'I don't want to be part of this.' Aiken backed away, shaking his head. 'I wouldn't want Farmer Quick to find out I helped her to escape. Down in the village us all knows what he's like.'

Caroline thought for a moment. 'How far is it to the village, Aiken?'

'Two mile or so, miss.'

'And you could walk that far easily.'

'I could.'

'Then we'll take the ponies and you'll be able to say in all honesty that you were tricked. You wouldn't mind walking back to the inn, would you?'

'If it means being saved from a beating I'd walk twice that distance.'

'Very well, then we'll ride back to the inn, pay our bill and be on our way. You don't need to know any more.' Caroline put her hand in her pocket and took out a silver half-crown. 'I'd give you more if I had it, Aiken, but you have my heartfelt thanks.'

He pocketed the coin with a nod and a smile. 'Best get moving, miss. The sooner you leave Wolf Tor the better. I'll set off when you've gone.' He glanced at the dog seated at his side. 'He seems to have attached hisself to me, miss. I think I found a friend.'

'Take him and give him a good home,' Caroline said firmly. 'I wouldn't leave a sewer rat in Mr Quick's care.'

Grace was silent during the ride to the village, but it soon became obvious that her presence would not go unnoticed. People stopped to stare and they nudged each other, no doubt eager to pass on the news that Mrs Quick was seen out riding with the two strangers who were staying at the inn. Caroline could guess what they were saying even though she could not hear the actual words – their shocked and excited expressions said it all.

She left Maria to pack their bags, keeping an eye on Grace, who was still wavering and terrified that her husband would find her and drag her back to the farm. Caroline took her purse and went to find the landlord.

'You'll discover soon enough that we have Mrs Quick with us, Mr Brewer. That poor woman has been abused by her husband and we are taking her back to her family in London. If Mr Quick tries to follow I'll set the police on him.' She counted out the coins to settle their bill and laid them on the bar counter. 'Aiken is an innocent bystander, so please don't blame him. We borrowed his pony and left him to walk home. I'm sorry for that, and I hope you don't punish him because it wasn't his choice.'

Brewer puffed out his ruddy cheeks and exhaled loudly. 'Well, I'll be . . .' He shook his head. 'There's a to-do, miss. I wouldn't like to be in your shoes when Quick finds out his missis has gone.'

'We're leaving right away, but we need transport to get to the railway station.' Caroline placed a golden guinea on the counter. 'It would be in your best interests to have us far away before Farmer Quick returns from market, don't you think?'

'I couldn't agree more, miss. I'll drive you to the station myself.'

Grace sat in the corner of the railway carriage, pale and silent, with a dazed look like a sleepwalker awakened suddenly.

'Where are we going?' Maria asked in a whisper. 'I can't take my mother home to Pier House.'

'No, and I can hardly burden Sadie with the three of us,' Caroline said in a low voice. 'The only place I know we'll be safe is with Lady Bearwood at Daumerle.'

'Where is Daumerle?'

'It's on the coast near Dawlish. It's her ancestral home and summer retreat. She married the richest man in England and they have several properties, but I think Daumerle is still her favourite, and my mama is there with her.'

'Esther Manning is staying at the place you mention?' Grace spoke for the first time since they boarded the train.

'I suppose you must know my mother,' Caroline said, smiling. 'Were you friends, despite company rivalry?'

'We weren't friends. I knew of her, but I never met her.'

'I'm sure that Mama will be very sympathetic.'

Grace shook her head. 'You don't understand.'

'Are you worried because the Mannings and the Colvilles were rivals?'

'Something of that nature.' Grace turned her head away and stared out of the window. 'It wouldn't do for me to ask Mrs Manning for help.'

Maria put her head on one side. 'Are you afraid that Farmer Quick will follow you and cause trouble, Mama?'

'Don't call me that,' Grace said angrily. 'I might have given birth to you, but I abandoned you. We are strangers, Maria. The gap between us is too wide to bridge easily.'

'That's not true. I understand why you had to give me up. I would have been forced into an arranged marriage if I hadn't run away, so I can see how it must have been for you.' Maria reached out to grasp Grace's hands. 'Can't we start at the beginning and get to know one another?'

Grace withdrew her hands as if Maria's touch had burned her skin. 'It's too late for that. I don't think I'm capable of loving another person. Elias beat that out of me, and all that's left is a shell.'

'I'm afraid we will have to visit Daumerle,' Caroline said gently. 'My mother is a very generous woman and she won't hold the fact that you're a Colville against you. The very opposite, I should think, especially when she hears how you've suffered for all these years.'

'No. I'm sorry, but you're wrong. I have my reasons, but I cannot and will not throw myself on her mercy.'

'You make it sound so dramatic.' Caroline sat back in her seat, eyeing Grace curiously. 'Is there something you haven't told us?'

'Leave her alone, Caroline,' Maria said urgently. 'Can't you see that she's exhausted and doesn't know what she's saying? We'll have to find somewhere else to go.'

'We're running out of money.' Caroline's fingers curled around her reticule. Her purse was considerably lighter after she had paid their fares as far as Dawlish, and there was not enough to take them much further, let alone to pay for food and lodgings. 'We have to be practical.'

Grace sat bolt upright. 'I knew I shouldn't have

come with you. I am just a burden and an embarrassment.'

'Don't say things like that, Mama.' Maria's cheeks flooded with colour and she bit her lip. 'I'm sorry, what should I call you if you don't want to be my mother?'

'I have grown accustomed to being called Grace, so you might as well use that name, but I don't intend to burden you with my presence for any longer than necessary. I'll find work and make my own way in the world.'

'You are a very ungrateful woman,' Caroline said angrily. 'Maria needs you and she loves you, although you haven't given her any reason for doing so. Whether you care to acknowledge it or not, she's your daughter.'

Grace raised her hand as if to fend off a blow and turned her head away. 'I failed at love and I failed as a mother. Leave me alone.'

They lapsed into silence, broken only by the clickety-clack of the wheels rumbling over the tracks, and the occasional hoot of the steam whistle as they approached a junction. Grace had closed her eyes and Caroline could not decide whether she was feigning sleep or if she was dozing, but Maria was alert and fidgety and obviously upset.

'What will we do, Caroline?' she asked in a whisper. 'It's obvious we can't take her to meet your mama. She's in such a state I think she would run away before we got there.'

'There's only one other place that comes to mind, although I haven't been there since I was a child. Starcross Abbey is only a few miles from Daumerle.'

'An abbey? Do monks live there?'

'Not for centuries,' Caroline said, laughing. 'My uncle Freddie lives there with a few servants to keep the place going. He's an artist and quite well thought of.'

'Is he very rich?'

'I don't think so, and he's not really my uncle, it's just that I've always called him that. He's Lady Bearwood's cousin, and I believe the estate belongs to his brother, who lives in Australia. Mama often mentions him; I think she was rather sweet on Lord Dorincourt at one time, but then she met my father.'

Maria's eyes shone with excitement. 'I can't wait to see the Abbey. It sounds so romantic and mysterious.'

'I don't know about that, but there is a secret passage down to a cave where smugglers used to hide their contraband. It's the stuff of penny novelettes, but it's true.'

'Will we get there soon?'

'We'll have to change trains at least once, maybe twice, I'm not sure, and we'll have to find transport to take us to the Abbey, but we should get there before dark.'

The sun was low in the sky when the farm cart dropped them off outside the gates of Starcross

Abbey. After a long wait at the station it had been sheer luck that Caroline spotted a farmer unloading boxes of vegetables onto a porter's wagon. He had not been very forthcoming at the start, but the sight of a handful of coins had brought forth the better side of his nature and he had, somewhat grudgingly, agreed to take them to Starcross.

Caroline stood outside the closed gates, breathing in the pine-scented air, laced with the salty tang from the sea. The sound of waves rhythmically pounding the shore and the cries of seagulls flying overhead reminded her of holidays spent in Devonshire when she was growing up. She had always loved the gothic Abbey, and had a special soft spot for Uncle Freddie, although her father had always said that Freddie Dorincourt was a useless sort of fellow and spent far too much time splashing oil paint onto canvas. Her mother had always taken Freddie's side, and Caroline had loved to sit quietly in his studio, watching him concentrate on his latest work.

'Well, are you going to open the gate?' Maria said, chuckling. 'Or are we going to stand here all night admiring the scenery?'

'I'm not sure I should be here.' Grace dumped the small carpet bag containing all her worldly goods on the ground at her feet. 'Maybe I should have stayed in the town.'

'It appears that the gatehouse is empty.' Caroline chose to ignore Grace's self-pitying remark, just as she had done during most of their journey. She sympathised with the poor woman, but at times Caroline's patience was wearing thin and she had felt like shaking her and telling her how lucky she was to have a daughter like Maria.

'Do you think that your uncle is away from home?' Maria peered through the ornate ironwork scrolls.

'There's only one way to find out.' Caroline slipped her hand through the bars, and found to her relief that the padlock was hanging loose and the gates opened easily. They walked the last hundred yards to the carriage sweep at the front of the ancient mansion. With a tower at each corner of the building, Starcross Abbey had obviously seen many changes during its hundreds of years of existence, but it still retained a timeless, peaceful atmosphere.

Maria dropped her bag and clasped her hands together, her eyes shining. 'It's so beautiful.'

'This part is fairly new.' Caroline pointed to the left side of the building. 'Mama said the original wing was burned down in a fire caused by a disgruntled servant, who died from the burns he received.' She hammered on the door. 'Let's hope Uncle Freddie is at home. I'm not sure that the housekeeper will remember me.'

They did not have long to wait. Hurried footsteps pitter-pattered across the stone floor and the door was opened by a plump, middle-aged woman dressed in black bombazine.

'Is that you, Jenifry?' Caroline asked tentatively. 'It is, isn't it? I'd know that smile anywhere.'

'Miss Caroline. This is a surprise. Come in, please.'

Jenifry Grimes had been employed at Starcross for as long as Caroline could remember.

'Your mother used to spoil me when I was a child. She was the most amazing cook and used to bake my favourite dishes.' Caroline stepped over the threshold, taking in the serene ambience of the old building with its aura of peace and contentment. It felt like coming home, even though she had never lived here for longer than a few weeks at a time. She could almost feel the house wrapping its arms around her and suddenly she was fighting back tears. She had pushed all thoughts of her old home to the back of her mind, but now they came flooding back and threatened to swamp her.

Jenifry ushered them all inside. 'Ma decided to give up work a few months ago. She's got rheumatics and this old place is a bit damp in the winter, so she stays at home in the cottage and sits by the fire, knitting and generally making a nuisance of herself by telling me what to do.'

'That sounds lovely,' Maria said wistfully. 'I'm Maria Colville, by the way, and this is my mama.' She indicated Grace, who was hanging back, gazing round as if she could hardly believe her eyes.

'What a beautiful house,' Grace murmured. 'I never thought to see the like again.'

Jenifry gave her a cursory glance. 'You're very welcome, ma'am. I'll tell the master that you're here. We don't get many visitors these days, so you'll have to excuse the fact that your rooms won't be ready for a while.'

'That's quite all right. We turned up unexpectedly and I'm sure we could share a room if that would help.' Caroline glanced round, half expecting to see her uncle materialise. 'Where is Mr Dorincourt?'

A wry smile curved Jenifry's lips. 'Where he be always – in his studio. I'll show you to the drawing room and get Cook to make up a tray of tea for you. Dinner will be at eight.'

'Don't put yourselves out for us. We're truly grateful for anything,' Caroline said hastily.

'If you leave your luggage there I'll get Dickon to take it up to your rooms.'

'Dickon?' Caroline followed Jenifry across the entrance hall. 'He's new, I think.'

'Not so very new, Miss Caroline. Dickon is my son.'

'I didn't know you were married, Jenifry.'

'My husband is a seaman, miss. He sailed away more years ago than I like to remember and never returned. I don't know if he's alive or dead.'

'I'm so sorry.'

'Thank you, miss. Anyway, I'm known as Mrs Grimes, just like Ma, so everything changes and everything stays the same, as they say.' Jenifry opened the drawing-room door and they filed into the oak-panelled room. 'I'll be back dreckly.'

Caroline breathed in the scent of wax polish and the perfume from a vase filled with garden roses set on a low table in the middle of the room, but that was the only feminine touch visible. Books were scattered on every available surface and a pair of leather slippers had been abandoned in the empty grate. The padded leather sofa and armchairs would not have looked out of place in a gentleman's club, and a pair of shotguns were propped up against a wooden settle. It was every inch a man's room and Caroline stood on the red Turkey carpet, wondering whether to sit down and try to make herself comfortable, or to stand there in readiness to greet her uncle.

Maria looked equally uncomfortable and Grace had begun, as if out of habit, to tidy up the piles of books and periodicals that had fallen on the floor.

'There's no need to do that, Grace,' Caroline said hastily. 'I'm sure the servants will see to it.'

Grace straightened up, standing to attention. 'I'm sorry, miss. It's force of habit.'

'It's Caroline. You're not a servant. You're a guest in this house, Grace.'

'I'd be happier below stairs. It looks as though they need help.'

Caroline was saved from answering by her uncle, who burst into the room, bringing with him the aroma of linseed oil, turpentine and cigar smoke. Frederick Dorincourt came to a standstill, looking from one to the other with an appreciative smile.

'Well then, Carrie, my love. What a wonderful surprise.' He enveloped her in a hug that almost squeezed the breath from her lungs, then held her at arm's length, taking in every detail of her appearance. 'You are a sight for sore eyes. You get more beautiful every time I see you. In fact, I must paint you. I insist upon it.'

Caroline looked him up and down. It was several years since they had last met, and he must be at least forty-five, but he had not lost his youthful zest for life and his face was unlined apart from laughter lines at the corners of his blue eyes, which were set beneath straight black brows. The only sign of ageing was the streaks of silver in his long, dark hair, which curled around his head giving him the appearance of an elderly angel, which Caroline knew was far from the truth. Uncle Freddie had a reputation with women and she could see that his roving eye had fallen on Maria.

'May I introduce my friend Maria Colville?' Caroline said, remembering her manners. 'And her mother, Mrs Grace Quick.'

Freddie released Caroline, bowing to Grace and Maria with a courtly gesture. 'Delighted to make your acquaintance, ladies. It's a pleasure to have such charming company.'

Maria bobbed a curtsey, but Grace remained aloof, eyeing him suspiciously.

Caroline cleared her throat, sensing the underlying tension in the room, although Freddie seemed totally oblivious to anything other than the fact he was surrounded by pretty women.

'I'm sorry to descend on you like this, Uncle. It's a long story, I'm afraid.'

'Then save it until we are relaxed over a bottle or two of wine at dinner,' Freddie said, beaming. 'It was getting devilish dull here and to tell the truth I couldn't be more pleased to see you. I am in desperate need of models to paint and here you are, lovely ladies descended from artists' heaven.'

'Really, Uncle.' Caroline shook her head. 'The things you say.'

'I only speak the truth.' Freddie took a step backwards, gazing thoughtfully at Grace, who looked away. 'You, madam, are the most interesting in my eyes. I see pain and suffering etched onto beauty. Come with me now and I'll start making a few sketches.'

Caroline laid her hand on the sleeve of his velvet smoking jacket, which was splashed with paint. 'No, Uncle Freddie. I'm sure that can wait until morning. We've been travelling all day and we're all exhausted.'

He sighed and shrugged. 'Oh, well, I suppose you're right, but we'll start first thing in the morning. Do you rise early, Mrs Quick?'

'I'm a farmer's wife, sir. I rise at dawn and my name is Grace.'

Freddie took her hands in his, turning them palm upwards. 'Such lovely hands, worn and calloused by hard work. They tell a story in themselves.' He raised them to his lips. 'I should call you Graziella – it suits you much better than Grace, which is a name for serving maids.'

Grace snatched her hands free, giving him a suspicious look. 'If you're laughing at me, sir, I don't think it's very nice.'

'I never joke about the serious things in life.' Freddie sauntered over to a table set with cut-crystal decanters and glasses. 'Will anyone join me in a tot of the best Armagnac? Or do you ladies prefer to coddle your bellies with tea?'

'Uncle Freddie, you are impossible,' Caroline said, chuckling. 'I can only speak for myself but I would prefer tea.'

'And I,' Maria added.

'I'll take brandy, sir.' Grace crossed the floor to join him. 'After the day I've had I think I need something stronger than tea.' She accepted the glass he proffered and tossed the drink back in one. 'Thank you.'

Freddie stared at her in amazement and a slow smile lit his eyes and curved his lips. 'By God, a woman after my own heart. I knew it the moment I saw you. I love a challenge.'

Caroline was beginning to think that coming here was a serious mistake, but Maria was laughing and the colour had returned to Grace's pale cheeks. Freddie was refilling her glass when the door opened to admit a boy carrying a tray of tea and cake. The aroma of warm saffron buns reminded Caroline of previous visits to Devonshire, and she moved swiftly to clear the table.

'So they've got you doing women's work, have they, Dickon?' Freddie said, laughing.

'I don't mind, sir.' Dickon placed the tray carefully on the table. He straightened up. 'I remember you, miss,' he said, grinning at Caroline. 'You don't remember me, though.'

She shook her head. 'I'm afraid not. You're Jenifry's son, but I didn't know she had any children.'

'Just me, miss. I'm the one and only.'

'And a cheeky young scamp to boot,' Freddie said casually. 'Be off with you, boy. Go and help your mother.'

'Yes, sir.' Dickon left the room, chuckling to himself.

'That boy has the cheek of Old Nick,' Freddie said, topping up his glass with brandy. He raised it in a toast. 'Welcome to Starcross Abbey, ladies. I hope your stay will be a long one.'

The door opened and Dickon bounced back into the room. 'I nearly forgot to say that Ma has made your old room ready, Miss Caroline. The others will be ready soon.' He retreated before anyone had a chance to comment.

'Why do you allow him such freedom, Uncle?' Caroline asked as she poured the tea. 'I can't imagine Mama allowing a servant to behave like that.'

'He's my son,' Freddie said calmly. 'Illegitimate, of course. I'm sorry if that offends you ladies, but these things happen.'

Maria's hand flew to cover her mouth and her eyes widened in horror. 'No, really?'

Freddie smiled. 'You've led a sheltered life, Miss Colville. We will have to broaden your education.'

'You men are all the same.' With a flick of her wrist, Grace tossed her drink in his face. 'Touch that girl and you'll be facing the wrong end of one of those shotguns, and I'm no mean shot, believe me.'

There was a horrified silence. Caroline sat with the teapot poised over a cup and Maria sank down on the nearest chair, staring at her mother in a mixture of shock and amazement. Freddie was the first to recover and he threw back his head and laughed.

Grace glared at him, her lips tightened into a pencil-thin line and her eyes flashing angrily. 'You are old enough to be her father,' she hissed. 'I suppose you think that seducing a servant is your right – well, it isn't.'

'Madam,' Freddie said humbly, 'I apologise for my coarse remark, and I apologise for being a mere male. I've done many things to be ashamed of, but I've never forced myself on a woman. I can assure you that Dickon's mother and I had a passionate relationship that gradually burned itself out. She has my total respect and she will never want for anything. In fact it was she who tired of me, and for that I cannot blame her.'

Grace turned her back on him and went to sit beside Maria. 'Don't imagine that I'll apologise, because I won't.'

'I respect your decision.' Freddie placed his empty glass back on the tray. 'I will return to my studio, but I will join you for dinner.' He was about to leave the room, but he hesitated in the doorway. 'I hope you will still sit for me, Graziella. I long to capture the fiery spirit that you've just demonstrated. I knew you were a powerful woman the moment I set eyes on you.' He left them, closing the door softly behind him.

'Well!' Caroline said, sipping her tea. 'Who would have believed it? You are a dark horse, Grace Quick.'

'I'll never use that name again as long as I live,' Grace said firmly. 'From now on I am Grace Colville.' She raised her head to give Maria a long look. 'You see where uncontrolled passion leads you. Men like Freddie prey on young innocent women.'

'I don't think that's fair,' Caroline protested. 'He has stood by Jenifry, and he said that it was she who ended their relationship.'

'But she's still a servant.' Grace stood up. 'I would like to rest. Would you allow me to use your room until they find somewhere for me to sleep?'

Caroline put her cup and saucer down and rose to her feet. 'Of course. It's a long time since I last stayed here, but I think I can remember how to find my old room. Come with me, Grace.'

'Would you like me to go with you, Mama?' Maria asked anxiously.

'No, but thank you anyway. I need to be on my own for a while. I have to think and decide what I ought to do next. I can't remain here indefinitely.'

Maria jumped to her feet, holding out her hand. 'We'll work it out together, Mama.'

'You don't understand; neither do you, Caroline. If the truth came out it would be a disaster for all concerned.'

Chapter Eleven

Satisfied that she had done everything she could to make Grace comfortable, Caroline left her lying down on the four-poster bed in her old room. She hesitated on the landing, wondering whether to venture to the kitchen and offer Jenifry some help, or return to the drawing room. Freddie's casual acknowledgement of his former relationship with his housekeeper had come as a shock, as had his announcement that Dickon was his illegitimate son. Caroline did not consider herself to be a prude, but she realised now that she had led a sheltered existence, and knew little of the world outside the elegant walls of the house in Finsbury Circus. What secrets Grace had yet to divulge were still a mystery, but Caroline had a feeling of foreboding, and she suspected that what had happened in the past had something to do with the rivalry between the

Colvilles and the Mannings. She decided to leave the domestic arrangements to Jenifry and hurried back to the drawing room.

Maria looked up from the copy of *Punch* magazine she was reading and replaced it on the table. 'Is she all right?'

'Your mother is resting. We need to give her time to adjust to simply being free from that hateful man. She's been through a lot, Maria.'

'I might not know the identity of my father, but at least it wasn't that person,' Maria said, shuddering. 'But what will we do if that horrible man comes looking for her?'

'Grace is safe here for the time being, but we need to think carefully about what to do next.'

'I'm afraid she offended your uncle, Caroline. She has quite a temper.'

'I think he was more amused than angry,' Caroline said, smiling. 'Uncle Freddie is a dear, if a little eccentric, but we can't stay here for ever.'

'I suppose we must return to London, but I can never go back to my grandmother's house.'

'I'll visit Daumerle tomorrow and see Mama. I hope she's recovered her spirits by now – she was brought so low after my father's death. I really thought she might die of a broken heart.'

'Do you think she will be able to help? After all, you said your family has lost everything. It seems to me that we're all in a terrible fix.'

Caroline went to the window, gazing out at the

sweep of lawn surrounded by tall trees, and a glimpse of the sea, gleaming like a silver ribbon laced between the branches. 'I will find a way, Maria. I just don't know how I'm going to do it, but I refuse to be beaten.'

'If all else fails I'll ask Phineas for help.'

'Let's hope it won't come to that. He made it perfectly clear what he thought of me and my family. Heaven knows what he would say if he saw your mother now, and I don't think he'd approve of the goings-on here at Starcross Abbey either.'

A gurgle of laughter escaped from Maria's lips. 'I'd love to see Grandmama's face if confronted by your uncle.'

'He would probably charm her into sitting for her portrait. Uncle Freddie has had a colourful past, including several years in exile in Italy, as well as gold mining in Australia. We must get him talking about it at dinner – that will cheer everyone up.'

At eight o'clock Caroline took her seat at the dining table next to Maria, but Grace had refused to leave her room. What was even more surprising was the fact that Jenifry and Dickon were apparently going to join them for the meal. Jenifry served the soup and then sat down at the far end of the table with Dickon on her left.

'Where is Graziella?' Freddie demanded, gazing round as if expecting to see her lurking in a corner of the candlelit room.

'She begs to be excused,' Caroline said tactfully. 'She has a headache and is very tired.'

'Nonsense. I don't believe that for a moment.' Freddie leaped to his feet. 'Don't start until I return.'

He left the room and everyone sat still and silent, as if in a tableau, until he returned minutes later, carrying Grace over his shoulder. He dumped her unceremoniously in a chair on his right.

'I told you I don't want any food,' Grace said angrily. 'I won't be treated like this.'

'You will sit and eat, if only to please my excellent cook, who will be mortified if this soup goes to waste.' Freddie shot her a sideways glance. 'You need meat on your bones, woman.'

Caroline glanced at Jenifry and Dickon, but neither of them seemed to be upset or even surprised by Freddie's unconventional behaviour.

'Eat and enjoy,' Freddie said, picking up his spoon. 'Tomorrow morning I will make a start on your portrait, Graziella. I've already made a preliminary sketch, from memory, of course, but I have a feeling that this will be my masterpiece.'

Grace gave him a stony stare. 'If you call me Graziella once more I'll empty the damn tureen over your head. Do you understand me?'

Freddie shrugged and blew her a kiss.

'I thought I might go to Daumerle tomorrow,' Caroline said tentatively. 'I'm quite a good rider, Uncle Freddie, so I wonder if I might borrow one of your horses.'

'Of course you may. Dickon will accompany you. I can't allow you to roam the countryside on your own.'

'I'll be glad to,' Dickon said cheerfully. 'I'll get all the gossip from the stable lads at Daumerle. Ma enjoys a bit of tittle-tattle from the big house.'

Jenifry shook her head, smiling. 'Hush now, Dickon. Your pa isn't interested in such nonsense.'

'That's right,' Freddie said airily. 'My mind is on higher things.' He turned to stare at Grace. 'Have you anything less ragged to wear, my dear? Something a little more revealing, perhaps?'

Caroline stifled a gasp and Maria began to giggle.

'One more word from you, Mr Dorincourt, and I'll walk out of that door and never return,' Grace said, sniffing. 'Don't worry about me, girls. I've dealt with old goats like this man many times in the past, and they've always come off the worst.'

Freddie hooted with laughter. 'Whatever you say, Grace. I love you.' He threw his spoon down. 'She's amazing, isn't she, Mrs Grimes?'

'Indeed she is, sir.' Jenifry rose from the table. 'Dickon, help me clear the plates and we'll fetch the next course.'

Maria leaned closer to Caroline. 'How can she bear living like this?'

Jenifry stopped to give Maria a stern look. 'Other people might think the way we live is odd,' she said calmly, 'but Freddie and I have an understanding. We like things the way they are; it suits us both.' She swept out of the room carrying the tureen.

Dickon followed her, winking at Caroline as he passed her chair.

'You'll have to watch that young man,' Freddie said, puffing out his chest. 'A chip off the old block, except that he did not inherit my artistic talent. Keep him in order tomorrow, Caroline.'

'Don't worry, Uncle. I have two younger brothers – I know exactly how to handle difficult boys.'

The mention of her brothers at dinner was still on Caroline's mind as she lay in her bed that night. She was almost too tired to go to sleep – her mind was racing and her limbs felt restless. What had started out simply as finding work in order to survive had become a quest to seek revenge on the Colvilles, and now she was more deeply involved with that family than she could have imagined possible. She turned on her side, listening to the distant swish of the waves lapping on the shore. The scent of garden roses wafted in through the open window, bringing tears to her eyes at the memory of the father she had lost, and the home that had been wrested from her. She felt as though she would never sleep again, but her eyelids were heavy and she closed her eyes.

Next morning Dickon was waiting for her outside the stables, holding the reins of two horses.

'Good morning, miss. Are you ready for a hack across the fields?' His berry-dark eyes gleamed with mischief and his lips curved in a mocking grin.

'No, I prefer to go by road, like a normal person,' Caroline said coldly.

'Shall I give you a hand up?'

Caroline took the reins from him and led the frisky bay mare to the mounting block. 'I can manage on my own, thank you, Grimes.'

His smile did not waver. 'It's Dickon, miss. Everyone, including the master, calls me Dickon.'

Caroline mounted the horse with ease. 'Then I suggest we get going, Dickon. I have important business at Daumerle.'

'Yes, miss.' Dickon vaulted onto the saddle and swiftly mastered the black stallion, bringing the animal to a sedate walk as they left the stable yard and headed for the road.

Caroline had ridden this way many times when she was younger, and she rode on ahead, urging her horse to a canter when they were going uphill and slowing her down to a walk on the descent. Dickon seemed content to ride on in silence and they reached Daumerle in just over half an hour. Caroline dismounted and handed him the reins.

'I don't know how long I'll be, Dickon.'

He nodded. 'Just send word to the stables when you're ready to leave, miss.'

Caroline shot him a suspicious glance. She did not know what to make of Freddie's son. Sometimes he was over-familiar, and at other times he was almost subservient, although she suspected that he was secretly laughing at her. She turned away and headed up the stone steps to the front entrance.

The butler, who answered her insistent rapping on the door, looked her up and down and was obviously unimpressed by a young, unaccompanied woman who demanded to see Lady Alice, but he ushered her into the entrance hall and asked her to wait. Caroline remembered Garner, Lady Alice's formidable former butler, who must have been close on ninety when he eventually retired to a cottage on the estate, but this was the first time she had come across the equally stately and relatively new member of the staff. Garner might have thought he was king of the servants' hall, but at least he would have recognised her and she would not have been told to wait or made to feel she should have used the tradesmen's entrance. She waited impatiently for the butler's return.

'Lady Alice will see you now, Miss Manning,' he said stiffly. 'Follow me and I'll show you to the garden room.'

'Thank you, but there's no need. I know my way.' Caroline walked past him, holding her head high. She was familiar with the wide corridors and twisting passageways in Daumerle, and she made her way to the garden room where she found her mother and Lady Alice seated in the midst of tall palms and exotic blooms.

'Carrie!' Esther rose to her feet and rushed towards her daughter, arms outstretched. 'My darling girl, how lovely to see you.' She gave her a hug and then held her at arm's length. 'But what are you doing here? Has something terrible happened to my boys?'

'No, Mama. They are safe and well. There's nothing for you to worry about.'

'But why are you here? Why aren't you at home?'

'There's something you should know, Mama,' Caroline said gently.

Alice gave Caroline a searching look. 'That sounds serious.'

'It is, Aunt Alice. I didn't want to burden you with the truth just yet, Mama, but I'm afraid I can't keep it from you any longer.'

'What's happened to you, Carrie?' Esther sank back onto her chair, staring up at her daughter. 'You look different somehow, and why are you dressed so shabbily?'

Caroline sank down on the padded seat of an ornate wrought-iron chair. 'I didn't want you to find out until you were feeling stronger, but apparently the rent on our home was due and there was no money to pay it, or the tradesmen's bills. The bailiffs came in and took everything and we were evicted.'

'Why wasn't I informed of this?' Esther cried angrily. 'Why didn't my solicitor do something to prevent such a catastrophe?'

'Don't upset yourself, Esther,' Alice said sternly. 'I'll send for some tea, or perhaps a glass of brandy would be more to the point?' Alice rang a silver hand bell, and, as if she had been hovering behind one of the giant plants, a maid appeared.

'We'll take tea, and you can fetch the brandy decanter from the drawing room, and three glasses.' Alice waited until the maid was out of earshot. 'You'd better start at the beginning, Caroline. Your mother needs to know everything.'

'We're homeless,' Caroline said, shrugging. 'It's no use pretending otherwise. The *Esther Manning* is overdue and there haven't been any sightings of her for weeks.'

Esther's eyes widened with shock. 'She can't have been lost at sea. George is an excellent shipmaster – he'll bring her home safely, you can depend on that. Something must have happened to delay them.'

'I hope that's all it is, Mama. But things are very serious – we are virtually bankrupt and there was no money to pay the school fees.'

Esther fanned herself with her hands. 'Oh my goodness. This gets worse. Where are they now? Where are my boys?'

'Sadie took us all in. We've been living at the Captain's House. Max and Jimmy are being taught by Mr Bromley, who was one of their tutors at Rugby. Sadie invited him to stay and continue the boys' education and he intends to take on more pupils.'

'And all this is happening at the Captain's House? Are you telling me that Sadie is living with this man?'

Delighted to have given her mother something to think about other than her own problems, Caroline smiled. 'He's a lodger, Mama. But it wouldn't be such a bad thing if there was something going on between them. Mr Bromley is a nice man and the boys think a lot of him. It's time that Aunt Sadie had a life of her own, instead of living in your shadow.'

'I don't know what you mean, Carrie. Sadie is like a sister to me.'

'Of course she is, Mama. All I meant to say is that she has devoted herself entirely to our family, and maybe it's time for her to think more about what she needs and wants.'

Esther pursed her lips, frowning. 'I hope the old captain doesn't mind having his house turned into a school. He might not like having rowdy boys living in his home.'

'At least you can be sure that Max and Jimmy are being looked after, Mama.'

'But you still haven't explained why you've come all this way,' Alice said, giving Caroline a puzzled look. 'You say you're short of funds, and I'll be only too happy to help you.'

'That's very kind of you, Aunt Alice. But it's a little more complicated than that.'

'It most certainly is,' Esther added crossly. 'We're

homeless, Alice. If only Jack had left the Captain's House to me we would have a roof over our heads. I'm not too proud to return to Wapping.'

'Bearwood owns properties all over London,' Alice said airily. 'I'm sure we can find suitable accommodation for you both until George returns. When your ship comes in you'll be comfortably off again, won't you?'

'I should never have left London.' Esther fumbled in her reticule, taking out a hanky and dabbing her eyes. 'If our last vessel has foundered it will be the end of everything. I can't bear the thought of losing my only brother so soon after Jack was taken from me.'

'Please don't upset yourself, Mama,' Caroline said anxiously. 'We'll manage somehow.'

'That's easy for you to say.' Esther's lips trembled. 'We're ruined, and everything your father and I worked for is lost. It will affect us all and you'll never find a husband. Who would want to marry a penniless girl?'

'That's hardly to the point, Essie.' Alice was suddenly alert, looking towards the door. 'What is it, Digby?'

Caroline looked round to see the pompous butler standing in the doorway.

He cleared his throat. 'There's a gentleman who wishes to see Mrs Manning, my lady.'

'Really?' Alice turned to Esther, eyebrows raised. 'Are you expecting anyone?'

Esther shook her head. 'No, of course not.'

'Who is it, Digby? Do you know this person?'

He proffered a silver salver. 'His card, my lady.'

Alice studied the visiting card and her lips tightened. 'Phineas Colville.' She turned to Esther with an anxious frown. 'Do you want me to send him away, Essie? Or I could see him on my own and find out why he has come all this way.'

'I have nothing to say to that gentleman,' Esther said icily. 'I can't imagine what brought him to Devonshire.'

'I know why he's here.' Caroline stood up, smoothing the creases from her cotton skirt. 'I was going to tell you everything in my own good time, but you'll find out anyway.'

'What do you mean by that?' Esther's voice rose sharply. 'What else has been going on in my absence, Caroline?'

'Allow her to explain later,' Alice said hastily. 'Let's see what Mr Colville has to say for himself. Send him in, Digby.'

Digby bowed out of the room, narrowly missing a giant potted palm in his retreat. Caroline giggled nervously, but the situation was far from amusing and Phineas Colville was the last person she wanted to see.

'He has a nerve, coming here when he knows very well that his company's dealings were responsible for our huge losses.' Esther's cheeks flamed with angry spots of colour and she rose to her feet. 'I'm afraid I'll be very rude to him, Alice. Perhaps I'd better go to my room.'

'Too late, Mama,' Caroline said in a low voice. 'You'd better sit down.'

'Mr Phineas Colville, my lady.' Digby ushered Phineas into the room.

Alice acknowledged Phineas with a gracious smile. 'Mr Colville, welcome to Daumerle.'

'It's very kind of you to see me, my lady. I wouldn't have troubled you were it not a matter of some urgency.' He shot a glance at Esther and bowed. 'Mrs Manning, we haven't met since your husband's untimely death, but might I offer my sincere condolences.'

Esther's lips trembled but she held herself very straight and looked him in the eye. 'It's just words as far as you're concerned, Mr Colville. It's a pity you were not more generous in your treatment of my husband when he was alive.'

Caroline had not intended to say anything, but this was a step too far. 'That's not fair, Mama. There were circumstances of which you know nothing.'

'How do you know that, Caroline?' Esther demanded crossly. 'What have you been up to in London since I was forced to leave?'

'You chose to come here, Mama. I don't recall anyone exerting any pressure on you, and you left me to cope with everything that happened afterwards.'

'We have a guest,' Alice said pointedly. 'Please

take a seat, Mr Colville, and tell us why you are here.'

'Miss Manning knows very well why I've travelled all the way to Devonshire. I doubt if she's told you about her exploits, including the forging of your signature on a reference, Lady Alice, in order to obtain a position as companion to my cousin Maria.'

'My daughter wouldn't do such a thing.' Esther turned to Caroline. 'Did you?' she added in an undertone.

'I was going to tell you, but Mr Colville's sudden arrival forestalled me. Yes, I did write myself a reference, signing your name, Aunt Alice. I was desperate for money and I couldn't impose any longer on Sadie's good will.'

'As I recall she did very well from your father's generosity,' Esther said through gritted teeth.

'Go on, Carrie,' Alice said eagerly. 'This sounds very diverting. I was growing rather bored with country life and considering a return to London.'

'Yes, do continue, Miss Manning.' Phineas pulled up a chair and sat down.

'I saw that Maria Colville was being treated abominably by her grandmother. The poor girl was virtually a prisoner in her own home, and the unfortunate circumstances of her birth were constantly being thrown at her.'

'Maria Colville?' Esther said faintly. 'You say she's your cousin, Mr Colville. Do you mean that she is your aunt's child?'

'It's a scandal that my family has had to live with for the past twenty years, Mrs Manning. It's common knowledge that my aunt, Grace, was seduced by a man who took advantage of her when she was only fifteen, and she gave birth to a child, my cousin Maria.'

'I remember hearing about the scandal when I returned from Australia.' Esther eyed him thoughtfully. 'Although it was said that Grace Colville was as much to blame as the man who fathered her child.'

'How can you say that, Mama?' Caroline demanded. 'Did you know Grace? More importantly, did you know the man who led her astray and then abandoned her? I don't call that the act of a gentleman.'

'This has nothing to do with you, Carrie.' Esther stood up, facing Phineas with a haughty toss of her head. 'I am not interested in your family problems, Mr Colville. The fact is that your company drove our business into the ground. You set out deliberately to ruin us and now you have. I hope you're happy with the result.' She stormed out of the room.

'Why did you have to come here today?' Caroline asked angrily. 'I was about to tell them everything and now you've made matters worse.'

The maid chose that precise moment to arrive bearing a tea tray, followed by a younger servant carrying a decanter and three glasses.

'May I offer you some refreshment, Mr Colville?' Alice said with an attempt at a smile. 'I'm afraid that Esther is still very upset by the death of her husband. You must forgive her outburst, although I can't think what could have brought you here today.'

Phineas shook his head when the maid offered him tea, and he waited for the servants to leave before responding.

'Two things, my lady. First, I knew that Mrs Manning was here and I wanted to give her some good news for a change. Her brother's ship was sighted off the coast of Cuba. The *Esther Manning* is apparently safe and sound, presumably on her way home.'

Caroline stared at him in astonishment. 'Are you certain? There hasn't been any news for so long I was certain she was lost.'

'The ship has had two verified sightings. By my reckoning she should arrive in a couple of weeks' time.'

'That's wonderful news, Mr Colville,' Alice said earnestly. 'Esther should be informed immediately. But you said there were two pieces of information you had for us.'

'That's right, and Miss Manning will be able to help me here – I came to find my cousin, Maria, and take her home, where she belongs.'

'You want to take her back to that ice palace you call home?' Caroline jumped to her feet, clenching her fists at her sides. 'Maria was virtually a prisoner in that place. She won't go with you.'

'But you admit that you took her without her grandmother's knowledge?'

'Yes, I helped her to escape, and she's happy to be free from you both.'

'Where is she? I want to hear it from her lips.'

'You want to browbeat her into returning with you.' Caroline shook her head. 'I won't allow it.'

Phineas remained seated, looking up at her with calm disdain. 'You can't speak for Maria.'

'Yes, I can. She's my friend and I won't allow you to bully her. Anyway, it's not me you have to deal with now. Maria is reunited with her mother. You'll have to answer to your aunt Grace for allowing her daughter to suffer so badly.'

Alice uttered a sharp gasp. 'Where are they, Carrie?'

Caroline turned to her in surprise. 'They are together and they're safe.'

'Oh, my God!' Alice struggled to her feet. 'You shouldn't have interfered.'

'Where are they?' Phineas also rose from his seat, towering above Caroline. 'Are they here?'

'Certainly not,' Alice protested. 'I'm as shocked as you are, Mr Colville.'

'I don't understand,' Caroline said wearily. 'I thought you would be pleased to know that Maria has found her mother at last.'

'I don't know how you engineered their meeting,

but it was the worst thing you could have done,' Phineas said angrily. 'The whole sorry, sordid story will be made public once again, especially if the newspapers get hold of it. Where are they, Caroline? What have you done with them?'

Chapter Twelve

'I'm not telling you,' Caroline said firmly. 'They've been through enough.'

'This is serious.' Phineas caught Caroline by the hand, his fingers holding hers in a vice-like grip. 'Don't play games with me. I need to see my aunt and cousin. This is my family business, not yours.'

'And it must remain so,' Alice added sternly. 'You mustn't get involved. Heaven knows your mother has had enough to bear these past months, if what you tell us is true, Carrie. She's lost everything, including her home.'

Caroline snatched her hand free, but she could still feel the imprint of Phin's cool fingers on her flesh. She turned her back on him, addressing herself to Alice. 'At least Uncle George is safe and Mama has a half-share in the *Esther Manning*, so she won't be destitute. I'll look after her.'

'I'm sure you will.' Lady Alice moderated her tone. 'And Mr Colville needs to take care of his family. You must understand that.'

'I think there's something you aren't telling me,' Caroline said, glancing from one to the other.

'I suggest you talk it over later.' Phineas made a move towards the doorway. 'I've outstayed my welcome, but I'm not leaving without you, Miss Manning. I need you to take me to my aunt.'

'I don't think she wants anything to do with you.'

'That may be how she feels at the moment, but I need to see her and make sure she is all right. I visited the farm late yesterday afternoon, so I know what went on. Or, at least, I heard Quick's version of events and now I want to see what Aunt Grace has to say.'

'Caroline?' Alice raised an eyebrow. 'What is your part in all this?'

'Maria was desperate to find her mother. Surely you can both understand that?' Caroline glared at Phineas. 'Even you could not wish Grace to remain with that brute.'

'I admit that I didn't take to the fellow,' Phineas said slowly. 'Go on. I'm listening.'

'We went to the farm and found Mrs Quick in a terrible state. She looked half-starved and ill, and her clothes were little more than rags. Despite what her husband might have told you, she has suffered abuse and brutality at his hands for the past twenty years. That man is evil and he should be locked up.'

'How awful,' Alice said, shuddering. 'Whatever she has done in the past, she didn't deserve to be treated like that.'

'No,' Caroline agreed. 'She was terrified of him, and Maria and I rescued her.'

'So where are they now?' Phineas asked in a more conciliatory tone. 'I want to see them, Miss Manning. I need to make sure that my aunt is all right and to offer any help she wishes to accept.'

'Do you?' Caroline faced him angrily. 'Or do you merely want to keep her out of sight so that she doesn't upset your grandmother?'

'My grandmother is an old woman. She's set in her ways, and although I often disagree with the manner in which she does things I have to respect her as the head of our family.'

'Mr Colville has a point, Carrie,' Alice said softly. 'You can't save every lame dog you come across. I see shades of your mother in you, although you probably won't recognise her good qualities yourself. I think you should allow him to see his aunt and cousin. After all, what harm could it do?'

'I'll take you to them,' Caroline said reluctantly. 'But only if you promise not to coerce them into anything.'

'Despite what you may think of me, I'm a reasonable man and I only want what's best for both of them.'

Caroline looked him in the eye and decided that he was speaking the truth. Perhaps she had misjudged him so far as his own family were concerned, but it would be impossible to forgive him for the way in which he had treated her father. Perhaps it was time for a truce.

'All right. I'll take you to them.' Caroline turned to Alice with a weary smile. 'We're staying with Uncle Freddie at Starcross Abbey.'

'I might have guessed it,' Alice said, chuckling. 'I'm sure Freddie is thoroughly enjoying your company. He always had a weakness for pretty women.'

'I rode here with Dickon,' Caroline added. 'He's waiting in your stables.'

'I sometimes wish that Freddie had done the decent thing and married his housekeeper after she gave birth to his son,' Alice said, sighing. 'I don't trust that young man, and I think he could cause trouble for my cousin.'

'What makes you say that, Aunt Alice?' Caroline asked, frowning. 'Dickon seems reasonable enough.'

Alice shrugged and rose to her feet. 'It's just a feeling I have whenever I see that boy. There's something about him that I find disturbing, and he's sly.' She held her hand out to Phineas. 'I'm glad to have met you at last, Mr Colville. I think perhaps we have all done you a great injustice, and I hope we might become better acquainted in the future.'

'I would hope so, my lady. Please forgive me for leaving so abruptly.'

'Of course,' Alice said graciously. 'And I hope the

rift between your family and Mrs Manning can be overcome in time.'

'I promise to do all I can.' Phineas turned to Caroline. 'I hired a nag at the inn where I stayed last night, so we can ride together. Is it far?'

'Four miles at the most.' Caroline turned to Alice. 'Will you make things right with my mother, please? I don't understand why she was so upset, and I know she's keeping something from me, but I'll do my best to make it up to her.'

'Don't worry about Esther. She just needs more time to recover from the terrible blows that life has dealt her, but she's a strong woman and she'll come round.'

'Perhaps then she'll trust me enough to tell me everything.'

'Give her time, that's all I can say, and give my love to Freddie. Tell him I'll see him soon.'

Caroline and Phineas stood at the top of the steps, waiting for Dickon to bring the horses to the front of the house. The sun was high in the sky and the air was filled with citrus scent from the huge creamy-white flowers of the magnolia standing tall at the side of the house, and an achingly sweet perfume floated on a gentle breeze from the rose garden. Deer grazed beneath shady oaks in the park that surrounded Daumerle, and Caroline was suddenly aware of birdsong so sweet that it touched her heart. The cheeping of sparrows and the chattering of starlings coming home to roost at night were the sounds she was most accustomed to hearing, but their country cousins' songs were honeyed and soothing. This beautiful house was paradise, compared with Wapping and Limehouse, and yet those places were home and she missed the hustle and bustle, the noise, and even the stench of the city.

She shot a wary glance at Phineas. 'You did promise that you wouldn't force your aunt to return to her husband, didn't you?'

'I wouldn't condemn an animal to live with that brute. I can't imagine why my grandfather thought he was a suitable match for his only daughter.'

'Why was she left to suffer for so many years? Didn't anyone think to visit her and make sure she was all right?'

'Apparently not. Don't blame me, Miss Manning. I was only six years old when Aunt Grace married that man. Her name was never mentioned after that day, and I was sent away to school when I was eight, so I only saw my cousin Maria during the holidays.'

'But you're a man now. Didn't you think it unfair the way your grandmother treated Maria?'

He turned to give her a steady look. 'I was pitched into the shipping business the moment I graduated from Cambridge. I didn't have time to think of anything other than building the company back to its former glory. My grandfather had let matters slide after the death of my father. I suppose I should have paid more attention to Maria, but I just accepted the situation, and for that I am sorry, but she was such a quiet little mouse that I barely noticed her.'

'That's no excuse.' Caroline paused. She could hear the sound of the horses ambling towards them, although they were still out of sight, but there was one question that she had to ask. 'Do you know the identity of Maria's father?'

Phineas shook his head. 'I don't, and it's really none of my business, or yours either, come to that. If my aunt wishes to keep it to herself, I think we must respect her right to privacy.' He descended the steps ahead of her as Dickon and a groom came round the corner of the house leading their mounts.

During the ride to Starcross Abbey Caroline's thoughts were occupied mainly with worries as to how Grace and Maria would react to coming face to face with Phineas, and she could find no easy solution. They rode mainly in silence with Dickon riding on ahead, but Caroline suspected that he was keen to eavesdrop on anything that was said, and she did not want to give him the satisfaction of discussing family matters within his hearing. The heat was intense at midday, but the narrow lanes were shaded by tall trees forming cool tunnels sheltered from the direct rays of the sun. The horses plodded on at little more than walking pace, as if they, too, found the excessive warmth oppressive.

When they arrived at Starcross Abbey they were greeted by Maria, whose face fell when she saw her cousin.

'What are you doing here?' she demanded anxiously. 'I'm not going back to London with you, Phin. You can tell Grandmama that I've found my mother and we're staying together.'

Phineas handed the reins to Dickon. 'I only want to talk, Maria.'

'Good, but I'm not sure that Mama wants to speak to you.'

Caroline mounted the steps to give Maria a hug. 'Don't worry. Phineas promised to listen to what you both have to say, or I wouldn't have brought him here. Where is Grace?'

'She's sitting for her portrait,' Maria said in a whisper. 'He made her take her clothes off, Carrie. She's lying on a chaise longue with a sheet draped around her body. I don't think Phin ought to see her like that.'

Caroline glanced round to see Phineas standing behind her and it was obvious from his amused expression that he had overheard. 'It sounds very artistic,' he said mildly.

Maria blushed rosily. 'I didn't mean you to hear what I said about Mama posing for the painting. Mr Dorincourt is a very good artist, and it's all very proper, Phin.'

'I'm intrigued, and I'm not a monster, Maria. If I've neglected you in the past, I'm really sorry and I hope I can make up for it in the future.'

'You won't make me go back to Pier House, will you?'

He shook his head. 'Of course not. We'll sort something out for you and your mother.'

Caroline gave him a grateful smile. 'Thank you.'

'Don't thank me, Caroline. I may call you Caroline, mayn't I? It seems we've crossed the barrier of formality, and I'd appreciate it if you would call me Phin. It would make me feel less of a threat. There is no reason why we can't be on more friendly terms.'

'I agree.' Caroline turned away, aware that she was blushing. 'And now I'd better introduce you to Uncle Freddie. Let's hope he's finished the morning painting session.'

'Shall I go on ahead and warn them?' Maria asked anxiously.

'No,' Phineas said firmly. 'I think I'd like to see how an artist works.'

Caroline shot him a wary glance, but he seemed more amused than shocked. This amenable person was not the man she had briefly known in London, and she was intrigued.

'Lead on, Maria,' she said hastily. 'I think I'd like to see Uncle Freddie at work, too.'

Maria's relief was palpable as she danced on ahead to the East Wing and flung open the studio door. Caroline followed her into the large room with its high vaulted ceiling and tall windows designed to let in the maximum amount of light. She came to a halt, staring at Grace, who was reclining on the chaise longue with a sheet draped artistically around her otherwise naked body, leaving one shoulder and

217

both arms bare. Her feet and ankles peeped out from beneath the cloth in a decidedly provocative fashion, and her dark hair hung loose, framing her oval face. Despite her harsh existence, there was a look of innocence and faded beauty about her, and Caroline could see why Freddie had wanted to capture her on canvas.

At the sight of them Grace clutched the sheet to her throat and curled up in a ball. 'Who are you?' she demanded, staring at Phineas. 'I'm not going back to Quick, if it was he who has sent you here?'

'It's all right, Grace,' Caroline said hastily. 'This is your nephew, Phineas Colville.'

'He's nice, Mama,' Maria added. 'Phin was always kind to me.'

'I won't look if it embarrasses you, Aunt Grace.'

Grace shrank even further down into the folds of the sheet. 'You were a little boy when I last saw you.'

'So I was, but I'm a grown man now, and I've come to help.' Phineas turned to Freddie, holding out his hand. 'I apologise for arriving uninvited, Mr Dorincourt.'

'Delighted to meet you, sir. I'd shake your hand, but as you see, I'm covered in paint.' Freddie wiped his hands on his stained smock. 'Anyway, I've finished for now, so let's go and celebrate your arrival with a glass or two of wine.'

'Wouldn't a cup of tea be more suitable at this hour of the day, Uncle?' Caroline picked up a blanket and draped it over Grace, whose face was scarlet with embarrassment.

'You women can coddle your innards with tea, but us men like something stronger. Come to my study, Phineas, my boy. I have a bottle of Madeira hidden from my housekeeper. She doesn't approve of my drinking habits.'

'Thank you, sir. That's very kind of you, but first I would like to have a word with my aunt and cousin.'

'Plenty of time for that later. I suggest the lady would be more comfortable if she were dressed, if you know what I mean. Caroline will look after her.'

'Of course, Uncle,' Caroline said, stifling the desire to giggle. She waited until they had left the studio. 'Where are your clothes, Grace? I'll fetch them for you.'

Grace struggled to her feet, her movements hampered by the voluminous folds of the sheet. 'Behind the screen. It's all right, I don't need anyone's help.'

'That's your trouble, Mama,' Maria said, sighing. 'I'm sure if you'd written to Grandmama and told her how that man was treating you, she would have done something about it.'

Grace paused, one hand holding the sheet, the other clutching the screen. 'You're wrong, Maria. My mother wouldn't have lifted a finger to help me. She would have said it was God's way of punishing me for my wickedness.' She slipped behind the screen, leaving a heap of crumpled cotton sheeting on the floor.

'Stay with her, Maria,' Caroline whispered. 'I'd better find Jenifry and tell her that we might have another guest for dinner this evening.'

Freddie, it seemed, was delighted to have male company, even though he loved being surrounded by women. He treated Phineas like a life-long friend, insisting that he stayed for dinner that evening, and when the meal was over and they had drunk copious amounts of wine, he suggested that Phineas might like to stay the night instead of riding back to the inn.

Grace and Maria exchanged wary glances, but Caroline nodded in agreement. 'I think that's an excellent idea, Uncle Freddie.'

Jenifry frowned, but said nothing, and Dickon looked on. He was grinning, but there was a calculating look in his dark eyes that sent a shiver down Caroline's spine, and she decided that Lady Alice had been right – Dickon was not to be trusted.

Freddie rose from the table and leaned over to seize the bottle of claret that they had just opened. 'Let's go to my study, Phineas, my boy.'

Phineas turned to Grace with an apologetic smile. 'You'll excuse us for defying convention, I hope, Aunt?'

'Freddie is our host,' she said softly. 'This is his home and I'm grateful to him for giving me refuge.'

'Say no more, dear lady.' Freddie hooked two wine

glasses in one hand. 'I am only too pleased to oblige, and tomorrow morning we will have another sitting. I'll bid you all good night.' He staggered towards the door and Phineas leaped to his feet, but Dickon forestalled him and he was already at his father's side.

'I'm accustomed to this, sir.' Dickon looped Freddie's arm across his shoulders and helped him from the room.

'Come on, Colville, don't dawdle,' Freddie called from the depths of the hall.

Jenifry had been watching with tight-lipped disapproval, but she rose from her seat at the far end of the table. 'I'll make some coffee. If you ladies would like to go to the drawing room it will be brought to you.'

'I think Uncle Freddie needs it more,' Caroline said, smiling.

Jenifry paused in the doorway. 'He shouldn't drink too much. The doctor was quite clear as to the dangers of overindulgence.' She whisked out of the room, leaving Caroline, Grace and Maria still seated at the table.

'I suppose we'd better go to the drawing room, although I am quite exhausted and I'd really like to go to bed.' Grace glanced anxiously at her daughter. 'I'd like to spend more time with you, Maria, but Frederick is not someone to be gainsaid.'

'That's all right, Mama,' Maria said hastily. 'I understand, and we'll have plenty of time to get to know each other when we return to London.'

'No one has mentioned that to me.' Grace had been about to rise but she subsided onto her seat. 'Why would I want to go home? My mother made it clear that she wants nothing to do with me.'

'That was a long time ago,' Caroline said cautiously. 'She might change her mind when she learns about your years of suffering.'

'You don't know my mother, Miss Manning. Clarissa Colville is the most stubborn woman in London, and the least forgiving. I can't go home, ever.'

'We will find a way, and Phin has promised to help you both.' Caroline raised her glass in a toast. 'Fate threw us together, and together we'll get through this difficult time.'

Grace and Maria joined in the toast, clinking glasses as they sat amongst the debris of the meal. Caroline set her empty glass down on the table. 'I suggest we leave the gentlemen to their wine and brandy, or whatever Uncle Freddie has hidden in his study. If you want to go to bed, then please do so, Grace. You must be exhausted.'

'I will, if you don't mind.'

Maria jumped to her feet. 'I'll come too, Mama. We could talk for a while, if you aren't too tired.' She glanced at Caroline. 'That's if you don't mind being left on your own.'

'It's a lovely evening. I think I might take a walk in the rose garden. They were my father's favourite flowers and the scent of them always reminds me of him.' Caroline stood up to embrace Maria and then Grace. 'I hope you sleep well. Tomorrow we'll make plans and perhaps Phin will have some helpful advice for you.'

The last remnants of a fiery sunset were being stalked by darkness, but there was still enough light for Caroline to make her way easily amongst the well-kept rose beds. The air was heavy with perfume from the full-blown blooms and even more intoxicating than the wine she had drunk at dinner. The alcohol had left her with a slight headache, but, fanned by a light breeze she began to feel refreshed and more optimistic about the future, although when they left Starcross Abbey, as they must, it would be like leaping off a precipice. She could stay with her mother at Daumerle, but they could not remain there for ever, and she would have to find a way to earn her own living. Being dependent on friends was not an option that she would even consider.

She was deep in thought, listening to the sound of the leaves rustling in the trees and the ever-present action of the waves on the shore, when, without warning, someone clamped their hand on her shoulder. She spun round.

'Dickon! You gave me a terrible fright.'

A saturnine grin curved his lips but his eyes were pools of darkness. 'You shouldn't roam outside after dark, miss.'

'Surely I'm safe enough in the garden?' She was shaken by his sudden appearance and unaccountably nervous. 'What do you want?'

'Ma sent me to find you, miss. There's coffee in the drawing room. You'd best come with me.'

It was more of an order than a request and Caroline could not think of an excuse that would not sound feeble or childish in the circumstances. 'You go first, I'll follow.'

'Of course, miss. As you wish.' He bowed and ambled off, but she had the inexplicable feeling that he was laughing at her. Perhaps it was the tone of his voice or the arrogant way he held his head as he walked on, stopping every few seconds to make certain that she was following.

'You don't need to escort me, Dickon,' she said at last. 'I know the way to the drawing room, but I think I'd prefer to go straight to my room.'

He came to a halt, moving closer to her so that his face was just inches from hers. 'My mother wishes to speak to you, miss. It wouldn't be wise to ignore her, if you get my meaning.'

Caroline drew herself up to her full height. 'Are you threatening me, Dickon? I don't think my uncle would like to hear that.'

'Of course not, miss. I am just saying that Ma wants to speak to you. She requests the pleasure of your company in the drawing room.'

'Then I will go to the drawing room on my own.' Caroline met his gaze with a determined lift of her chin. She was not going to allow a mere boy to frighten her, although she felt the menace beneath his softly spoken words. There was something not quite right about the situation in Starcross Abbey – she felt it with every fibre of her being. She walked past him, keeping to a measured pace, although she was tempted to run. Without looking back she knew that he was standing where she had left him, watching her like a wolf eyeing his prey. But as she reached the house and let herself in through the side door, she managed to convince herself that her fears were ridiculous and must be due to tiredness, exaggerated by the eerie silence away from the sounds of the city. She collected the oil lamp she had left burning on the windowsill and made her way to the drawing room. Jenifry Grimes might hold a special place in Freddie's heart, but she was still a servant, and not the mistress of the house. Perhaps she would do well to remember that fact.

The sound of male laughter brought Caroline to a halt outside the study, and she was tempted to join them. Freddie's loud voice, fuelled by the wine he had imbibed at dinner and possibly a generous tot or two of brandy, was followed by monosyllabic answers from Phin, but it seemed a pity to interrupt them, and she made her way to the drawing room. If they were to remain at Starcross for an indefinite period, or at least until Freddie had finished his painting, perhaps it was time to put Jenifry and Dickon firmly in their place.

Caroline placed the lamp on a side table and entered the drawing room, ready for a constructive conversation, but she came to a halt in the doorway, staring in horror at the man seated in a chair by the fireplace.

'What are you doing here?' she demanded angrily. 'Why did you allow this person into the house, Mrs Grimes?'

Chapter Thirteen

Elias Quick stood up abruptly. 'Where's me wife? I've come to take her home.'

'How did you know she was here?' Caroline demanded breathlessly. She looked to Jenifry, who was seated on the sofa as if she were the lady of the house. 'Was this your doing?'

'This gentleman was hammering on the front door, demanding to see his wife. What else was I supposed to do but let him in and sort matters out face to face?'

'That's not your choice, madam,' Caroline said angrily. 'You should have gone to Mr Dorincourt and told him what was happening. This fellow would not have been admitted.' She rounded on Elias. 'I'm asking you politely to leave, or else I'll have you thrown out.'

'I ain't going nowhere until I've got me wife. I'll

have the law on Mr Dorincourt if he don't give her up to me. It's a case of kidnapping, that's what it is. We're married legal and proper.'

'Someone must have told you where to find her.' Caroline backed towards the door. 'I'm going to fetch my uncle and Mr Colville.'

'They'll be too drunk to deal with the matter, Miss Caroline,' Jenifry said slyly. 'Best give her up to her husband, I say.'

Caroline stared at her and suddenly all the pieces slotted into place. 'Dickon was in on this, wasn't he? You knew where we had found Grace. Did you send your son to fetch this man?'

'It's only right and proper that a wife should know her place.' Jenifry folded her hands in her lap, glaring at Caroline with narrowed eyes.

'I hardly think you're in a position to criticise anyone for their morals.' Caroline turned to Elias. 'I'm asking you once again to leave this house, Mr Quick.'

'And I say I won't. Fetch the gentlemen and the constabulary, if you're so minded, but I won't go without my wife.'

'We'll see about that.' Caroline stormed out of the room to find Dickon barring her way, his arms folded and a smug grin on his face.

'Are you going somewhere, miss?'

'You knew he was here, didn't you? Why did you interfere in matters that don't concern you?'

'But it do concern me, miss. I am the son and heir

to my father's fortune, that's what Ma says. I see the way he looks at that woman you brought here, and if he marries her we'll be sent packing.'

'But that's nonsense.' Caroline stared at him, hardly able to believe her ears. 'What makes you think that Mr Dorincourt would want to marry Mrs Quick? Anyway, she's a married woman.'

'He be an old goat when it comes to pretty women. Ma knows that to her cost, but she's managed to keep him safe from the clutches of others when it comes to marrying. Even so, there's something different in the way he treats Mrs Quick, and us don't like it. 'Tis best that she goes home with her old man.'

'That's not for you to say. Now get out of my way. I'm going to speak to my uncle and settle this once and for all.'

She made a move to pass him but still Dickon barred her way. 'No, maid. You go back in there and sit down. I won't ask you again. I'll carry you if necessary.'

Incensed, Caroline stamped on his foot with all her might and he howled with pain, hopping around and swearing volubly. Taking advantage of his temporary incapacity she ran off in the direction of the study, arriving breathless with her hair flying around her face in wild confusion.

'What on earth is the matter?' Phineas demanded, rising to his feet as she burst into the room.

'Is the house on fire again?' Freddie asked with a drunken laugh. 'I can't smell smoke.'

'Come quickly.' Caroline grasped Phin's hand. 'That boy has brought Grace's husband here. He's in the drawing room with your housekeeper, Uncle Freddie.'

'The devil he is.' Suddenly sober, Freddie raised himself from his seat. 'We'll see about that. I'm not about to send Grace back to live with that brute.'

'Perhaps you'd better leave this to me, sir,' Phineas said calmly. 'Grace is my aunt and I should be the one to stand by her. I'm afraid that hasn't been so in the past, but I want to make amends now.'

'Go on ahead, old boy. I'll follow. Not as quick on my pins as I used to be, especially on a bellyful of strong drink. Kick the fellow to kingdom come.'

But Phineas had already left the study and Caroline had to run to keep up with his long strides. When they reached the drawing room they found Dickon standing guard, and when he refused to move, Phineas simply picked him up and tossed him aside as if he were a featherweight. Dickon sprawled on the floor, shouting obscenities that at any other time would have made Caroline blush, but she ignored him and hurried into the drawing room.

Elias leaped out of his chair, fisting his hands and dancing round as if he were in the boxing ring.

'Stop that, you're being ridiculous,' Phineas said icily. 'I'm asking you politely to leave this house, sir, but if you refuse I might have to use force.'

'I ain't afraid of a toff like you,' Elias said bellig-erently. 'Give me the woman and I'll be on me way.'

At that moment Freddie arrived, huffing and puffing and red in the face. He lunged at Elias, catching him off guard, and grabbed him by the collar. Aided by Phineas he marched the protesting Elias Quick from the room.

'You'll be sorry for interfering in matters what don't concern you,' Jenifry cried passionately. 'We were doing fine until you came along and spoiled everything.'

Caroline could see that Jenifry was genuinely upset and she felt a moment of sympathy for her, but it was short lived. 'You acted out of self-interest and sheer malice,' she said angrily. 'You know nothing of the life that Mrs Quick led with that man. If you did you wouldn't have brought him here. I just hope for your sake that he takes heed of what Mr Dorincourt said and stays away.'

'This is my home, and I'm the real mistress of Starcross Abbey.' Jenifry rose to her feet. 'I under-stand the master. I know his ways and I've warmed his bed for nearly twenty years. He needs me.' She walked past Caroline with her head held high, pausing when she reached the doorway. 'I have been more of a wife to him than any high-born lady could have been.' She left the room, closing the door behind her.

Caroline sank down on the nearest chair. The situation was even more complicated than she had thought, and she had a feeling that they had not seen the last of Elias Quick. He did not seem to be the sort of man who would give up easily. Grace ought to be told that her husband knew of her whereabouts, but somehow Caroline did not relish the task. Perhaps she would let her enjoy a good night's sleep before breaking the news.

Caroline awakened early from a troubled sleep. She could only hope that Grace would feel strong enough to stand up for herself if Elias returned, as she was certain he would. She rose from her bed, washed and dressed and went downstairs, intending to have an early breakfast before taking a walk to clear her head.

To her surprise, she found Freddie was already at the table when she entered the dining room. He was seated at the head with a white linen napkin tucked into his collar as he munched his way through a large plate of bacon, egg, devilled kidneys and a couple of fat sausages. The aroma of freshly made coffee mingled with the savoury smells from the silver serving dishes, which were laid out on the sideboard. Caroline's mouth watered – she had not breakfasted like this since their troubles began.

'Good morning, Carrie,' Freddie said cheerfully. 'Help yourself while the food is hot. I recommend the kidneys, they're Mrs Grimes' speciality. She knows just how I like them.'

Caroline nodded. She could imagine Jenifry making herself indispensable by pandering shamelessly to her master's appetite for good food.

'Good morning, Uncle.' She spooned some buttered eggs onto a plate before taking her seat at the table.

He wiped his lips on the napkin. 'Mrs Grimes is a good cook and a good woman, too. Don't judge her too harshly, Carrie.'

She reached for the silver coffee pot and filled her cup. 'It's really none of my business, Uncle.'

'Carrie, you're a grown woman now, and I think we can dispense with the honorary title "Uncle". If I were in fact your uncle there might be a case to continue its use, but the time has come to acknowledge that you are a young lady. From now on I insist that you call me Freddie.'

'It would feel odd. I'm used to thinking of you as my uncle.'

'To tell the truth it makes me feel a hundred years old, my dear. I'm sure that your mother would agree. She was always down to earth and ready to embrace change. You remind me of her in many ways.'

'You make it sound as though she's passed on. She's very much alive.'

'I've only seen her once since she came to stay with Alice. Poor Esther was a shadow of her former self. I hardly recognised her.'

'She's still grieving for my father. Surely you must understand that?'

'I find it hard to comprehend such devotion. I'm shallow, Carrie. I don't think I have any deep feelings for anyone.'

Caroline took a sip of her coffee. 'Not even Jenifry?'

'You're a saucy minx,' Freddie said, chuckling. 'But I suppose I asked for that, and yes, I admit I've taken advantage of the poor woman, although I am fond of her in my own way. She's an obliging soul, but the boy is a disappointment. I'm truly sorry that he interfered by bringing that oaf Quick here. I've had words with young Dickon and I threatened to pack him off to the army if he doesn't shape up.'

'I was going to ask you about that, Uncle – I mean, Freddie.' Caroline shot him a sideways glance and saw that he was smiling. 'I'm sorry, I've been calling you Uncle for as long as I can remember, so it will take some time for me to get used to the change.'

He mopped his plate with a slice of bread. 'It will come in time. What were you going to say about Dickon?'

'I was going to say that someone ought to tell Grace that her husband knows where she is. I don't think he'll give up without a fight, and we really ought to move on.'

'What?' Freddie dropped the bread onto the plate and pushed it away. 'No, you can't take her away, at least until I've finished her portrait. She's a marvellous subject, so fragile and world-weary and yet so beautiful. She must remain here.'

Caroline eyed him curiously. 'Are you falling in love with her, Freddie?'

'What, me? I told you I don't have the capacity for love and devotion, but I admit she has touched something in me, and I have to put it onto canvas. I refuse to allow that brute to take her from me.'

'Then you might have a fight on your hands. That's all I can say.'

Freddie pushed back his chair and stood up. 'I'm going to my studio. Tell Grace to join me as soon as she's had breakfast.'

Caroline waited until everyone had finished their meal to break the news to Grace, who was naturally distraught when she heard what had occurred the previous evening, as was Maria, and they were both convinced that Elias would return.

'The only solution,' Phineas said firmly, 'is for us to return to London today. I've been absent far too long as it is.'

Maria's soft chin hardened into a stubborn jaw. 'I won't go back to Pier House, Phin. I'm sorry, but I'd rather live anywhere than there.'

'We could go to the Captain's House,' Caroline said doubtfully. 'But it would be a terrible squash, and it doesn't seem fair to burden Sadie with our problems, even though I'm sure she would make us welcome.'

Phineas shook his head. 'It seems to me that you have little choice. After all, it might be a temporary arrangement, Caroline. Your uncle's ship should dock very soon and then he will be able to take care of you.'

'Uncle George lived with us in Finsbury Circus. He had his own set of rooms, and he won't be aware of what's been happening in his absence. Besides which, I don't want to be passed from hand to hand like an orphaned child,' Caroline said firmly. 'I am never going to depend entirely on anyone ever again. People let you down and sometimes they treat you badly, but I intend to save my father's shipping company, if it's humanly possible.'

'Don't you think it's too late for that?' Phineas said seriously. 'The failure of the company was not your fault, Caroline. It's a difficult business at the best of times.'

'We still have one ship.' Caroline met his gaze with a defiant toss of her head. 'I'll do everything I can to help my uncle restore Manning and Chapman. We'll compete with you again, so you'd better beware.'

His eyes lit with a genuine look of admiration. 'I don't doubt you'll try, but you'll have a hard task ahead.'

'What about me?' Maria said plaintively. 'And Mama, too. You know she can't go home, Phin. Grandmama would never allow it.'

Phineas stared at them, frowning. 'The company owns a house in Great Hermitage Street. It was vacated recently by one of our employees and you may have it as far as I'm concerned.' He shot a sideways glance in Caroline's direction. 'It's large enough for all of you.'

Maria grasped her hand. 'You will stay with us, won't you, Carrie? Please say yes, because I don't know how to manage on my own.'

'You have your mother now,' Caroline said softly. 'You can look after each other.'

'Maria is right,' Grace added hastily. 'I'd be grateful if you would join us, too. It's so long since I lived in London that I'm afraid I won't be able to cope, and I'd feel safer if you were with us.'

Phineas met Caroline's anxious gaze with a nod and a hint of a smile. 'You see, you are very much needed.'

The idea that she might one day be dependent on the Colville family was something that had never occurred to Caroline until this moment, but her only alternative was to return to the Captain's House. She was eager to see her brothers and Sadie, but Great Hermitage Street was close enough for her to visit them as often as she wished, and it would only be a temporary measure. When Uncle George brought the *Esther Manning* into port she was certain that everything would change for the better.

'All right,' she said reluctantly, 'but only until I find a place of my own. I have my mother to consider as well as myself.'

'Then that's settled. We leave for London as soon

as you're ready.' Phineas rose from the table. 'I'll go and tell Freddie.'

'He'll be angry with me for leaving before he's had a chance to finish the painting,' Grace said anxiously. 'He's been so good to us, it seems very ungrateful to go running off like this.'

'We have little choice, thanks to that interfering woman.' Phineas opened the door and looked outside, as if expecting to find someone eavesdropping on their conversation.

'If she or Dickon find out where we're going they're sure to pass the information on to Quick.' Caroline glanced at the grandfather clock, ticking away busily in the corner of the room. 'Perhaps the portrait could be completed at a later date, Grace. Anyway, the sooner we leave the better.'

The house in Great Hermitage Street was, like most of its neighbours, tall and narrow, with three rooms on each of its four storeys, and a deep, dank cellar filled with broken chairs, empty tea chests, cracked china, broken glass and a sea of small unwanted and useless objects that had been tossed down the steps by the former residents. Whoever lived there before had not been house-proud, as Caroline noticed the moment she stepped over the threshold late that evening. In the half-light she could see wallpaper hanging in strips, filthy paintwork and bare floorboards littered with the empty carapaces of cockroaches, and their lingering odour rose in waves of nastiness. Damp, dry rot, mildew and the pervading stink of rodent droppings assailed her nostrils, which had become accustomed to the clean country air. If she had thought the Captain's House was dirty, then this residence was filthy.

Phineas brought their baggage in from the hackney carriage that had transported them from the station. He dropped the luggage on the floor in the front room, which, even in poor light, was in a dire state. The furniture was shabby, the upholstery torn and the curtains lacy with moth holes.

'It's a long time since I last saw this place,' he said angrily. 'I wouldn't have suggested it had I known it was in such a state.'

Grace took off her bonnet and the cape she had chosen from the supply of garments donated by Lady Alice. 'I've seen worse.' She laid her garment neatly over the back of a chair, which wobbled dangerously on three legs. 'I'm used to hard work, Phineas. But all this furniture will have to be replaced. I don't doubt it's running with fleas and I dare say the beds are crawling with bugs.'

Maria shuddered and wrapped her shawl round her slight figure. 'It almost makes me want to go home to Pier House, but I think I'd prefer bed bugs and fleas to living with Grandmama.'

'I know what you mean,' Grace said, chuckling.

Caroline stared at her in amazement. 'That's the first time I've heard you laugh, Grace.' She glanced round the room with a sigh. 'If you can find anything funny in this, you're a better person than I am.'

'I can't leave you here,' Phineas said firmly. 'I think I'd better find you rooms at the nearest respectable inn or lodging house.'

'I'll help to clean the place up,' Caroline volunteered, although it seemed like a Herculean task and it was getting late. They had been travelling for hours and she was tired, but she was determined to take as little as possible from the Colville family.

'If you're sure,' Phineas said doubtfully.

'I'm quite sure.' Caroline added her own bonnet and shawl to the pile on the chair. 'We need to make ourselves comfortable for tonight, and tomorrow we'll make a start on getting the place straight.' She winced at the sound of a high-pitched scream from the house next door, followed by shouts and loud male voices.

'No, this really isn't good enough.' Phineas picked up their luggage, tucking a valise under one arm. 'I told the cabby to wait, so I'll take you to my house in Princes Square.'

'I haven't seen your house, Phin,' Maria said eagerly. 'You've never invited me there before.'

'I have to have a life of my own, even if Grandmama doesn't acknowledge the fact that I'm a grown man. I bought the house in the square when I came into my inheritance.'

'And you managed to keep it from Mama?' Grace stared at him with something like admiration. 'But then you're a man, and you have money of your own. It's so different for women.'

'I refuse to leave you here, but if you still want this house, despite the neighbours, I'll have it cleared out and fumigated, which will have to be done anyway. You can decide then whether it's for you.' Phineas shooed them out of the room.

Caroline hesitated as she was about to climb into the cab. 'Perhaps it would be best if I go to the Captain's House tonight.'

'Indulge me this once, Caroline.' Phineas hefted the bags into the cab. 'You've gone out of your way to help my family. Go to your friend's house tomorrow, if you wish, but allow me to be host this evening. I have a business proposition to put to you, and we can discuss it after supper. My housekeeper is an excellent cook and she'll be delighted to show off her talents.'

'I think she might feel differently when faced with three unexpected guests for dinner.'

'Is that a yes?'

'Do get in, Caroline.' Maria leaned out, looking from one to the other. 'Why are you standing out there? We're tired and we're hungry.'

Caroline climbed in and sat down beside her. 'Phineas says that his housekeeper is an excellent cook. I'm eager to try her food.'

'Is she pretty, Phin?' Maria said archly. 'Have you got a secret like Freddie?'

Phineas took his seat next to Grace. 'One more

word from you, Maria, and I'll deposit you on Grandmama's doorstep.'

'Why haven't you told my mother that you have your own establishment, Phin?' Grace leaned back against the leather squabs, looking relaxed for the first time since they left Devonshire.

'You of all people know the answer to that question.' Phineas closed his fingers around his aunt's small hand. 'It's good to have you home, Grace. You must decide whether or not you wish to visit Pier House. It's entirely up to you, but for now you're safe from that oaf you were forced to marry, and your daughter is restored to you.'

Caroline turned her head to look out of the carriage window. She did not want them to see the tears that threatened to spill down her cheeks. At least this family were reunited, now all she had to do was to perform a miracle that would bring her mother and brothers together. All her hopes were pinned on the return of the *Esther Manning*, after what she hoped might have been a successful and profitable voyage.

The lamplighter was doing his rounds when they reached Princes Square. Caroline was encouraged to see that the neat Georgian terraces were well kept, as was the central garden. It was obvious that the residents took pride in their surroundings and highly polished door furniture gleamed in the light from the newly lit streetlamps. A warm breeze rustled the leaves of the trees cloistered behind the iron railings and, if it weren't for the inescapable noxious smells, she could have imagined herself back in the country.

Phineas had already alighted, paid the cabby and deposited their bags on the pavement outside his house. The door was opened by a middle-aged lady, whose neat figure and appearance fitted in nicely with her surroundings.

'Mr Colville, I wasn't expecting you tonight, sir.'

'I'm sorry, Mrs Morecroft. A sudden change of plans brought me home earlier than I expected, and I've brought three guests with me.'

'Will the young ladies be staying, sir?' Mrs Morecroft stood aside, eyeing them warily.

'Yes, they will. I hope it's not too much for you, Moffie.'

'No, sir. Of course not.'

'This is my aunt, Mrs Quick, and her daughter, Miss Maria Colville, and their good friend, Miss Caroline Manning.'

Mrs Morecroft bobbed a curtsey to each of them in turn. 'It's not often we have guests, so I hope you'll bear with me. It will take a while to make dinner, and then I'll see to your rooms.'

Caroline realised that the poor woman was struggling, and she laid her hand on Mrs Morecroft's arm. 'You must allow us to help you, ma'am. I can't cook, but I do know how to make up a bed.'

'I'm quite handy in the kitchen,' Grace added.

'I'm afraid I'm not much help at all,' Maria

confessed. 'But I will do my best to make myself useful.'

Mrs Morecroft sent a pleading glance to Phineas. 'I can't allow that, sir. It wouldn't be proper.'

'I'd give in now, if I were you, Moffie,' he said, smiling. 'Accept the help offered.'

'Very well, sir.' Mrs Morecroft turned to Caroline. 'I'll show you to your rooms, miss. There is plenty of clean linen in the oak chest on the first landing.' She eyed Grace warily. 'I was just going to have some bread and cheese for my supper, madam.'

Grace smiled. 'That sounds delightful. If you have eggs and maybe some herbs, I could make an omelette, too.'

'That sounds excellent,' Phineas said enthusiastically. 'You wouldn't have learned to cook had you remained at home, Grace.'

She pulled a face. 'It's my only talent, Phin. Although I can do the laundry and scrub floors as well.'

'You won't be required to do anything like that in this house, madam,' Mrs Morecroft said stiffly. 'I'll be glad to allow you all to assist me this evening, but tomorrow things will get back to normal.'

Caroline met Phin's amused gaze and smiled. 'I suppose you will sit down and let us all wait on you, Mr Colville.'

'That's how it should be, miss.' Mrs Morecroft opened the door to the front room. 'I keep the parlour ready for use at all times.' She shooed

Caroline and Maria towards the staircase. 'The master bedroom is the largest and my room is on the top floor, but you may have your pick of the other bedchambers.' She glanced over her shoulder at Phineas. 'Perhaps you would like to make yourself comfortable, sir. I think I can remember how to make an omelette, but I will, of course, call upon madam if I need help.' She marched upstairs ahead of Caroline, who had seen the funny side of things and was trying hard not to laugh.

'You've met your match there, Grace,' she said in an undertone. 'I feel as though Nanny Robbins has returned, disguised as Mrs Morecroft.'

'Are you coming, Miss Manning?' Mrs Morecroft peered over the banister. 'Chop-chop.'

'Now I'm certain of it,' Caroline said, mounting the stairs. 'You'd best come, too, Maria, or you might find yourself sent to bed without any supper.'

'Really, Phin, do you always allow your housekeeper to boss you around?' Grace put down her knife and fork, and reached for her wine glass.

'I was only twenty when I took her on,' Phineas said, sighing. 'An inexperienced young chap who was used to being dominated by Nanny and Grandmama, so I saw nothing odd about dear Moffie.'

'You created a monster, I think.' Caroline crumbled a slice of bread and popped it into her mouth. The omelette had been delicious and they had finished their meal with bread and cheese, accompanied by a fine claret. The dining room was small, but cosy. The red and gold wallpaper created a warm effect and the highly polished mahogany furniture glowed in the light of a gasolier hanging above the table.

Phineas raised his glass in a toast. 'Here's to people like Moffie, who has a heart of gold beneath her granite exterior.'

'A bit like you, cousin,' Maria said, giggling.

'I think you're a bit tipsy.' Grace reached across the table to pat her daughter's hand. 'It's time for bed, Maria. It's been a long day and I'm exhausted.'

'Yes, Mama.' Maria rose from her chair, swaying slightly. 'It's not the wine, I'm just sleepy.'

'We'll say good night then.' Grace stood up and slipped her arm around Maria's waist. 'We can help each other up the stairs. Heaven knows, we don't want to fall and break our bones.' She glanced over her shoulder. 'Are you coming, Carrie?'

'Yes, in a minute. I think Phineas has something he wanted to discuss with me.' Caroline gave him a searching look. 'You said you had a business proposition for me. I'm eager to know what it is.'

Chapter Fourteen

Phineas waited until the door closed and they were alone. 'You don't think much of me, do you, Caroline?'

Startled, she spilled some of her wine on the table and hastily mopped it up with her napkin. 'What gives you that idea, sir?'

'Perhaps the fact that you've reverted to calling me "sir" and not Phin is an indication that all is not well between us.'

'What do you expect? I'm grateful, of course, for the invitation to stay here for a while, which I won't impose upon any longer than necessary, but . . .' She paused, looking him in the eye.

'But you still blame me for your father's early demise, even though it was caused by illness.'

'Which no doubt was made worse by his state of mind. I remember how tired and drawn he looked before he was taken ill, and the long hours he worked in an attempt to turn the business round. I know now that he was struggling to repay his debt to you.'

'Your father was an excellent person, but a poor businessman. I'm sorry if the truth offends you, but it is a fact. He made some ill-judged decisions and lost a lot of money, which is why he was forced to come to me for a loan.'

'You told me that before, and I accept what you say, but you can't deny that you were in competition with my father and Uncle George.'

'Nor do I, but that is the way it is in the world of commerce. The strong survive and prosper and the rest struggle along or fail completely. Your uncle is a good shipmaster, but he has no head for business.' Phineas leaned forward, resting his elbows on the table. 'The one person who could have pulled the company together is your mother, but I strongly suspect that her opinions were often overruled, simply because she is a woman.'

'I know that my mother helped to build the company,' Caroline said slowly. 'But I never heard her complain about the way she was treated.'

'I was very impressed with her on our first meeting. She's a woman to be reckoned with, and if you have inherited her abilities, you might be able to make a good living for yourself and your family.'

'So what is your proposition?'

'Straight to the point. I like that.' Phineas sat back

in his chair. 'The *Esther Manning* is due back in port after what will hopefully prove to be a profitable trip. I'm offering to buy a half-share in your company.'

Caroline was momentarily speechless. She stared at him in disbelief and she reached for her glass, downing the last of her wine. 'You want to be a business partner? Why would you want to invest in a company that is virtually bankrupt?'

'What better time to invest cheaply? I'm a hardheaded businessman, Caroline. You still have one vessel that should be giving a good return. It makes sense to buy up my competitor.'

'Even so, I'm not in a position to say yes or no. I suppose it would be down to my mother and Uncle George.'

'Bring your mother back to London. From what I know of her she'll rise to the challenge, and she's too young to hide away for ever.'

'She's nearly forty; that's quite old.'

'Your mama is ageless, and she's the one you have to convince. I suggest you return to Devonshire and talk my proposition over with her, but you need to do it before the *Esther Manning* arrives in port.'

'You're forgetting my uncle. He would have to agree, too.'

'I've no doubt that Mrs Manning has a great deal of influence over her brother.' Phineas reached for the decanter and refilled both their glasses. He raised his in a toast. 'Shall we drink to success?'

Caroline was already feeling light-headed. It had been a long day and a trying one. Then Phineas had come up with this extraordinary plan, which in normal times she would have thought laughable. Whether it was the wine, or simple fatigue, she felt a sudden surge of optimism. Together they might resurrect the fortunes of Manning and Chapman, but there was one obstacle that had to be overcome.

'I'll drink to it,' she said slowly, 'but to be honest I don't hold out much hope. My mother is still in deep mourning and I doubt if she will want to return to London so soon, or to think about business.'

Despite exhaustion, Caroline found it hard to sleep. The bed was comfortable and the house was silent, but she tossed and turned, unable to put their conversation out of her mind. She fell into a fitful doze in the early hours of the morning, and her last memory before sleep claimed her was the chiming of the grandfather clock in the entrance hall. The third stroke had barely faded away when she drifted off.

She was awakened by someone shaking her by the shoulder.

'What time is it?' Caroline opened her eyes and found Maria bending over her.

'It's nine o'clock, sleepyhead,' she said cheerfully.

Caroline sat up, groaning. 'Oh Lord! I meant to get up early this morning.'

'You must have been so tired. We thought it best to let you sleep, but I couldn't wait any longer. I have a favour to ask.' Maria thrust a cup of tea into Caroline's hand. 'This will help you to wake up.'

Caroline took a sip. 'What do you want, Maria? What's so urgent that you're waiting on me like this?'

Maria perched on the edge of the bed. 'Phineas told me at breakfast that Captain Barnaby's ship is still in port, and I thought if we went down to the docks we might happen to see him.'

'As a matter of fact I intended to visit the Captain's House to see my brothers, so we could go together. Just give me time to get washed and dressed and we'll be on our way.'

'You must have breakfast first. Mrs Morecroft has been up since the crack of dawn, baking the most delicious bread, and there's strawberry jam, too.'

'We'll see, but go away and leave me in peace, and I promise to be as quick as I can.'

Caroline had the satisfaction of leaving Maria and Grace in the capable hands of Captain Barnaby. He had, almost as if he had been expecting a visit, been conveniently on deck when they walked past his ship, which had been moved from the dock at high tide and was now moored alongside the Colville wharf. He had invited Caroline to join them but she had declined, explaining that she was eager to see her brothers. Barnaby had promised to see Grace and Maria back to Princes Square, leaving Caroline with the rest of the morning free to do as she pleased.

She hurried on to the Captain's House, but when Sadie opened the door Caroline knew immediately that something was wrong.

'It's Jimmy,' Sadie said tearfully. 'He got measles, so the doctor says, and I knew it anyway. I recognised the symptoms because I had it when I was young, and you contracted the disease when you were fourteen.'

'I must see him,' Caroline said anxiously. 'Where is Max?'

'He's at his lessons with Laurence. He's had measles, in fact he caught it from you, but for some reason Jimmy didn't get it until now.'

'You look worn out.' Caroline shed her shawl and took off her bonnet, hanging them on the row of hooks next to the boys' overcoats and hats. 'I'll look in on Max first, and then I'll go and sit with Jimmy for a while.'

A faint smile lit Sadie's red-rimmed eyes. 'It's good to see you. I'll make a pot of tea and then you can tell me how you and Maria got on in Devonshire.'

'I'll tell you everything. You won't believe half of it, Sadie.'

'You saw Esther, didn't you?'

'Yes, I did and she's on the mend, but I need to get her back to London as soon as possible.'

'I sent for her yesterday. Jimmy has been calling for her and she should be with him, not hiding away in the country. Laurence went to the telegraph office for me and sent a message to Daumerle and she replied by return, promising to come straight away.'

'Is he that poorly, Sadie?'

'Who knows, my dear? You and Max got over it quite quickly, but Jimmy is more delicate. I blame myself for allowing him to associate with those ragamuffins who scavenge the foreshore. Dirty, rude boys who should be in school.'

'He'll recover, I know he will.' Caroline headed for the stairs, her heart hammering against the whalebone of her stays. To lose her father and then her home had been bad enough, but if Jimmy was taken from them it would be too much to bear.

She poked her head round the door of the schoolroom and Max leaped to his feet, knocking over his chair in his haste. He flung his arms around her and almost squeezed the breath from her lungs in a bear hug.

'I'm so glad you're back, Carrie. Have you seen Jimmy? He's covered in a rash.'

'No, I came to see you first.' Caroline sent an apologetic smile in Laurence's direction. 'I thought you wouldn't mind the interruption, but I had to see Max.'

Laurence rose to greet her with a tired smile. 'I'm glad you're back. Sadie has been out of her mind with worry.'

'Jimmy is a fighter,' Caroline said with more conviction than she was feeling. 'I'll go and see him now.' She turned to Max, giving him a hug. 'Thank goodness you've already had measles.'

Despite the tears that sprang to his eyes, Max managed a grin. 'I'd be the man of the house if we were still at home. Sir sent a telegram to Mama yesterday – did Sadie tell you?'

'Yes, she did, and I'll be as glad to see her as you will.'

Max clung to her hand. 'You won't go away again, will you?'

'No, I won't, and that's a promise.' Caroline hurried from the room, controlling the urge to cry with difficulty. She did not want to break down in front of Max, who was obviously struggling to control his own emotions. They had all been under a considerable strain, and it was beginning to tell on everyone.

She made her way upstairs to the room the boys shared. The curtains were drawn, but there was enough light to see the small shape tossing feverishly in the bed.

'Jimmy,' she whispered. 'It's me, Carrie. I've come home.' She went to kneel at his bedside, taking hold of his hot little hand as it rested on the counterpane. She held it to her cheek and this time she could not prevent the tears from falling. He was mumbling incoherently and although his eyes were open, he did not seem to recognise her. She stood up and went to the washstand where a bowl of tepid water had been left, together with a face cloth. She returned to the bed and bathed his face and chest with the damp cloth, and it seemed to calm him, temporarily at least. His lips were dry and cracked and she reached for the cup of water on the side table and propped his head up so that he could take a sip or two. Having settled him down again there was little else she could do other than talk, hoping that he could hear her, even if he could not understand what she was saying.

She lost track of time completely, but she could not bear to leave her younger brother to fight the illness on his own. She talked until her mouth was dry and her voice began to crack, watching and waiting for him to show some sign that he knew she was there, but the fever held him in its vicious grasp. Sadie brought her a cup of tea, which was more than welcome, and she offered to take a turn at Jimmy's bedside, but Caroline would not be moved. She blamed herself in part for his illness, although there was nothing she could have done to prevent the contagion. Bowed down by feelings of guilt for leaving the boys in the care of others while she herself went careering off to Devonshire in an attempt to reunite Maria with her mother, Caroline knew that she would never forgive herself if Jimmy suffered any of the dire complications of the illness.

She must have dropped off to sleep still holding her brother's hand, but she could hear her mother's voice and she felt Jimmy's fingers twitch. Caroline opened her eyes with a start to find her mother leaning over the bed.

'Mama.' Caroline released Jimmy's hand and rose

stiffly from her seat. Her limbs were cramped and her head ached, but she could have cried with relief. 'You've come home. I'm so glad.'

Esther gave her a hug. 'I came as soon as I could, Carrie. How is my poor baby?'

'I'm sure he'll be better when he realises that you're here, Mama.'

Esther sank down on the chair. 'I'll stay with him for a while. You look exhausted, my dear. Go downstairs and talk to Freddie. He insisted on accompanying me because he wanted to find Grace. I've had to listen to him going on about her ever since we boarded the train for London.'

'Did Aunt Alice travel with you?'

'She wanted to stay at Daumerle a while longer.'

'I'm so glad you've come home, Mama. I have so much to tell you, but the most important thing is getting Jimmy better, and having you here is the best medicine he could have.'

Esther shook her head. 'I hope so, but I shouldn't have left the boys, or you, come to that. I ran away and I'll never forgive myself for leaving you to deal with matters that were beyond your control. I realise that I was being selfish in my grief, thinking only of the pain I was suffering and ignoring the fact that you three were going through something similar.' She turned her head, at a small sound from the bed. 'Jimmy, can you hear me, sweetheart? It's Mama.'

'He seems calmer,' Caroline whispered. 'Keep

talking to him. I'm sure he can hear you, even if he can't tell you so.'

'I think he squeezed my fingers.' Esther looked up, her eyes magnified by unshed tears. 'I'll never leave my family again, never.'

Caroline bent down to drop a kiss on her mother's smooth forehead. 'I love you, Mama,' Caroline said softly. 'I'll be downstairs with Sadie if you need me.'

Freddie was in the front parlour deep in conversation with Sadie when Caroline entered the room. He looked up, frowning.

'Was it really necessary for you to leave the Abbey in such a hurry? I would have protected Grace from that villain who treated her so badly.'

'You've met him, Freddie. Quick is a brute and he's vicious.'

'I'm still in my prime, I'll have you know, and I could knock the wretched fellow's block off, if I so wished.'

'At least Grace is safe from him in London.'

'But I haven't finished the portrait,' Freddie grumbled. 'She must come back to Starcross Abbey.'

'I've more important things to worry about than a painting.' Caroline was in no mood to talk about portraits and she spoke more sharply than she had intended. 'Perhaps you could make some sketches of Grace while you're here,' she added hastily. 'I know she won't want to return to Devonshire, at least not for a long time.'

'I suppose you're right.' Freddie cleared his throat noisily. 'Er – how is the boy? I should have asked that the moment you came into the room. I'm sorry, Carrie. I'm a selfish man and always was.'

'Jimmy is very unwell, Uncle. But I'm sure he'll rally when he realises that Mama is here.'

'Of course he will – I've no doubt about that.' Freddie put his head on one side, giving her a searching look. 'Out with it, Carrie. I've known you since you were a small child. There's something else bothering you, so what is it?'

Sadie rose from the window seat. 'I have bread to bake, so I'd best get on. I'll be in the kitchen if you need me.' She whisked out of the room, closing the door behind her.

'Phineas Colville has been very helpful,' Caroline said carefully. 'Surprisingly so, considering the rivalry between our two companies, although I still hold him partly responsible for Papa's death.'

'Come now, my dear. Your father died from an illness that had nothing to do with his financial troubles. Colville cannot be held responsible.'

'You're probably right,' Caroline conceded reluctantly. 'Anyway, he's offered to go into business with us by taking a half-share in the company, which would allow us to continue trading when the *Esther Manning* finally reaches port.'

'That sounds like a good proposition, and one not to be missed.'

'I'm not in a position to accept or refuse it, Uncle.

The business belongs to Mama and Uncle George, and I don't know if either of them would relish working with a Colville.'

'I'm not well versed in the world of commerce, Carrie. But as I see it, they would be fools to turn him down. You must discuss it with Esther.'

'I know, but with poor Jimmy so ill I don't like to bother her.'

Freddie reached out to grasp Caroline's hand. 'I've seen your mother go through hardships that would have broken a lesser woman. I think a challenge such as this is just what she needs to help her recover from the bitterest of all blows. Tell her everything, that's my advice.' He squeezed her fingers. 'And now I think it's time for me to go to my club. I'll only be in the way if I remain here, but I'll be staying for a night or two at Bearwood House so you can contact me there. I've already told Esther of my plans.' He picked up his top hat and cane just as Max burst into the room. 'Ah, my boy. You can assist me by going out and hailing a cab. There's a silver sixpence in it for you.'

Max nodded. 'Yes, sir, I will, but I came to tell Carrie that Mama wants her to bring something for Jimmy to eat. She said the fever has broken and he's hungry.'

Caroline jumped up from her chair and threw her arms around her brother's neck. 'I knew it. The moment he realised that Mama was there was better than all the medicine in the world.' She rushed out of the room, forgetting everything other than the urgent need to speed Jimmy's recovery.

Sadie was standing at the range and she looked up from the pan she was stirring. 'What is it? Is he worse?'

'No, far from it. Jimmy's hungry.'

'Thank God.' Sadie closed her eyes, taking a deep breath. 'I love that boy as if he were my own.' She unhooked a ladle from the beam above the range and filled a bowl. 'This broth is just the thing. Tell your mother to come down and have something to eat as soon as she's ready, or she'll be the next one laid up in bed. I know Esther and I'll wager she hasn't eaten a bite since she heard that her son was ill.'

'I'll send her down,' Caroline said firmly. 'And then I need to have a long talk with my mother.'

Jimmy was over the worst. The doctor came next day and pronounced that his patient was out of danger, and there was no congestion of the lungs or any other complication that might have occurred. Caroline and her mother took it in turns to sit with Jimmy, and he became crotchety and demanding, which Esther said was a sure sign that he was getting better. Max was less than sympathetic, although Caroline was not fooled by his casual attitude – she had seen the panic in his eyes when he had told her of his brother's illness, and she knew that the boys loved each other, despite their tendency to fight and argue over the silliest things.

Jimmy was definitely on the mend and Caroline's relief was such that she could think of nothing else, but the time passed quickly and she had not been able to find a moment for a private conversation with her mother. It was early evening when Esther announced that since Jimmy was so much improved she intended to spend the night at Bearwood House.

'But you need to stay here,' Sadie said, frowning. 'I assumed you would want to be close to Jimmy, at least until he's up and about again.'

'And so I do, but I can't impose on you and they're expecting me. Carrie will look after Jimmy tonight.'

'I thought she would be returning to Princes Square,' Sadie said impatiently. 'You can't abandon the child again so soon, Essie.'

'I'm not abandoning Jimmy.' Esther turned to Caroline, eyebrows raised. 'I must have missed something. What's been going on in my absence, Carrie?'

Caroline and Sadie exchanged worried glances and Laurence rose hastily from the table. 'I have to set the school work for the morning, if you'll excuse me, ladies.' He tapped Max on the shoulder. 'I believe I set you some studying for this evening, or would you rather go upstairs and sit with your brother?'

Max leaped to his feet. 'I'll keep Jimmy company, sir.' He rushed out of the room, followed more slowly by Laurence.

'Is there something I should know?' Esther demanded, frowning.

'I'll leave you two to have a talk.' Sadie hurried

261

from the room, leaving the door to swing shut in her haste.

'Now I know there's a conspiracy of some kind.' Esther sat back in her chair, fixing Caroline with a hard stare. 'Come along, Carrie. Out with it.'

There had been no time to talk about anything with Jimmy so poorly, but now there was nothing for it, but to tell her mother everything.

'It is just business, Mama.' Caroline came to a sudden halt, gazing anxiously at her mother, who had remained rigid and silent, listening intently. 'When the *Esther Manning* returns we will have one ship, but we haven't the money to pay for a fresh cargo, and we don't know how the voyage went, or what Uncle George has brought back, if anything.'

'But to give the Colvilles a half-share in the company is ridiculous,' Esther said slowly. 'Your poor papa would be spinning like a top in his grave.'

'Papa isn't here to say yes or no, Mama. Everything is up to us now, and Uncle George, of course, although . . .' Caroline could not bring herself to tell her mother that Phineas had said George was a poor businessman.

Esther remained calm, her cheeks pale, but there was a militant spark in her hazel eyes. 'You don't have to dissemble, Carrie. I love my brother, but I know very well that he has no head for business. He's a good shipmaster, but that is all.'

Her words echoed those of Phineas, and Caroline breathed a sigh of relief. 'So I believe, Mama.'

'I dare say you heard that from Phineas Colville as well, but don't take everything he says as gospel truth.'

'I don't,' Caroline said hastily. 'But you worked alongside Papa and you helped to build the business. I think if anyone can turn things around it's you.'

'I had your father to back me up in those days. Now I'm on my own.'

Caroline reached across the table to grasp her mother's hand. 'No, Mama. You are not on your own – you have me. I believe I could learn from you, and I have a fair idea of how the company should be run. If you'll just give me a chance to prove myself, I'm sure that we could work together. What do you say?'

Chapter Fifteen

The meeting between Esther Manning and Phineas Colville took place in the boardroom of the Colville Shipping office, as arranged by Caroline. The atmosphere was formal, if not frigid, but Esther had her emotions under control and Caroline saw a different side to her mother. The woman, dressed entirely in black, who talked on a business level equal to that of any man, laid down the conditions she expected from the proposed merger, and Phineas was coolly professional in his responses. Caroline sat quietly, listening and occasionally putting in a point, but her respect for her mother was growing with every passing minute. As a child she had seen little of either parent as they were both deeply involved in running the company, and now she could see why her father had relied so much on her mother for sound common sense and a pragmatic approach to any problems that might have arisen. The reasons for their finances falling into such a parlous state were not mentioned, but Caroline had a feeling that her mother was keeping something back. Phineas did not press the point and she was grateful to him for that small mercy.

The boardroom clock struck midday and Phineas rose from his seat at the head of the table. 'It seems that we are largely in agreement on everything, apart from a few minor details, Mrs Manning.'

Esther stood up, shaking the creases from her voluminous skirts. 'Your financial backing will allow me to reopen the office and employ a clerk. We will start off in a modest way, but I intend to rebuild the company.'

'I admire your spirit, Mrs Manning.' Phineas shot a sideways glance at Caroline. 'I sincerely hope we can put the past behind us.'

Esther proffered her hand. 'This is a business arrangement only, Mr Colville. I prefer to keep things formal and then there is no danger of misunderstandings, as happened before.'

He shook her hand. 'My sentiments exactly.'

Caroline had risen unnoticed but she was not going to be ignored. 'There is one more matter to discuss, Mr Colville. You poached two of my father's employees, Mr Parkinson and Mr Masters.'

A faint smile lit his eyes. 'I wouldn't put it like that exactly.'

'You can keep Parkinson,' Caroline said shortly.

'I caught him emptying the safe in my father's office. However, I believe Mr Masters was a trusted clerk, and he would be an asset to our company.'

Esther turned to stare at her daughter, eyebrows raised. 'You have been busy in my absence, Carrie.'

'I only want what is best for us, Mama.'

'I will arrange for Masters to be seconded to your office,' Phineas said easily. 'We're working together now. Don't forget that, Miss Manning.'

Esther made a move towards the door. 'Thank you for your time, Mr Colville. I expect you to have the contract drawn up speedily as I'm eager to recommence trading as soon as the *Esther Manning* reaches port.'

He nodded and moved swiftly to open the door for her. 'It will be sent to your office as soon as it's ready, and the money will be paid into your bank on signature.'

Caroline held out her hand as she was about to walk past him. 'Might I have a word in private?'

'Of course.' Phineas glanced at Esther. 'If you have no objections, Mrs Manning?'

'None at all. I'll wait for you in the vestibule, Carrie.' Esther left the room, her silk petticoats swishing as she moved.

'What can I do for you?' Phineas asked gravely. 'Aren't you satisfied with our agreement?'

'It has nothing to do with that.' Caroline met his curious gaze with a steady look. 'I can't continue to live under your roof, and the Captain's House will be overcrowded when the new pupils take up residence.'

'Yes, I see that. What are you suggesting?'

'If you agree, my mother and I could rent the house in Great Hermitage Street. My uncle has always lived with us and he'll be home soon. We need somewhere permanent to set up home.'

'Maria will miss you.'

'Maria has her mother now, and she is very taken with Captain Barnaby, as he is with her, or so I believe.'

A frown creased his brow. 'I could wish a better match for my cousin, although Barnaby should have left port by now, and hopefully Maria will forget him and settle on someone more suitable than a mere seafarer.'

'Maybe, she will,' Caroline said doubtfully. 'But the house, Mr Colville. What do you say?'

'You may have it with pleasure. Anticipating your acceptance, I've had it cleaned from top to bottom, so it won't take much to make it more liveable.'

'We'll take it, thank you.'

'On one condition.'

'And that is?'

'Outside the boardroom I hope we can drop the formalities, as we agreed previously.'

Caroline hesitated. 'I think I prefer to keep matters on a more formal level, for the time being at least. We're business partners, and I think my mother would find it distasteful if you and I were to be too friendly.' She opened the door, pausing on the threshold. 'But thank you, anyway. I'll go and give my mother the good news that we will have a roof over our heads.' She turned on her heel and left the room without waiting for his response.

'Why did you want to speak to him in private?' Esther demanded as Caroline climbed into the cab and sat down beside her.

'We have to be practical, Mama. I've arranged for us to rent a house in Great Hermitage Street. It belongs to the Colville Shipping Company and it's not what you're used to, but it's close to the office and you'll be near the boys, presuming you wish them to continue their schooling with Laurence.'

'I grew up in the slums of Limehouse, Carrie. I doubt if it's worse than the house where I was born and raised. As to the boys, they must continue their education and I have to be realistic – there is no money for school fees, although I will contribute to their board and keep as and when I am able.'

'That should be fairly soon, Mama. When Uncle George returns we will begin all over again, and this time you'll have me to help you.'

'I just hope that the *Esther Manning* arrives soon, and I'll have a few words to say to that brother of mine for failing to keep us notified as to their where-abouts.'

'I'm sure there must be a good reason for the delay.'

'You are a lot more charitable than I am.' Esther

leaned back against the squabs with a heavy sigh. 'But I am not in a position to criticise my brother. I ran away, nursing my grief like a wounded animal, and I left you to shoulder the responsibilities that were mine.'

'Don't think about it, Mama.'

'We must look to the future, Carrie. That's what your father would have wanted.'

'We'll be all right, Mama,' Caroline said firmly. 'I'll see you safely back to the Captain's House and then I'll go to Princes Square and break the news to Maria that I'm leaving. Poor girl, I'm afraid she'll be very sad because her sea captain has sailed away.'

'She's probably better off without him,' Esther said drily. 'In my experience seafarers are an unreliable breed of men – the sea is in their veins and they never settle well to life ashore.'

Her mother's words were still ringing in her ears when Caroline reached Princes Square.

Mrs Morecroft opened the door. 'Oh, it's you, miss. Come in, please. There's been such a to-do this morning, I don't know if I'm on my head or my heels.'

Caroline could hear Freddie's unmistakable tones droning on in the front parlour and she opened the door to find Grace slumped on the sofa, weeping into a sodden hanky, while Freddie paced the floor.

'Oh, it's you, Carrie,' he said, unconsciously repeated Mrs Morecroft's greeting. 'I thought it might have been that silly girl returned, having thought better of it.'

Caroline looked from one to the other, slowly taking off her bonnet and shawl. 'What have I missed? Where is Maria?'

'It's history repeating itself,' Grace sobbed. 'Like mother, like daughter – that's what they'll all say.'

'Pull yourself together, woman,' Freddie said crossly. 'It's hardly your fault if the girl is infatuated with a bounder. What sort of fellow takes a young woman away from her loving mother to sail the seven seas without making an honest woman of her first?'

'Don't say things like that,' Grace wailed, dabbing her eyes. 'Maria has bad blood, which she inherited from me. I was a reckless little fool and I thought I was in love. I disgraced my family and spent twenty-one years of my life married to a brute, who punished me daily for my youthful mistake.'

'Are you telling me that Maria has run away with Barnaby?' Caroline gasped. 'His ship sailed today. Phineas told me so this very morning.'

'Don't get too friendly with that man,' Freddie said sternly. 'Look at poor Grace, see how the Colvilles made her suffer all these years.' He took a large silk hanky from his pocket and thrust it into Grace's hand. 'You can't change what's happened, my dear, but we can look to the future. You're coming back to Starcross Abbey with me – I have a portrait to finish.'

Grace threw the hanky back at him. 'You're just the same as all men. You make out you want to paint my picture and then next thing you know I'll be warming your bed.'

'How can you say such a thing?' Freddie stared at her in horror.

'I can because it's true. You slept with your house-keeper and she bore you a son. You treat both of them like servants, and that's how I'll end up.'

'That's not how it will be. Jenifry is married to a seaman who sailed away years ago and has yet to return. I offered to do the right thing by her when she had Dickon, but she refused and believes her husband might yet return. I'm not a bad man.' Freddie turned to Caroline, shaking his head. 'You've known me since you were a child. Have I ever said or done anything to hurt anyone?'

'No, Uncle Freddie, but Grace has a point. You can't just take women into your home and treat them like chattels. Grace would be swapping one master for another, albeit a much nicer and kinder master,' she added hastily. 'What would people think of her?'

Freddie paled visibly. 'I've lived so long in my own little world that I've never considered what others might think of me. I thought Jenifry was happy with the way things were.'

Grace rose shakily from the sofa. 'Well, that's all you know, you stupid man. And that son of hers is evil. You might be his father but it's obvious that he hates you, and he hates me, too. If – and I say if – I were to come with you to the Abbey, young Dickon would do his best to get rid of me. He thinks he is going to inherit your estate when you die, and I wouldn't put it past him to plot your sudden demise.'

Freddie sank down in an armchair by the fireplace. 'That's nonsense, Grace. You are a wonderful woman, and a beautiful one, too, but you are quite wrong. Jenifry is devoted to me, as was her mother before her, and Dickon is a dolt, but he's harmless.'

'Think that if you like, but you're mistaken,' Grace cried passionately. 'I saw it all when I was there, and it was Dickon who betrayed me to my husband. Don't forget that I'm still married to Elias Quick. If I return to Devonshire he'll find out and come after me. I'd rather kill myself than go back to him.'

'I wouldn't allow that to happen.' Freddie looked to Caroline as if for encouragement. 'Tell her she's wrong, Carrie. I need Grace – she's my muse.'

'I'm not sure what that is, Uncle. But I think she's right, and all this isn't helping Maria. Could we send a telegram to a port somewhere downriver? Perhaps the ship could be intercepted and Maria could be persuaded to return home?'

He shook his head. 'I doubt if that's possible, but I'll speak to Colville. He should be informed anyway, because she's his responsibility.'

'Oh dear, this is all my fault,' Caroline said sadly. 'I knew she was infatuated with Captain Barnaby, but I didn't realise that it had gone so far. How did it happen, Grace? You were with her.'

'I am to blame.' Fresh tears spurted from Grace's eyes and she buried her face in her hands. 'She said she wanted to purchase some ribbons for her bonnet, and I let her go out on her own.'

'Are you sure she went with Barnaby?' Caroline said urgently.

Grace pulled a crumpled piece of paper from her pocket and handed it to Caroline. 'This was delivered by a street urchin, who demanded a penny for his trouble.'

The note was brief and to the point.

Dearest Mama,
    Please don't worry. Theo and I plan to marry as soon as we reach our first port of call.
    Your loving daughter,
    Maria

'That is all she said,' Grace sobbed. 'We've only just found each other and she's left me for a man she barely knows.'

Freddie cleared his throat. 'Sometimes it happens like that, Grace. In fact quite frequently in my case – but then,' he added hastily, 'I am not an impressionable young woman. That fellow should be horsewhipped.'

'It was obvious that the attraction was mutual,' Caroline said thoughtfully. 'Maria knows nothing of life outside the walls of Pier House. It's no wonder she's seized a chance of happiness, even if it is against all odds.'

'You encouraged her.' Grace leaped to her feet. 'This is your fault as much as mine.'

'I admit my part and I'm sorry, but the baby you abandoned grew up in that unhappy house with an uncaring grandmother, so I'm not surprised that she fell in love with the first man who paid her any attention. I think all of you are to blame, including Phineas, who admitted that he devoted all his time to building the business. He knew how Maria was being treated and yet he did almost nothing to make her life easier.'

Freddie laid his hand on Grace's shoulder. 'The girl has gone. Face the fact, Grace, and come back to Starcross with me.'

She turned on him in a fury. 'Don't say things like that. I won't leave her again.'

'It seems to me that she's left you this time, my dear.' Freddie took the note from Caroline and studied it. 'You'll never catch up with them, Grace. You'd best get used to the idea that your daughter has made her choice.'

'As if I haven't suffered enough,' Grace murmured, sinking back onto the sofa. 'I might as well go back to Elias. There's no point to anything now.'

Freddie sent a mute plea for help to Caroline and she sat down beside Grace.

'I think you might consider returning to the

Abbey,' Caroline said gently. 'There really isn't much we can do now. Freddie's right – Maria has chosen the life she wants.'

'Phineas will have details of the next port of call. I'll follow them and maybe I can prevent her from marrying this fellow and making a terrible mistake.' Grace rose slowly to her feet. 'Find me a cab, Freddie. I'm going to the office.'

'All right, Grace, have it your own way, but I think it would be a grave mistake. Maybe your nephew can talk some sense into you.' Freddie turned to Caroline. 'Will you accompany us? You seem to be the only sensible person in this room, apart from myself, of course.'

Caroline nodded. 'Yes, of course I will.' She slipped her arm around Grace's shoulders. 'We'll do everything we can, but Maria is a grown woman – she's capable of making her own decisions.'

Freddie left the room, muttering beneath his breath.

Phineas listened to Grace's outpourings, his rigidly controlled expression giving nothing away.

'I need to follow them and persuade her to come home,' Grace finished breathlessly. 'You could arrange that, couldn't you, Phineas?'

'The *Colville Star* is en route to Australia, Aunt Grace. There's no possibility of anyone making chase, and Barnaby is a good man. He's sober and reliable and an excellent shipmaster.'

Caroline nodded in agreement. 'I'm so sorry,

Grace, but there really is nothing you can do. I think you have to trust Maria to know her own mind, hard though it seems.'

'What will I do? Where will I go?' Grace murmured dazedly. 'I found my child, only to lose her again.'

'You are welcome to stay with me for as long as you like,' Phineas said calmly. 'You might even try to make your peace with Grandmama. She's mellowed over the years.'

'I don't believe that for a moment.' Grace tossed her head. 'My mother has a heart of granite, like Wolf Tor. She will never forgive me, and I will never forgive her. We are strangers and that's how it will be for ever.'

'My offer still stands,' Freddie said solemnly. 'Come back to Starcross Abbey and allow me to finish your portrait. If, after that, you wish to leave you may do so with my blessing, but I hope you might decide to stay on.'

Grace turned on him in a fury. 'And what happens to your housekeeper and her bastard son? They'll make my life unbearable and I'll be regarded for ever as a kept woman. I've just escaped one man's clutches; I won't put myself in that position again.'

'I agree with Grace,' Phineas said angrily. 'That's a shoddy suggestion, Mr Dorincourt, and unworthy of you. Despite what ignorant people might say, my aunt is a respectable woman from a good family, and I won't allow her to be subjected to humiliation at your hands.'

'Hold on, old chap. I'll marry Grace if she'll divorce that blackguard she wed all those years ago. I'm perfectly serious.'

Caroline rose to her feet. 'This is family business. I think I should leave now, Phineas. I've been away from the Captain's House for too long anyway. My younger brother is just recovering from measles and I should be there to help look after him.'

'You should have told me,' Grace said humbly. 'My problems are of my own making. I'm sorry to have involved you, Caroline.'

Freddie raised himself from his chair. 'I'll escort you home, Carrie. I need to speak to Esther, anyway.' He turned to Grace. 'I'll leave you to think over my offer. I plan to return to Starcross in a day or two, so please let me know if you change your mind.'

Phineas was already at the door, holding it open. 'I've sent Masters to open up your father's premises, Caroline. He'll carry out any instructions that you or your mother give him, but if you find that he's unhelpful in any way just tell me, and I'll deal with him.'

Caroline held her head high. 'Thank you, but I'm sure that won't be necessary.' She treated him to a frosty smile.

'You were a bit hard on the fellow,' Freddie said as they left the building. 'He seems to be bending backwards in his attempts to help you and Esther out of the mess Jack left.'

'My father made mistakes, but Phineas Colville

took advantage of his misfortune. I've tried, but I can't forget that.'

'Even so, you might find it in your heart to forgive him,' Freddie said with a wry smile. 'I'm much older than you, Carrie, and I've made plenty of mistakes in my lifetime. Everyone deserves a second chance.'

'Even Elias Quick?'

He chuckled, taking her arm as they crossed the street. 'Maybe not everyone, but I'd say that Phineas is trying to make amends.'

Caroline broke free from his guiding hand, pointing a shaking finger towards the river. 'I know that ship – it's the *Esther Manning*, and what a state she's in, but at least she's here. I'm going to tell Mama.' She broke into a run, arriving at the Captain's House, breathless and with her bonnet hanging by its ribbons as she hammered on the door.

'Mama, Sadie, someone, open the door and let me in.'

Her urgent summons was answered by Max. 'What's up, Carrie? Where've you been all this time?'

Caroline clutched her hands to her bosom as she struggled to catch her breath. 'Fetch Mama. Tell her the *Esther Manning* has arrived in port.'

'What?' Max pushed past her and ran to the edge of the wharf. He hallooed loudly, waving madly.

'Come inside, boy.' Flushed and breathless, Freddie put his arm around Max's shoulders. 'They can't hear you. Let's go and give your mother the good news.'

Caroline hurried into the house and made her way to the kitchen where she found Sadie at the sink, washing dishes.

'You missed luncheon,' she said grumpily. 'I kept yours warm for a while, but then I gave it to the seagulls – noisy, dirty beggars, but they're useful sometimes.'

'The *Esther Manning*. She's at the moorings, Sadie. Uncle George has brought her home – we'll be all right now. We're back in business.'

Sadie dropped the plate she was holding and it plopped back into the water. 'Heaven be praised.' She wiped her hands on her apron. 'Your mother is with Jimmy. Go and tell her, Carrie. She deserves to have some good news for a change.'

An hour later the whole family, including Jimmy, who had insisted on joining them, were waiting on the wharf for the lighter to bring George Chapman ashore. Caroline shaded her eyes from the sun, but as it drew closer she realised that her uncle was not one of the men on board.

'Where is George?' Esther's voice shook with emotion. 'What's happened? Why isn't he coming ashore?'

Caroline grasped her mother's hand. 'I'm sure there's a good reason why he's remained on board, Mama.'

Max peered into the distance, moving perilously close to the edge of the wharf. The muddy water lapped greedily at the stanchions as the incoming tide battled against the fast-moving river water flowing down to the sea. The lighter bobbed up and down, the lighterman using all his muscle and sinew to bring the craft alongside.

'Uncle George isn't on deck,' Max said over his shoulder. 'I don't recognise the captain either, Mama.'

'Neither do I,' Caroline said grimly. 'Something isn't quite right.'

Chapter Sixteen

Caroline glanced at her mother, who was swaying on her feet, supported by Freddie and Sadie. Laurence moved forward to drag Max away from the edge and Jimmy clung to Caroline's arm. She gave him a hug.

'I think you ought to go back to bed, Jimmy,' she said gently. 'This is your first time up, isn't it?'

'I'm all right, Carrie. Don't fuss. I'm not a baby.'

She released him reluctantly. 'Of course not. But Mama doesn't look very well. Perhaps you could take her indoors and we'll find out why Uncle George hasn't come ashore.'

Jimmy looked as though he was about to rebel, but Laurence took him by the hand. 'Come on, old chap. We'll find out soon enough.' He turned to Max. 'You, too. Set a good example to James, if you please.'

Max nodded, eyes downcast. 'Yes, sir.' He followed his brother and Laurence into the house.

'Let's go indoors, Essie,' Sadie said gently. 'There must be a good reason why George has remained on board.'

Esther nodded dully. 'Yes, you're right.' She shook free from Freddie's restraining hand. 'I'm fine now, thank you. It was a dizzy spell, that's all.' She returned to the house, walking briskly with Freddie and Sadie close on her heels.

Caroline stood alone on the wharf, the cool breeze whipping her hair into tangles, and her skirts billowing around her. The sun had disappeared behind a bank of grey clouds and the first spots of rain had begun to fall, creating tiny dimples on the surface of the water. She ignored the weather as she waited eagerly for the lighterman to manoeuvre his craft alongside, but the man who climbed the stone steps was neither her uncle nor the captain.

'Why hasn't Mr Chapman come ashore?' she asked anxiously.

'Are you Miss Manning?'

'Yes, I am. Who are you?'

'Gilbert Reid, captain of the *Esther Manning*.'

'What happened to Captain Daniels?'

'It would be best if I speak to Mr Manning in private.'

Caroline felt her throat tighten and she willed herself not to cry. The mention of her father as if he were still alive was like a dagger thrust into her heart. She cleared her throat. 'My father died some weeks ago, Captain Reid. My mother is now head of Manning and Chapman, but she is still in deep mourning. Perhaps it would be best if you told me what has happened.'

'Yellow fever,' he said grimly. 'We took a cargo from Baltimore to Trinidad, and half the crew, including Captain Daniels and your uncle, went down with the fever on the trip out from there. The ship was quarantined and, sadly, many died.'

'My uncle?'

'He was one of the first to succumb, and Captain Daniels shortly afterwards. I'm very sorry, Miss Manning.'

The rain had started to fall in earnest, but Caroline barely noticed that she was getting soaked. She stared at him, stunned by the enormity of what he had just told her. Yet another tragic death in the family was almost too much to bear. She took a deep breath. 'You'd better come inside and speak to my mother, Captain Reid.' Bracing herself for what was to follow, she led him into the house.

Esther was in the front parlour, staring out of the window. She turned to face them with a worried frown. 'What's happened? Where is my brother?'

'Maybe you should sit down, Mama,' Caroline said gently. 'This is Captain Reid, and I'm afraid he has some bad news for us.'

Esther sank down on the sofa. 'I can see by your

expression that it's dire, Captain. You'd better tell me everything.'

'Please take a seat, Captain Reid.' Caroline sat down beside her mother, holding her hand tightly.

Esther listened intently, and was outwardly calm, but Caroline winced as her mother's fingers tightened around her hand.

'I don't understand why the ship sailed for Trinidad,' Esther said slowly. 'They were supposed to return to London with a cargo of wheat and raw sugar.'

'I can't say, ma'am. I was only first mate at the time and the decision was made by Mr Chapman and Captain Daniels. We did an extra run from Baltimore to Trinidad, where we delivered our goods and took on another cargo. We were there for a few days and all was well, but the crew started to fall sick soon after we set sail. We headed for Jamaica and anchored offshore, flying the yellow flag.'

'I've heard enough, thank you, Captain. I know how these things work and the laws surrounding quarantine. I take it that the ship has a clean bill of health now.'

Caroline exchanged anxious glances with Gilbert Reid. Her mother's acceptance of the situation was even more disturbing than an outpouring of grief.

'Yes, ma'am.'

'Our office has been closed temporarily.'

'But it's about to reopen,' Caroline said hastily. 'I have Mr Colville's word on that, Mama.'

'I'm glad to hear it.' Esther inclined her head graciously. 'Until then, Captain, you should return to the ship, and you'll receive instructions as to where to berth and unload the cargo.'

'The crew need to receive their pay, ma'am.'

'It will be arranged.'

'Do I take it that you approve of my captaincy, ma'am? Will it be a permanent promotion?'

'Yes, I'm sure it will. You've brought the ship home and you've done an excellent job under very difficult circumstances.' Esther stood up, facing him with an attempt at a smile. 'Thank you, Captain Reid. Now, if you'll excuse me, I have to go and break the news to my two younger children. They will be devastated by the loss of their uncle, as am I.'

Caroline jumped to her feet. 'Are you sure you're all right, Mama? You've had a terrible shock.'

'My heart is already broken, Carrie. The loss of my brother is something more I have to bear, but we have to rebuild the business. I'm going to devote all my energy into making sure that the company your father and your uncle loved so much will continue in a way they would have wished. Good day to you, Captain Reid.' Esther glided from the room, leaving the door to swing on its hinges.

'Your mother is a remarkable woman,' Reid said in a low voice. 'I've been dreading this meeting but both of you have made it much easier for me.'

'We lost virtually everything, but I discovered that

I am a fighter, and I know now that I must take after my mother. She almost gave up after my father died, but we'll work together to rebuild Manning and Chapman.' Caroline held out her hand. 'Welcome aboard, Captain Reid.'

'I'll return to the ship and await orders, Miss Manning.'

'Come to the office tomorrow morning at ten o'clock. Anyone will be able to direct you.'

'I've been there once or twice in the past.' Reid smiled and nodded. 'Your father took me on as third mate when I was eighteen, and I'm sorry to hear of his demise. He was a good man.' He hurried from the room and Caroline went to stand by the window, watching him as he paused at the bottom of the steps to put on his hat. Reid's praise for her father had brought tears to her eyes and she needed a moment to compose herself before she went to find her mother. Although she had suspected something dire had happened to their vessel, she had fully expected her uncle to return. His jovial presence had always made her feel happy, and it was almost impossible to believe that he was gone for ever. How her mother must be feeling was something she could barely imagine, and then there were the boys. Max and Jimmy had been fond of Uncle George, and now they were doubly bereaved.

Caroline squared her shoulders and headed for the kitchen, where she thought everyone would have congregated, but when she opened the door she found Freddie seated at the table, drinking brandy, and Sadie was sitting opposite him with a cup of tea clutched in her hands.

'Where are the others?' Caroline looked to Sadie for an answer.

'Jimmy was very upset when Essie broke the news. She took him to his room and Laurence insisted that Max returned to his lessons. I dare say he thought that keeping the boy occupied would take his mind off what's happened.'

'I'm just having a tot before I return to the Bearwood House,' Freddie said hastily. 'It's a bit early for me, but I felt I needed something after the upset. Essie's being very brave – too brave, in fact. She's bottling it all up inside and that's no good.'

'Mama has the business to think about,' Caroline said stoutly. 'We'll be all right, Freddie.'

'I know everyone is suffering but I'm a selfish sort of fellow, Carrie. I'm used to living my own way and the sooner I return home the better, although I'm not giving up on Grace yet. I'm going to do my best to persuade her to accompany me to the Abbey.'

Sadie put her cup down on the saucer with a clatter. 'Then you'd best get rid of your housekeeper. I know all about her and her bastard son, and I don't blame Grace for being wary. You might think you're one of them Eastern potentates, Freddie Dorincourt, but you are just a younger son, living like a lord. If your brother decides to return to

England and claim his inheritance, you'll find your-self put in your place.'

Caroline held her breath. She fully expected Freddie to explode with anger, but he threw back his head and laughed.

He turned to Caroline, grinning broadly. 'Don't look so shocked, Carrie. Sadie knows me only too well.'

'But she's right,' Caroline said firmly. 'You need to choose between Grace and Jenifry, and you have to watch out for Dickon. I don't trust him at all.'

'So you keep saying, but he's just a boy. I can handle my son.' Freddie drained his glass and stood up. 'I've said all I can say by way of commiserations to your mother, Carrie. But if either of you needs me I'll do anything I can to help.'

'Thank you,' Caroline said, giving him a hug. 'We may not be related by blood, but if I could choose anyone to be my uncle, it would be you.'

A sudden rush of scarlet coloured Freddie's cheeks and he gave an embarrassed chuckle. 'Come now, Carrie. You've made me blush for the first time in my life. I didn't think any woman had that power over me.'

'It's time you grew up, Freddie.' Sadie rose to her feet. 'Go home and sort your romantic problems out and leave us in peace.' She hustled him out of the kitchen, returning moments later with a satisfied smile. 'You caught him off guard, Carrie. That will serve him right. Ever since I've known him, Freddie

Dorincourt has thought he could get away with anything as far as the ladies were concerned.'

'He's a dear, but he does need to be honest with Jenifry. She's not a bad person, but that son of theirs is horrid. I can't like him, no matter how hard I try.'

'And how do you feel about Phineas Colville? You seem to be getting on with him now.'

'He's a difficult man to get to know, but he's been very helpful recently.'

'Don't tell me that you're beginning to like him?'

Caroline shook her head. 'A little perhaps, but we need his backing or we won't be able to pay the crew, or meet the other expenses that are bound to occur. Mama should be the one to work out the details with Phineas, but I'm not sure she's up to it at the moment.'

'She was very fond of George and it's going to hit her hard when she allows herself time to think. Perhaps you ought to negotiate with Mr Colville.'

'You're right, Sadie. The crew will be desperate for their pay. We can't let them down, especially after what they've been through.'

Phineas was seated behind his desk, going through a leather-bound ledger when Caroline was ushered into his office next morning.

'Did we forget something?' he asked brusquely.

'No, but circumstances have changed. The *Esther Manning* has arrived in port and I need money to pay the crew.'

289

Phineas closed the ledger with a snap and sat back in his chair, eyeing her curiously. 'Did Captain Daniels explain why the ship was delayed?'

'Captain Daniels died of yellow fever – and so did my uncle . . .' Caroline broke off, unable to stem the tears that she had been holding back since she received the sad news. She sat down on the nearest chair, wiping her eyes on the back of her hand. 'I'm sorry. I didn't mean to cry, it's just that it's been a terrible shock.' She looked up to see a white hanky held in front of her.

'Take it,' Phineas said abruptly. 'I should have been more tactful. It was obvious that something had gone wrong.'

Caroline blew her nose and mopped her eyes. 'Thank you. I'm all right now.'

'No, you are not. You should go home and rest. Leave business matters to Masters. I'll see that he has enough money to pay the crew. Who brought the ship home?'

'Captain Reid. Do you know him?'

Phineas leaned against his desk, a wry smile curving his lips. 'Yes, I do. As it happens, Gilbert Reid is my cousin.'

'Your cousin?'

'He's my aunt's son. She married beneath herself, or so Grandmama thought.'

'I didn't know that.'

'Why would you? It's of little interest to anyone outside the family. Unfortunately Grandmama disapproved intensely and that caused a rift between them. My parents died within months of each other and I was sent off to boarding school. I spent the holidays with my grandparents.'

'I'm sorry.'

'There's no reason why you should care. I survived, although as I said before, I didn't particularly want to run a shipping company, but it was my grandfather's last wish that I take over from him. Gilbert was too young, of course, and his only ambition was to go to sea. It was your father who helped him then.'

'I can't believe that I knew nothing of all this. Why did my parents keep it from me?'

'I doubt if it would have been of interest to you when you were younger.' He straightened up and went to sit behind his desk. 'It really doesn't matter now. What is important is to keep both companies going. We'll be stronger and more profitable if we work together.'

Caroline nodded dully. 'I agree.'

He studied her face, as if attempting to gauge her emotions. 'Do you feel able to talk business? I quite understand that Mrs Manning might feel herself unable to take part in such a discussion at the moment.'

'My mother has been under a considerable strain recently.'

'And we won't add to it.' Phineas reached for a pen and flicked open the silver top of the inkwell.

'I'll arrange for the berthing and unloading of the *Esther Manning* in due course. What cargo did she carry?'

'Cocoa from Trinidad, which is where they contracted yellow fever.'

He nodded, making a note on a sheet of paper. 'It should fetch a decent price.'

'I know nothing about the running of my parents' business,' Caroline admitted reluctantly. 'But I want to learn.'

'You need a good manager, not one like Parkinson. I confronted him with what you told me and he admitted it. I've given him notice, but don't be tempted to take him on again. I can suggest one or two candidates and you will be able to choose the one you think will be best for the position.'

Caroline was about to thank him when the door burst open and a worried-looking clerk rushed into the office. 'I'm sorry to interrupt, sir. But I thought you would want to see this telegram.'

Phineas stood up to take it from him and scanned its contents. 'I'll deal with this, Simms.' He waited until the door closed. 'The *Colville Star* is laid up in Dover with engine trouble. I have to leave immediately.'

'Maria is on board.' Caroline leaped to her feet. 'I'm coming with you.'

He hesitated and then nodded. 'All right, but I'm going straight away.'

'I should tell my family.'

'I'll send someone with a message.' Phineas grabbed his hat from the stand behind his desk and jammed it on his head. 'Are you sure you want to do this?'

'I don't want you to bully her into coming home.'

Phineas opened the door, holding it to allow her to pass. 'As if I would.' He issued a stream of instructions to the surprised clerk as they left the building.

It was late afternoon by the time they reached the port and discovered the *Colville Star* was berthed. Phineas strode up the gangway with Caroline hurrying after him.

'I don't need permission to come aboard,' he snapped when an unfortunate seaman tried to stop him. 'I own the damn ship.'

'Begging your pardon, sir.' The man backed away. 'I ain't never seen you afore.'

'Well, you have now. Is Captain Barnaby on board?'

'Aye, sir.'

'I know my way.' Phineas headed for the master's cabin with a purposeful stride.

Caroline caught up with him, catching hold of his sleeve. 'Wait a moment, Phin.'

'What's the matter?' He turned to her, scowling.

'Take that look off your face,' Caroline said severely. 'You'll scare Maria and ruin any chance we might have of persuading her to return home.'

He hesitated. 'I won't allow her to ruin her life.'

'It's her choice.'

Phineas knocked on the door and entered without waiting for a response. 'Barnaby, I want a word with you.'

Captain Barnaby looked up from the log book, dropping his pen on the desk as he rose to his feet. 'Mr Colville.'

Caroline pushed past Phineas, placing herself between them. 'Where is Maria, Captain? I'd like to see her.'

'She's in her cabin, I believe.' Barnaby fingered his tie nervously. 'I can explain everything, sir.'

'You will, indeed, and I'm relieving you of your command.'

'That's a bit harsh, isn't it?' Caroline protested. 'Let me speak to Maria. She should have a say in all this.'

'Her cabin is in the passenger accommodation,' Barnaby said hastily. 'I'd better show you the way.'

'There's no need.' Maria stood in the doorway. 'I saw you both coming on board.'

Caroline grasped her hand. 'Are you all right?'

'Of course I am. I wasn't kidnapped, Carrie. I chose to come with Theo.'

'What were you thinking of?' Phineas demanded angrily. 'Your poor mother is distraught.'

'My mother gave me up when I was a baby.'

'She didn't want to. You know that.' Caroline squeezed Maria's cold fingers. 'She loves you. We all do.'

'I believe you,' Maria said slowly. 'But I love Theo and he loves me.'

'It's true.' Barnaby moved to Maria's side. 'I'm sorry for behaving in such an ungentlemanly way, Mr Colville. But we had no choice.'

'Of course you did.' Phineas clenched his fists at his sides, flexing his fingers. 'You could have asked her to wait for you, man. You could have observed the proprieties and married her when you returned to London, but you took advantage of an inexperienced young girl. You turned her head and ruined her reputation at the same time.'

'No, Phin.' Maria clutched Barnaby's arm. 'I didn't have a good name to lose in the first place. You're forgetting that I am a bastard. Don't flinch – it's the word that all those good God-fearing people at home use behind my back. I may be young and naïve but I'm not stupid.'

'Nobody thinks you're stupid,' Caroline said quickly. 'We were worried about you. If you'd decided that this was all a mistake it would have been terrible.'

'Not to mention the worry you put everyone to,' Phineas added.

'It wasn't a mistake.' Maria looked up at Barnaby with an expression of pure adoration.

Caroline could see that Phineas was unimpressed. 'Hear them out, please,' she urged. 'Don't turn this into a battle of wills.'

'I've no intention of doing that, Caroline.' Phineas

turned to Barnaby, fixing him with a hard stare. 'Let's put an end to this charade now. You must both return to London, and, if you insist on getting married, it will be done properly.'

'But I can't leave the ship, sir,' Barnaby protested. 'We'll be putting to sea again when the engine is repaired.'

'You will stay on board tonight and I'll send a relief captain to take over your duties. Maria will accompany us.'

'But I don't want to leave Theo.' Maria's bottom lip trembled and her eyes reddened. 'I think you're trying to separate us, Phin.'

'Only for tonight,' he said, moderating his tone. 'Barnaby can travel to London tomorrow.'

'Does this mean that I'm no longer captain of the *Colville Star*, sir?'

'Is that more important to you than marriage to my cousin?'

'Don't push them into saying things they'll regret later,' Caroline said softly.

'Don't interfere.' Phineas lowered his voice. 'I need to discover this man's true feelings towards my cousin.'

'I heard that,' Maria cried passionately. 'You have no right to come here laying down the law. I will do as I please.'

Barnaby shook his head. 'This has gone far enough. Your cousin is right, Maria. I've been selfish and I was wrong to take you away from your family, especially on such a short acquaintance.'

Maria's hands flew to cover her mouth and her eyes widened with shock. 'What are you saying, Theo?'

Caroline placed her arm around Maria's shoulders. 'Don't upset yourself. We all want what is best for you, and I think Phin is right.'

'He is, I'm afraid,' Barnaby said reluctantly. 'I'll do anything that will make you happy, Maria. And if that means resigning as captain of this ship, it's a price I'm willing to pay.'

'Fine words, but hardly practical.' Phineas leaned over the desk and closed the log book. 'I didn't say anything about your resignation, Barnaby. You're a good captain and you'll be even more reliable when you have a wife and family to support, but if you are sincere in your desire to marry my cousin, you will take what comes.'

Barnaby nodded. 'I will, sir.'

'Theo, no.' Maria's voice broke on a sob. 'I know how much this ship means to you.'

'You are far more important to me. Go with Mr Colville and Miss Manning, and I'll join you as soon as I can.'

'Go and get your things, Maria,' Phineas said firmly. 'We'll catch the first train back to London.'

'How do I know you'll keep your word?' Maria eyed him warily.

'You'll just have to trust me.'

It was close to midnight when they reached Victoria Station, and Caroline decided that it would be best to accompany Maria and Phineas to his house in Princes Square. Her family had had enough disturbances that day and she did not want to add to them by waking them up at such a late hour. Maria had been unusually quiet during the journey, but Caroline's decision brought a smile to her lips for the first time since she had left the ship.

Mrs Morecroft had gone to bed, but their old rooms were in readiness for them, almost as if the redoubtable Moffie had been waiting for their return. Caroline fell into bed and closed her eyes.

She was awakened next morning by Maria, who was fully dressed. 'Get up, please, Carrie. I don't want to go down to breakfast on my own.'

Caroline sat up, brushing her hair back from her forehead. 'What time is it?'

'Eight o'clock, and I can hear Grace and Mrs Morecroft chatting away in the dining room. I don't want to face them without you to support me.'

'All right. Give me five minutes and I'll be with you.' Caroline swung her legs over the side of her bed. 'No, make it ten minutes. I need a wash.'

It was almost half-past eight when Caroline entered the dining room, followed by Maria. Grace was seated at the table, drinking coffee. She replaced her cup on its saucer.

'So you've decided to come home, Maria.'

The tension in the room was tangible, making Caroline apprehensive. She had hoped the reunion between mother and daughter would be a happy one, but Grace's expression was not welcoming. 'Maria realised that you might be worried,' she said tactfully. 'There's no harm done.'

'I'm sorry if I've disappointed you, Mama,' Maria said miserably. 'Theo and I fell in love.'

Grace rose to her feet, her features pinched and pale. 'You silly girl. Haven't you learned anything at all from my plight?'

'That's not fair,' Maria protested. 'This isn't anything like what happened to you.'

'Is it not?'

'Perhaps we should all sit down and talk this over calmly.' Caroline took her seat at the table, hoping the others would follow suit, but mother and daughter faced each other like combatants in the ring.

'You stupid little fool,' Grace hissed through clenched teeth. 'You allowed yourself to be despoiled by a man who had little thought for anything but his own pleasure.'

Maria collapsed onto the chair next to Caroline. 'That's not true.'

'How do you think you came to be born?' Grace paced the floor, wringing her hands. 'I was seduced by a man who gave me compliments and made me feel that I was the only one for him, and then he walked away.'

'I – I'm sorry,' Maria faltered. 'But that won't happen with Theo.'

'No? Where is he now? Phineas told me everything before he went to the office this morning. It wouldn't surprise me if your sea captain sailed away, leaving you sullied and disgraced.'

Caroline jumped to her feet. 'Stop it, Grace. This is so unfair. You can't say things like that.'

Grace turned on her in a fury. 'Have you any idea who Maria's father was?'

'No, of course not.'

'Then I think it's time I told you and my daughter the truth.'

Chapter Seventeen

Caroline sank back on the chair she had just vacated. 'Go on then, Grace. Since you're so eager to confess. Who was it?'

'Yes, Mama,' Maria added. 'Tell me, please.'

'No. Not yet. I think it's time to make a clean break and I want everyone to hear it from my own lips. I'm sick and tired of being labelled a harlot by my family.' She glanced at the clock. 'I want Freddie to be present as well, because I'm not going to repeat myself. Once the secret is out that will be the end of it.'

'Why must Freddie be told?' Caroline asked, frowning.

'Because then he might leave me alone. I'm not going to be his "muse", as he calls it. If he wants me it must be done properly, with respect. That woman and her evil son must go, and I want a divorce from Elias. If Freddie is sincere he will have to place a wedding ring on my finger and make me a respectable woman.'

Maria stared at her mother as if seeing her for the first time. 'Do you love Freddie?'

'Love isn't always about romantic trysts and fluttering hearts. I like Freddie – he makes me laugh, and he's a kind man. I think we would do well together, but I'm not prepared to live as a kept woman.'

'In that case, I suggest we send for Freddie and ask him to meet us at the Captain's House.'

'Perhaps we'd better include Phin,' Maria added in a whisper. 'You said you wanted everyone to know, Mama. Do you want Grandmama to be there, too?'

'I never want to see my mother again,' Grace said bitterly. 'She disowned me twenty years ago. She allowed my father to give me to Elias Quick, and for that I can never forgive either of them.'

Mrs Morecroft appeared suddenly in the doorway. 'Do you young ladies want some breakfast?'

'A cup of coffee would be more than welcome, Mrs Morecroft,' Caroline said before Maria had a chance to refuse. 'I don't think another hour or so is going to make any difference after twenty years, do you, Grace?'

'Carrie!' Maria whispered. 'Can't you see she's upset?'

'I can, but there's no need for us to starve because

of it.' Caroline nodded to Mrs Morecroft. 'Some bread and honey would be marvellous, too.'

'Of course, miss.' Mrs Morecroft sniffed and tossed her head, and was about to leave the room when the sound of someone rapping urgently on the front door make them all jump.

'I'll see who that is.' She hurried from the room, leaving the door ajar.

'I wonder who it could be at this early hour?' Maria glanced anxiously at her mother, who had come to a sudden halt, standing rigidly as if she had been turned to stone.

'It's Elias,' Grace whispered. 'I'd know that voice anywhere. How did he know I was here?'

Caroline leaped to her feet as Elias rushed into the room.

'You crafty bitch.' He grabbed Grace by her arm. 'You thought you could hide away in London, did you? Well, you were wrong.'

'How did you find me?'

'I went straight to the Colville office and it cost me a half-sovereign to get this address from that Parkinson fellow. He'd been sacked by that cousin of yours and was just leaving when I arrived. He was more than happy to tell me what I wanted to know.' He twisted Grace's arm so that she howled with pain.

'Let her go,' Caroline cried angrily.

'You're hurting her,' Maria screamed as Elias dragged Grace across the floor.

'She's my wife,' he snarled. 'And she's coming with me. I've got the law on my side, but if you try to stop me I'll break her bones. Don't think I won't.'

'He will,' Grace sobbed. 'I don't want to go with you, Elias.'

'You ain't got a choice, my dear.' Elias pushed her into the hall, turning his head to give the others a warning glare. 'Follow me and she'll get the worst of it.'

Caroline moved swiftly to the front entrance and was in time to see Elias bundling Grace into a waiting cab. 'Waterloo Bridge Station.' He climbed in after her and clamped his hand over her mouth to mute her cries for help.

'What will we do?' Maria sobbed. 'We can't let him take her away like this.'

Mrs Morecroft had emerged from the kitchen wielding a rolling pin, but she allowed it to drop to her side. 'Now we'll never know what she was going to tell you girls.'

'I think that's the least of our worries,' Caroline said grimly. 'That man is a maniac. He should be locked up.'

'If only Theo were here,' Maria sobbed. 'He would have stood up to him. He has a sword and a pistol in his cabin. He's not afraid of anyone.'

'Well, he isn't here.' Caroline spoke more sharply than she had intended and regretted it when she saw the ready tears spring to Maria's eyes. She gave her a hug. 'I'm sorry. Of course Theo would stand up for you and your mother, but he's not here, so it's up to us to do something.' She frowned, thinking hard. Where would Quick take Grace? There could be only one answer. 'Wolf Tor Farm. He'll take her there, I'm certain.'

'Oh, no! Not that dreadful place.' Maria clasped Caroline's hand. 'We'll never get her away from him now.'

'Get your things, Maria,' Caroline said firmly. 'We're leaving right away. We'll send a message to Phineas and tell him what's happened. We're going to Devonshire.'

'I can't,' Maria wailed. 'I'm getting married.'

Caroline took her by the shoulders and gave her a shake. 'Theo will wait, but your mother is in real danger. Who knows what cruel punishments Quick will inflict on her? It's your choice, Maria.'

'If your man loves you, he'll understand,' Mrs Morecroft said, nodding. 'You only have one mother, miss. Do you want to lose her for ever?'

Maria's lips trembled and she shook her head. 'We were just getting to know one another, but Phineas might send Theo to Australia without me. He'll be gone for months.'

Caroline threw up her hands. 'Well, I'm going to find Freddie and tell him what's happened. Stay here if you wish, Maria, but if it were my mother I know what I'd do.'

'I will come,' Maria said slowly, 'but first I must tell Phin, and he'll have to explain things to Theo.'

Mrs Morecroft tut-tutted, tucking the rolling pin under her arm. 'I'll just put this back in the kitchen and then I'll fetch your luggage, Miss Colville.'

'It's lucky I left some clothes here,' Caroline said, making for the stairs. 'I'll throw a few things into a valise and then we'll go to the office. I'll send a message to Bearwood House to let Freddie know what's happened.'

They arrived at the office to find that Phineas was out on business and not expected back until noon at the earliest. Caroline scribbled a message to Freddie, and the desk clerk agreed to have it delivered to Bearwood House as a matter of urgency.

'Will you wait for Mr Colville's return, miss?'

'Yes, we will,' Maria said hastily. 'I have to see Phin. He's the only one who can tell me when Theo is due to arrive in London.'

'Might I suggest you wait in Mr Colville's office?'

'Yes, that's what we'll do.' Maria hurried off without waiting for Caroline's response.

Caroline caught up with her. 'We can't afford to lose time. We'll have to leave a note for Phineas. Every second we waste gives Quick an advantage.'

'I don't care, Carrie. I'll wait because I want to speak to Phin.' Maria opened the door and marched into the office.

Caroline was close on her heels, but they came to a sudden halt at the sight of Gilbert Reid, who was seated in front of the desk, reading a copy of

Lloyd's List. He dropped the paper and leaped to his feet. 'Miss Manning and Cousin Maria. This is an unexpected pleasure.'

'Captain Reid! What are you doing here?' Caroline eyed him curiously. 'I thought you were employed by us, not the Colvilles.'

'It seems that we are virtually one and the same company now, but I'm on two days' leave while the *Esther Manning* is in dock. I came to see my cousin.'

'This isn't a social call. We need to speak to him urgently.' Caroline glanced at the desk where everything was laid out neatly, from the pen placed at right angles on the inkstand to the piles of documents tied with red tape. 'If I might have a sheet of paper I'll leave a message.'

'I'm not leaving until I've seen Phineas,' Maria said mutinously. 'My whole life depends on what happens today, Carrie.'

Gilbert looked from one to the other, a smile curving his lips. 'This sounds intriguing. Maybe I can help?'

Caroline met his amused gaze with a steady look. 'I very much doubt it, Captain. We have to travel to Devonshire as a matter of urgency.'

'Might I ask why?'

'Maria's mother is in imminent danger.'

His smile faded. 'How so?'

'Her husband, Elias Quick, has been ill-treating her for years. We rescued her and brought her back to London, but he found out where we were and has taken her back by force.'

'The devil he did.' Suddenly alert, Gilbert looked from one to the other. 'I've never met Aunt Grace, although of course I've heard my parents speak of her.'

'No doubt blackening her name,' Maria said angrily. 'I've had to live with her legacy all my life, and now I have the chance to get away from the misery her youthful mistakes have caused me. I'm to be married, Gilbert.'

'But only if Phineas manages to relieve Theo from his post,' Caroline said pointedly. 'You are going to have to choose, Maria. Will you wait here on the off-chance that Theo will get to London, or will you accompany me to Wolf Tor Farm to save your mother from that vicious brute?'

Maria subsided onto a chair, burying her face in her hands. 'That's not fair, Carrie. You mustn't make me choose.'

'Captain Reid is here,' Caroline said more gently. 'He could tell Phin what's happened, and we could be on our way.'

'What do you hope to achieve by following them?' Gilbert leaned against the desk, and for the first time Caroline could see a likeness between him and his cousin.

She met his questioning look with a toss of her head. 'I don't know, but we have to do something. You haven't met this man, Captain. He's a brute and a bully.'

'But without a definite plan of action you'll be wasting your time,' Gilbert said reasonably. 'And if they're married he has the law on his side.'

'That's what he said.' Maria grasped Caroline's hand. 'I want to help my mother, but Gilbert is right. What could we do?'

'Freddie will help us. If he's sincere about his feelings for Grace he'll do anything he can to free her.'

'Who is Freddie?' Gilbert asked.

Caroline was tempted to tell him to mind his own business, but it was obvious that his interest was genuine. 'Freddie Dorincourt is a friend of the family,' she said, resigning herself to an explanation that would satisfy his curiosity. 'He's the younger brother of the Earl of Starcross, and he lives at Starcross Abbey, not too far from Bovey Tracey, which is where we took Grace when we rescued her from Elias.'

'And what is his interest in my aunt?'

'Freddie is an artist,' Maria said proudly. 'He was painting her portrait and I think he wants to marry her, but—'

Gilbert held up his hand. 'Please stop, Maria, you're confusing the issue. According to the law Grace belongs to Quick and he can do more or less as he pleases. I think you have to accept that.'

'Whose side are you on?' Caroline demanded angrily. 'Would you beat a woman black and blue and keep her a prisoner in her own home?'

'Of course not.'

'Then why would you stand by and allow some other man to do exactly that?' Caroline fixed him with a stony look. 'Anyway, we're not asking you to do anything other than pass on a message to Phineas. Maria and I are going to Devonshire. I'd be grateful if you could let my mother know that we don't plan on being away for long, and tell her that I'll explain everything on my return.'

'Oh, Carrie, I'm not sure about this,' Maria said in a low voice. 'What will Theo say if he arrives in London to find me gone?'

'He'll understand. Anyone with any decency would agree that we're doing the right thing.' Caroline made a move towards the door. 'Goodbye, Captain Reid.'

'Wait.' Gilbert's note of command made Caroline hesitate. He reached for his hat and cane. 'I can't allow you to travel on your own. Phineas would never forgive me if I did. I'm coming with you.'

Caroline gazed at him in amazement. 'You? Why would you do that, Captain?'

'You're forgetting that I'm related to both Grace and Maria. Of course I care about what happens to them, as does Phin, only he's not here at the moment.' He reached across the desk to pick up the pen and dipped it in the ink. 'Write a note for him and one for your mother. I'll see that they're delivered, and we'll be off.'

'Are you sure about this, Gilbert?' Maria said worriedly.

'We can't wait for you to pack a bag,' Caroline added.

He placed two sheets of paper on the desk in front of her. 'As it happens I stayed on board last night and I have some of my things with me. I'd intended to visit my mother's home in the country, but she isn't expecting me, so I'm free to come and go as I please.' He moved to open the door as Caroline hastily finished scribbling her notes. 'Shall we?'

They arrived at the Wolf Tor Arms too late to make a journey onto the moor a safe option. Mr and Mrs Brewer welcomed Caroline and Maria as if they were old friends, and, if they were surprised to see them with a male escort they were too experienced in the trade to allow it to show. Aiken, however, had no such scruples. He was acting as potboy that evening, and he was openly curious.

'I never expected to see 'ee back so soon, miss. Let alone accompanied by a gentleman.' He brushed a lock of tow-coloured hair back from his brow. 'Do 'ee want to venture onto the moor again?'

Caroline held her finger to her lips. 'Yes, but don't tell anyone. Word mustn't get round.'

'You can trust me, miss. I never let on last time and I won't now.' Aiken puffed out his chest, turning to Gilbert, who was still in uniform. 'You can trust me, Cap'n.'

He slipped a coin into Aiken's palm. 'I can see

that. We'll need your services in the morning and the hire of three horses.'

'Ponies is best on the moor, Cap'n. Dartmoor born and bred, but broken to the saddle, so they're as gentle as lambs.' Aiken sauntered off, pocketing the money.

'It's a pity we can't go this evening.' Caroline shook her head. 'Poor Grace will think we've abandoned her.'

'If she's managed to survive twenty years of marriage to Quick, I don't think one more night will break her.' Gilbert raised his glass in a toast. 'Here's to success, and with luck we'll have Grace safe and sound and back in London by this time tomorrow, although quite how we'll manage it I have yet to work out.'

'It's not like plotting a course at sea, Captain.' Caroline sipped her coffee, eyeing him over the rim of her cup. 'I suggest we go there tomorrow morning first thing, and hope to find her on her own. It's a slim chance, but one I think we'll have to take.'

'We'll have to be careful,' Gilbert said, frowning. 'Quick sounds like a nasty piece of work.'

Maria clutched his hand, holding it to her cheek. 'The sooner we rescue my mother, the sooner we return to London.'

Next morning they set off immediately after breakfast with Aiken, once again, as their guide. Caroline thought she knew the way, but even in high summer the boggy areas were dangerous and she did not entirely trust her memory to get them to the isolated farm without his help.

They came to a halt some way from the house, sending Aiken to reconnoitre, but he returned with bad news. He told them that Quick was seated outside the front door with his shotgun at his side, as if he were expecting them or perhaps a representative of the law. After a swift discussion they dismounted and settled down to wait, detailing Aiken to take a look every so often, but he returned each time with the same story.

The sun rose higher in the sky and they all grew hot and thirsty. The song of the skylark and the scent of gorse and heather had seemed delightful at first, but now Caroline was past caring about the beauties of nature. She was hungry and there were damp patches beneath her armpits. She could feel the sweat running down between her breasts – tight stays and voluminous skirts and petticoats were not the most comfortable mode of dress when the wearer was exposed to the merciless rays of the sun. Gilbert had had the forethought to bring a bottle filled with water, but when that was gone they were tortured by thirst. He strolled off, returning minutes later with it refilled from a spring.

'We should return to the village,' he said, having been the last to take a drink. 'I'm afraid you'll both suffer from sunstroke if we stay here.'

'But the longer she's with him, the worse it will be for Grace,' Caroline protested.

'I realise that, but Quick is on the alert. Short of an armed boarding party there's very little we can do. I think we'll have to return to the inn and try again tomorrow.'

'Maria and I have only a small amount of coin,' Caroline said slowly. 'We can't afford to stay there very long.'

'Don't worry about that. I'm doing this for my family so money doesn't come into it – not yet, anyway.' Gilbert signalled to Aiken, who was sitting on a granite slab, smoking a clay pipe. 'We won't give up, Maria. But we have to be sensible.'

They returned to the inn and tried again next day, but the result was the same. Quick was taking no chances and he did not stray more than a few yards from the house. There was a mangy dog tied to a post close to the front door and it barked at the slightest sound or movement, forcing them to retreat to the village.

The third morning dawned wet and a thick mist enveloped the moor. Brewer advised against travel that day, but, with each passing hour, Caroline was becoming more worried, and Maria was openly fretting. Gilbert seemed to be the only member of the party who was optimistic, especially when Aiken announced that it was market day in Bovey Tracey.

'Quick is a farmer,' he said, smiling. 'I'm fairly certain he would want to go to market.'

'Of course,' Caroline said eagerly. 'I should have

remembered – that's when we managed to get into the house before. Quick goes to Bovey Tracey, leaving Grace at home.'

'As my husband said, it would be best not venture on the moors in this weather, miss.' Mrs Brewer placed a basket of hot rolls on the table in front of them. 'I doubt if Aiken would want to risk such a venture.'

'I might be persuaded,' Aiken said, grinning. 'I know the way blindfold, if it's made worth my while.'

Caroline turned to Gilbert. 'What do you think?'

He nodded. 'With the enemy out of the way and under cover of a thick fog, we might just have a chance.' He put his hand in his pocket and took out a half-sovereign. 'Would this make the mist lift just a little, Aiken, my boy?'

After the frustration of their previous attempts, it seemed all too easy. Aiken, as he had boasted, knew his way across the moor despite the swirling mist, which left Caroline feeling dizzy and disorientated. He also showed a talent for picking locks, having kept the guard dog busy with a large juicy bone he had pilfered from the inn kitchen. They entered the house, calling out to Grace. After an unsuccessful search of the ground floor they went upstairs calling her name, and a faint response led them to a locked room at the back of the house. Gilbert put his shoulder to the door and, after a couple of attempts, it flew open to reveal Grace tied hand and foot and chained to the iron bedstead. Once again, Aiken exerted his magic on the padlock, and Gilbert used his pocket knife to slice through the cords that bound her. She was in a dire state, battered and bruised, half-starved and shaken by the viciousness of the beatings that she had suffered at Quick's hands. Gilbert carried her downstairs to the kitchen, where they attempted to revive her with sips of water and mouthfuls of porridge, which had been left in a saucepan on the range.

'We must get her out of here before he returns,' Caroline said in a low voice.

'Perhaps it's not a good idea to take her to the inn,' Gilbert whispered. 'That's the first place Quick would come looking for her.'

'Aye, master.' Aiken nodded sagely. 'That's what he did afore.'

'She can't travel in this state,' Caroline said worriedly. 'Starcross Abbey is the nearest place we could take her, but Elias would work that out for himself.'

Aiken glanced out of the window. 'No matter where you'm thinking of taking the lady, I say us had better move soon, miss. The fog is getting thicker.'

'There's Daumerle,' Caroline said thoughtfully. 'Aunt Alice would take us in, and Quick knows nothing of our connection there.'

'Then I suggest we head for the inn and collect our things. Perhaps we can hire some sort of transport to take Grace to Daumerle, and when she's well enough we'll travel back to London.' Gilbert turned to Maria, who was trying to persuade her mother to sup a little more of the cold porridge.

'We have to leave now, Maria,' he said gently. 'Best find a coat or something to wrap around Grace. She can ride my pony and I'll walk. Aiken will go on ahead, making sure we don't get stuck in the mire.'

By some miracle they made it off the moor without getting lost or being trapped in the boggy ground. The only good thing about the fog that Caroline could see was that it would hamper Elias Quick's return home, giving them more time to get Grace as far away as possible.

Gilbert settled their bill at the inn and arranged the hire of a somewhat rickety wagonette drawn by an aged carthorse, handled by an equally ancient driver, who bellowed at them, demanding payment in full before they set off. Aiken explained that the man was unlikely to pass on any information to Quick as he was stone deaf, and Gilbert paid up without a murmur. They left for Daumerle, having dosed Grace with a generous amount of brandy to ease her pain. Caroline suspected that her injuries included several broken ribs, but there was no time to consult a doctor, and they made Grace as comfortable as possible, with a blanket wrapped around her knees.

The fog had lifted and the sun appeared briefly as they set off, but then clouds rolled in from the west and it started to rain. They were all soaked to the skin by the time they reached Daumerle, except for the driver, who had wrapped himself in a tarpaulin and was oblivious to the requests of his passengers for similar cover. The gates were closed and the gatekeeper took one look at the shabby equipage and refused to open them, despite Caroline's angry assertion that she was a close family friend. Her embarrassment deepened when the gatekeeper chose to pay heed to Gilbert and grudgingly unlocked the side gate, allowing the passengers to enter on foot. Grace was barely able to walk and had to be supported during their trek up the tree-lined drive. The rain was lashing down, soaking them further, and Caroline could see that Maria was growing weary. Grace was virtually a dead weight, and when Maria stumbled and only just managed to save herself from falling, Gilbert abandoned the luggage he had been carrying and lifted Grace bodily in his arms.

'Leave the cases,' he said firmly. 'I'm sure someone will be sent to collect them.'

Caroline nodded and dashed the rainwater from her eyes. 'Hold on to me, Maria. We're nearly there.'

It was a bedraggled party who arrived at the grand entrance, sheltering from the teeming rain beneath the columned portico, and perhaps hardly surprising that Digby, Lady Alice's butler, was about to turn them away.

'I am Miss Manning. You must remember me,' Caroline protested. 'My mother was a guest of Lady Alice, who is a close family friend. Please inform her that I am here.'

'Lady Alice left for London two days ago, miss. I'm afraid you've had a wasted journey.' He was about to close the door when Caroline heard a familiar voice.

'Is that you, Carrie?'

'Yes, it is. Tell your man to let us in, please, Delia.'

Cordelia Bearwood appeared in the doorway. 'For heaven's sake, what are you about, Digby? Let my friends in.'

'Of course, Miss Cordelia.' He stood aside, staring over Caroline's head with a pained expression.

Ignoring him, Caroline stepped over the threshold, ushering the rest of the party into the vast entrance hall. 'Thank you, Delia. As you see, we're rather wet, and we had to leave our baggage beneath a tree.'

'Digby will send someone to collect it.' Cordelia looked from one to the other. 'Perhaps introductions had better wait until later,' she said, smiling. 'I felt rather chilly so I had a fire laid in the drawing room.' She turned to Digby. 'We'll take tea and cake, and perhaps a tot or two of brandy wouldn't go amiss.'

He inclined his head and stalked off, as if walking barefoot on hot coals.

'Digby thinks he rules the house in my parents' absence,' Cordelia said cheerfully. 'He doesn't and I have to remind him of that every now and again. Follow me, everyone.' She shot a wary glance in Grace's direction. 'Who is that and what on earth happened to her, Carrie? Has there been an accident?'

'Not exactly,' Caroline whispered. 'I'll tell you everything later.'

'Who is that handsome man you've brought with you?' Cordelia's eyes twinkled with anticipation. 'Is he your latest beau?'

'Captain Reid? Good heavens, no. I'll introduce you in a minute.'

Cordelia's laughter echoed off the ornately decorated high ceiling. 'I can't wait. This is the most exciting thing that's happened since I left London. I've had the most boring summer imaginable at Euphemia's house, and yet here you are in the middle of an adventure. You must tell me everything.'

Chapter Eighteen

They crowded round the elegant Carrara marble fireplace in the drawing room with steam rising from their damp clothes. The refreshments were more than welcome, but Caroline's main concern was for Grace, who was obviously in a great deal of discomfort, although saying very little.

'Of course you may stay as long as you like,' Cordelia said in answer to Caroline's tentative request. She glanced anxiously at Grace. 'I've sent a maid to make your rooms ready. The poor lady looks as though she ought to be in bed. Should I send for the doctor?'

Caroline was about to reply when she realised that Gilbert was trying to attract her attention. 'What is it, Gilbert?'

'If you summon the doctor it would draw attention to our presence here. You don't want Quick to discover Grace's whereabouts.'

'I think that's a chance we'll have to take,' Caroline said firmly.

'I agree.' Cordelia treated him to a charming smile. 'We have a small army of servants to protect us, Captain, and you look like a man who could defend us, should the need arise.'

'I'm flattered, Miss Bearwood.'

Cordelia laid her hand on his sleeve. 'I think we can drop the formalities, Gilbert.'

A groan from Grace put a stop to Cordelia's flirtatious behaviour, much to Caroline's relief. Delia collected men's hearts in the way others collected fans or seashells, and she discarded them just as easily. Gilbert Reid was obviously impressed, and Caroline suspected that he was an innocent when it came to dealing with such blatant feminine flattery.

'I think we ought to take a risk and send a servant to fetch the doctor. Perhaps you could do that, Delia?' Caroline said pointedly. 'Will you help me take her upstairs, Gilbert?'

'Yes, of course.' Gilbert leaned over Grace, lowering his voice. 'I'm going to lift you up and take you to your room. I'll try not to hurt you.'

Grace's eyelids fluttered and her lips moved soundlessly.

Cordelia was suddenly serious. 'I'm hopeless when it comes to dealing with sick people.'

'I can help put Mama to bed,' Maria offered.

'That's even better.' Cordelia hurried to open the door. 'I told them to make the Jade Room ready for her, Carrie. You see to Grace and I'll send for the doctor.'

The doctor was visibly shocked when he saw Grace's injuries, but after he had examined her he said that they were superficial and there was no evidence of broken bones. He advised arnica for the bruises and laudanum for the pain, but he said that rest and nourishing food were what the patient needed most.

His advice was followed to the letter and Grace received the best attention possible. Maria spent a great deal of time at her mother's bedside and Caroline was pleased to see their relationship improving, but their respite at Daumerle could only be temporary. She sent a message to Starcross Abbey, informing Freddie that Grace was staying at Daumerle, and she invited him to join them for dinner, but, to her surprise and annoyance, she received a curt response from Jenifry stating that Mr Dorincourt had paid a brief visit to the Abbey, but had now returned to London. Caroline read the scrawled note twice, and was suspicious. She wondered if Freddie had received her letter, or if Jenifry had intercepted it in an attempt to keep him from seeing Grace. If that were so, it did not take a leap of imagination to picture Dickon riding post-haste to Wolf Tor Farm to inform Grace's husband of her whereabouts. Her fears were justified when, after breakfast one morning, Quick arrived at the gatehouse, accompanied by a police constable.

'I've given orders not to admit them,' Cordelia said urgently. 'From the injuries inflicted on poor Grace I'd say the man is a fiend.'

'I'll speak to the constable,' Gilbert moved to the door. 'Quick should be reported for ill-treating his wife.'

'Wait a moment,' Caroline said urgently. 'That won't do any good. Quick will deny everything and twist things so that it looks as if we kidnapped her.'

'Grace will tell the police what happened.' Cordelia peered out of the window. 'They're still there, and it looks as if they're arguing with Rawlings.'

'Grace isn't in a fit condition to stand up to that brute.' Caroline pushed past Gilbert and opened the door. 'I'll speak to the constable. He might just believe me.'

Maria hurried to her side. 'I'm coming with you, Carrie. I'll vouch for everything you say.'

'All right,' Gilbert said reluctantly. 'But don't allow Quick into the grounds.'

'You may depend on that.' Caroline slipped her shawl around her shoulders. 'Are you coming, Maria? We'll sort this out together.'

'They're lying, Officer,' Quick said angrily. 'My wife was kidnapped from our home.'

'He's the one telling untruths.' Maria clenched her small hands into fists. 'You should have seen the state my mother was in, Constable. That villain beat her black and blue.'

The constable glanced from one to the other. 'Mr Quick has the law on his side, miss. He wants to see his wife and that is his right.'

'She doesn't want anything to do with him,' Caroline said icily. 'You wouldn't treat a dog in the brutish way he abused his wife. She's been ill for days and it will take her a long time to recover completely.'

'You've only their word for it, Officer.' Quick made an aggressive move towards Caroline and Maria, who had ventured out through the side gate, but he was restrained by the constable.

'There's no need for violence, Mr Quick. I suggest you remain here while I go to the house and speak to the lady in question.'

Rawlings had been standing silently with his muscular arms folded across his chest, but he stepped forward, placing a large hand on Quick's shoulder. 'The policeman said you was to stay here, mister.'

Caroline ushered Maria and the constable into the grounds. 'Don't let him follow us, Rawlings.'

'You'll regret this,' Quick muttered beneath his breath, but just loud enough for Caroline to hear.

She ignored him and shut the gate with a clang of metal against metal.

The constable stood in the doorway of Grace's room, cap in hand, staring in horror at her bruised face. He cleared his throat nervously. 'Er – the gentleman,

Mr Quick, said you fell downstairs, ma'am, and that's how you come to get your injuries.'

Grace twisted her swollen lips into a semblance of a smile. 'He's lying. He did this to me.'

'Surely you can see that she's telling the truth,' Caroline said softly. 'This poor lady has been through hell for years, and no one has lifted a finger to help her, until now.'

'Well, miss, it's like this, you see. We're not empowered to intervene in what is a domestic issue.'

'Do you mean to tell me that a man can brutalise his wife, and you can't do anything about it?'

'I don't make the law, miss. I just do me best to uphold it.'

'I'm not going back to him,' Grace said feebly. 'I'd sooner kill myself.'

Maria went down on her knees at her mother's bedside. 'Don't say that, Mama. We won't let him near you, will we, Carrie?'

Caroline edged the constable out of the room. 'You can see how it is, Officer. I'd be grateful if you could tell Mr Quick what his wife said. He won't be admitted here, no matter what threats he uses.'

'I've done my duty, miss. I'll pass on the message and I'll advise the gentleman to abide by the law as it stands. I can do no more.'

Caroline grabbed his hand and shook it. 'We can't ask any more of you than that, but if he should try to break in he will be forcibly ejected and sued for trespass.' Caroline spoke with authority although she was bluffing, but the constable seemed a little vague, and was obviously impressed by her manner and overawed by his surroundings. She led the way downstairs and let him out of the house, ignoring Digby, who was hovering in the background.

'Do I take it that I am not to admit a certain person to the house, miss?'

She closed the door, meeting Digby's disapproving gaze with a steady look. 'That's right. Under no circumstances is Mr Quick to be allowed access. You may call a constable should he give you any trouble. Miss Bearwood will confirm that.' Caroline headed for the drawing room to join Cordelia and Gilbert.

'Well?' Cordelia raised her delicate eyebrows. 'What did the constable say?'

'I think he was shocked when he saw Grace's injuries, but there is very little he can do other than warn Quick not to trespass on your mother's property.'

Gilbert rose from his seat and went to look out of the window. 'It seems to me that the sooner we get Grace back to London, the better.'

'I agree.' Caroline sank down on the sofa. 'Although I'm not sure whether she's well enough for a long train journey.'

'And you can't take her to Starcross Abbey,' Cordelia added, frowning. 'I didn't tell you before, but I've had a letter from Mama ordering me to join her in London. I'm sorry, but I'll be leaving tomorrow.'

Gilbert turned away from the view. 'Unfortunately I've almost come to the end of my leave, so I too must return to the city.'

'I doubt if Quick will give up easily, and who knows what he'll do next?' Caroline said urgently. 'I suppose we could hire a carriage and take Grace by road, but that will take longer and be more arduous than travelling by train.'

'In the old days people would have gone by boat,' Gilbert said thoughtfully. 'There are plenty of ships in these waters, and a sea voyage might be good for her. At least she would be safe from that husband of hers.'

'Would that be possible, Gilbert?' Caroline eyed him hopefully. 'I'd do anything to keep the poor woman away from that brute.'

He turned to Cordelia. 'If you'll allow me to take one of your horses, I'll ride to Teignmouth straight away and see if I can find a suitable vessel.'

'Of course you may take any animal you wish. Just tell the head groom you have my permission.' Cordelia tilted her head, giving him a sweet smile. 'I promised Mama that I would join her very soon, so we could travel to London together; otherwise I'll only have my maid for company, and you are much more entertaining.'

A dull flush coloured Gilbert's face and he hurried from the room.

'Don't tease him, Delia,' Caroline said sternly. 'He's a good man, but he's not one of your London beaux. I don't think he realises that you're simply flirting.'

'How do you know that's the case?' Cordelia tossed her head, smiling impishly. 'I might be falling in love.'

'Don't break the poor man's heart, that's all I ask. He doesn't deserve that.'

'Oh, Carrie, you take things too seriously.' Cordelia's smile faded. 'As a matter of fact I'm spoken for, or at least my mother thinks I am.'

'Why didn't you mention it before?'

'I've been trying to pretend that I have a choice, but Lord Bridechurch has made an offer for my hand, and both Mama and Papa think it's a wonderful match. That's why I have to return to London.'

'Who is he? I don't think I know him.'

'He's middle-aged and seems quite amiable. His family own great tracts of land and he's never been married, so there are no children to complicate matters.'

Shocked by Cordelia's cool and calculating attitude, Caroline was almost at a loss for words. 'But do you like him, Delia?'

'I can't say that I know him very well. I've danced with him at balls and we've met at dinner parties and the theatre, but that's all. He's pleasant enough and I dare say I could twist him round my little finger, if I chose to do so.'

'And your parents consider this is a good basis for marriage?'

'Don't look so appalled, Carrie. The aristocracy

have been making marriages of convenience for centuries. Apparently Bridechurch is willing to settle a huge dowry on me, and he has a house in London and a large estate somewhere in the Midlands, as well as a villa in the South of France.'

'But you wouldn't marry for money, would you, Delia?'

'I don't know. I've never been in love so perhaps I have no heart, in which case it cannot be broken. Maybe I'm the sort of person who has to use her head, and I would certainly lack for nothing if I married Bridechurch, and I do love luxury.'

'Maybe you're right, and that's the best way to be,' Caroline said, sighing. 'After all, you just have to look at Grace and see what terrible things can occur if you fall in love with the wrong person.'

'Does Maria know the identity of her father?'

'No, she says that her grandmother refused to tell her, and I can believe that. Mrs Colville is a hard woman. I think she has a block of ice where her heart should be.'

'She sounds a bit like me,' Cordelia said, giggling. 'Don't look so worried, Carrie. I promise not to upset Gilbert. I'll try not to flirt with him, but he is rather sweet.'

Caroline rose from her seat on the sofa. 'You are impossible, Miss Bearwood.'

'Miss Bearwood – it doesn't have the same ring as Lady Bridechurch, does it?' Cordelia subsided into a fit of giggles, making it impossible for Caroline to keep a straight face, but at that moment the door opened to admit Gilbert.

'I'm leaving now and I hope to return by early evening.'

Caroline came to a sudden decision and she jumped to her feet. 'I'm coming with you, Gilbert. If you'll send for another mount I'll change quickly and be with you in ten minutes.'

'Really, Carrie,' Cordelia protested. 'Is this necessary?'

'I can't sit about any longer, Delia. I'm sorry, but I have to do something useful.' Caroline turned to Gilbert with a persuasive smile. 'You needn't worry. I'm a good horsewoman. Teignmouth is only four miles or so from here and I promise I won't slow you down.'

'You can't desert me,' Cordelia said angrily. 'What will I do if Quick returns?'

'You have plenty of people to protect you.' Caroline headed for the doorway. 'You don't mind, do you, Gilbert?'

He smiled. 'I can pick a seaworthy vessel, but you would be a better judge of what you need to make Grace comfortable. I'll send to the stables for a suitable mount.'

They reached Teignmouth in the middle of the afternoon and made straight for an inn situated close to the harbour, and a groom rushed out to take care of their horses.

'I can't go any further without something to eat and drink,' Caroline said, sniffing hungrily as the aroma of roast beef wafted from the kitchen.

'We can make enquiries about the ships in the harbour.' Gilbert shielded his eyes as he scanned the forest of masts. 'The landlord will probably have an idea of what ships are in port and where they are bound.' He led the way into the taproom and went straight to the bar, leaving Caroline standing in the middle of the crowded room – an object of curiosity. The male drinkers turned their heads to stare, making her feel like a sideshow in the fairground.

Gilbert hurried to her side. 'I've ordered food and there's a dining parlour at the back of the bar. We'll be more private there.'

'Lead on. I don't think they're used to seeing women in the taproom.'

'I doubt if many ladies frequent this place.' Gilbert took her by the arm, forging a path through the interested onlookers. 'It will give them something to talk about other than the price of fish.' He opened the door to the dining parlour and ushered her inside.

Caroline came to a halt, realising that they were not alone. One of the tables was occupied by three men, who, judging by their salt-stained garments, must have come off one of the ships moored in the harbour. The two older men glanced over their shoulders and then turned back to concentrate on their meal, but the man with the look and bearing of a gentleman rose to his feet, staring at Caroline as if he could not believe his eyes. She knew she ought to ignore such blatant rudeness, but she found she could not tear her gaze away. He was undoubtedly a person of some standing, and he could be any age from forty to fifty. His dark hair was streaked with silver and his eyes were startlingly blue, set beneath straight black eyebrows.

Gilbert pulled up a chair for Caroline, but she remained standing – the stranger's expression was both embarrassing and unsettling. 'Do I know you, sir?'

He shook his head. 'I believe not, and I apologise for my rudeness, but you remind me of someone I once knew.'

One of his companions turned his head. 'You must excuse my friend, *signorina*. The poor man has been living in Australia for so many years, he has quite forgotten his manners.'

'Are you off one of the ships that we saw in the harbour, sir?' Caroline asked eagerly.

He stood up, bowing theatrically. 'Captain Enrico Falco at your service, *signorina*.'

'Captain Falco?'

His dark eyes sparkled with pleasure. 'My name is still known in these parts?'

'Who is this, Caroline?' Gilbert asked in a low voice. 'Do you know these men?'

Caroline shook her head. 'I don't think so, but I've heard the name Falco somewhere.'

The oldest of the three, who had so far sat in silence, stood up slowly. 'You're from London, miss?'

'Yes, sir.' Caroline met his curious gaze with a smile. 'And so are you, if I'm not mistaken.'

Gilbert stepped forward. 'Perhaps I should introduce myself. I am Captain Gilbert Reid and my companion is Miss Caroline Manning.'

After a moment of stunned silence, Falco was the first to speak. 'Who could forget that face – so like that of her mama. I knew it the moment I saw her.'

The dark-haired man held up his hand. 'That's enough, Falco. You're jumping to conclusions.' He moved around the table, coming to a halt in front of Caroline, his blue eyes scanning her face as if trying to read her thoughts. 'You must forgive my friend, Miss Manning, but either this is the most amazing coincidence or you are who I think you are.'

'You're talking in riddles, sir,' Gilbert said warily. 'Who are you?'

'I'll tell you who he is.' The oldest man in the group leaped to his feet. 'This is Lord Dorincourt, the Earl of Starcross, and he's come home to claim what's his. I'm Jacob Chapman.' He seized Caroline's hand and clasped it to his chest. 'And unless I'm very much mistaken, you are my granddaughter.'

Caroline looked into his eyes and saw something of her mother in their hazel depths. Despite the wrinkled skin, the colour of tanned leather, and thinning white hair, there was something familiar in his voice and in the smell of salty air, mingling with a faint whiff of tobacco and lye soap that stirred a distant memory.

'Grandpa?' she murmured. 'You once read me a bedtime story.'

His eyes reddened and his lips trembled. 'You was four years old and as pretty as a picture.'

'You are Essie's daughter?' Dorincourt threw back his head and laughed. 'Well, I'm damned. For a moment I thought the years had rolled back and Essie had come into the room.' He held out his hand. 'How do you do, Caroline?' His handshake was firm, but brief.

'How do you do, my lord?'

'My friends call me Raven,' he said, smiling. 'I knew and respected your mother. Is she well?'

'She is in mourning for my father and her brother . . .' Caroline hesitated, eyeing her grandfather warily. 'I'm afraid I have some bad news for you, Grandpa.'

Jacob sank down on his chair. 'George is dead?'

'Yes. I'm so sorry.'

'What happened to my boy?'

The old man was clearly moved and Caroline struggled to hold back the tears that threatened to overcome her.

'Mr Manning was struck down by yellow fever, sir,' Gilbert said hastily. 'We took a cargo to Trinidad and it was after we left that certain members of the crew came down with the disease.'

Jacob shook his head. 'Yellow fever. Poor George.'

'That's hard, Jacob,' Raven said, frowning. 'Is Essie all right? It must have been a terrible blow.'

'Mama is coping.' Caroline dashed a tear from her cheek. 'It's been a difficult time.'

'Many commiserations.' Falco shook his head. 'Life is hard.'

'I must see my girl,' Jacob said urgently. 'I can't hang around here when Essie needs me.' He turned to glare at Caroline. 'Anyway, what brings you here? This ain't no place for a young lady like you.'

'I was going to ask that same question,' Raven added, frowning. 'Why are you travelling without a chaperone, Caroline?'

Gilbert cleared his throat, facing Raven squarely. 'It's not what it looks like, sir.'

'No, indeed,' Caroline said hastily. 'We were hoping to book a passage to London for two friends and myself. One of the ladies is in desperate need.'

Falco's waxed moustache quivered. 'How so, *signorina*? We might be able to help.'

'It is a very long story.'

'Perhaps we should sit down and allow Carrie to tell you in her own way?' Gilbert suggested.

'I never thought I'd live to see this day.' Jacob pulled a grubby hanky from his pocket and blew his nose. 'I've been away too long, and I've neglected my daughter and I've lost my son. It's a judgement on me for the way I treated him when he was a boy.'

Caroline reached out to pat him on the shoulder. There was nothing she could say that would take away his pain. She sat down, waiting while the landlady served their food, but even though the plate of roast beef and potatoes looked tempting, she realised that her appetite had deserted her. There was silence in the room as everyone waited for her to continue. Desperate to find the right words, she glanced at each of them in turn. These men had been so much a part of her mother's life that she felt she knew them all, even though she had never met Raven or Falco, and her memory of her grandfather was vague like a half-forgotten dream. Her mother had talked endlessly of her time with Raven and their voyage to Italy on Falco's rusty old ship, and of the months they had spent in the mining town of Ballarat. She had lulled Caroline to sleep at bedtime, recounting the events that had culminated in her return to London with a fortune in gold. And now here they were, the three most important people from her mother's younger days – all of them hanging on her every word. She began, haltingly at first, and then growing more confident she told them everything. When she came to a halt Jacob leaned over to give her a hug. Raven's expression was inscrutable and Falco's eyes were moist.

Jacob sat back, shaking his head. 'I was a bad father, and I've been a neglectful grandfather, Caroline. I want to make amends.'

Falco downed the last of his ale. 'You are my first

mate, Jacob. The *Bendigo Queen* is due in London in two weeks and I need you on board.'

Momentarily diverted, Caroline turned to Falco. 'What happened to the *Santa Gabriella*?'

'She was an old lady,' Falco said, sighing. 'She slipped away peacefully to the bottom of the Indian Ocean, where she still slumbers.'

'How did that happen? Was there much loss of life?'

Falco grinned. 'Maybe a few rats that did not get away from the sinking ship. No, *mia cara*, it was not far off shore and everyone was saved.'

'Be honest, Falco,' Jacob said, chuckling. 'She was scuttled deliberately and you claimed the insurance money.'

'I had to purchase another vessel. It was the only way.'

'Forget that for a moment.' Raven met Caroline's curious gaze with an even look. 'Why do you think travelling by sea is the best way to get your friend back to London?'

'Her husband is a vicious brute and he's determined to get her back, no matter what. She would be safe on board your ship and it would give her time to recover from the beatings he inflicted on her.'

'I would like to meet this man,' Falco said, flexing his fingers. 'I would make him think twice before he harmed a woman.'

'I second that.' Jacob shook his head. 'The man should be horsewhipped.'

'Wouldn't it be best to bring Grace to the Abbey?' Raven said thoughtfully. 'I'm going there to visit my brother.'

'The last I heard of him he was in London.'

'Then I'll send for him. Your friend would be safe with us until she is well enough to travel.'

'I don't think you understand the situation at Starcross.' Caroline leaned forward, lowering her voice. 'Jenifry and her son, Dickon, want Grace out of the way.'

'What have they to say in the matter?'

Caroline eyed him curiously. 'Didn't Freddie tell you?'

'What is it that I should know?'

'Freddie is Dickon's father. He's allowed Jenifry to live with him as mistress of Starcross Abbey, although she is supposed to be his housekeeper.'

'The dirty dog,' Jacob said, grinning. 'Begging your pardon, Caroline.'

'Freddie always had a way with women,' Falco added.

Raven held up his hand. 'We all know about my brother's weakness for a pretty face. Are you telling me that he is romantically inclined towards Grace?'

'I think he really cares for her, but Dickon and his mother could see that Freddie had a soft spot for Grace, and they did their best to get rid of her.'

'That's not good,' Falco said darkly.

'If he's made advances to you, Caroline, he'll have to answer to me.' Jacob's jaw hardened. 'I may be an old man, but I can still handle meself in a brawl.'

'No, Grandpa,' Caroline said hastily. 'Freddie is a perfect gentleman. I think he has genuine feelings for Grace, but Jenifry and Dickon see her as a threat.'

Raven rose to his feet. 'It's definitely time that I returned home. Falco, you'll take the *Bendigo Queen* to London, and, Jacob, you'll sail with him. I intend to hire a horse and travel to Starcross, and I'll join you later. In the meantime I'll do what I always do and sort out my brother's mess.'

Falco and Jacob rose to their feet, exchanging mutinous glances, but saying nothing.

'What about Grace?' Caroline asked anxiously.

'You've explained that you must leave Daumerle,' Raven said seriously. 'I suggest that you bring Grace to the Abbey first thing tomorrow morning. I'll deal with Jenifry and her son, never fear.'

Caroline stood up to give her grandfather a hug. 'I'll see you in London, Grandpa. You'll find Mama and the boys at the Captain's House. You know where that is.'

Jacob's weathered face creased into a smile. 'Aye, and I have a lot of lost time to make up for. I've lost the son I treated so badly, which I'll regret until my dying day, but I have two grandsons and I want them to think well of their old grandpa.' He gave her a whiskery kiss on the forehead before shambling out of the parlour following in Falco's wake.

'I can't believe this is happening,' Caroline said slowly.

Raven laid his hand on her shoulder. 'In my life I've had many regrets, Caroline, but I've a feeling that things have come full circle. I'm a very wealthy man, thanks to my goldmine in Bendigo, and I promise that you and your mother and brothers will never want for anything, ever again.' He turned to Gilbert with a grim smile. 'Take care of her, Reid. She's as important to me as if she were my own daughter.'

Chapter Nineteen

Next morning Daumerle echoed with the sound of running footsteps and the excited chatter of voices. After a long discussion the previous evening, it had been decided that Maria would return to London with Cordelia and Gilbert. Maria had wanted to accompany her mother to the Abbey, but she was equally anxious to see Theo again. Even though the cuts were healing and the bruises were beginning to fade, Grace was still suffering mentally from the vicious treatment she had received at the hands of her husband, and Caroline suspected that peace and quiet during her convalescence was what Grace really wanted. It was left to Caroline to take her to Starcross Abbey in the Bearwoods' barouche, while the others travelled to the railway station in the family brougham, which had seen better days, but was still roadworthy.

The journey to Starcross Abbey was uneventful, although the nightmare Caroline had endured persisted even in daylight. She had dreamed that Quick, dressed as an eighteenth-century highwayman, had held them up at gunpoint and had dragged Grace physically from the vehicle, with Dickon and Jenifry waiting to take her away in a tumbril. What might have happened next was left to her imagination, as she had been awakened by the appearance of a maid bringing her a cup of chocolate.

Grace was calm and accepted everything that was done for her, smiling as much as her swollen face would allow, and she dozed off during the carriage ride, which saved Caroline from making conversation. Her thoughts kept straying to the meeting with her grandfather, Falco and Raven. They were part of her parents' past, and until yesterday had been shadowy figures, but suddenly they were flesh and blood. Caroline wondered how their unexpected reappearance would affect her mother, but if Raven had been sincere in his promise to help them financially, it could mean an end to hardship and homelessness. Maybe they could rent somewhere in a more respectable area than Great Hermitage Street, and they would not be dependent on the Colvilles. She settled back against the leather squabs, closing her eyes. The sooner Grace was fit enough to return to London, the better.

Half an hour later the barouche drew to a halt

outside the Abbey, which, despite its harsh granite walls, looked mellow in the brilliant sunlight. Raven met them with a welcoming smile and ushered them into the drawing room. A young parlour maid was instructed to fetch refreshments and, to Caroline's relief, there was no sign of Jenifry or Dickon. When Grace was comfortably ensconced in an armchair by the window, with a view of the sunlit parterre garden, Caroline sat down to pour the coffee. She shot a covert glance at Raven, and it was easy to see what had attracted her mother to him all those years ago. He might be closer to fifty than forty, but he was still a commanding figure, and dressed in a tweed jacket and riding breeches he looked every inch a country gentleman.

Caroline rose from the table to take a cup of coffee to Grace, who accepted it with a nod and a crooked smile. Her facial injuries were beginning to heal, but the deep purple bruises had taken on a rainbow effect and her lips were still very swollen. Caroline returned to her seat and Raven sat down next to her.

'Where are Jenifry and Dickon?' she asked in a whisper.

'I paid them off,' Raven said simply. 'Everyone has a price and I gave Jenifry enough money to purchase her mother's cottage, which is large enough to house both herself and that son of hers. He may be my nephew, but I didn't take to him at all.'

'I can't imagine that Dickon would give up so

easily. He seemed to think that he was heir to the estate.'

Raven threw back his head and laughed. 'Don't worry – I soon put him straight.' His expression darkened and he leaned closer. 'To tell the truth I don't think we've heard the last of that young man, despite my generosity. On my way here yesterday I stopped off to send a telegram to Bearwood House in London, assuming that my brother is staying with Alice, and I've asked him to return home as quickly as possible.'

'That's good. Freddie should be here in case Dickon tries to make trouble.'

'I know he's acknowledged the boy as his son, but I sent a groom to the local superintendent registrar with a request for a copy of Dickon's birth certificate. I want to find out if Freddie's name is on it. If he is named as the boy's father it could complicate matters.'

'I don't trust Dickon. He's not a nice person.'

'Are you talking about Elias?' Grace's querulous voice made them both turn to look at her.

'No, Grace,' Raven said firmly. 'We were speaking of Dickon.'

Grace shuddered and turned back to the view. 'He's a bad lot. Freddie should be warned.'

'Don't worry,' Caroline said gently. 'That's just what we're saying. Whatever happens, we'll keep you safe from him – and from Quick. All you have to do is to get well again.'

'I should be with my daughter. I don't want Maria to make a fool of herself over a man, as I did when I was her age. She hardly knows that sea captain, but she's besotted and I'm afraid it will end in disaster.'

'We can only hope she decides to wait a while.' Caroline rose to her feet and went to relieve Grace of her empty cup. 'Would you like some more coffee?'

Grace shook her head. 'No, thank you, dear. I'd like to sit a while and enjoy the peace and quiet, but I'm determined to get better quickly. In a day or two I'll be fit to travel to London. I just hope I'm in time to stop Maria doing something she'll regret.'

Caroline turned to Raven. 'Is there anything I can do to help now that you've lost your cook-housekeeper?'

'I hired a woman from the village to take over in the kitchen, but perhaps you could keep an eye on her. I had to take her word for it that she can make a decent meal.'

'No need for you to trouble yourself, Carrie.' Grace heaved herself from the chair. 'That's somewhere I can make myself useful. I'll be able to tell in an instant if the woman knows what she's doing.'

'Are you sure?' Caroline asked anxiously. 'You're supposed to be recuperating.'

'Don't try to stop me. I can do this.' Grace limped from the room, clutching her side as if every step caused her pain.

Caroline was about to protest when Raven laid his hand on her shoulder. 'Let her go. She might save us from being poisoned by Mrs Duffin. I think Grace is sensible enough to know when to rest, and having something to do will take her mind off her worries.'

'You're right, and I can help by getting our rooms ready. I think I can remember where everything is.'

'Freddie should be here later. I need to have a serious talk with my brother.'

Despite the fact that she was supposed to be working upstairs, Caroline could not resist the temptation to venture into Freddie's studio. His portrait of Grace was on a large easel in the middle of the room, and a shaft of sunlight played with the tones and texture of her naked flesh. He had caught on canvas the essence of her fragile, faded beauty and the haunting sadness of her expression. Caroline knew little about art, but she was suitably impressed and also deeply touched. It was as if Freddie had captured the soul of the woman he painted and had saved this fragile beauty for posterity. Caroline had walked past the portraits of the Dorincourt ancestors each time she had used the main staircase, but those people with their lifeless faces and dead eyes were simply images from history – the portrait of Grace, even in its unfinished state, spoke as much of the emotions of the artist himself as those of the sitter. It was, as Caroline had suspected, proof of Freddie's deep feelings for Grace. Perhaps now, with Jenifry and Dickon out of the way, Freddie and Grace could be together as fate seemed to have intended.

Caroline closed the door on Freddie's private domain and went about her tasks with the hope that he would come soon, and that everything would fall into place. She could then return to London with Raven, who had promised to find a new home for her family. Perhaps he would invest in the business and make her an equal partner with Phineas. It was an idea that both excited and pleased her. She paused with a pile of bedding in her arms as she caught sight of herself in the cheval mirror, and a smile curved her lips. She looked more like a chambermaid than the part owner of a shipping company, but looks could be deceptive and she would prove the doubters wrong. Phineas had been helpful, but, despite warming to him a little, she still could not bring herself to trust him and she suspected that he was simply humouring her. He might be waiting for her to lose interest in the business, intending to make a takeover bid for Manning and Chapman. She tossed her head – the young woman who scowled back at her from the mirror was not going to be bested, neither would she give up easily. As soon as Grace was well enough they would return to London.

Freddie did not come home that day, and Raven did not try to conceal his annoyance. 'He hasn't bothered to reply to my telegram,' he said at dinner that evening. 'I'm sure that Maria will have explained the situation by now, but Freddie always does exactly what he wants. My brother never changes.'

Grace put her knife and fork down with a clatter. 'Maybe they haven't seen him,' she protested. 'I'm sure he wouldn't deliberately ignore your message.'

'You have more faith in my brother than I have.'

Caroline and Grace exchanged wary glances. 'Give him a little more time,' Caroline said hastily. 'We don't know how things are in London.'

'I intend to find out.' Raven reached for his glass of wine and took a sip. 'I'll travel up to London tomorrow morning. You'll be quite safe here, ladies, and I'll make sure the gatekeeper and the outdoor servants know that Dickon and Quick are not to be allowed anywhere near the house.'

'We'll be all right,' Caroline said stoutly. 'Do what you must, my lord.'

Raven shot her an amused glance. 'I thought we'd agreed that you would call me Raven. I never use my title these days, or at least I don't in Australia, although if it works to my advantage I might throw it into conversation now that I'm home.'

'Do you intend to stay in England?' Grace asked.

'No, at least not permanently. I've worked hard and I've had a certain amount of luck, which has enabled me to have a house built to my exact requirements. I own a gold mine and I have a half-share in the *Bendigo Queen*, but what I'm really interested in are the reefer ships that the Americans use to transport frozen meat. If we could perfect the use of refrigeration in shipping there would be a huge trade between England and the Antipodes.'

'That's amazing,' Caroline said eagerly. 'I wish our company had the money to invest in such a wonderful idea.'

Raven smiled. 'Who knows? Maybe you will.'

True to his word, Raven left for London early next morning. Grace had virtually taken over in the kitchen, having found that Mrs Duffin was next to useless. Her only talent was burning everything to a crisp, for which she blamed the range, but as Grace managed to use it without setting fire to the bacon or serving the porridge blackened and lumpy, it seemed that the fault lay firmly with Mrs Duffin. However, she claimed to be a good laundress and was relegated to the wash-house to light the fire under the copper in readiness to deal with the soiled bedding, towels and table linen.

'Everyone is good at something,' Grace said philosophically. 'You just have to find out where their talents lie. Maybe Freddie will keep me on as cook general. I won't be his mistress, but I think I'd like to live here and look after him, on the understanding that Jenifry and that boy of hers are kept away, of course.'

Caroline was about to take a basket of towels to the laundry room, but she hesitated. 'Don't you want to go back to London, Grace? I thought you were eager to spend more time with your daughter.'

'Of course I want to be near my girl, but if she's set on marrying that sea captain there'll be no stopping her. She'll be off with him on his ship and I'll be on my own in London.'

'Is there no chance of a reconciliation between you and your mother?' Caroline voiced the question, although she felt she already knew the answer.

'None at all. My mother has a heart of pure granite. My brother Everard, Phin's father, was her favourite, and my sister Clarice, Gilbert's mother, wouldn't say boo to a goose. Mama never liked me because I stood up to her.'

'I'm sorry.' Caroline was at a loss as to what else to say.

'It doesn't matter now, Carrie. I've been through worse since I married Elias. I'll never go back to him. Never.'

'Of course not,' Caroline said firmly. 'There's no question of that.' She left Grace in the kitchen and took the washing to Mrs Duffin, who was in the wash-house, stirring the contents of the copper with a wooden stick. Her round cheeks were flushed from the heat and exertion, but she was singing at the top of her voice and Caroline placed the basket on the table and left unnoticed.

She was cheered by the improvement in Grace's mood and her pragmatic approach to the life she might expect to lead if she chose to stay at the

Abbey. Freddie would have his muse and would have a good cook into the bargain. If he was genuinely fond of Grace it would be up to him to sort out his tangled relationship with Jenifry, but then, lurking in the background, was Elias Quick. Divorce proceedings were expensive and even though she knew little of the law, Caroline suspected that it would be very difficult for Grace to prove that she had been so cruelly abused.

The day passed pleasantly and in the afternoon Caroline took a pair of rattan chairs from the old orangery and placed them on the lawn. Grace dozed off beneath a large straw hat she had found in a cupboard, and Caroline opened the book she had selected from Freddie's library, which, surprisingly, included works by Miss Austen and Mrs Radcliffe. Caroline had read the first page, but she found her mind wandering. The air was filled with birdsong and the sweet scent from the rose beds brought back memories of the garden in Finsbury Circus. The terrible events that had followed her father's death had left an indelible impression on Caroline, but the atmosphere in the former monastery garden was both soothing and serene. With the sun high in the sky and the sound of the waves breaking softly on the sand at the foot of the cliffs, it was almost possible to put the past behind her. She relaxed against the silk cushions and closed her eyes.

She was awakened by the maid. 'There's a message from his lordship. Billy Davey brought it from the station. It must have come on one of them electric machines that tap out messages.'

Blinking against the bright sunlight, Caroline took the piece of paper that was creased and crumpled as if it had been screwed up in a ball and spent some time in Billy Davey's pocket. A piece of toffee was still stuck in the fold. She read the message carefully.

'Billy says is there an answer, miss?'

'No answer, but thank him anyway.' Caroline reached out to give Grace a gentle shake. 'Raven and Freddie will be arriving in time for a late supper.'

A rosy blush coloured Grace's cheeks. 'I'll make a pie that can be eaten hot or cold, then it doesn't matter if they're late. I'd best start now.' She raised herself carefully from the chair. 'The gardener's boy brought in a pair of rabbits this morning. I was going to stew them for us, but a pie is better in this hot weather. Would you fetch me a handful of herbs from the kitchen garden, please, Carrie?'

Caroline pulled a face. 'I would, of course, but I don't know one herb from another. We left that sort of thing to Cook.'

'Of course, silly of me. I would have been the same before I married Elias. Now I have a very good grounding in all things that grow wild, including plants that will cure ailments and others that are poisonous.'

'I wonder you didn't concoct a deadly brew for Quick,' Caroline said, smiling.

'Don't imagine I didn't think of it once or twice, but that would have brought me down to his level, and I would have been hanged for my pains.' Grace started walking in the direction of the kitchen garden. 'Come with me and I'll show you what parsley and thyme look like. I hope there's a bay tree or even a rosemary bush. Look, Carrie – I'm walking without a limp. Isn't that wonderful, and the pain is getting less and less. The magic of Starcross Abbey is healing my injuries.'

The kitchen garden was bathed in sunshine and Caroline was impressed with Grace's knowledge of herbs and medicinal plants. They gathered what they needed and made their way back to the house, accompanied by the deafening sound of Mrs Duffin's throaty contralto and clouds of steam billowing from the open wash-house door. Grace started to laugh, and, although she tried to keep a straight face, Caroline was giggling helplessly by the time they reached the kitchen.

'I don't know why Mrs Duffin's awful out-of-tune attempt at singing is so funny,' Caroline gasped.

'The Abbey is so quiet and peaceful until she shatters the silence with that truly terrible voice of hers. She sings out of tune and I'm sure she makes up half the words, but she seems to imagine that she sings like a lark.'

Caroline wiped her eyes on her apron. 'It's so good to see you laughing, Grace.'

'I feel happy for the first time in twenty years,'

Grace said seriously. 'Whatever the future holds nothing can be as bad as being married to that brute.' She laid the herbs out on the table. 'If you'll be kind enough to fetch the rabbits from the larder I'll show you how to prepare them for the pot. This will be the best pie that Freddie and Raven have ever tasted.'

The rest of the afternoon passed in a flurry of activity. Caroline did what she could to help Grace prepare the meal that would welcome Freddie home, and the savoury aroma of rabbit pie filled the kitchen. Mrs Duffin had made excuses to come indoors, but it was obvious that their sudden burst of activity had made her suspicious, but Caroline had not chosen to satisfy her curiosity. She had sent Mrs Duffin home early, and, for the same reason, had given the maid the evening off. The less the servants knew of their business the better – gossip would soon reach Jenifry's ears and that was the last thing that Caroline wanted. If Freddie was sincere in his desire to keep Grace at his side he must be given a chance to do so away from prying eyes. Raven might think that his money could buy Jenifry's silence and Dickon's loyalty, but Caroline was not so sure.

She sent Grace upstairs to change into her best gown and was just putting the finishing touches to the dining table, when she heard raised voices outside. The dining room overlooked the front of the house, and, to her horror, Caroline saw a group of men struggling with one of the ageing groundsmen and the head groom. It was an unequal fight as the intruders were younger and stronger, and their leader was Dickon with Elias Quick in the background, wielding a cudgel.

Caroline ran into the hall shouting for Grace, who appeared at the top of the stairs, pale-faced and trembling. 'I knew it,' she cried. 'He's come to get me.'

'I'm afraid so, but we won't let them in.'

Grace hurried downstairs as fast as her long skirts would allow. She clutched the newel post, breathing heavily. 'What do we do now? They'll get in somehow, and he'll kill me this time.'

'No he won't.' Caroline grabbed her by the hand. 'I know a place where we can hide. Raven and Freddie will be here soon, and then we'll be safe.' She dragged Grace through a maze of corridors to Freddie's study.

'Why here?' Grace demanded. 'This is no better than any other room. We should escape through the kitchen and into the woods.'

'Dickon knows every inch of the estate. That's the first place he'll look and we wouldn't stand a chance. Just keep quiet and let me find the hidden catch.' Caroline ran her fingers over the panelling in the far wall.

'What are you doing?'

'Found it.' Caroline turned to give Grace a triumphant smile. 'Freddie showed me the secret passage when I was a child and we used to get to the beach this way. Sometimes we took the rowing boat and went fishing for dabs.'

'A secret passage?' Grace's hand flew to cover her mouth.

'Yes, it was used by smugglers in the last century, and we're going to escape through it now. It's only half a mile or so to the railway station. We'll be safe if we can get there and we'll meet Raven and Freddie off the train.' She held her hand out to Grace. 'Come on. It's a lot safer down there than it is in the house. I think I heard breaking glass.'

Grace needed no second bidding and she squeezed through the narrow opening. 'It's very dark.'

'Hold on a moment. I'll light a candle.' Caroline snatched a chamber candlestick from Freddie's desk and struck a match. Holding the candle high above her head she followed Grace into the passage and closed the door behind them. 'I'll go first. There are steps leading downwards so mind how you go.'

'I can hear the sea. It sounds very close,' Grace whispered.

Caroline could feel the cold air rushing towards her and condensation dripped off the tunnel roof and walls. She remembered asking Freddie who had hewn the red sandstone, carving the passage through the cliff, but he protested that history was not his forte and she had better ask someone who was better informed. But then he had sworn her to secrecy and she had never discovered the answer to her question.

It was irrelevant now – all she knew was that it provided a means of distancing them from the intruders who meant them harm. However, it was only a matter of time before Dickon would realise where they had gone. He might not have been present during her past visits to the Abbey, and Freddie had good reason for keeping his love child a secret, but Dickon would know every nook and cranny in the old building and he would soon find them.

'It's not much further.' Caroline made an effort to sound positive, but Grace was right, the sound of the waves crashing on the rocks was growing louder.

'I think I can hear them in the study,' Grace said in a low voice.

'Dickon would be the only one to know about the tunnel. Best hurry now.'

Caroline led the way, slipping and sliding on the wet stone steps, and grazing her knuckles on the rough walls as she tried to stop herself from falling. She must not allow the candle flame to be extinguished. Grace stumbled and righted herself by clutching Caroline's arm and for a moment it seemed that they would both tumble into the blackness, but Caroline wedged her elbow against the rock and managed to steady both of them. Her arm was bruised and sore but she ignored the pain, breathing a sigh of relief when she realised that they had come to the bottom of the steps.

'It really isn't far now,' she whispered. 'I can see a glimmer of daylight.'

'Thank goodness, because my legs are shaking so badly I think they might give way beneath me.'

'The passage ends in a cave. We'll be there very soon.' Caroline felt the salt air on her cheeks and she pressed on with Grace clinging to her hand. 'Not far now. When we get to the beach we are almost there.'

'The waves are very loud. Can you see the mouth of the cave, Carrie?'

Caroline came to a sudden halt. The mouth of the cave was clearly visible now, as was the water that was lapping around her feet. She had not bargained for a high tide and she could hear shouts echoing off the walls of rock. Their pursuers were coming, but they were cut off by the sea.

'I'm so sorry, Grace. The tide is in – we're trapped.'

Chapter Twenty

The waves were lapping gently round Caroline's feet and the water seemed calm, almost inviting. Through the mouth of the cave she could see the sky, rose pink in the sunset, and the wet sand beneath her feet suggested that the tide was on the turn.

'I can't swim.' Grace clutched Caroline's arm. 'But I'd rather drown than go back to Elias.'

'You won't have to.' In the dark shadows of the rocky cave wall Caroline caught sight of the rowing boat, moored to an iron ring. She bundled her skirts up round her waist. 'Wait there, Grace.'

'You can't go into the water.'

'I've done this once before and it only came up to my waist.' Caroline cocked her head on one side, listening. 'Can you hear them? They'll be on us in a few minutes. Let go of me.' She wrenched free from Grace's frantic clutch and waded into the water.

The sudden chill made her stomach clench and she could feel the undertow as the water receded, but she reached the boat and after a couple of unsuccessful attempts, managed to heave herself on board. Her fingers were numb with cold but she untied the painter and manoeuvred the boat towards Grace.

'You'll have to get your feet wet,' Caroline said through chattering teeth. 'Hurry, Grace – they'll be here any moment now.'

Quick's voice echoed off the walls of the tunnel and Grace flung herself into the boat. Caroline thrust an oar into her hands. 'Do as I do. The tide is on our side.'

Quick and Dickon had reached the end of the tunnel and they waded into the water but they were soon waist deep, and a combination of desperate sculling and the ebb tide helped the small craft out to sea.

'It's no good, Carrie.' Grace bent double over the oar, gasping for breath. 'My ribs hurt and I can't row any quicker.'

'We need to get away from the shore.' Caroline grabbed the oar from Grace and began rowing furiously.

'Where are we going?' Grace clutched the sides of the boat, glancing anxiously over her shoulder.

'They can't follow us, unless they can swim like porpoises,' Caroline said, chuckling. 'But they'll probably make for the beach where they think we'll put ashore.'

'Where are we going then?'

'Let me concentrate on rowing.' Caroline was beginning to struggle as the tide and currents were taking them further and further from the shore. She had not handled the oars of a boat for several years, and she could feel a change in the weather as the wind increased and the sky darkened. The sun was obscured by dark clouds and spots of rain landed like pinpricks on her cheeks, numbing her fingers as they curled around the oars. Grace huddled, petrified in the stern, covering her face with her hands.

A sudden flash of lightning was followed by a rumble of thunder and a gust of wind seized the boat, sending it scudding out of her control. Caroline struggled to hold on to the oars, but one of them snapped in two and she was left holding a broken spar. She tossed it into the sea, attempting to scull, using the remaining oar, but she was no match for the elements and they bobbed about on the waves like a child's toy.

The sky visible between the heavy black clouds was sulphurous yellow and the boiling black mass of water had them at its mercy. Caroline shipped the oar and held on to the gunwales for dear life. The flashes of lightning were followed seconds later by ear-splitting crashes of thunder, loud enough to waken the dead. The boat was bouncing off the waves, plunging into troughs and then by some miracle came up head to the wind. Then, even more terrifying, Caroline was aware of a dark shape looming above them, and they were heading for it at an alarming speed. The keel grated on shingle and for a moment it seemed as though they were safe, but then a huge wave flipped the boat over and they were flung into the water.

Gasping for air, Caroline crawled up the beach, raising herself to her knees as she struggled for breath. 'Grace.' She scrambled to her feet and stumbled over to where Grace lay face down in the surf. Caroline used the last of her strength to pull her clear of the water. 'Grace, speak to me.'

Grace retched and turned her head as she coughed up seawater. Caroline raised her to a sitting position. 'You're all right. We're safe on shore.'

'Where are we?' Grace looked round dazedly.

A flash of lightning illuminated the small cove surrounded on three sides by high cliffs. A wooden jetty jutted into the water, and across the dark expanse of the bay Caroline could see pinpricks of light from the mainland.

'It's Bear Island,' she said softly. 'I remember coming here for a picnic when I was a child. We're about half a mile off shore.'

'That's not very far,' Grace said hopefully.

Caroline stood up, wringing water from her sodden skirts. 'Help me to drag the boat above high-water level or we'll lose it.'

'Are you telling me we'll have to stay here all night?'

'I'm afraid so. We won't get very far with only one oar, and no one knows we're here.'

'But Elias and Dickon know that we took the boat.'

'Yes, but they won't know that we were washed up on this beach, and the island is uninhabited.' Caroline could see that Grace was close to tears, and she made an effort to sound positive. 'We'll move the boat first and then we need to get dry.'

Grace helped Caroline drag the boat higher up the beach, but having done so she collapsed onto her knees. 'I can't go any further, Carrie. I'll have to stay here.'

'Don't give up now.' Caroline glanced up into the darkening sky. 'It's stopped raining, thank goodness.'

'I'm so wet I don't think I'll ever get warm again.' Grace covered her face with her hands and her shoulders heaved.

'You've got to keep moving.' Caroline helped her to her feet. 'Freddie and Raven should be at the Abbey by now and when they discover we're missing they'll send out a search party. We're safe here, for now, but we have to find shelter.'

'I can't go any further, Carrie. I'm sorry, but I'm done in.'

'If I remember rightly there's a path that leads from the beach to the top of the island, and there's a hut that the fishermen used to use to watch for shoals of fish, or that's what Freddie told me. Anyway, if it's still there we'll be able to shelter until morning.'

'I don't think I can walk that far. My gown is so wet I can hardly stand.'

Caroline began to unbutton her bodice. 'I'm going to take mine off. It'll make walking easier and it's not cold.'

'My teeth are chattering.'

'Then take off your dress and start walking. There's no one to see us and we'll die of lung fever if we don't get warm.' Caroline allowed her soaking garment to fall to the ground. She picked it up and looped it over her arm. 'Are you coming? Or are you going to spend the night on the beach?'

It was a long walk up the steep incline and they had to keep stopping to allow Grace to catch her breath, but eventually they reached the top of the island, and, as Caroline had said, there was a stone hut perched on a vantage point overlooking the whole bay. The storm had abated and in the moonlight the small building looked lonely and dilapidated. The door creaked and opened, although it hung precariously on one hinge, and Caroline stepped inside. There was no glass in the windows, and, judging by the smell, birds had obviously been nesting in the rafters, but it was shelter of a sort and reasonably warm. A shaft of moonlight filtered through the small windows, revealing wooden benches built along two of the longest walls.

'At least we can lie down.' Caroline heaved the door shut and clicked the latch into place. 'I'm almost dry after that walk. How about you, Grace?'

'I'm so tired I could sleep anywhere.' Grace sank

down on one of the benches. 'I suppose I should be thankful that we're alive, but I'm starving, and I keep thinking of that pie we took so much trouble to make.'

Caroline hooked her wet gown over one of the window frames and did the same with Grace's equally sodden dress. 'I'm hungry, too.'

Grace stretched out on the rough planks. 'How will we let them know where we are?'

'We could make a flag from our clothes. We'll think of something, and Freddie will see that the boat is gone. We've survived so far, haven't we?' Caroline eased herself onto the bench and lay back. She was certain that she would not sleep a wink on such an uncomfortable bed, but she was exhausted and she closed her eyes.

She awakened suddenly and found herself lying on the floor in a pile of dried moss and straw. For a moment she did not know where she was and then she remembered. She raised herself to a sitting position and glanced anxiously at Grace, who was still asleep although it was daylight and sunshine streamed through the windows. Caroline scrambled to her feet and stretched. Every bone in her body seemed to ache, but she was alive and for that she had to be thankful. She was also very hungry and she decided to leave Grace to sleep while she went outside to look for something to eat. Perhaps she would find some blackberries, although, born and bred in the city, she had very little knowledge of what she might find growing in the wild. She opened the door carefully so that she did not disturb Grace and went outside, taking deep breaths of the salty air and inhaling the scent of sea thrift. The tussocky grass was spangled with dew and the sun had risen, turning the distant sandstone cliffs to a deep crimson. Across the water she could see the square towers of the Abbey rising above the trees, and she wished she could fly like the gulls that soared effortlessly overhead, but that was just fantasy and she must be practical. She stood on the top of the treeless windswept island, trying to think of a way to attract the attention of those who were maddeningly near, and yet out of reach. A signal fire would certainly make someone on land sit up and take notice, but, lacking the means to light one, it was out of the question. A flag made out of her chemise might catch someone's eye, but they needed to get off the island quickly. Grace was still recovering from her injuries and they had neither food nor water.

Caroline decided to inspect the boat to find out if it was seaworthy. From her vantage point the waters looked calm enough and maybe she could scull across the narrow strip of sea using the remaining oar.

She made her way down the steep path to the beach, hoping that they had left the boat well above the high-water mark. It was there, but the bright sunlight revealed a huge hole where the rotting timbers had crunched on the stony foreshore. Despondent and desperate, she picked up the oar and returned to the hut.

Grace was wide awake and she attempted to stand, but sank down again on the hard wooden bench. 'Where have you been, Carrie? I thought you might have fallen over the cliff or something equally terrible.'

Caroline laid her hand on Grace's forehead. 'I think you have a fever.'

'It's hardly surprising after what we've been through.' Grace sat back against the rough stone wall. 'Where were you?'

'I went to see if the boat was seaworthy, but I'm afraid it came off badly when we were washed ashore. We'll just have to make a flag out of a petticoat or something. I've brought the oar with me as it's the only thing we could use as a flagstaff.'

'You're going to tie your chemise to an oar?' Grace began to giggle uncontrollably.

Caroline smiled. 'Well, it should attract someone's attention. Unless you have a better idea.'

'You'd best use mine, which is cotton and yours is silk.'

Caroline lifted Grace's dress from the window. 'This is almost dry. You should put it on.'

'I'm too hot as it is. Hang my dress on the pole, Carrie. I never liked that shade of yellow anyway, it makes me look sallow.'

'You sound just like Maria,' Caroline said, chuckling.

Grace lay down again, balancing precariously on her side. 'Do as I say, please, Carrie.' She closed her eyes.

Caroline covered Grace, using the offending yellow gown as a blanket, and left her to sleep. She took her own dress outside and tied it to the oar, which she stuck into the soft ground at the highest point on the island. Occasionally a playful breeze tugged at the long skirts, but at other times the air was still, and the dress dangled limply, steaming slightly in the warmth of the sun. Grace was feverish and kept calling out for something to slake her thirst, but Caroline was unable to help her. Despite searching every inch of the island she soon realised that there was no source of fresh water. She wished it would rain again, but the sky was an unrelenting blue and the heat was intense. There was little she could do other than to divide her time between her attempts to soothe Grace's feverish cries and keeping a lookout for a passing vessel. It was frustrating to see trains wending their way along the coastal line and being unable to attract the attention of anyone on board. She waved frantically at each one, but they were far away and she doubted if any of the passengers could see her.

The hours passed slowly and the sun was high in the sky, making it uncomfortable to sit outside for any length of time. Grace was babbling incoherently and the only relief that Caroline could offer was to snatch a handful of grass and wipe the minute residual drops of dew onto Grace's cracked lips. She had just done so and had gone outside to shake the grass from her hand, when she saw clouds swirling in from the west. A warm breeze ruffled her hair and for the first time in her life she prayed for rain. Then, as quickly as often happens in the middle of an English summer, the clouds darkened and giant spots of rain fell on her upturned face. She cupped her hands and held them up to collect as much of the life-giving water as was possible, moistening her own lips before attending to Grace. Having repeated this several times, Caroline stood outside allowing the rain to cool her hot body. It was only a passing shower, but the relief it had brought was huge. Then, just as her sense of optimism was returning, the sun broke through the clouds and it was even hotter than before.

Caroline was beginning to give up hope of being rescued when she spotted a boat heading for the cove. She snatched her dress from the oar and waved it frantically. In her excitement she had quite forgotten that she was wearing nothing but her chemise, and her stays were inside the hut where she had left them the previous evening. It might be Quick or Dickon standing in the bows, but at this moment she would have supped with the devil in order to get off the island.

'Halloo!' she shouted at the top of her voice. 'Halloo! We're here.' She dropped the soggy garment, raced down the path at a reckless speed, and arrived on the beach just as the vessel slid alongside the jetty. The relief of seeing another human being over-came all thoughts of modesty and she ran to meet her rescuer, coming to a sudden halt when she recog-nised the first man to step off the boat. It was only then that she realised her state of undress and she took a step backwards, folding her arms across her bosom.

'What are you doing here, Phineas?'

'We were all worried about you. I came down on the train with Raven and Freddie. I hoped to take you and Grace back to London with me.' Phineas took off his jacket and wrapped it around her. 'Are you all right?'

'I'm fine, but Grace is unwell. She's in the hut on top of the island.'

'Let's get you on board and you can tell us what happened later.'

Caroline stood her ground. 'No, we must get Grace first. I'll take you to her.'

'No, you won't.' Raven hurried up to them, followed by Freddie. 'Do as Phineas tells you, Caroline. I know the island well. We'll find Grace and bring her to you.'

'That's right.' Freddie patted her on the shoulder. 'Raven and I used to swim out here to escape our tutor. We know every inch of the place – we'll fetch Grace.'

'My gown,' Carrie whispered. 'I was using it as a flag. I can't go ashore in my shift.'

'Never mind that now.' Phineas boarded the boat first and held out his hand. 'Freddie will bring your gown, and I promise not to look.' His lips twitched and the twinkle in his eyes brought a blush to her cheeks.

'My mother would have forty fits if she could see me now,' she said, smiling ruefully as she took his hand and stepped onto the deck. 'How did you know we were here?'

'We found Quick and his friends sleeping off the effects of drinking everything they could lay their hands on in Freddie's cellar. We left the local police sergeant and a constable to deal with them.'

'Quick is a dangerous man,' Caroline said wearily. 'I think he might have killed Grace had he got his hands on her last night.'

'Raven said he'll press charges. They behaved like common criminals, breaking and entering, damaging private property and threatening you and Grace with bodily harm. That will do for a start.'

'But if they were dead drunk how did you know where to find us?'

'Freddie guessed that you'd escaped through the secret passage. He went to check and saw that the boat had gone.'

'We could have drowned.' Caroline's teeth were chattering, despite the heat. 'Grace is very poorly.'

Phineas slipped his arm around her shoulders and guided her to a seat. 'Sit down, Caroline. You've been through a nasty experience, and you need to rest.'

She collapsed on to the hard wooden bench. 'I need food, and a cup of tea wouldn't go amiss.'

He took a hip flask from his pocket and unscrewed the silver stopper. 'It's not tea, but this will help.' He held it to her lips, smiling gently. 'You gave us a fright, you know. Freddie knew that the rowing boat was in a poor state of repair. You and Grace were lucky it got you this far.'

Caroline coughed as the brandy hit the back of her throat, but the alcohol had an almost instantaneous effect and she began to feel better. 'The wind and tide helped, but I learned to row when I was a child, and I remember coming here for a picnic with Freddie. I think the sea must be in my blood, which is why I'll be a good business partner.'

Phineas handed her the flask. 'Have another sip. It's brought the roses back to your cheeks.'

She smiled up at him. 'Are you evading the issue? We are still partners, aren't we?'

'Why else would I have come all this way to find you?'

Caroline was inexplicably disappointed by Phineas' response. She took another sip of brandy, knowing that it was a mistake to drink on an empty stomach, but she was beginning to feel pleasantly light-headed.

'I thought perhaps you were worried about me,' she said recklessly. 'But then I know you have a block of ice where you heart should be – just like your grandmother. All you think about is profit and loss.' She was about to take yet another sip from the flask when Phineas snatched it from her.

'Maybe a cup of tea would have been a better option.' His lips were smiling but his eyes darkened, and he turned to help Freddie, who had made his way down the steep path with Grace held firmly in his arms. With Raven's assistance they managed to get her on board and sat her down next to Caroline.

'My gown,' she said anxiously. 'I can't go ashore like this.'

'It's all right, Caroline. I rescued a gown from your makeshift flagpole, and the other one was on the floor of the hut.' Raven tossed the garments to Phineas. 'Ready to cast off?'

'Yes, all aboard safely.' Phineas passed the dresses to Caroline. 'I wouldn't worry about what your mother would say. You look quite charming.'

'A gentleman would pretend he hadn't seen me in such an embarrassing situation.' She grabbed the gown and slipped it over her head before turning her attention to Grace.

'I'm a Colville,' he said drily. 'You've made your opinion of me and my family crystal clear.'

Freddie moved aside to make room for Raven as he leaped onto the deck. 'This is like old times, Raven. We used to come over to Bear Island all the time when we were boys. It's good to have you home.'

'I won't be staying much longer,' Raven said casually.

'But the Abbey still belongs to you.'

'It's yours for your lifetime. I don't think I could ever settle down to the life of a landed gentleman. You handle such matters much better than I do.' Raven slapped him on the shoulder. 'We'll talk about it over dinner this evening.'

Caroline cleared her throat. 'Excuse me, gentlemen. Aren't you forgetting something? Grace is poorly and I haven't eaten since noon yesterday.'

Freddie's face crumpled with concern. 'Poor Graziella. Don't worry, Carrie, she'll have the best possible care when we get her home. I'll make sure of that.'

'I should think so, too.' Caroline's attempt at a smile faded when she spotted her stays lying on the deck, and she whisked them up, placed them on the seat next to Grace and sat on them.

Phineas was at the wheel during the short trip to the harbour and, although she knew she owed him an apology, Caroline could not bring herself to speak to him. The insulting words had tumbled from her lips for no apparent reason, and it would have been easy to blame the alcohol, but she knew that was a half-truth. Deep down she still believed that Phineas was responsible for the collapse of her parents' business, and that his demands for repayment of the loan had contributed to her father's early demise. She glanced at him occasionally, wondering why he had chosen to accompany Raven and Freddie to Devon. She found it hard to believe that he had travelled all this way because he was worried about her personal safety, and she suspected his motive might have something to do with his proposed half-share in the *Esther Manning*. If he had changed his mind it would prove disastrous. She looked away, wishing she had held her tongue.

Grace stirred, raising her head and looking round dazedly. 'Water,' she murmured through cracked lips.

Freddie leaped forward, holding a flask to her lips. 'Don't worry, Carrie,' he said, catching her eye. 'It is water, nothing stronger.'

Grace drank thirstily. 'Thank you, Freddie,' she murmured, smiling. 'I'm starving.'

Freddie wrapped his arms around her, hugging her to him and rubbing his cheek in her salt-stiffened hair. 'Don't ever give me a fright like that again, Graziella. My nerves won't stand it.'

The Dorincourts' carriage was waiting at the harbour and the short journey back to the Abbey was uneventful. Freddie sent a groom to fetch the doctor and Caroline helped Grace to her room.

'I thought we would die on that wretched island,' Grace said wearily as Caroline helped her into her nightgown. 'Even if we were rescued, I was afraid that it might be Elias who came for us.'

'Don't think about him now. You'll be fine, Grace. I expect it's just a chill, but the doctor is on his way.'

'I've caused so much trouble. Perhaps you should

have let Elias take me, because I fear I will have to return to him sooner or later.'

'Indeed you won't. Freddie won't allow it and neither will I. We'll fight Quick through the courts if necessary, so stop thinking about him. Concentrate on getting better and remember that you have a daughter. Think of Maria.'

Grace nodded and closed her eyes. 'There's something you should know, Carrie.'

'Tell me later. I think I hear footsteps on the stairs. I expect it's the doctor.'

It was, as Caroline had suspected, a chill that Grace had caught from exposure to the elements, but nothing that could not be cured. The doctor left a bottle of laudanum and a list of instructions as to Grace's care and wellbeing, but Caroline already had everything in hand. She went straight to the kitchen and was horrified by the mess that Quick and his friends had left. They had eaten the pie that had been intended for Freddie, and they had strewn rubbish everywhere. It looked as though they had been throwing eggs at each other – the smashed shells were scattered all over the floor and yellow yolk ran down the walls. Mrs Duffin and the young housemaid were attempting to rectify matters, but they lacked direction and Caroline had little option other than to step in and organise their efforts. They had just finished when Freddie entered the room.

'I wondered where you were, Carrie,' he said,

gazing round at the spotless kitchen. 'You've done wonders.'

'I've had help.' Caroline nodded to Mrs Duffin. 'I sent Mary to the farm to fetch eggs, butter and milk, and if you would bring me vegetables and herbs from the kitchen garden, Mrs Duffin, I'll make some broth for Mrs Quick. We'll have an omelette.'

'Yes'm.' Mrs Duffin bobbed a curtsey. 'I could walk to the village and fetch bread, miss. They ruffians have ate everything in the larder.'

'Get what we need, Mrs Duffin.' Caroline waited until she heard the scullery door open and close. 'She's willing enough, Freddie. She's just a terrible cook.'

'You shouldn't be working in the kitchen, Carrie. Come and join us in the drawing room.'

'I will, when I've got the broth started. We all have to eat.'

Freddie gave her a searching look. 'You may think I'm a buffoon, my dear, but I noticed a coolness between you and Colville. Has he said anything to upset you?'

Caroline shook her head. 'On the contrary, Freddie, I was rude to him, which was unforgivable in the circumstances. I didn't mean to liken him to his grandmother, but she is such a tyrant.'

'He came with us because he was concerned about you, Carrie. I think the fellow likes you more than he lets on.'

'No. You're mistaken. Phineas Colville lives and

breathes business. If he was anxious about anything it would be pounds, shillings and pence. I suspect an ulterior motive, although I'm sure that Mama would handle company matters far better than I ever could.'

'Your mother is doing well, but her main concern is for your brothers. I think she feels that she has spent too little time with them in the past. She told me that she devoted all her time to working with Jack and her brother to make Manning and Chapman a success, but that now they're gone she doesn't feel the same enthusiasm for the business.'

'That's probably why Phineas came for me. I believe that he wants complete control of our company and he'll offer to buy us out.'

'He could do that anyway, Carrie. Some people would think it a good thing for all concerned and I'm sure he would be generous.'

'Whose side are you on, Freddie?'

'I'm strictly neutral in this matter, but I think you might be missing the point. Could it be that he cares just a little for you, my dear? I'm well versed in affairs of the heart – I've had enough in my lifetime. I think I know the signs and symptoms.'

'No, Freddie. You're quite mistaken.' Caroline turned away, unable to look him in the eye. 'Ours in a purely business arrangement.'

'If you say so, my dear. Anyway, I want to thank you for everything you've done for Grace. I intend to press charges against Quick, but I'll let Dickon off if he promises to join the army. I've had enough of that young man's conniving and posturing. He might be my son, but what he needs is discipline and that's what he'll get.'

'What about Jenifry?'

'She has the cottage, and I'll give her an allowance. I can do no more. She wasn't a child when we got together, and she has a husband somewhere in the background.'

'How does Grace fit in with your plans?'

A wry smile curved his lips. 'My intentions are strictly honourable. I will marry her as soon as she is free from that vicious brute.'

Caroline gave him a hug. 'You are a good man, Freddie. I love you as if you were my uncle. Anyway, I have work to do or no one will get fed today. I'd better see to the soup before Mrs Duffin has a chance to meddle.'

'Grace is a wonderful cook,' Freddie said wistfully. 'But of course it wouldn't do for her to work in the kitchen after we're married.'

'I'm sure she'll have time to train someone to take over from her.' Caroline managed to keep a straight face as she hurried from the room. Freddie was an improbable mixture of gallant knight and greedy little boy, but she would not hurt his feelings by telling him so.

'What's so funny?'

Caroline looked round to see Phineas coming towards her. 'It's just my odd sense of humour. It was nothing.'

His expression was grave. 'You can trust me, Caroline. I know we got off to a shaky start, but I really do have your best interests at heart.'

She met his serious gaze with a straight look. 'No, Phineas. Your family business comes first and foremost – the rest of us have to follow your lead.'

'I can see that you won't be persuaded otherwise.'

'I'm busy. I have work to do.'

'I've just been upstairs to see Grace. She insists that she'll come down to dinner tonight. Apparently she has something to tell us all that simply won't wait.'

Chapter Twenty-One

Grace refused to stay in bed and insisted on joining them for dinner that evening. Caroline had tried to dissuade her, but Grace was adamant.

'I can see that you have the Colville stubborn streak,' Caroline sighed, shaking her head. 'I'll help you to dress, but I really think you ought to obey the doctor's orders.'

'Phineas said that he intends to leave for London first thing tomorrow morning. What I have to say affects everyone. I've kept quiet for too long and it's time I spoke up. It's for your sake as well, Carrie. Believe me.'

'All right, but I think perhaps you ought to concentrate on sorting things out with Freddie. He's desperate for you to remain here.'

'I'll do that, too.'

*

The meal would have consisted mainly of the vegetable broth followed by an omelette, had Mrs Duffin
not been so determined to prove her worth. She had
gone in person to the nearby farm, and, if her account
were true, had selected and wrung the neck of the
chosen bird. Returning in triumph she had plucked
and prepared the chicken for the oven, acknowledging Caroline's praise with a sly grin. Grace would
have a battle on her hands if she decided to take
over the kitchen permanently, but it was her own
problems that were uppermost on Caroline's mind.
She had been away from her family for too long,
and she must return to London as soon as possible.

Having left Mrs Duffin and Mary to serve dinner,
Caroline stood with the ladle poised over the tureen,
waiting for everyone to be seated at the dining table.
Freddie insisted that Raven took his rightful place
at the head, and Grace sat on his right. With everyone
settled, Caroline began serving the soup, but was
interrupted by Grace, who rose to her feet.

'I have something very important to say.' She
reached for her wineglass and sipped, as if to give
her courage to continue. 'I'm only revealing this now
because I think it's absolutely necessary.'

'Speak up then, Grace,' Phineas said, smiling. 'I'm
glad you're feeling better, but be quick or the soup
will be cold.'

'This isn't a laughing matter.' Grace shot him a
baleful glance. 'I've kept this secret locked away in
my heart for over twenty years, but I have to tell

you now that I was young and very much in love with Maria's father.'

Caroline sank down on her chair. Whatever it was Grace had to say was obviously causing her a great deal of pain and Caroline was suddenly nervous. 'You don't have to do this, Grace. You've been through a terrible ordeal. Don't make things worse for yourself.'

'I have to tell you, Caroline. This affects you particularly, and you, Phineas, and Maria, my daughter.' She drank more wine, placing the glass on the table with a shaking hand. 'This isn't easy to say.'

'Come on, old girl,' Freddie said cheerfully. 'It can't be that bad, and I'm hungry.'

'I'd had a crush on Maria's father since I was fifteen,' Grace continued dreamily. 'We met occasionally at social events, and I imagined myself to be in love with him, even though I knew he was engaged to someone else.'

'It was a childish attachment,' Freddie said casually. 'I expect whoever it was felt flattered. I know I would be in similar circumstances.'

Phineas shot him a disapproving glance. 'Go on, Grace. You can't stop now.'

'One evening after my chaperone had been taken ill in the middle of a ball and she left early, the man I hero-worshipped took pity on me and escorted me home. Everyone was asleep, apart from the maid who let us in, and my parents always went to bed

on the stroke of ten.' Grace reached for her glass
and drained the last drop of wine. 'We'd both drunk
too much champagne, but he was about to leave
when I begged him to stay. I kissed him and he
kissed me back – I knew he didn't really want me,
but I was mad with love for him. I realised afterwards that what I'd done was wrong, and I was
ashamed, which is why I never told him that I
was with child.'

'Who was this fellow who took advantage of a
young and innocent girl?' Phineas demanded angrily.

'I told you that it was my fault, Phin. I take full
responsibility for my actions and I've paid for my
mistake over and over again.'

'Who was he, Grace?' Caroline found her voice
at last, but she had already guessed the answer to
her question.

'I'm so sorry, Caroline. It was your father, Jack
Manning. I promised myself I would never tell a
living soul, but now I see that I was wrong.'

'You should have told our father,' Phineas said
angrily. 'He would have made Manning face his
mistake and make reparation.'

'Essie will be heartbroken,' Raven said slowly. 'I
would have horsewhipped him, had I known.'

'Stop it, all of you,' Caroline cried passionately.
'What's done is done, and I have a sister.' She turned
to Grace with a watery smile. 'I knew from the start
that Maria was special.'

'Half-sisters.' Grace nodded tearfully. 'Your papa

wasn't to blame. I'm sure that he loved your mother with all his heart.'

'Raven is right,' Caroline said softly. 'My mother will be devastated.'

'It happened only once,' Grace insisted. 'It meant nothing to Jack.'

'That's easy for you to say now, Grace. But this changes everything.' Phineas turned to Caroline. 'You're related to the Colvilles whether you like it or not.'

'This has nothing to do with Caroline,' Raven said angrily. 'What Jack did was wrong, but he's not here to defend himself.'

'I agree.' Freddie reached for the decanter and refilled Grace's glass. 'It all happened twenty-odd years ago. Time to let it go.'

'Have you told Maria?' Caroline asked anxiously. 'She'll have to know.'

Grace shook her head. 'We've spent so little time together, and my problems with Elias have come between us. I want to make amends, but I don't know if she will want to see me again when she discovers the truth.'

Caroline shot a wary look in Phineas' direction. 'Don't worry, Phineas. I'm not a threat to the Colville shipping dynasty. I don't want anything to do with your wretched business.'

'We'll discuss this at a later date,' he said coldly. 'This isn't the time or the place.'

'I agree with Phineas.' Raven took the ladle from

Caroline's hand and filled her bowl with the steaming broth. 'As a concerned friend I would say that Essie's feelings ought to be considered before this becomes widely known.' He served himself before passing the tureen to Freddie.

'My mother will have to know before word gets out,' Caroline said worriedly. 'Heaven knows how Maria will take the news. Will you tell her, Phineas?'

'She's fond of you, Caroline, and I think it might be best if you tell her.' Phineas turned to Grace, shaking his head. 'You should have been honest from the start. Your silence hasn't helped anyone.'

'I am so sorry,' Grace whispered. 'I thought I was doing the right thing, but it seems that everything I do is wrong.'

'You were little more than a child at the time.' Freddie grasped her hand and held it to his cheek. 'Jack should have known better, although I must say I'm surprised to hear that he behaved so badly. I was a young reprobate, but Jack always struck me as being the epitome of a solid citizen.'

Raven cleared his throat. 'I suggest we leave the matter there and enjoy our meal. I intend to return to London in the morning. Will you come with me, Caroline?'

She nodded. 'Yes, I will.'

'I'll travel with you.' Phineas held his hand out to take the tureen from Freddie, and he ladled a generous helping into Grace's bowl. 'You must keep your strength up, Grace. We aren't here to judge you.' He turned his head to give Caroline a steady glance. 'And we mustn't allow this to affect our business agreement.'

She met his intense gaze with an equally cold stare. The warmth had gone from their relationship and it was like looking into the eyes of a stranger. 'No,' she said dully. 'I agree. As always, Colville Shipping comes first.'

Caroline barely slept that night and was up early. Grace and Freddie opted to remain at the Abbey while Raven, Phineas and Caroline were to travel to London by train.

Conversation was brief during the journey, each of them apparently immersed in their own thoughts. Grace had begged Caroline to tell Maria of their close relationship as soon as possible, and, albeit reluctantly, she had agreed. But how she would break the news to her mother was something that Caroline hardly dared imagine. Phineas had been quiet during the journey, but Caroline sensed that he, too, was disturbed by Grace's admission. Raven slept most of the time, waking only when the train pulled into Waterloo Bridge Station. They shared a cab to Wapping where Phineas alighted outside his office, leaving Raven and Caroline to travel on to the Captain's House, where she hoped to find her mother.

The sparkling clean windows seemed to wink in the sunlight as if the old captain was welcoming her home when Caroline ascended the steps to the front door, followed by Raven. She had always felt comfortable here, and, despite being the bearer of such shocking news, it was no different now. It was high water and the wharfs on both sides of the river were hives of activity – cranes worked tirelessly, hefting goods from the lighters tied up alongside. The shouts of the dock workers were all but drowned out by the sound of barrels rolling over cobblestones, and the flapping of stays and the hoots of steamships. The door to the Captain's House was only locked last thing at night and Caroline knocked and entered, certain of a welcome.

'It's a long time since I was last here,' Raven said thoughtfully. 'I should have returned to London long ago, if only for a brief visit.'

'Well, you're here now. I'm sure that Mama will be delighted to see you. She's often spoken of you.'

'Really? Nothing bad, I hope?'

'Of course not. I think she was very fond of you.' Caroline opened the door and stepped inside. Sadie popped out of the front parlour with a big smile on her face, putting Caroline in mind of the little wooden lady on a weather house that her father had brought back from Germany. The happy little woman only came out when the sun was shining. Today it was glorious outside, but Caroline could feel a big black cloud looming over them.

'It's good to see you, Carrie.' Sadie gave her a hug, but her eyes widened when she saw Raven.

'Good Lord! You're the last person I expected to walk through my door, Raven Dorincourt.'

He kissed her on the forehead. 'How are you, Sadie? Although I hardly need to ask. The years have been kind to you.'

Sadie flapped her apron at him, spots of colour staining her cheeks. 'Oh, get on with you.'

'No, I mean it. You were a skinny little thing when I first met you, but now you're a handsome woman, Sadie Dixon.'

'Soon to be Mrs Laurence Bromley,' Sadie said smugly.

'I must congratulate the lucky man,' Raven said smoothly. 'I hope he is worthy of you, Sadie.'

She giggled, blushing like a girl. 'Shut up, Raven. I know it's Essie you've come to see, but she's at the office.' She led the way to the kitchen with Caroline close on her heels.

'Is Jimmy well now?' Caroline asked anxiously.

'Fully recovered, I'm glad to say. Quite back to his old mischievous self.'

'It's very quiet.' Caroline glanced at the clock above the range. 'It's time for lunch, but surely they aren't studying on a day like this?'

'Laurence has given them all a holiday, and he's taken your brothers and the two new boys, who started yesterday, on a fishing trip upriver.'

'It's good that Laurence has new pupils, but it seems a strange time for them to start,' Caroline said, momentarily diverted.

'To tell the truth I think their parents simply wanted them out of the way.' Sadie heaved a sigh and her eyes darkened. 'If I had children I would want to keep them with me.'

'They're in safe hands with you, Sadie.'

'Of course they are. I'll look after the little souls as if they were my own. Anyway, where are my manners, Raven? I'm sure you'd like something to eat and drink.' She filled the kettle and replaced it on the hob.

Caroline was about to speak when the door that led on to the back yard opened and a young girl staggered in, carrying a bucket filled with coal.

'Shut the door, Edna. Put the scuttle down and fetch the gingerbread from the larder, there's a good girl.' Sadie waited until Edna had disappeared into the larder. 'I got her from the orphanage. She's a bit simple, but she's willing.' She beamed at Edna, who reappeared carrying a plate of cake. 'Put it on the table, please.'

'Yes'm.' Edna placed the plate in front of Raven and stood stiffly to attention.

'Thank you,' Raven said, smiling.

Edna's freckled face flushed scarlet and she giggled.

'Go and see to the boys' rooms, Edna. Then you can come down for your luncheon.' Sadie sent the girl off with a wave of her hand. 'I'm training her,' she said, smiling. 'Who would have thought that Sadie Dixon would one day have a servant of her own?'

Raven cleared his throat. 'The gingerbread looks

very tempting. I'll help myself, if you don't mind.'

Caroline shook her head when he offered her the plate. She had other things on her mind than food. 'Have you seen Maria recently, Sadie?' she asked urgently. 'Did she marry her sea captain?'

'No, dear. She decided to remain in London. She's been staying in Mr Colville's house in Princes Square. Such a lot has happened in a very short time.'

Raven pulled up a chair and sat down, stretching out his long legs. 'I've missed all this while I've been living a bachelor existence in Bendigo.'

'It was your choice.' Sadie bustled about taking cups and saucers from the dresser. 'I always thought you and Essie would make a match of it, but you didn't.' She reached for the teapot. 'Where was I? Oh, yes, I remember now. I was saying that the company couldn't find a replacement for Theo, and Maria was supposed to travel down to Dover to get married, but she changed her mind. A good thing, too, if you ask me.'

'I don't suppose that Captain Reid had anything to do with her change of heart?'

'He is rather dashing, apart from being related to the Colvilles, which makes him quite a catch, and they do seem to get on very well together.' Sadie threw back her head and laughed. 'Oh, to be young again. Mind you, I prefer to be my age and have all that silliness behind me. Laurence and I have named the day and the first of the banns was read last Sunday. At my age I can't afford to wait.'

'You're not old, Sadie. What are you, thirty-two or thirty-three?'

'My mother was a grandmother at thirty-two. Would you like some more gingerbread, Raven? I've just made another batch – the boys love it.'

'I haven't tasted gingerbread for years,' Raven said, smiling. 'My cook in Bendigo is an ex-convict and has only just mastered the basics.'

Caroline took a seat at the table. 'I have something to tell you, Sadie. Although I really wanted to tell Mama first, but you'll know soon enough.'

Sadie's smile faded. 'What is it, dear? You're not sick, are you? Has anything happened to Grace or Freddie?'

'No, I'm well and so are the others, but this concerns Grace and Maria.'

Caroline repeated what Grace had told them the previous evening, and when she finished speaking there was a moment of stunned silence.

'Well, I never did.' Sadie shook her head. 'Who would have thought it of Jack? He loved your mother so much, I can't believe that he'd do a thing like that.' She dabbed her eyes with her apron. 'It will break Essie's heart. She mustn't know, Carrie. Don't tell her.'

'It's no use,' Caroline said gently. 'Now that Grace has let her secret out there's no stopping it. Maria will have to know and it would be cruel to keep it from my mother. I dread telling her, but I feel I must tell Mama first.'

Sadie stood up, ripping off her apron. 'Then I'm coming with you. Essie will need her friends standing by her.' She glowered at Raven. 'You were Essie's friend – you'd better come as well.'

Sidney Masters was seated in his usual position at the front desk. The office looked neat and clean, but there was none of the hustle and bustle Caroline remembered from the old days when she had come to visit her father and mother. Masters greeted her with a wary look, as if expecting trouble, but he relaxed a little when she made it plain that she had come to see her mother. He rose stiffly from his chair.

'I'll just check to see if it's convenient, Miss Manning.'

Caroline was too nervous to wait. 'It's all right, Mr Masters. She won't be too busy to see us.' She walked past him and let herself into the main office, which had once been the centre of their shipping operation – the walls covered with charts and lists of ship movements, and clerks working at their desks. Esther sat in solitary state behind the desk where Ezra Parkinson had once ruled the department. She rose to her feet, smiling and holding out her hands as she walked towards them.

'Caroline, darling.' She came to a sudden halt when she saw Raven. 'No, I don't believe it. What are you doing all this way from Bendigo?' She rushed past Caroline to grasp Raven's hands. 'You're really here?'

'Are you pleased to see me, Essie?'

The warmth in his voice and the teasing smile in his eyes as he raised her hands to his lips came as yet another shock. Caroline had been used to seeing her parents together, but now she was seeing her mother in a new light. Until this moment Esther Manning had been a mother figure, slightly remote during Caroline's younger days, but much loved and respected. It came as a surprise to realise that men still found her mother attractive, and Sadie had a smug smile on her face, as if she was party to a well-kept secret. Caroline was intrigued.

'Why didn't you let me know that you were coming, Raven?' Esther demanded, breaking free from his grasp. 'Has my pa come with you? And what about Falco, the old rogue?'

'They'll be here in a few days' time. I left the ship to visit Freddie, and became embroiled in the most bizarre set of circumstances involving your daughter and people who were complete strangers to me.'

'Dear me, how fascinating. Sit down everyone and tell me what's been happening?' Flushed and looking suddenly ten years younger, Esther motioned Caroline and Sadie to take a seat while she led Raven to the chair reserved for important clients. 'Who is going to speak first?'

Caroline met Raven's quizzical glance with a frown. 'I have something to tell you, Mama. But perhaps it would be better if we leave it until later.'

Sadie nudged her in the ribs. 'No, it won't. Essie doesn't need to hear this second-hand.'

Esther resumed her seat behind the desk. 'It can't be so very bad, darling. We've been through so much recently, what could be worse than losing my dear husband, my home and having to rely on the Colvilles for business?'

'This concerns the Colvilles, Mama.' Caroline began tentatively, but somehow she could not bring herself to say anything that would spoil her mother's obvious happiness on being reunited with such an old friend.

'There's no way to say this other than to come out with the truth, Essie.' Raven leaned forward, reaching across the desk to take Esther's hand in his. 'Last evening, at dinner, Grace told us that Jack was Maria's father. I'm sorry, but it happened before you were married, and, according to Grace, it was a brief moment of drunken madness, for which she has paid a terrible price.'

Esther's cheeks paled and her eyes widened. She gazed at Raven, shaking her head. 'No. I don't believe it. Jack wouldn't – he couldn't have – not Jack.'

'I was going to tell you, Mama,' Caroline murmured. 'I'm sorry, but I'm afraid it is true. Maria is my half-sister.'

'You're wrong.' Esther shook her head, her eyes magnified by unshed tears. 'Jack loved me.'

'He did,' Raven nodded emphatically. 'He was a good man, Essie. You were happy with him, weren't you? Tell me that you were.'

'Of course she was, Raven.' Sadie jumped to her

feet. 'They were well suited and it was a happy home until Jack got into financial trouble.'

Esther snatched her hand away and rose unsteadily to her feet. 'I want you all to go. Leave me on my own. I have to think.' She began pacing the floor, wringing her hands. 'It can't be true. Maria can't be Jack's daughter.'

Caroline was about to argue when the door burst open and Phineas strode into the office. 'Go away, please, Phin,' she said urgently. 'My mother is very upset.'

'Upset?' Esther was trembling visibly as she spun round to face Phineas. 'Your family are to blame for all our ills. I hate you, Phineas Colville. I loathe the very sight of you.'

Raven leaped to his feet and wrapped his arms around Esther, holding her despite her struggles to free herself. 'Calm down, Essie,' he said softly. 'It's not this man's fault.'

'Yes, it is. He loaned money to Jack and then demanded it back when he could see that we were in trouble. Jack might still be here had the Colvilles not put pressure on him to repay his debt.'

'That's not entirely true,' Phineas said icily. 'I came to talk business, but I see that you are out of sorts and perhaps we should leave it until another day.'

Esther broke free from Raven's arms, holding her head high. 'I've just learned that my husband was Maria's father. I don't want anything to do with you or your family.'

'I know, and I'm truly sorry, Mrs Manning,' Phineas said gently. 'It came as a shock to all of us.'

'I don't want your sympathy,' Esther cried passionately. 'Your family have been the ruin of us.'

Caroline had had enough. She felt her mother's pain, but this was not the time to fall out with Phineas. She could only hope that he had forgiven her for her ill-judged remarks on the day of the rescue from Bear Island. She stepped in between them.

'As my mother is clearly upset, I think you'd better deal with me, Mr Colville.'

'You are not the head of the company, Caroline,' Esther said icily. 'That dubious honour falls to me.'

'That's something we need to discuss at a later date, Mama. But we have a ship in dock, as yet without a cargo and it's losing us money. Phineas has agreed to help, and if we don't act soon we will lose what little we have.' She met Raven's enquiring look with a lift of her chin. 'Would you be kind enough to take my mother home?'

A gleam of admiration lit his blue eyes and he smiled. 'I think that's eminently sensible, but where is home?'

'I offered them a house in Great Hermitage Street,' Phineas said calmly. 'I've had it cleaned from top to bottom and it might suit as a temporary base. It's unfurnished at the moment, but that could easily be rectified.'

'Great Hermitage Street.' Raven frowned. 'I think

I know it and it's not the sort of area that would suit Mrs Manning.'

'I can speak for myself,' Esther protested. 'I don't need you to tell me what I can and cannot do, Raven. I've been staying with Alice at Bearwood House, and that's where I intend to go now.'

'You should, by rights, own the Captain's House,' Sadie said in a low voice.

'Nonsense.' Esther turned on her with an angry frown. 'It was I who advised Jack to leave it to you. Anyway, it would have been sold to pay off our creditors had it not been your property. You are part of my family, Sadie, and we look after each other.'

Sadie nodded. 'You'll always have a roof over your head while I live there, Essie. I'll never let you down.'

Phineas made a move towards the doorway. 'You don't have to worry about your ship, Mrs Manning. A cargo will be found and the crew will be paid.'

'And I'm sure whatever you do will be for the benefit of your own company,' Esther said angrily. 'I neither trust nor like you, Phineas Colville. I know who my friends are and that doesn't include you.'

Caroline opened her mouth to protest but Raven forestalled her. He tucked Esther's hand in the crook of his arm. 'This is getting us nowhere, my dear. Maybe you could stay with Alice for a few more days while we look for somewhere more suitable.'

'All right.' Esther turned to Carrie. 'Do what you

must, but I want nothing more to do with the company. I'm handing it over to you, Caroline. It's caused me nothing but grief.' She marched out of the office, leaving a shocked silence in her wake.

Raven was the first to recover. 'A sensible decision,' he said firmly. 'Don't worry, Caroline. I'm sure that your mother will see things differently when she's calmed down.' He patted Sadie on the shoulder. 'Essie will be all right. I'll look after her.'

Sadie managed a tight little smile. 'You always knew how to handle her. I was convinced from the start that she was too spirited for Jack, and she would have done much better to marry you.'

'I was a fool to let her go.'

Caroline stared at him in surprise. 'You and my mother?'

He smiled ruefully. 'It was a long time ago, and I was chasing rainbows, but I never discovered the rainbow's end, and perhaps I never will.' He strode out of the office, calling to Esther to wait.

'I'd best get home, too,' Sadie said hastily. 'I have to prepare supper for Laurence and the boys. Will you join us, Carrie?'

'I suppose I ought to go to Bearwood House and make things right with Mama, but I must see Maria first.'

Sadie straightened her bonnet and looped her shawl around her shoulders. 'The boys will be disappointed if you don't stay with us. I've kept your room in readiness.'

'Thank you, I will, but Mr Colville and I have some business to discuss, and then I have to find Maria.' Caroline shot a sideways glance at Phineas. 'I think I owe you an apology.'

'I'll see you at supper.' Sadie walked to the door, but, before she could reach out for the handle the door opened and Masters rushed into the room.

'Miss Dixon, there's a young girl here who says she's got an urgent message for you. Something about an accident upriver.'

Chapter Twenty-Two

'Laurence!' Sadie shrieked, heading for the door. 'And the boys.'

'Oh, no.' Caroline hurried after her. 'Wait, Sadie. We don't know it's their boat.'

Sadie was already in the outer office and she grabbed the young girl by the shoulders. 'Tell me what happened.'

The child's eyes almost popped out of her head as Sadie shook her. 'Pa hires out the boats,' she said on a sob. 'Number 5 was late coming back and then we had news that it was turned turtle in the shallows upriver.'

Sadie uttered a strangled cry. 'How far upriver? We need to know. Tell me, you stupid child.'

'Stop shaking me, lady. Me brains will be addled.'

'That won't help.' Caroline put her arms around

the terrified child. 'Did they tell you where they'd seen the upturned boat?'

'On the foreshore, close to Battersea Park. Don't let the madwoman get me, miss.'

Phineas stepped forward. 'I'll take you there, Caroline. My steam launch will get us there quickly.'

'You're prepared to help us?' Caroline stared at him in surprise. 'Even after I was so horrible to you.'

'Don't waste time talking,' Phineas said briskly. He bent down so that he was more on the child's level. 'What's your name?'

'Who cares? Sadie gasped. 'Hurry.'

'It's Rose, sir.'

'Do you know the exact spot, Rose?'

'Yes, sir. I think so.'

Phineas took her by the hand. 'Show us the way and I promise to pay for the repairs to your pa's boat.'

Caroline grabbed Sadie by the arm. 'They'll be fine, I know they will. Come on, Sadie.'

Despite Phineas' assertion that his launch would get them upriver faster than any other means of transport, the steamer puttered along at a maddeningly slow speed, belching smoke from a single funnel amidships. Phineas took the helm and Rose stood in the bows like a figurehead on a sailing ship, puffed up with importance as the designated lookout.

Caroline sat beside Sadie, trying hard to keep up her spirits, although inside she was just as anxious. Her only comfort was the fact that Papa had insisted on teaching both Max and Jimmy to swim. If, for whatever reason, their craft had capsized, the boys should have been able to get ashore. The long hot summer had kept the water levels low, and the Thames slithered towards the sea like a sleepy serpent.

Caroline tried to think positive thoughts, focusing her mind on Max and Jimmy and willing them to survive, while Phineas steered the boat expertly through the busy river traffic. The steam-powered engine battled valiantly against the ebb tide and they had almost reached the newly built Albert Bridge when Rose called out, pointing frantically. Caroline turned her head and saw the unmistakable shape of an upturned rowing boat, stranded above the high-water mark on the south side of the river.

Sadie stood up, causing the craft to rock dangerously and Phineas ordered her to sit down. Caroline had expected an argument, but Sadie subsided onto the wooden seat, clamping her hands over her mouth. It was an agonising few minutes before they reached the rickety wooden jetty. Rose leaped ashore like a young gazelle and Caroline followed more cautiously with Sadie clutching her sleeve. Phineas made the boat safe before joining them on the muddy foreshore.

'There's no sign of them. Where could they be?' Sadie looked round, pale faced and desperate.

Caroline bit her lip to prevent herself from crying. The hull of the boat was a stark reminder that the deceptively calm waters were deep and dangerous with hidden currents.

Phineas laid a hand on her shoulder. 'I don't know how this happened, but the structure isn't damaged, so it doesn't look as though they were involved in an accident.' He turned to Rose. 'Who reported seeing this?'

She shook her head. 'I dunno who he was, guv. A boy come running into the office downriver and told my pa. He got tuppence for his trouble.'

'Did he say he'd seen anyone near the boat?' Phineas asked gently. 'Can you remember anything else he said?'

'No, sir. He were a bit of a simpleton, if you ask me. He had big sticking-out teeth and ears. My gran would have said that only a mother could love a face like that.'

Rose's words brought a reluctant smile to Caroline's face and she could see that Phineas was also amused, although he managed to keep a straight face. 'Thank you, but if you think of anything, please tell one of us.'

Caroline turned away. 'If they made it to the shore they can't be too far away. Can they?'

Phineas shrugged. 'It depends how long the boat was in the water and how far upstream it was when it capsized.' He glanced over the hedge. 'That's Battersea Park. It might be worth making enquiries to see if anyone has seen them.'

'They're drowned,' Sadie said dully. 'Otherwise they'd be here, or making their way home.'

'Or in the dead house,' Rose added. 'My gran told me about them. They stack the corpses on shelves like wet fish and wait for someone to claim the bodies.'

Sadie gave her a withering look. 'Your gran has a lot to say for herself, young lady.'

'I suggest we take a quick look in the park,' Caroline said hastily. 'We can't search the whole river.'

'I agree. We should split up and meet back here, but we can't take too long or the fire will have gone out in the boiler and it takes a devil of a long time to get up steam.' Phineas headed for a break in the hedge, leaving the others little option other than to follow him.

Caroline and Rose walked the twisting paths, stopping anyone they saw to make enquiries, but Sadie ran on ahead, shouting Laurence's name at the top of her voice, and Phineas strode off in the opposite direction. All too soon Caroline realised that there were no witnesses and they were wasting time. Phineas gathered them together and, hot, tired and dispirited, they made their way back to the boat.

'We can't give up yet,' Sadie said tearfully.

'We could search all day and still be in the wrong place.' Phineas untied the painter and climbed on board. 'We'll take Rose back to her father and I'll make sure that the authorities are alerted. We can do no more than that.'

Caroline pressed Sadie down on the seat. 'We'll find them. Max and Jimmy are strong swimmers and I'm sure that Laurence will have made sure they were all safe.'

Sadie nodded dully. 'Maybe they'll be waiting at home.'

Caroline glanced at Phineas, hoping he might agree, but he was focused on getting the engine back to full throttle.

Rose had been reluctant to go ashore and Caroline suspected that she had enjoyed the adventure, but Phineas delivered her safely to her father and returned to the launch looking even more serious than before.

'No news, I'm afraid, but Rose's father has reported the matter to the Thames River Police.'

'Is there nothing else we can do?' Caroline asked anxiously.

'If anyone comes forward with information we'll be notified.' Phineas resumed his position at the helm. 'Who knows? They might be at home waiting for you.'

Despite his optimism, it was a largely silent journey back to Wapping. When they disembarked

Phineas helped Caroline ashore, holding her hand in a firm clasp. 'They will be found,' he said in a low voice. 'Don't give up.'

She met his unsmiling gaze with a nod. 'I won't.'

'We need to talk business, but this isn't a good time.'

'I agree.' Caroline glanced at Sadie, who was standing on the wharf, staring into the water. 'I'd better take her home. I'll stay with her until we have news, but I don't want my mother to hear about this, at least not yet. I won't tell her what's happened unless it's absolutely necessary.'

He raised her hand to his lips. 'The weather was good. There haven't been any reports of an accident upriver, so there's every reason to hope for the best.'

Caroline was about to withdraw her hand but he tightened his grasp. 'I just wanted to say that you mustn't worry about the company. As far as I'm concerned you are a Colville, whether you like it or not. That makes you one of us and entitled to your fair share of everything.'

She snatched her hand away, raising it to her cheek. 'I can't think about that now.'

'I understand. What I'm saying is that you are assured of an income. A cargo will be found for your ship, but nothing will be done without your approval.'

'Thank you.' She hesitated, frowning as the memory of Grace's confession came back to her. 'I need to see Maria.'

'Your sister is safe in Princes Square with Gilbert dancing attendance. He's on leave until the *Esther Manning* is ready to sail, and another day isn't going to make any difference. You need to rest.'

'Why are you being so kind?' Caroline demanded. 'I don't think I know this Phineas Colville.'

'I'm not all bad, Caroline. Maybe if you get to know me better you might begin to like me.'

'Sadie is waiting for me. I must go.' Caroline hurried after Sadie, who had set off at a brisk pace, and was breaking into a run.

'They might be at home,' she muttered breathlessly when Caroline caught up with her. 'I must start supper anyway. They'll be hungry. Maybe I'll have time to bake. Laurence and the boys love my ginger-bread, or I might make a chocolate cake.'

Caroline could not resist the temptation to glance over her shoulder, and, as she had half hoped, Phineas was standing very still, staring after her.

The Captain's House was filled with the aroma of baking. Sadie had thrown herself into a cooking frenzy as if, by doing so, she could tempt Laurence and the boys to return home. A large pan of beef stew simmered on the hob, the cake was in the oven and bread dough was set aside to prove. Caroline had given up her attempts to comfort Sadie and, as her offer to help had been rebuffed, she made her way up to the attic and stepped out onto the balcony. It was early evening, but the heat was still intense. It radiated out of the bricks and the cobble-stones, and the breeze that followed the incoming tide fanned her cheeks with unusual warmth. She had visited the Thames River Police station and had left her name and address with the desk sergeant, but there was still no news of Laurence and the boys. She felt a presence in the room behind her, but a quick glance over her shoulder revealed nothing out of the ordinary. Perhaps the shadows were a little deeper, or it might be that her imagi-nation was playing tricks on her – or, maybe, the old captain was as anxious as she herself. The sun was low in the sky, and midsummer's eve was a distant memory; summer was almost over and soon it would be autumn.

She felt a shiver run down her spine and she sighed. The events of the day had left her exhausted both mentally and physically. She had discovered a sister, but she might have lost her much-loved brothers. She closed her eyes and prayed silently for their safe return. Then, as if by a miracle, she heard Jimmy's unmistakable voice calling her name, followed by a chorus of shouts. She opened her eyes and leaned over the railing. Down below, on the muddy foreshore, she saw a rowing boat crammed with people. Jimmy was waving frantically and then she spotted Rose, who leaped out first, followed by Jimmy and then Max – she did not wait to see more. Picking up her skirts she raced downstairs, calling out to Sadie as she wrenched the front door open.

Jimmy arrived first, throwing himself into her arms, followed by Max. Two small boys followed, accompanied by Laurence, and Rose hovered at the foot of the steps, gazing up at them with a huge grin on her face.

'Come in, everyone.' Caroline had to shout to make herself heard. She beckoned frantically to Rose and the tall, thin man she had seen at the boatyard, who must be Rose's father.

Sadie was hugging Laurence with tears running down her cheeks and the small entrance hall was crowded with people, large and small, hugging, crying and laughing.

'Come inside, please.' Caroline shooed the boys into the kitchen. She held out her hand to Rose's father. 'Thank you for bringing them home, Mr . . .? I'm sorry, I don't know your name.'

He shook her hand. 'Ted Munday, miss.'

'I'm Caroline Manning. Do come into the kitchen, Mr Munday. You must need a rest after rowing all the way from Chelsea.'

'I'm used to it, Miss Manning.'

'My pa is a champion rower, miss,' Rose said proudly.

Sadie released Laurence, wiping her eyes on her pinafore. 'I don't know how you did it, sir, but you've brought my intended home. I thought I was widowed before I was a bride.'

Laurence patted her on the shoulder. 'There, there, Sadie. It wasn't as bad as that.'

'Maybe not for you.' Sadie slapped him on the arm. 'We were worried sick, weren't we, Carrie?'

'Yes, we were. Anyway, why are we standing here? You must all be hungry and Sadie has made enough stew to feed an army. There's chocolate cake to follow.'

'I must have known it was going to be all right,' Sadie said happily. She hurried off in the direction of the kitchen, dragging Laurence by the hand. 'Don't ever give me a fright like that again, Laurence Bromley.'

'I really should be getting home.' Ted Munday held his hand out to his daughter. 'Come on, Rosie. We don't want to keep these good folk from their supper.' He grinned ruefully. 'It does smell good.'

'I'm hungry, Pa,' Rose protested. 'We only got bread and a heel of cheese for supper.'

'Hush, Rosie. You don't tell people things like that.'

'Please join us,' Caroline said, smiling. 'We owe you that at least for bringing the boys home safely. I can't thank you enough.'

'Well, if you're sure.'

'She's sure, Pa.' Rose tugged at his hand. 'Follow the pretty lady, Pa, or those boys will have scoffed the lot.'

Food came first. It was obvious that Laurence and the boys were famished, as were Ted and Rose. The stew vanished like summer lightning, mopped up with bread still warm from the oven. The cake disappeared almost as quickly, although it seemed that bellies large and small were stretched almost to capacity as the boys licked the last delicious crumbs from their sticky fingers.

'That was the best cake I've ever tasted.' Ted beamed at Sadie. 'Thank you, Miss Dixon. I haven't eaten a meal like that since my wife passed away four years ago.'

'I'm glad you enjoyed it,' Sadie said briskly. She turned to Laurence, who was pouring boiling water into the teapot. 'Now that we've finished our meal, I want to know what happened and why we've been left to worry all day.'

He placed the teapot on the table and sat down. 'I'm not quite sure how it happened, Sadie. One minute we were fishing happily . . .'

'And then a paddle steamer came downriver,' Max added without giving Laurence a chance to finish. 'I don't think the captain saw us because we were partly hidden by a weeping willow.'

'That's just about it,' Laurence said, nodding. 'We were caught in the wash and I was standing in the bows. I overbalanced and fell in and the boys tried to pull me on board, but our combined weight and the turbulence left by the paddle steamer, caused the boat to turn turtle.'

'We had to swim for the bank.' Jimmy wiped his mouth on the back of his hand. 'Can I have another slice of cake, please?'

'It's "May I have another slice of cake, please?"'
Laurence said severely. 'You know that, Jimmy.'

The two young boarders sniggered, but were
quelled by a warning look from Sadie. She cut the
last slice of cake into four, handing the boys a piece
each. 'That's enough for tonight,' she said severely.

Caroline smiled at the two small boys. 'It's Billy
and David, isn't it?'

'Yes, miss,' they chorused.

'It's lucky that both of you could swim.'

'I can,' Billy said proudly. 'But David never learned.
Mr Bromley helped us to the bank.'

'The river currents can be dangerous in that
stretch.' Ted accepted a cup of tea. 'You did well to
get the lads ashore, sir.'

'What happened then?' Caroline asked eagerly.
'Was there anyone around to help you?'

Laurence shook his head. 'No, we were soaked
to the skin and the tide took the boat downstream.
We had to walk, which is why it took so long to
get to Ted's yard. I had to let him know what
happened to his boat.'

'The bailers will come in now, for sure,' Rose said,
sighing. 'The bailers take everything you've got. Pa
said so.'

Ted frowned at her, shaking his head. 'You mean
"the bailiffs".' He glanced round the table, his face
flushing beneath his tan. 'It's not quite as bad as
that, but business has been poor recently.'

'Pa used to go to sea,' Rose said proudly. 'He

sailed in big ships, like the ones out there on the river.'

Sadie took a sip of tea, eyeing Ted curiously. 'Did you have a fancy for life ashore?'

'My wife took sick and passed away.' Ted stared down into his cup. 'There was nobody to care for my little girl.'

'I ain't so little now, Pa,' Rose said, puffing out her chest. 'I can handle a boat better than them boys.'

Caroline could see that Jimmy was about to argue. 'You've done a wonderful job of raising your daughter, Ted. She's a credit to you.'

'And it's high time she was tucked up in bed. Thank you for the wonderful meal.' Ted pushed his chair back and stood up. 'We're going home, Rosie.'

'We must do something to pay for the loss of your boat,' Laurence said hastily. 'But I'm afraid you might have to wait while we raise the money.'

'I'll salvage it as best I can, sir. Anyway, it's not the first time it's happened. That's the trouble when you let people take boats on the water who aren't used to the river, present company excepted, of course,' Ted added. 'You were just unlucky.'

'I'll see you out, Ted.' Caroline followed him to the door with Rose clutching her hand. She bent down and dropped a kiss on the child's coppery curls. 'You did well today, Rose. Thank you.'

'Good night, miss.' Ted held his hand out to his daughter. 'Let's get going, love.'

Caroline watched father and daughter as they made their way down the front steps and she had a sudden idea. She hurried after them. 'I'm part owner of the *Esther Manning*. If you should decide to return to sea, I'm sure we could find room for a man of your experience.'

Ted's lined features creased into a grin. 'I worked for your rivals, miss. I started as a seaman on the *Colville Star* when I was little more than a boy – worked my way up to third mate. But I won't leave my girl. She's more important to me than money.'

'If you change your mind you know where to come, Ted.' Caroline shook his hand. 'Good luck.' She retraced her steps and found Sadie standing over Billy and David as they washed their hands and faces at the kitchen sink.

'That's the last time I let you take these children fishing, Laurence Bromley.' Sadie shot a sideways glance at Laurence. 'It'll take me days to get their clothes washed and dried. They stink of river mud.'

Laurence smiled vaguely. 'It was a lesson well learned. I'll keep clear of willow trees if I take a boat upriver again.'

'You'll stay on land from now on.' Sadie glared at him, arms akimbo. 'You scared me half to death.'

'I'm going outside to smoke my pipe, dear.' Laurence stood up, stretched and strolled out of the kitchen.

Sadie shook her head. 'Men! They're all the same and we women get stuck with all the work.'

She scrubbed David's face with a coarse towel. 'That'll do. Take your brother upstairs, Billy. I'll come up and tuck you in later.' She advanced on Jimmy, brandishing a flannel, but he snatched it from her.

'I can wash myself, thank you, Sadie.' He went to the sink and splashed about in the water.

'I'll bet they have a proper bathroom at Bearwood House,' Max said, backing away. 'Don't come near me with that wet flannel. I'd rather go to the public bath house.'

'You're a spoiled boy. You wouldn't last five minutes in the goldfields,' Sadie said scornfully. 'Your mama could tell you some stories of the privations we suffered in Ballarat.'

Max yawned. 'I've heard it all before, Sadie. You can give the flannel to Jimmy, because I'm going outside to sit with Laurence. At least he treats me like a man.'

'You're still a baby to me,' Sadie called after him.

'He's nearly fifteen,' Caroline said, chuckling. 'He's growing up fast.'

Sadie inspected Jimmy's neck, checking behind his ears. 'You'll do,' she said briskly. 'Up to bed with you and no larking around.' She gave him a brief hug and a gentle push towards the door. 'You can go to the baths with your brother tomorrow, if you want to.' She waited until he was out of earshot. 'I'm going to take their smelly clothes to Mrs Spriggs, the laundress, despite the cost.'

Caroline picked up a pile of dirty crockery and placed it on the wooden draining board. 'What happened today has made me think, Sadie. I wasn't going to tell Mama, but she needs to know. It's time she stopped moping about and thought of her children.'

Sadie was silent for a moment and then she nodded. 'You're right. It's not like Essie to give in when things don't go to plan. When I think back to our time in the goldfields, and how she was then, it's as if I'm seeing a different person. She's allowed you to shoulder everything to do with the business and she's left me to look after the boys.'

'You're right, and it's got to stop. I'll go to Bearwood House tomorrow and see if I can talk sense into her. If I can't, I think I know who can.'

Sadie met Caroline's gaze with a knowing grin. 'Raven.'

'Exactly. I saw how she reacted when he took her by surprise, and I think he's still in love with her. If anyone can bring her back to the real world, it will be Raven Dorincourt.' Caroline turned her head to see Max standing in the doorway and for a moment she thought he might have overheard all or part of their conversation, but he was breathing heavily as though he had been running. 'What's the matter?' she asked anxiously.

'What was the name of Raven's ship? Was it the *Bendigo Queen*? I think it's just arrived at the moorings.'

'Yes, I think so.' Caroline hurried to his side. 'Are you sure?'

'Yes, I took a look through the captain's telescope in the front parlour. A lighter is on its way to her, so maybe I'll meet our grandpa at last.'

Chapter Twenty-Three

The sky was livid with streaks of scarlet and purple, and clouds that were tinged a fiery orange by the setting sun. The river seemed to boil with reflected colours like a witch's cauldron as the lighter picked up its passengers and returned to the wharf. Caroline and the boys waited eagerly at the top of the steps with Sadie and Laurence close behind them.

Caroline peered into the gathering dusk, and, as the boat drew near, she could see her grandfather and Falco. She pointed excitedly. 'There you are, Max. Your wish is granted. The older man is our grandfather, and the one with the brass buttons on his jacket is Captain Falco.'

Max turned to her with a broad grin. 'That's what I want to do, Carrie. I want to go to sea like Grandpa and Uncle George, or maybe I'll join the army. I haven't quite decided.'

'I like the water, but I don't want to go to sea,' Jimmy said thoughtfully. 'Maybe I'll be a lighterman so that I can come home every night and sleep in my own bed.'

Caroline ruffled his hair. 'That sounds like a much better idea.'

They waited impatiently and minutes later the lighter came alongside and Jacob Chapman climbed ashore, followed by Falco.

'Grandpa,' Caroline held out her hand. 'Welcome home.'

Jacob enveloped her in a hug. 'I didn't expect to find you waiting for me, duck.' He released her, staring up at Max. 'Am I to assume that this tall fellow is one of my grandsons?'

Max grabbed his grandfather's hand and pumped his arm enthusiastically. 'I'm Max, sir. I'm nearly fifteen.'

'And tall for your age, I think,' Falco said, smiling. 'A handsome fellow, Jacob. You should be proud.'

'Indeed I am.' Jacob patted Max on the shoulder. 'A good, firm handshake, my boy.' He turned his attention to Jimmy, who was standing close to Caroline, apparently overcome by shyness. 'And this must be young James. How d'you do, Jim?'

Jimmy eyed him warily. 'How do you do, sir?'

'Tolerably well, thank you, my boy. And, if I'm not mistaken, that's young Sadie lurking in the background.' He made his way across the cobblestones with a rolling gait, as if he were still on board ship. 'Give an old man a big hug, Sadie, love.'

'You never change, Jacob.' Sadie obliged, but pulled away quickly. 'I want you to meet my intended, Laurence Bromley.' She gave Laurence a gentle shove. 'He knows all about you, Jacob, and you, too, Falco. I'm sure he feels as if he's known you all his life.'

'She's a good girl,' Jacob said, glowering at Laurence. 'I hope you'll look after her as she deserves.'

'I'll do my very best, sir.'

Jacob glanced over his shoulder. 'Where is Essie?'

'Mama is staying with Lady Alice – for the time being, anyway.' Caroline mounted the bottom step, holding out her hand. 'Come inside. I'll tell you everything that's happened since I last saw you, and tomorrow we'll go to Bearwood House.'

Caroline's first mission next morning was to walk to Princes Square. It was still early and, if Mrs Morecroft was surprised to see her, she disguised her feelings with a welcoming smile.

'It's good to see you, miss. Come in, please.'

Caroline stepped over the threshold. 'I know it's early but I wanted to see Miss Maria.'

'She is in the dining room, but the master has already left for the office.' Mrs Morecroft shot her a calculating look. 'You might catch him there should you wish to see him.'

'My business is with Maria.' Caroline could see

that Mrs Morecroft was curious, but some things were best kept within the family circle. 'I didn't have time for breakfast,' she added in an attempt to divert the housekeeper's attention. 'I would love a cup of your excellent coffee.'

Mrs Morecroft beamed at her. 'Of course, miss. I'll bring a fresh pot and some toast.' She bustled off in the direction of the kitchen, leaving Caroline free to enter the dining room where she found Maria finishing off a slice of toast and marmalade.

'Carrie. This is a nice surprise.' Maria dabbed her lips on a napkin. 'What brings you here so early in the morning?'

Caroline pulled up a chair, laid her shawl over the back and sat down. She had rushed here without giving a thought to how she would break the news to an unsuspecting Maria, but now they were face to face she was suddenly at a loss for words. 'I have something to tell you,' she said nervously.

'Is it bad news? Has Elias done something dreadful?'

'As far as I know your mother is safe at the Abbey with Freddie. Jenifry and Dickon have been sent packing and Elias was carted off by the police, but you know this already. Phineas will have told you.'

'Yes, he did, and I was glad.' Maria eyed her steadily. 'But what else is there to say?'

'Grace told us something important, and she wanted me to pass it on to you.'

'She gave you a name?'

'We share the same father.'

Mrs Morecroft chose that moment to breeze into the room with a pot of coffee and a silver rack filled with daintily sliced toast. She placed them on the table. 'Is everything all right, Miss Maria? You're very pale.'

Maria gazed at Caroline, her stunned expression replaced by a dazzling smile. 'We're sisters, Carrie. We really are sisters – I knew it from the start.'

Mrs Morecroft folded her arms, looking from one to the other. 'Might I ask how this came about?'

Maria leaped to her feet and danced Mrs Morecroft around the table. 'I've just found out that Caroline's father is my father, too. Isn't it wonderful?'

'Stop, stop. You're making me dizzy.'

Maria released her with a hug. 'I'm going to Pier House to tell Grandmama that I have a proper family – people who truly care for me.'

'Phineas loves you,' Caroline protested. 'He has stood by you throughout, don't forget that.'

'Yes, of course, but now I can hold my head up. From this moment on, I refuse to allow my grand-mother to make me feel inferior, or to mock me because I didn't know who my father was. My parents might not have been married, but I'm certain they must have loved each other. Don't you think so, Carrie?'

Caroline was torn between loyalty to her father's good name, her mother's tender feelings and the desire to make Maria happy. 'Your mother loved my father, she said so.'

'Are you feeling all right, Miss Maria?' Mrs Morecroft asked anxiously. 'Should I send for the doctor?'

'I've never felt better.' Maria sank down on a chair beside Caroline. 'Will you come to Pier House with me, dear sister?'

Caroline was about to refuse on the grounds that she had promised to take her grandfather to visit Lady Alice's mansion in Piccadilly, but Maria was so excited that she had not the heart to disappoint her. 'Of course I will.'

'But not until you've had breakfast,' Mrs Morecroft said severely. 'I can't abide wasting good food, and you need some meat on your bones, Miss Caroline. You'll forgive me for saying so, but now you're part of the family I consider it my duty to take care of you, too.'

'I'll go upstairs and put on my best gown.' Maria rushed to the door. 'You must do as Moffie says, because we're family.'

'Family!' Clarissa Colville's voice rose to a shriek that made the crystal chandeliers tinkle like fairy bells. She rose to her feet. 'You are the bastard daughter of a slut, Maria Colville.' She turned her malefic gaze on Caroline. 'And your father was a despoiler of an innocent young woman, and you should be ashamed of him.'

'Have you no heart, Grandmama?' Maria cried passionately. 'Have you no feeling at all for the terrible price that my mother paid in order to prevent the family name from being sullied by her disgrace?'

'I have a heart, but it was broken by my elder daughter – shattered into a million tiny shards. Clarice is a weakling and my beloved son Everard died young. Now Phineas spends so little time at home that I hardly see him. I am alone.'

Caroline had been sitting in silence, keeping her temper in check, but this was too much. She stood up, placing her arm around Maria's shoulders. 'You are an evil old woman, Mrs Colville. You are cruel and unfeeling, and, if you are lonely perhaps you should ask yourself why people shun you. Grace is a brave woman and Maria is a loving daughter. I'm proud to call her my sister.'

Mrs Colville's thin lips curled into a snarl. 'You are your father's daughter, Miss Manning. I heard that you've wheedled your way into my grandson's good books, and who could blame a fortune-hunting little trollop for trying to get her hooks into one of the wealthiest men in London?'

'That is a lie,' Caroline snapped. 'Phineas and I have a business relationship and there it ends.'

'I don't believe a word you say.' Mrs Colville leaned towards Caroline, eyes narrowed. 'But your machinations are all in vain. My grandson is going to marry Agatha Booth, the daughter of a Liverpool shipping magnate. It was arranged a long time ago.'

Caroline turned to Maria. 'Is this true?'

'I don't know.'

'I see it matters to you, Miss Manning.' Mrs Colville sat back in her throne-like chair, a smug smile on her thin features.

'Not at all,' Caroline said icily.

'I don't believe it,' Maria protested. 'She's just saying that to upset you, Carrie.'

'Phineas can do as he likes. It has nothing to do with me.'

'You can tell him so, face to face.' Mrs Colville chuckled, but it was a humourless sound as she pointed to the doorway.

Caroline spun round to see Phineas standing behind them. Maria ran to him and seized him by the hand. 'Phin, come and speak to Grandmama. She's been hateful to me and to Caroline.'

'Mrs Morecroft told me that you'd come here, Maria. What did you hope to achieve by telling Grandmama?'

Maria's bottom lip trembled. 'I wanted her to know that I am someone, Phin. I'm not a nameless illegitimate embarrassment. I have a father and now I have a sister, too. I'm part Manning and I'm proud of it.'

'Then I wash my hands of you. You are Maria Manning from now on because you've forfeited the right to use our family name.' Mrs Colville waved her hand towards the door. 'You may leave now and don't bother to come back. I want nothing to do with you, or that trollop I used to call my daughter.

Neither of you will get a penny from me.' She turned to Caroline. 'My grandson will tell you now that he is engaged to Miss Booth from Liverpool. Isn't that so, Phineas?'

'You are a bully, Mrs Colville,' Caroline said angrily. 'I don't care if Phineas is engaged to a royal princess. It's of no concern to me.' She left the room without giving Phineas a chance to respond.

Gilroy was hovering outside the door. 'You got your comeuppance, snooty bitch,' she hissed.

'Mind your own business.' Caroline marched to the front door and opened it, hesitating at the sound of running feet.

'I'm coming with you,' Maria said breathlessly. 'I've left Phin to sort Grandmama out. He's always good with her.'

'He's welcome to her, and Miss Booth from Liverpool.' Caroline stepped outside into the sunshine. Her hands and feet were as cold as if she had been standing on a frozen lake. 'I'm going to find my grandfather and take him to Bearwood House.' She turned to Maria with a sympathetic smile. 'I'd take you, too, but I doubt if my mother will be any more forgiving than Mrs Colville. My papa has a lot to answer for.'

Maria nodded. 'I understand.' She glanced over Caroline's shoulder at the ships making for the docks and a slow smile spread across her pretty face. 'Phin told me that the *Colville Star* was diverted to Calais at the last minute and is due to arrive back in port any day now. Gilbert expects to take over as captain for the next trip.'

'I thought that you were keen on Gilbert.'

'He's my cousin, Carrie. We get on splendidly, but there's nothing romantic in our relationship.'

'Do you still feel the same for Theo?'

'I'm not sure. I've had time to think and I want to see him again. It was a *coup de foudre*, as the French say, and I was scared, but if we both feel the same perhaps we do belong together.'

Caroline leaned over to kiss Maria on the cheek. 'Good luck. I'm entirely on your side.'

'I'll go to the office and wait for Phin. Why don't you come with me?'

'No, I don't think that's a good idea. I must see my mother. There are so many things we need to discuss – the main one being where we'll live. There isn't room for us all at the Captain's House, and Sadie's getting married soon – she'll want a bit of privacy. I'm hoping that Raven might help out until we get the business up and running again.'

'Didn't Phin offer you the house in Great Hermitage Street?'

'He did, but Mama turned it down.'

'You could suggest that she takes a look at the place. She might change her mind.'

Caroline laid her hand on Maria's arm. 'I have to go, but good luck with Theo. I'm sure it will all fall into place when you see him again.'

'You'll be the first to know, dear sister.'

Caroline sighed as she headed towards the wharf and she quickened her pace when she saw a lighter pull away from the *Esther Manning*. She was not looking forward to the interview with her mother, but they needed to have a serious talk about business matters. Everything had been left in limbo since her mother had been told about Maria's parentage.

Jacob glanced around the elegantly furnished drawing room in Bearwood House, twisting his cap in his hands. 'I don't feel comfortable here, girl.'

Falco lounged on one of the damask-covered sofas. 'It suits the gentleman in me, Jacob. I could happily live like this, instead of in a cramped cabin on the *Bendigo Queen*.'

Caroline glanced at the French ormolu clock on the mantelshelf. 'Where is Mama? We've been waiting a good half an hour.'

'Ladies,' Falco said, smiling. 'They like to keep us gentlemen waiting.'

'I'm getting nervous.' Caroline paced the floor, clasping her hands so tightly that her knuckles whitened. 'I'm hoping that Mama will have had second thoughts. She was very upset last time I saw her.'

'Just keep her happy,' Jacob said, sighing. 'At least wait until I've left the country.'

Caroline came to a halt, staring at him. 'Are you returning to Australia so soon?'

'Don't get me wrong, duck. I'm glad to see you

and the boys, but my life is in Bendigo now.'

'He has a lady friend,' Falco said, grinning. 'The widow of a prospector who struck it lucky, as they say.'

'Grandpa! Really?'

'Don't look at me like that, Carrie. I ain't too old for a bit of a cuddle every now and then, and Mrs O'Neill is a fine cook. Her steak and kidney pie is the best I've ever tasted.'

'But she don't know how to cook Italian.' Falco pulled a face. 'I'm thinking of giving up the sea and going back home to Italy.'

Caroline was about to question him when the door opened and Esther glided into the room followed by Cordelia and Raven.

'It's good to see you, dear girl,' Jacob said, holding out his arms.

She gave him a peck on the cheek and stepped away, making a show of arranging her silk skirts as she sat down. 'It's been so many years since we last saw each other, Pa. I don't suppose you've given me a thought in all that time.'

'That's not true, *mia cara*,' Falco said hastily. 'Jacob often speaks of you.'

'Now that the fond greetings are out of the way, I suggest we get down to business,' Raven said, chuckling. 'I expect your grandpa has told you that this will be a short visit, Caroline?'

'He's just mentioned it, but why come all this way for such a brief stay?'

'I think it's very touching,' Cordelia said cheerfully.

'To travel halfway round the world to see loved ones must be the ultimate gallant gesture.'

'You read too many penny dreadfuls, Delia.' Caroline sank down on the sofa next to her mother.

'You are unromantic, Carrie.' Cordelia slipped her hand through the crook of Raven's arm. 'Anyway, I have an announcement to make, since you are gathered here under my parents' roof.' She waved her left hand under Caroline's nose. 'I'm engaged to be married.'

'Is it the old man you mentioned when I last saw you?' Caroline said faintly. 'I didn't think you liked him.'

'Bridechurch proposed last evening, and I accepted.' Cordelia looked up at Raven, her pretty lips making a *moue*. 'My parents will be very happy and I will be a titled lady.'

He patted her hand. 'You are a minx, Cordelia. You remind me of your mother's younger sister.'

'Is that a compliment? I don't quite know how to take you.' Cordelia withdrew her hand, gazing at him with a puzzled frown.

'I believe it is,' Caroline said hastily. 'You were named after her.' She turned to her mother. 'Isn't that so?'

'Cordelia was beautiful, but she died at a tragically young age. But enough of that.' Esther dismissed the subject with a wave of her hand. 'We were talking about the brevity of your stay in London, Raven.'

'Aunt Essie!' Cordelia's large eyes filled with tears. 'Don't you care that I've made a good match?'

'Congratulations, of course, Delia. I'm very happy for you. Now, would you do something for me, please? I want you to find your mama and bring her here. I'm sure she'd like to see my pa and the Captain. They won't be staying long.'

Cordelia rolled her eyes and flounced out of the room.

'That was a bit unkind, Mama,' Caroline said in a whisper. 'You might have pretended to be pleased for her.'

'She's marrying a much older man purely for financial gain and a title. I would never have done that when I was her age.'

Raven's lips quivered and his eyes twinkled. 'Does that mean you're open to offers now, Essie?'

'If that's a proposal it's in very bad taste, Raven. I'm in deep mourning.' A mischievous twinkle lit Esther's hazel eyes.

Caroline stared at her mother, startled by the sudden change in her demeanour. It was becoming clear that there was a deeper understanding between her mother and Raven than she had ever suspected.

'If it were, Essie, I would have chosen my timing better. But I rule nothing out.' Raven laughed and pulled up a chair. 'First of all I want to tell you why I returned to England. I wanted to make certain that everything was running smoothly at the Abbey, and to ensure that Freddie has enough funds for the upkeep of our ancestral home. Who knows? Maybe I'll decide to return for good one day, and face up to my responsibilities at Starcross.'

'All that aside, why did you return to London?' Esther eyed him curiously. 'You never do anything without good reason.'

'I decided to invest some of my money in the stock market, and, of course, I wanted to see you and your family.' His gaze rested for a moment on Caroline, and then he turned back to Esther. 'I didn't know that your business was in trouble, but it seems I've arrived at an opportune moment.'

'Are you going to buy me out, Raven? If so, make me an offer I can't refuse.'

Both Esther and Raven seemed to have forgotten that there were others in the room and Caroline was suddenly anxious. 'Just a minute, Mama. Don't forget that Phineas has offered to take half-shares in the *Esther Manning*.'

'Has he now?' Raven met Caroline's defiant gaze with a smile. 'Would that be because he has a personal interest? After all, you are rivals.'

'He's a very astute businessman.' Caroline found herself defending Phineas, even though she had to agree with Raven. Her recent visit to Pier House and the meeting with Mrs Colville had left her feeling bruised and angry, but Phineas had offered to help them out of an impossible situation.

'Indeed,' Raven said slowly. 'Well, I might consider

making a better offer. I intend to invest sufficient money in the shipping industry.'

'In what way?' Caroline demanded.

'The future will be in freezer ships. The Americans are already doing this using harvested ice, but that doesn't work for long voyages. Experiments are being carried out and I'm betting that refrigeration will come within the next ten years, which will revolutionise world trade in meat and dairy products. I want to be in at the start.'

'Is this just a wild idea or do you really think it will come about?' Esther's voice quivered with excitement.

'It will come,' Raven said seriously. 'There will be a fortune to be made and we will have the opportunity to get in at the very beginning. I have the capital and the energy and drive to make it happen.'

Esther raised her hand to grasp his. 'I believe you,' she breathed.

'Just a moment,' Caroline said slowly. 'Does this mean that you want to take over our business, Lord Dorincourt?'

He turned to her with an amused smile. 'I told you before that titles mean nothing in the goldfields – money is king.'

'But it doesn't buy everything.'

Jacob yawned and stretched. 'It gets you most things, duck. You should listen to Raven. He knows what he's talking about, and I'll bet he could buy your Mr Colville's company lock, stock and barrel.'

Raven laughed. 'It won't come to that, Jacob. But if Essie and Caroline will consider my offer I'll start by finding them a house of their own.'

Caroline jumped to her feet. 'Just a minute, sir. Who do you think you are to come here and take over our lives like this?'

'Sit down and be quiet, Caroline.' Esther's face paled and her voice shook with anger. 'Raven is trying to help us.'

'Yes, girl. You're ma's right,' Jacob added sternly. 'You should be grateful.'

'Grateful?' Caroline had suffered enough that morning, first of all from Mrs Colville and now a man she barely knew was attempting to order their lives. 'You are just as bad, Grandpa. Where were you while I and my brothers were growing up? Where were you when our pa died and we lost our home? The same goes for you, Raven Dorincourt. You might be the wealthiest man in the world but you can't buy us.'

'Caroline!' Esther cried passionately. 'Enough.'

'No, Mama. You, Papa and Uncle George worked together to build up Manning and Chapman. Are you going to allow this man, whom you haven't seen for twenty years, to decide our future? I, for one, will not. I say that half-shares in the company are better than giving it away to someone we don't know.'

Falco cleared his throat noisily. 'That is a little harsh, *mia cara*.'

Caroline rounded on him. 'This has nothing to do with you, Captain.'

'Surely you want what is best for your mother, Caroline?' Raven's voice was icy and his eyes steely blue.

'Why should I listen to you?' Caroline demanded angrily.

Esther rose majestically to her feet. 'Do you really want to learn the truth, Carrie? Are you a woman, or merely a child crying out for attention?'

'After everything I've been through recently, I doubt if there's anything that you could say or do that would shock me.' Caroline dashed angry tears from her eyes.

'What's all this about, Essie?' Jacob asked warily. 'Don't upset things now.'

'This doesn't concern you, Pa.' Esther drew herself up to her full height, holding up a warning hand as Raven opened his mouth to interrupt. 'Caroline needs to hear this. You all need to know the truth, and I'm sick to death of keeping it to myself.'

Chapter Twenty-Four

All eyes were on Esther as she clasped and unclasped her hands in a state of agitation.

'What is it, Essie?' Raven demanded anxiously. 'Are you ill?'

She met his look with a direct gaze. 'You once said that you loved me, Raven. Do you remember?'

His eyes clouded and he nodded wearily. 'Yes. I do, but . . .'

'But you added that you were still in love with Cordelia, your cousin who died in tragic circumstances.'

'I did say that.'

'And I believed you.'

He rose swiftly to his feet and grasped her hands. 'I lived to regret it, Essie. For twenty years I've paid the price for being such a damned fool.'

'I knew it,' Falco said triumphantly. 'I am a true romantic.'

'You never mentioned this to me, Essie.' Jacob stroked his beard, scowling. 'As for you, Raven, I don't approve of your playing fast and loose with my daughter's affections – even if you are a toff.'

'If anything I was too much of a gentleman.' Raven clasped Esther's hand to his chest. 'I should have swept you off your feet there and then, instead of condemning myself to lonely bachelorhood.'

'A very wealthy one,' Falco said softly. 'You made a lot of money, my friend.'

'As I said, I intend to do some good with it now.' Raven gazed into Esther's eyes, seemingly oblivious to those watching. 'Will you allow me to help you? I know that you loved your husband, and I can never take his place, but . . .'

Esther slipped her free arm around his neck and kissed him.

'I think we should leave.' Embarrassed by this outward display of affection, and touched by Raven's obvious devotion to her mother, Caroline jumped to her feet. 'You don't need us here.'

'Wait.' Esther freed herself from Raven's embrace, blushing rosily. 'I didn't mean to give way to my emotions, but I had to know what it felt like to kiss the man who was my first love. He'll be gone again soon . . .' She shot a wary glance in Caroline's direction. 'I'm sorry, my dear. I know this must look strange, and I really did love your father.'

Caroline could feel the tension in the air as everyone waited for her to respond. She was shocked and yet somehow she was not surprised. Deep down, even as a child, she had sensed that her mother was not entirely happy. Perhaps it was the odd wistful look, or the way in which Mama had thrown herself into the business that had made her suspicious, but now it was as if the curtains in a theatre had been drawn back and she was seeing her mother and Raven in their younger days – two star-crossed lovers, kept apart by the ghost of a dead girl.

'I know you did, Mama,' Caroline said softly.

Jacob cleared his throat noisily. 'This is all very well, but what does this mean? You're in mourning, Essie. Why have you spoken out now?'

Falco nudged him in the ribs. 'She thinks he will go away and she will never see him again, you old fool. You English have no romance in your souls.'

'I think Essie and I deserve some privacy,' Raven said sternly. 'We need to talk.'

'Come with me, Jacob.' Falco grabbed him by the arm. 'I should be back on board, anyway. We'll take a cab back to Wapping.'

'Sort yourself out, Essie,' Jacob said as he was propelled towards the doorway by a determined Falco. 'No need to push, Falco. I'm coming. Anyway, I suggest we stop by the pub on the way. I need a stiff drink after this.' His voice faded away as Falco opened the door and shoved him unceremoniously into the hallway.

Caroline was about to follow them when her mother barred her way. 'You do understand, don't you, Carrie? I had to speak out now, before it was too late. I couldn't live another twenty years without knowing how Raven felt.'

'Yes, Mama. I know exactly how you feel.'

'You do?' Esther took a step backwards. 'I thought you would hate me for being disloyal to your father's memory.'

'I could never hate you, Mama. I love you and I know you loved Pa, but nothing will bring him back, and I think he would want you to be happy. I can't tell you what to do, but whatever it is, I'm with you.'

Esther enveloped her in a warm hug. The scent of roses, jasmine, tuberose and vetiver was a fragrance that Caroline remembered from childhood. Every evening, her mother had come to her bedroom to kiss her good night, and the delicate perfume had lingered in the darkness as Caroline had succumbed to sleep.

'Thank you, Carrie,' Esther whispered. 'I love you and your brothers above everything.'

'I know you do, Mama.' Caroline kissed her mother's scented cheek and hurried from the room, closing the door behind her.

'What's going on?'

Caroline found herself face to face with Lady Alice, who seemed intent on entering the drawing room.

'I know this is your house, Aunt Alice, but please don't go in there for a while.'

'Why ever not?' Alice pushed past her and opened the door, but she closed it hastily.

'I see what you mean.'

'You don't seem surprised. Did you know how my mother felt about Raven?'

Alice shrugged. 'I knew that they had feelings for each other, but it was none of my business. Life is very hard in the goldfields, as I expect your mother has told you, and emotions ran high.'

'He said he was in love with your sister.'

'It's true and he was genuinely heartbroken when Cordelia died. I think he was afraid to let himself love again, and that's why he let Essie go. I've always thought he was an idiot, but now, it seems, he's going to stake his claim.'

'You make it sound as if my mother were a piece of lost property.'

'I didn't mean it like that,' Alice said, laughing. 'More importantly, would you mind if they got together at last? I know you worshipped your pa.'

'I did, and I do still, but I want Ma to be happy. She should live her life as she wishes and I'll be happy for her whatever she chooses.'

'You're a good daughter, Carrie. But what about you? I can see that you're worried, so if it isn't your mother's startling revelation, what is it? You can tell me, you know. I can be serious and sensible when I put my mind to it.'

'I'm worried about my mother. She was very upset when she learned about Maria. I suppose she's told you.'

Alice nodded. 'Yes, she has, and I told her to put it out of her mind. Jack was a good and faithful husband. What happened before they were married had nothing to do with Essie.'

'That's what I think, and I know that she was not quite herself, but she said she wanted nothing more to do with the business.'

Alice slipped her hand through the crook of Caroline's arm. 'Come to the Chinese Parlour. We'll have a glass of Madeira wine and you can tell me instead. We'll decide what to do together. After all, I am one of your mother's oldest friends.'

The wine sent a fuzzy glow throughout Caroline's tense body and she began to relax.

'Maybe it will all work out for the best,' Alice said, dabbing her lips on an embroidered napkin. She laid it back on the tray, and picked up her glass, taking a sip with a thoughtful frown. 'Maybe the knowledge that Jack fathered an illegitimate child will help her to come to a decision.'

'What do you mean, Aunt Alice?'

'Raven has made a life for himself in Bendigo, and I'm quite sure he'll want your mother to go with him when he returns.'

'It's all been so sudden. I'm not sure she's in a fit state to make such a decision.'

'Essie will do what she wants, no matter what anyone says. You ought to know that by now.' Alice put her head on one side, eyeing Caroline like an inquisitive robin. 'But what about you, Carrie? What's your position in all this? Your mother tells me that Phineas Colville wants to buy half-shares in the business.'

'He does, and Raven made a half-hearted counter offer.'

'What will you do?' Alice asked gently. 'Assuming that your mother allows you to choose.'

'I don't know, and that's the honest truth. But if I allow Raven to take over I think he would expect me to do exactly as he tells me.'

'And Phineas? Wouldn't he do the same?'

'That would be between him and me.'

Alice sat back in her chair, twirling her glass between her fingers. 'It seems to me that you've already decided.'

'What makes you say that?'

'Just a feeling, Carrie. If you want my advice I think you should speak to Phineas. Tell him about Raven, and see what he says.' Alice looked her up and down, shaking her head.

'What's the matter?' Caroline demanded. 'Why are you looking at me like that?'

'To be perfectly frank, you look a mess. It's quite obvious that you haven't got a lady's maid to care for your clothes, and that dress doesn't suit you at all.'

'This is my best dress – you gave it to me, Aunt.'

'Dear me. What was I thinking of? That shade of mauve does nothing for you, my dear. Come upstairs with me and we'll sort out something much more suitable.'

'I'll be meeting Phineas to discuss business, Aunt Alice,' Caroline said, smiling. 'I doubt if he'll notice what I'm wearing.'

Alice stood up, shaking crumbs from her silk skirts. 'Nonsense. He's a man, isn't he? You must look the part of a successful businesswoman.'

'But Phineas knows my circumstances.'

'Don't argue, Carrie. I have a dressing room filled with gowns that I will probably never wear again. You must allow me to know best.' Alice headed for the door, paused and beckoned. 'Come along, don't dawdle. You're worse than Cordelia.'

Caroline knew when she was beaten and she rose to her feet. 'Coming, Aunt Alice.'

Phineas looked up from his desk and his eyes widened. He smiled, rising to his feet. 'I wasn't expecting to see you today, Caroline.'

She could tell by his expression that her new outfit in pale grey tussore, trimmed with black fringing and draped over a fashionable bustle, had had the desired effect. Aunt Alice had been right, but then she nearly always was. Caroline sat down. 'I'm afraid I was rather abrupt when I saw you in your grandmother's house.'

'My grandmother has that effect on most people. She can be difficult at times.'

'That's one word for it,' Caroline said drily.

'Anyway, I didn't come to talk about Mrs Colville. I came to find out if your offer to buy half-shares in Manning and Chapman still stands.'

'Yes, of course. My solicitor is in the process of drawing up an agreement as we speak. I don't make idle promises.'

'I've received another offer.'

'I assume it must be a better one, or you wouldn't be here.'

She had to curb the desire to tell him everything. It would have been a relief to talk to someone about the sudden change in her circumstances, but she could not bring herself to admit that her recently widowed mother was in love with Raven Dorincourt. Perhaps it would be better for them all to try their luck in Australia and leave London for ever, but even as the thought entered her mind she knew that this was her home. Despite the dirt, the noxious odours and the huge social divide between almost obscene wealth and utter poverty, this was her part of the city, and, above all, she loved the river.

She met his intense gaze with an even look. 'I haven't come to bargain with you. I just wanted to be sure that our agreement still stands.'

'Why wouldn't it?'

She shrugged. 'Your grandmother must have told you that she disapproved of me and my family.'

'Grandmama doesn't run the company. It's sad

to say, but she is an embittered old woman, and, no matter how hard I've tried to persuade her otherwise, she refuses to allow the world into that cold house.'

He looked so sad that Caroline wanted to give him a hug, but she managed to restrain herself. 'I'm sure you've done your best.'

'So we have a deal? I will buy half-shares in your mother's company.'

'That's where there could be a problem,' Caroline said nervously. 'Raven wants to merge Manning and Chapman with his own shipping company, and I think my mother might be inclined to accept.'

'But you don't agree.'

'No, I don't. I think we need to have a measure of independence. After all, she hasn't seen Raven for twenty years and she might find that they've both changed too much to make a life together.' Caroline paused, trying to read his expression, but he was giving nothing away. 'I just wanted you to know that I'll do everything in my power to dissuade her. I think she will listen to me, but I can't be certain of anything at the moment.'

'Then I suggest we carry on as normal until your mother has reached a definite decision.' Phineas reached for a sheaf of papers and spread them out on the desk. 'As we agreed, my men have unloaded the *Esther Manning* and the goods are in your warehouse ready for sale. In your absence I'd already found a new cargo and it's being stowed away as we speak.'

'That's very good of you.' Caroline smothered a sigh of relief. She had given little thought to the business lately and she was genuinely grateful.

'Gilbert will captain her again, if that's agreeable to you.'

'Yes, of course. But what about the *Colville Star*? Maria seemed to think that Gilbert would relieve Theo Barnaby.'

'I don't want Maria to make a terrible mistake, but she's suffered enough and I won't stand in her way if she really loves Barnaby. I've given him a month's leave and another captain is taking the *Colville Star* on her next voyage.'

'You sound like Captain Falco, Raven's right-hand man,' Caroline said, smiling. 'He believes in romance above everything.' She faltered, not knowing what to say next. 'I'd better go now. I've taken up too much of your time and Sadie will be wondering what's happened to me.'

'Your brothers are well?' Phineas was already on his feet. 'They didn't suffer any ill effects from the soaking they got when the boat capsized?'

'I'm sorry,' Caroline said hastily. 'I should have thanked you for coming to our aid, but so much has happened in such a short time.' She eyed him curiously. 'How do you know they were found? I didn't mention it.'

He opened the door for her. 'I went back to see

Munday and told him to keep looking, and to let me know when the boys were safe.'

'You could have come to the Captain's House.'

'I didn't want to intrude, and as it happened I remembered Ted Munday. He was a good seaman and I offered him a job on the *Esther Manning*, but he couldn't accept because of his young daughter.'

Caroline stared at him in surprise. 'That's funny. I did exactly the same, but he refused because of Rose. It must be hard for him bringing up a child on his own.'

'He's a good man. I'm going to see him again in the morning to try to work something out that will suit both of us.'

'Be careful, Phineas,' Caroline said, laughing. 'I might begin to believe you have a heart after all.'

'I learned at a very young age to keep my feelings to myself,' he said with a rueful smile.

'I hope that I can persuade my mother to accept your offer. Now I really must go. Goodbye, Phineas.' She held out her hand and he raised it to his lips.

'That sounds too final. I will see you again very soon. We're business partners, for the time being at least.'

His words echoed in Caroline's head next morning as she made her way home from the market, carrying a basket of groceries. In the last few months her whole world had seemed to be spinning round, quite out of control. As she entered the Captain's House the sound of a familiar voice led her straight to the parlour to find her mother seated on the sofa, talking animatedly to Sadie.

Esther looked up and smiled. 'I thought you would be here, Carrie. I came to see my boys but they've gone to see Munday to thank him for saving them.'

'I'm surprised to see you here, Mama. I thought perhaps you were looking for a house to rent.'

'Raven had business in the city. He brought me in the brougham he's hired for the duration of his stay in London.' Esther leaned back against the shabby cushions and sighed. 'It's so wonderful to have money again. I'd almost forgotten what it was like to have one's own carriage.'

Sadie rose to her feet. 'I'll make a fresh pot of tea. I think you two need to talk.'

Caroline held out her hand in a vague attempt to stop her leaving the room, but Sadie was already out of the door and Caroline found herself alone with her mother.

'Do sit down, darling,' Esther said, smiling. 'Things are looking up for us, Carrie. Isn't it wonderful?'

'Mama, there's something we need to discuss.'

'Oh, don't spoil a lovely day talking about the business, Carrie. Can't it wait?'

'No, Mama. I saw Phineas Colville yesterday afternoon, and he's taken care of everything, but I need to know what your intentions are regarding the business. You said you wanted me to run it for you. Is that so?'

'I've had second thoughts, darling. You know that

450

Raven has offered to put up the money to rescue Manning and Chapman, and so I think we should get a manager in to run things. It's too much for a young woman to do on her own.'

'That's another thing, Mama.' Caroline rose to her feet, taking a turn around the room as she struggled to find the right words. She came to a halt in front of her mother. 'Aunt Alice seems to think that you're in love with Raven, and you certainly gave that impression.'

Esther shrugged and smiled. 'I was at one time. Maybe I still am, a little.'

'But you're in mourning for Pa. You loved him.'

'Yes, it's true. Even though I know he betrayed me, I did love your father, very much.'

'You weren't married to him then,' Caroline said gently. 'It was an act of madness, if you want to call it that. Pa was a good man, but he gave way to temptation.'

'Jack was always so quick to condemn others when they misbehaved. I can hardly believe that he did something so out of character.'

Caroline sighed, saying nothing. She had run out of excuses for her father's behaviour.

'Did he know about the child?' Esther asked after a moment's silence.

'Grace didn't tell anyone. She was separated from her baby at birth, and forced to marry the man her father had chosen for her. She had the most terrible life with him and he almost killed her.'

'For that I am sorry,' Esther said slowly. 'Does Maria know you are related?'

'Yes, she does, and I know it must hurt you, but I'm very happy to call her my sister.'

'You may do as you please, Carrie. Just don't expect me to welcome her into the family.'

'You're taking this more calmly than I expected, Mama.'

'It's been a shock, but in a way it releases me from my own guilt. I was in love with Raven before I met your father, and I realise now that I never stopped loving him. This makes it easier for me to do what is right now.'

'What are you saying?'

Sadie walked into the room at that moment. She put the teapot down on the small table next to the sofa. 'What have I missed?'

'We were talking about Maria, and my feelings.'

'I think you made it quite clear,' Sadie said, sniffing. 'Although I don't blame you. I would probably feel the same.'

'I've come through the worst, but now I feel free to follow my heart. Raven has asked me to marry him.'

Caroline stared at her in astonishment. 'Are you sure about this, Mama?'

Sadie sat down on the nearest chair. 'Well, I'm blowed. What did you say to him, Essie?'

'I haven't given him an answer. I wanted to talk to you about it, Carrie, but this piece of news has changed everything. I feel like my own woman again.'

'So you will accept Raven's proposal?' Carrie asked breathlessly.

'I will,' Esther said, smiling. 'We'll live in Bendigo, and you will come with us, of course, Carrie.'

'You want me to live in Australia?'

Esther threw back her head and laughed, looking so much like her old self that Caroline was astonished at the change in her.

'Of course I do, darling. The boys will love it and they'll have the chance to make their own fortunes in a young country.' Esther reached out to lay her hand on Sadie's arm. 'I'm not ungrateful for what you've done for them, Sadie. And I'll make certain that Raven pays you for their schooling as well as something for their board and keep.'

Sadie tossed her head. 'What I've done for you and the boys has been done out of love, not for money, Esther. You should know that.'

'Sadie's been like a second mother to us all, Mama,' Caroline said hastily. She could see that her mother's careless offer of money had hurt Sadie's feelings. 'I don't know what we would have done without her.'

'Sadie can come too,' Esther said brightly. 'You and Laurence could sell the Captain's House, and then you could use the money to buy a school in Bendigo. It would be wonderful if we all lived there.'

'Hold on a minute, Essie.' Sadie gave her a reproachful look. 'Don't let Raven's title and wealth go to your head. You can't order all our lives just to suit you, and this old house is mine. I'm a Londoner and I don't want to go to the other side of the world again.'

'Suit yourself, Sadie. It was just an idea.' Esther turned to Caroline with a persuasive smile. 'You will come with me, won't you, Carrie? I need my beautiful daughter by my side.'

Carrie shook her head. 'I don't think so, Mama. I have our business here, in London. As I said just now, I was talking to Phineas—'

'I don't want you to have anything to do with the Colvilles,' Esther said firmly. 'Maria may be your half-sister, but there's no need to pander to her whims. The Colvilles are and have always been our rivals, and Raven will do as I ask and buy back our share in Manning and Chapman.'

'Are you planning to dissolve the company?'

'It will merge with Raven's business. Poor George is no longer with us and if I decide to accept Raven's offer, I will no longer be a Manning.'

'I'll still bear the family name,' Caroline protested.

'I doubt if that will be the case for very long, my love. You are a very pretty girl and with a large dowry you will be the catch of the century. Young men will be queuing up to claim you for their own.' Esther shot her a sideways glance. 'And men in Australia far outnumber the women. You'll have the pick of the bunch.'

Caroline and Sadie exchanged baffled glances. 'I think all this has gone to your head, Mama,' Caroline said, rising to her feet. 'Shall I go and collect the boys? I'd like to see them and I'd like to thank Munday, too.'

'I sent a plate of my gingerbread with Max,' Sadie said, smiling. 'That family deserves some help, although there's very little I can do.'

Caroline picked up her shawl and wrapped it around her shoulders. 'Phineas offered Ted Munday work on the *Esther Manning*, but he couldn't take it because he has no one to care for Rose.'

'We'll have to rename the ship as well,' Esther said thoughtfully. 'The *Lady Esther Dorincourt* sounds rather splendid, don't you think?'

'It's considered bad luck to change the name of a vessel,' Sadie snapped. 'I'm losing patience with you, Esther. You're letting this business with Raven go to your head.' She jumped to her feet and followed Caroline from the room, closing the door behind her. 'I love your ma, but she seems to have taken leave of her senses.'

'She's been through a bad time, Sadie. I just want her to be happy.'

'You're a good girl, Carrie, and I'll miss you very much if you decide to go to Australia with your family.'

'You are part of that family, Sadie,' Caroline said, smiling.

'You'll be leaving me one way or another, my

duck. Some lucky man will snap you up sooner or later. Anyway, that's what made me think of little Rose Munday. She reminds me of you when you were that age, and I took a real liking to her. I had a word with Laurence last night, and he said he would be prepared to let her share some of the boys' lessons if we took her in. She could help me in the kitchen, too. I'd teach her to cook and sew, just as if she were my own daughter.'

'And that would leave Ted free to join the crew of the *Esther Manning*. I think that's an excellent idea.'

'I knew you'd approve, and so will Esther when she comes down from that cloud she's floating on. I've never seen her like this, Carrie. It must be true love.' Sadie's laughter was contagious and Caroline was still chuckling as she walked down the steps to the wharf. She paused, shielding her eyes from the sun as she focused on the deck of the *Bendigo Queen*. There was the usual activity of the seamen but no sign of either her grandfather or Falco. Her mother's seemingly outrageous suggestion kept running through her mind and she was slowly coming round to the idea. After all, if her whole family were to migrate to Australia it would seem logical for her to go with them. The alternative would mean living permanently in the attic room at the Captain's House and attempting to run the office virtually single-handed. Phineas might be willing to help, but she could not run to him every time there was a problem, especially if he was about to marry the heiress from Liverpool. She stared into the distance, biting her lip. If she left England she might never see him again, and that thought was unexpectedly disturbing.

She was brought back to earth by the sound of a familiar voice calling her name and she walked to the edge of the wharf.

Phineas smiled up at her. 'Where are you headed, Caroline?'

'I'm going to Chelsea to fetch my brothers.'

'You'll get there faster by boat. Come on board.'

Chapter Twenty-Five

Phineas handed her into the launch. 'I mentioned yesterday that I was going to see Ted Munday.'

'I'd forgotten.'

'Really?'

Caroline sat down, folding her hands primly in her lap. 'I suppose you think I was waiting for you to come along.'

'No such thing. But it's a happy coincidence that I was passing at that particular moment.'

She sighed. 'I'm not in the mood for banter, Phin. I've just had a talk with my mother.'

He returned to the helm and the launch chugged into motion. 'What did she say about my offer, or is she leaving it to you to decide?'

'She wants to merge our company with Raven's and allow him to take over, although that's so unlike her I can't believe she was in earnest.'

'Your mother is a remarkable woman. I remember my father saying so on many occasions when their paths crossed in business.'

'My mother isn't so complimentary about your family,' Caroline said, smiling. 'You are all evil, accordingly to Mama.'

'Do you agree with her?'

'No, of course not, although your grandmother is a difficult woman. I failed miserably there.'

'Grandmama isn't so bad when you get to know her. She has a softer side.'

'She frightens Maria to death.'

'My cousin is too sensitive for her own good. She is also very impressionable.'

'I suppose you're referring to Captain Barnaby. Has he returned to London?'

'I believe he's on his way. Maria was in quite a state when I last saw her. Perhaps you could find time to visit her this afternoon? I think she needs a little sisterly advice.'

'I don't want her to become too dependent on me,' Caroline said slowly.

Phineas had been concentrating on the river ahead, but he turned to look at her, eyebrows raised. 'Why is that?'

'My mother is thinking about migrating to Australia. She wants me to accompany her.'

'Is that what you want?'

'I suppose it makes sense. It would be a big under-taking for me to manage the business on my own, and we have no permanent home in London. I can't impose on Sadie and Laurence for ever.'

'The house in Great Hermitage Street is still at your disposal. You could stay there indefinitely.'

'It's far too big for one person,' Caroline said tactfully, which was true, but being totally dependent upon Phineas Colville might make things difficult when it came to business matters.

'Maria would love to share the house with you.'

'I'm sure she'll be married very soon, and Grace is unlikely to return to London, if Freddie has his way.'

'Is it certain that your mother and brothers will go to Australia?'

'I think her mind is made up, but anything could happen. I shouldn't have mentioned it.'

'You can tell me anything, Caroline. Above all, I want you to trust me.'

'You do?'

'We can't work together if you're suspicious of my motives.'

'Oh! Yes, of course,' Caroline said vaguely. 'I suppose it would suit you best to buy us out completely.'

'From a purely practical point of view, yes, it would. But I'm not in the business of taking over companies simply to further my own ends, and I don't want to see you and your family penniless and struggling to earn a living.'

'So buying half-shares in Manning and Chapman was a charitable act?'

'Don't put words in my mouth, and please stop

making me out to be a villain, when all I'm trying to do is to help you.'

'Thank you, but we don't need your financial backing. My mother wants Raven to buy you out.' Caroline turned her head away, staring ahead with unseeing eyes. The last thing she wanted was to be involved in a pointless discussion about the business over which she had no control. Phineas and Raven would have to argue it out between them, and she wished now that she had hired a cab to take her to Chelsea.

'I've always loved the river,' Phineas said, breaking the silence between them. 'When we were boys, Gil and I used to steal one of the launches and head upriver to do a spot of fishing. Sometimes we simply tied the boat up and went swimming. I can still remember the smell of the willows and fields filled with clover, and the feel of the mud oozing between my toes as I stepped ashore.'

'I've never learned to swim.' Caroline smiled to herself, captured by the vision of the young Colville boys enjoying their rare moments of freedom. This was a side of Phineas that she had not seen until now, and she found it touching.

'But you should. Everyone who lives and works on the water should be taught how to swim.'

'My mother would never have allowed me to paddle, let alone venture deeper into the water.'

'When I have a family my children will be taught how to swim as soon as they can walk.' Phineas steered the launch expertly alongside the small wooden jetty. 'We're here.'

Caroline allowed him to hand her ashore. 'I was forgetting that your grandmother told me of your engagement.' She had not intended to mention it, but she had to know the truth.

He held on to her hand a moment or two longer than was necessary. 'And you believed her?'

'Are you saying that she was lying?'

'Not exactly. She mooted the idea some time ago and I told her that I would prefer to choose my own bride.'

'Oh, I see.' Caroline snatched her hand away. 'Would you pass my basket, please? Sadie has been baking again,' she added smiling.

Munday's tiny boat yard was in an even more sorry state than Caroline remembered. She had not previously had the time or the interest to look around, but even a cursory glance revealed that the boats were patched and old, and it was clear that the business was failing badly.

Rose came running down the path to greet her and she grasped Caroline's hand.

'Your brothers are in the boathouse helping Pa to mend the boat,' Rose said happily. She eyed the basket covered with a clean white cloth. 'I can smell gingerbread.'

'Sadie sent it for you. But you'd better ask your pa if you may have some.'

'Oh, he won't mind,' Rose said, holding out her hand. 'I'll put it on a plate and then you can take your basket back with you.'

Caroline ruffled Rose's copper curls. 'That's very thoughtful of you.' She followed her into the shed.

Ted looked up from his work. 'Good morning to you both.'

'Look what Caroline has brought for us, Pa.' Rose thrust the basket under her father's nose. 'It's ginger-bread. Sadie made it especially for us.'

Jimmy sniffed the air. 'I like gingerbread.'

'Me, too.' Max lifted the corner of the cloth and grinned. 'No one makes it better than Sadie.'

'It's for Rose and her father,' Caroline said, laughing. 'Sadie will make some for you, I'm sure.'

'It was very kind of her, miss.' Ted glanced up at Phineas, eyebrows raised. 'Is anything wrong, sir?'

'A word in private, Ted,' Phineas said, smiling.

Caroline hustled her brothers and Rose outside, but she returned to find Phineas and Ted deep in conversation. 'Excuse me for interrupting, but I just wanted to pass on a message from Sadie. She would love to look after Rose should you decide to return to sea, Ted. She would be treated like a daughter and would share lessons with the boys.'

Ted's eyes misted and he clasped Caroline's hand. 'Thank her for me, miss. I might just take her up on her offer.'

'Then let's get down to business, shall we?' Phineas perched on a stool by the workbench. 'I'll happily take you on as third mate, if you're willing to accept the usual terms. What do you say, Ted?'

'I say, thank you, guvnor. Thanks from the bottom of me heart.' Ted glanced round at the chaotic mess of wood shavings, broken oars and pots of glue. 'This weren't never going to make me rich, and it barely feeds and clothes us, so I'll be more than glad to go back to doing something I know well.'

Caroline left them to talk over the details and went outside to join the children. She was delighted to think that Rose would benefit from Sadie's loving care, but space at the Captain's House was limited and Laurence wanted to take in more boarders. Caroline knew that staying there indefinitely was not an option.

Finding a home of her own was uppermost in her mind during the homeward journey, and she sat in silence while the boys chattered on excitedly about the prospect of migrating to Australia. It appeared to be an open secret and she had been the last to know.

There was little chance to talk to Phineas on the return journey to Wapping, and he dropped them off at the foot of the watermen's stairs. It was all rather hurried as the tide was on the ebb, tugging at the launch in an attempt to carry it downstream, and by the time Caroline reached the top of the wharf the craft was lost to her sight amongst the busy river traffic. So much had been left unsaid and she was left in an odd state of limbo with her future hanging in the balance, over which she had very little control.

She went indoors to pass on Ted's message of thanks to Sadie, who was thrilled at the thought of having a little girl to care for.

'She won't take your place in my heart, Carrie. No one could, but it will make up a bit for the fact that you'll be on the other side of the world in Bendigo.'

'That's not certain,' Caroline said, aghast. 'I haven't decided if I'll go with them or stay in London.'

'I expect Phineas would like you to remain here.'

Caroline sighed. 'All he wants is to get his hands on the company. I thought at first that he was being kind and generous when he offered to buy half-shares, but I'm still having doubts. I have a feeling that he wants to be king of the river.'

'Maybe he wants you to be his queen?'

'Don't be ridiculous,' Caroline said, chuckling. 'He's not the romantic type. I think he takes after his grandmother in his single-minded pursuit of power and wealth.'

'Isn't that a bit unfair, Carrie? You can't know that for sure.'

Caroline glanced at the kitchen clock. 'I really should go to Princes Square and call on Maria. Phineas thinks that she might need my support, but I don't think I ought to get too involved.'

'You're related to the Colvilles, whether you like it or not. Maybe you'd better get used to the idea.'

Caroline shook her head. 'I thought you agreed with my mother when it came to that family.'

'I've changed my mind about Phineas. "Handsome is as handsome does", as the saying goes, and I'll say this for him – he is very good-looking and he's proved that he has a kind heart by the way he's treated Ted and Rose.'

'I suppose you're right, but I have to go now. I'll see you later, Sadie.'

'Maybe your sister can help you to make up your mind,' Sadie called after her. 'I have no doubt that if your ma makes up her mind to accept Raven, she'll insist on taking you with her. You'd better think very carefully before you come to a decision, my love.'

Mrs Morecroft greeted Caroline as if she had not seen her for weeks, and there was no doubting the sincerity of her welcome. She ushered Caroline into the front parlour where Maria was attempting to darn a stocking, which she abandoned as she leaped to her feet and flung her arms around Caroline.

'I was hoping you'd come today. I expect you know that Theo is on his way from Dover, or at least he should be, providing everything went smoothly. I can't wait to see him again, but I must confess that I'm nervous. What will I do if he's had a change of heart?'

Caroline extricated herself from Maria's embrace. 'I don't think he would be coming here if he wasn't desperate to see you again. After all, it wasn't Theo who needed more time to decide.'

'It's true, and I wish I hadn't been such a coward. I knew he was the one for me the moment I saw him, and he said he felt the same. I should have been braver, Carrie. I was such a baby then.'

Caroline stifled a giggle. 'You've been apart for a short time – you can't have matured suddenly.'

'Oh, but I have. I had to think things over and Gilbert has helped me. If Theo's ship hadn't gone to Calais he would have been away for months, maybe a year or more. What would I have done then?'

'Maybe that's something you ought to think about before you commit to marrying a seafarer,' Caroline said gently. 'You would be on your own a great deal of the time.'

'I could sail with him.'

'What would you do when you start a family? You would have to bring them up virtually single-handed.'

'I'd have you to help and advise me,' Maria said shyly.

Caroline sat down beside her. 'Maybe not. My mother is going to marry the man she fell in love with before she met my father.'

Maria dropped her darning and clapped her hands. 'How romantic.'

'Maybe, but it means she will migrate to Australia,

taking my brothers with her. She wants me to go, too.'

'Oh dear.' Maria's lips trembled. 'Will you go with them?'

'I don't know what I'll do, and that's the truth.'

'Phineas would be upset if you went away.'

'Why do you say that?'

'Just a feeling I have.'

'I think you're wrong, Maria. Phineas wants to take over Manning and Chapman, but Raven wants to incorporate what's left of our company with his shipping line. He sees a future in exporting frozen meat from Australia and New Zealand to Europe.'

'The ice would melt.'

'I think they would use a more complicated method than blocks of ice, but that's where he thinks the future lies.'

'And your future, Carrie? What do you want?'

Caroline shook her head. 'I really don't know.'

'Will you wait with me until Theo arrives,' Maria asked urgently. 'I'm really nervous.'

'Of course I will.' Caroline patted her hand. 'I expect he feels the same way as you, so don't worry.'

'He probably thinks I'm a silly woman who doesn't know her own mind.'

'If he did he wouldn't be rushing up to London to see you.'

'You mustn't go to Australia, Carrie. What would I do without you?'

*

Caroline stayed in Princes Square until late afternoon when a hansom cab drew up outside and Maria almost fainted from nervous tension and excitement. Mrs Morecroft showed Barnaby into the parlour, and, having gone through the formal greetings, it became obvious to Caroline that she was not needed. She murmured an excuse and left the room, almost bumping into Mrs Morecroft, who was loitering outside the door.

'I was just coming to see if the captain wanted some refreshments,' Mrs Morecroft said feebly.

'I think food is the last thing on his mind.' Caroline laughed, and patted Mrs Morecroft on the shoulder. 'They only have eyes for each other. I doubt if they've even noticed I'm no longer there.'

Mrs Morecroft made a tut-tutting noise, shaking her head so that her mobcap wobbled from side to side. 'Miss Maria should be chaperoned. It's not proper for her to be on her own with a young man.'

'I have a feeling that they will be officially engaged before dinner is on the table.' Caroline reached for her bonnet and shawl. 'I have to go now, but no doubt I'll be back soon to congratulate the happy couple.'

'Mr Phineas wouldn't approve.'

'Mr Phineas isn't here.' Caroline fastened her bonnet and slipped her shawl around her shoulders. 'I hope I can find a cab quickly.'

'Where shall I say you've gone, should Miss Maria enquire?'

'I'm going to Bearwood House to see my mother. I need to have a serious conversation with her.'

Esther entered the drawing room at Bearwood House, waving her left hand in front of Caroline's face. 'I said "yes".' The diamond ring flashed in the sunlight. 'Raven insisted on rushing out to the jewellers in case I changed my mind. But, of course, I won't. Are you all right about this, sweetheart?'

'Of course I am, Mama.' Caroline gazed at her mother's flushed face and sparkling eyes and realised that she meant what she said. It was wonderful to see her mother happy again. 'I suppose this means that you'll live in Bendigo?'

'Yes, of course. You'll love Australia, Carrie. It was a hard life on the goldfields years ago, but Raven says that Bendigo is a thriving, modern city and he has a magnificent house. Even Pa says it's quite splendid.'

'You're assuming that I'll go with you, Mama. You haven't asked me if that's what I want.'

'You're my daughter, Carrie – of course I want you to come with us. Anyway, you're under age and you can't stay in London on your own.'

'I have Sadie to turn to, should I need anyone.'

'I'm trying to persuade Sadie and Laurence to come with us. Raven has offered to build a school and Laurence would be the headmaster. It means that Jimmy can continue his education and it gives Max time to consider what he wants to do.'

'He says he wants to go to sea or join the army, Mama.'

Esther rolled her eyes. 'He's never been on a long voyage. The journey out will test his resolve, and anyway, there will be plenty of opportunities for him in Raven's business empire.'

'You have it all worked out, haven't you?'

'Raven and I have had long talks about the future. We want to start afresh in Australia, and I have little love for London now.'

'But I have, Mama. This is my home.'

'Nonsense, Carrie. You're a beautiful girl and you'll meet plenty of eligible men in Bendigo. Now, I don't want to hear another word against our plans. It will be a good move for all of us, I promise you.'

'When will you go?'

'We leave in three weeks.' Esther looked up as Raven entered the room. 'I was just telling Carrie about our plans, my love.'

Raven walked over to the sofa and dropped a kiss on Esther's beautifully coiffed hair. 'How do you feel about living in Australia, Carrie?'

She stood up, facing him with a determined toss of her head. 'I don't want to leave London.'

'She'll come round,' Esther said hastily. 'Carrie knows that she can't remain here on her own.'

Raven met Caroline's mutinous look with a sympathetic smile. 'I hope you'll change your mind, Caroline. I know this is all very sudden, and probably difficult for you to comprehend, but I will do everything I can to make the transition easy for you.'

The twinkle in his blue eyes was almost irresistible, and Caroline felt herself warming towards him. She could see why her mother found him so attractive, but she was not going to give in without a fight. 'Thank you, but Phineas Colville has said I may rent the house in Great Hermitage Street and I intend to run my father's business to the best of my ability.'

'But you'll be alone in London,' Esther insisted. 'We're your family, Carrie.'

'I also have a sister,' Caroline said calmly. 'Maria needs me as much as I need her, and I can turn to Phineas for help, should it be necessary.'

Esther shook her head, sighing. 'You are a stubborn girl, Caroline Manning.'

'I wonder who she takes after,' Raven said, chuckling. 'You have three weeks to decide, Carrie. In the meantime I'm taking your mother and the boys down to Devon. We'll be staying with Freddie at Starcross Abbey, so if Maria wants to come with us she would be most welcome.'

'She might want to be with her mother,' Esther added. 'I'll make an effort to be nice, Carrie.'

'I'll mention it to her, although I think that she has other things on her mind at the moment, Mama, but give my love to Grace and Freddie. I hope everything goes well for them.' Caroline rose to her feet. 'I have to go now. Sadie will be wondering what's happened to me.'

Sadie was in the boys' room, throwing items into a large pigskin valise, with a scowl on her face. 'Your mother is impossible at times, Carrie. She expects to click her fingers and have everyone running round after her.'

'Let me help you.' Caroline picked up one of Jimmy's shirts and folded it neatly before adding it to the heap of garments in the case. 'I've just come from Bearwood House. Mama said she'd spoken to you about moving to Australia?'

'She turned up earlier and told me her plans, including taking Laurence and me with them. It was the first I'd heard of it.'

'I said I don't want to go, but Mama pointed out that I'm under age and I have to do what I'm told. It took me by surprise.'

'I must admit I'd never given it a thought, but I'll have to discuss it with Laurence.'

Caroline sat down on the edge of the nearest bed. 'Are you seriously considering such a move?'

'I've been there before, so I know what it's like. I think it could be a good life and Laurence would have a school built for him. That couldn't happen here.'

'Put like that it does sound as though it might be good for you.'

'But you don't want to leave London.' Sadie folded

the last garment and placed it in the already bulging valise. 'Is there a special reason for you to stay here?'

'It's my home, and Maria is here. I've only just found my sister.'

'I don't suppose your decision would have anything to do with Phineas Colville, would it?'

'What makes you say that?'

'He's rich and handsome, the king of the river, as you called him. He's kind to his employees, if you think about what he's doing for Ted and his little girl. Who in their right mind would not fancy a man like that?'

Chapter Twenty-Six

Maria was engaged to be married and Sadie was planning her wedding, which was to take place on the Monday following the last reading of the banns. Then, as if to eclipse Sadie's wedding arrangements, Maria announced that Theo had obtained a Special Licence and they were to be married at the end of that week. This meant that there would be two weddings, separated only by a few days and, as Caroline's help was needed on both occasions, she found herself in a flurry of dressmaking appointments for both brides. These had to be fitted in between other arrangements, including the sending of telegrams to Starcross Abbey to inform the family of the forthcoming nuptials. Fortunately both brides had decided to hold their weddings at the Church of St-George-in-the-East, which made life easier for Caroline, who was also responsible for ordering

flowers from Covent Garden, and finding somewhere
to celebrate the two wedding breakfasts. Added to
all this excitement, Sadie and Laurence had decided
to pack up and start afresh in Bendigo, and, as Ted
was going to be spending as much time in Australia
as he was in London, they had agreed to take Rose
with them.

Caroline concentrated all her efforts on the brides-
to-be, which relieved her of making any decisions
about her own future, although it was becoming
clear that to remain on her own in London would
present problems. She was still living in the Captain's
House but Sadie had put it up for sale, insisting that
they needed the money to keep them going until
Laurence's school in Bendigo was up and running.
Caroline tried every argument she could think of to
make Sadie change her mind, but it was no use. She
came home from market the next day to find a 'For
Sale' sign on the wall – the Captain's House was to
be sold. The old building held so many precious
childhood memories that it hurt Caroline to think
of strangers living in the house her father had occupied in his bachelor days, and where he and her
mother as newlyweds had set up home together. She
had been born in the master bedroom, and her
earliest memories were the sounds and smells of the
river. She remembered cosy teas, seated around a
roaring fire on cold winter days, eating buns baked
by Pa's cook-housekeeper, Mrs Cooper, before she
had retired and gone to live in the country. Then

there were the warm summer evenings when she used to sit on the balcony with her mother, watching the river traffic and listening to the flapping of sails and the soft sucking noise of the water caressing the stony foreshore at low tide. But when they moved to the grand house in Finsbury Circus everything had changed, and although some things were better it had meant seeing less and less of her busy parents, and, despite the luxury, Caroline had often wished herself back in the warm hug of the Captain's House.

Upset and angry, Caroline decided to leave the shopping basket for Sadie to deal with and she left for Princes Square. Mrs Morecroft met her with a worried frown and seemed oblivious to anything other than the forthcoming wedding arrangements.

'I don't see why Mrs Colville couldn't unbend for once and allow Miss Maria to have her wedding breakfast at Pier House,' she said crossly. 'That would have been the kindly thing to do, but she's a hard-hearted woman, even if I say so as shouldn't.'

'I agree,' Caroline said vaguely. 'Is Miss Maria at home?'

'She's in her room.'

Caroline headed for the stairs before Mrs Morecroft had a chance to detain her further, but when she entered the bedroom Maria gave her a searching look.

'What's the matter, Carrie? Are you unwell?'

Caroline shook her head. 'No, it's not that.'

'Then what's wrong?'

'Sadie has put the house up for sale. She won't even consider allowing me to rent it.'

'Would you really stay in the Captain's House on your own? I mean, the ghost of the old man roaming around day and night would frighten me to death.'

'I'm not scared of the captain, and living there would have solved all my problems.' Caroline laid her bonnet and shawl on the bed.

'Well, I'm glad you've come anyway. This gown doesn't fit properly.'

'Let me look. I might be able to do something about it.' Caroline picked up Maria's pincushion and set to work. 'How does that feel?' she asked, taking a step backwards and surveying her handi-work.

Maria peered at her reflection in the fly-spotted cheval mirror. 'That's lovely, Carrie. I didn't dare send it back to Miss Rafferty – the poor creature is so overworked and my wedding dress is absolutely beautiful. She's created the most beautiful gown I've ever seen.'

'And she will be handsomely rewarded,' Caroline said, laughing. 'You're lucky that Phineas is paying for everything.'

'I know. He's so generous, even though he didn't really want me to marry on such a short acquaint-ance, but I'm determined to sail with Theo on his voyage to New Zealand. It will be a wonderful honeymoon.' Maria clasped her hands together, her eyes wide and shining as she gazed into the mirror.

'The *Bendigo Queen* is bound for Australia, so you'll be following the same route as the *Colville Star*, at least part of the way.'

'I'll be able to wave to you when we pass you en route,' Maria said, chuckling. 'We're the faster ship.'

'Don't let Raven hear you saying that.' Caroline placed the pincushion on the dressing table. 'Slip the dress off and I'll take it home with me. I've got some other sewing to do anyway. Sadie wants me to take up the hem on the wedding dress she bought in Oxford Street, so that will keep me busy this evening.'

Maria stepped out of the gown. 'You've been wonderful, Carrie. I don't know how I'd have managed without you.'

'You're my sister. Of course I'll do anything I can for you.' Caroline folded the gown neatly while Maria slipped on her blouse and skirt. 'Have you seen your grandmother and spoken to her about the wedding?'

'No. I didn't have the courage to face her. I asked Phin to do it for me. He's the only one who can handle Grandmama.'

'Grace will be there. At least you'll have your mother to support you, and Freddie, of course.'

'She wrote to me, Carrie. It was such a lovely letter, and she said she'd agreed to marry Freddie as soon as her divorce comes through.' Maria sat down suddenly. 'It's all been such a rush, but I'm glad she'll be looked after, and she did sound happy.'

'Let's go downstairs. I could do with a cup of tea and some of Mrs Morecroft's seed cake. I didn't have time for luncheon and I missed breakfast because there was so much to be done.'

Maria rose slowly to her feet. 'What are you going to do? I know you want to stay in London, but with Sadie leaving as well as your family, I don't see that you have much choice.'

'I don't. It hurts to admit it, and the last thing I wanted to do was to give up my father's business, but Raven has other ideas.' Caroline turned with a start at the sound of someone rapping on the door. She skirted the bed and went to open it to see Mrs Morecroft outside on the landing.

'Mr Phineas is in the parlour, miss. He wants to see you. Says it's important.'

'Thank you, Mrs Morecroft. I'll come right away.' Caroline glanced over her shoulder. 'Did you hear that, Maria?'

'I'll be down as soon as I've tidied myself up. Anyway, it's you he wants to speak to. Perhaps it's good news.'

Phineas was standing by the window with his back to the door, apparently studying the view.

'You wanted to see me?'

He turned his head. 'I went to the Captain's House and Sadie told me you were here.'

Mrs Morecroft appeared in the doorway, breathing heavily as if she had raced down the stairs. 'Would you like some tea, Mr Phineas? Or something to eat?'

'Not for me, Moffie. But what about you, Caroline?'

She shook her head. 'Maybe later.' It was clear that Mrs Morecroft was bursting with curiosity, but Caroline was not going to give her the opportunity to barge in on their conversation, even though she was both hungry and thirsty.

Mrs Morecroft withdrew, closing the door so slowly that Phineas put his fingers to his lips, his eyes twinkling with amusement. He waited until the latch clicked into place. 'I am very fond of Moffie,' he said, laughing, 'but she does think she owns me.'

Caroline sank down on the sofa. 'What did you want to say to me? Don't keep me in suspense.'

'I had a letter from Lord Dorincourt's solicitor this morning. It contains a very generous offer for my share in the *Esther Manning*. I thought you would want to know.'

'I knew that my mother would get round him,' Caroline said, sighing. 'I don't blame her for wanting to start afresh in another country, or for agreeing to marry so soon after my father's death, but I wanted to prove that I could run the business successfully.'

'I told you that you could have tenancy of the house in Great Hermitage Street if you wished to stay in London.'

'I'm under age, Phineas. I have to follow my mother's wishes and she wants me to go with them.'

'And what do you want?'

'Perhaps I should wait until I'm twenty-one and I've seen a bit more of the world before I decide what I really want out of life. Everything has been so confused since Papa died and it's been one thing on top of another, and now Sadie has put the Captain's House up for sale, that's my last connection severed. I really don't have a choice other than to follow my family to the other side of the world.' Caroline rose hastily to her feet. Stating a simple fact had brought her close to tears and she did not want to embarrass herself or Phineas by breaking down and crying. 'I'll go and give Mrs Morecroft a hand with the tea. She never takes no for an answer.' She hurried from the room, almost bumping into Maria.

'What's the matter?' Maria demanded. 'What has Phin been saying to upset you?'

'Nothing,' Caroline said quickly. 'I was going to fetch the tea to save Mrs Morecroft the trouble. Go and talk to him, Maria. I won't be long.'

In the kitchen Mrs Morecroft appeared to have dropped the milk jug and was attempting to pick up the shards of china without trailing her long skirt in the debris. She looked up, red-faced and perspiring. 'I'm sorry, Miss Caroline. So clumsy of me.'

'Let me help.' Caroline bent down and retrieved the last tiny pieces, leaving Mrs Morecroft to fetch a mop. 'There you are – no harm done, apart from a broken jug, and I'm sure Mr Phineas can afford to buy a new one.'

If Caroline did not know her better, she would have thought that Mrs Morecroft giggled, although she turned it into a cough. 'You are a one, Miss Caroline. I'll miss you when you're gone to the other side of the world. So will Mr Phineas, I've no doubt.'

'I'm sure he'll be far too busy to even give it a thought.' Caroline took another jug from the china cupboard and filled it from a pitcher of milk. 'I'll take the tray into the parlour. I think you need to sit down for a while.'

'Thank you, maybe I will.'

Caroline stopped outside the parlour door, painting a smile on her face, which turned into a genuine chuckle as the old saying about there being no use in crying over spilled milk came to mind. She would miss London and she would miss her beloved river, but most of all she would miss . . .

She pushed the thought to the back of her mind, balanced the tray on one arm and opened the door. 'Sorry for the delay,' she said brightly. 'There was a small accident in the kitchen, but no one is hurt other than a china milk jug, which I'm afraid is no more.'

Maria jumped up to help clear a small tea table. 'I've told Phin how much you've done for me, Carrie. I'll really miss you when you go to Australia.'

Phineas gave Caroline a searching look. 'Are you set on going?'

She met his gaze with a determined lift of her

chin. 'My family means everything to me, Phin. I can't go against my mother in this.' She held her breath, waiting for his response, willing him to say something that would make it possible for her to follow her heart and not her head. There was a moment of silence that seemed to suck the air from her lungs.

'Oh, bother!' Maria cried as the lid of the teapot fell into the cup she had been filling, smashing it to smithereens. 'How clumsy of me.' She turned to Caroline with a stricken look. 'That's the second mishap this afternoon – there's bound to be a third.'

'Superstitious nonsense,' Phineas said, chuckling.

'I'll go and get a cloth.' Caroline sighed. The moment had gone and she would never know what Phineas had been about to say.

She returned moments later to find Phineas on his feet. 'Going so soon?'

He nodded. 'I've just remembered a very important appointment. Would you tell Moffie I won't be in for dinner this evening?' He glanced over his shoulder. 'I'll see you tomorrow, Maria. Don't wait up for me.' He hurried from the room.

'I suppose that saves me getting another cup,' Maria said, shrugging. 'I can't think where he could be going in such a rush – unless he has a lady friend we don't know about. What do you think to that, Carrie?'

'Ouch!' Caroline yelped with pain as a fragment of china sliced into her finger. She stared at the scarlet stain mingling with the spilled tea, and she realised that she was crying.

She did not see Phineas again until the day of Sadie and Laurence's wedding. The family had travelled up from Devonshire, including Freddie and Grace, and they were joined by Falco and Jacob at the church. Maria and Mrs Morecroft were already there, escorted by Captain Barnaby. Caroline watched him covertly as he introduced himself to his future in-laws, and she was impressed by the way he dealt with what might have been a tricky situation, and her fears that Grace might disapprove of him proved groundless. Maria's mother seemed to be as charmed by him as Maria had been at their first meeting, and it boded well for the future. Caroline tried not to dwell on the fact that she would be on the other side of the world, unable to share their joys and sorrows, but she forced such thoughts to the back of her mind and did her best to concentrate on the present.

Lady Alice arrived late, as usual, accompanied by Cordelia, who was wearing her diamond engagement ring, which was large enough to be classified as vulgar, although she was obviously enjoying the sensation it caused. Sir Henry had been called away on business, but Caroline had seen the cheque he had sent as a wedding present, and whatever anyone said about Sir Henry Bearwood, he could never be accused of being mean.

Raven had agreed to give Sadie away and Rosie was her only attendant as they entered the church and processed up the aisle to the accompaniment of an aged musician, who hit so many wrong notes on the organ that he seemed to be fighting with the mighty instrument. The vicar had told Caroline in a hushed voice that the resident organist had been taken ill at the last minute, and Mr Wilby had stepped in to replace him. As she listened to the discordant thundering on the keys Caroline suspected that Mr Wilby only knew one tune despite his attempts to cover up his lack of expertise by playing as loudly as was possible. The glass in the church windows rattled and Caroline could feel the vibrations running along the wooden pew as she took her seat next to Phineas. Standing so close to him she found it hard to concentrate on the words in the hymnal, most of which she knew by heart anyway, but somehow memory seemed to fail her, and it was not simply due to the noisy accompaniment. At last the vicar pronounced the happy couple man and wife and they disappeared into the vestry to sign the register before processing down the aisle and out into the late summer sunshine.

The party then made its way to the Prospect of Whitby where Caroline had hired a private room for the wedding breakfast. The food was plain, but excellent, and there was enough wine and champagne to keep everyone happy. Caroline was amused to see Max slightly tipsy, while Jimmy and Rose sat next to each other, whispering and giggling until a withering glance from Esther subdued them. Speeches were kept to a minimum and toasts were drunk to the happy couple. The cake was brought in and cut with due ceremony, and then Falco surprised those who did not know him by rising to his feet and singing, accompanied by a fiddler, who had been hired to entertain them. If the musician was surprised to end up as an accompanist to a slightly drunken Italian sea captain, he was too polite to refuse, or, perhaps it was the large tip that Raven had given him, unseen by anyone except Caroline.

The bride and groom left to spend their wedding night at Brown's Hotel in Albemarle Street, a wedding present from Raven and Esther, and the party went on until well into the evening. The tables had been pushed back and the fiddler struck up a jig. Maria and Theo took the floor and couples joined them. Caroline saw Phineas coming towards her but he was accosted by Cordelia, who pouted prettily and fluttered her long lashes, making it impossible for him to refuse to partner her. Caroline stepped outside onto the terrace. It was getting dark and gaslights were reflecting on the water. Lanterns on the small boats bobbed up and down as if floating independently above the surface of the oily black water as the Thames wound its way down to the sea. A cool breeze fanned Caroline's hot cheeks and she was about to return to the party when Phineas joined her.

'I saw you slip outside,' he said, smiling. 'I was going to claim you for a dance.'

'But Cordelia waylaid you. Yes, I saw.'

He held out his arms as the music of a waltz wafted out of the open door. 'May I?'

She took a step towards him but came to a sudden halt as her mother appeared in the doorway. 'Caroline, darling. Come here for a moment, please.'

The moment was shattered and Caroline murmured an apology. 'My mother wants me.'

'Of course.' Phineas stood aside.

'I'm sorry, Carrie,' Esther said, smiling. 'I didn't mean to interrupt, but Raven and I are just leaving with Alice and Cordelia, and I think you'd better take the children home.'

With a last backward glance over her shoulder, Caroline followed her mother into the crowded room. A cloud of cigar smoke greeted them and the fiddler was being plied with food and drink. The babble of conversation was punctuated by gusts of laughter. Max was half asleep with a glass of wine clutched in his hand, while Rose and Jimmy were dancing a jig. The fiddler had wandered into the taproom but strains of his lively music floated through the open door. Jacob and Falco were singing a duet despite Freddie's attempts to persuade them to leave, although they quietened down instantly when Grace spoke to them, and slunk off arm in arm.

Grace turned to Caroline. 'Maria and Barnaby

are waiting for us in a cab. Can you manage the children on your own, Carrie?'

Max opened his eyes, giving them a blurry smile. 'I'm fine, thank you, ma'am.'

'Of course you are,' Caroline said briskly. 'Get up, Max. We're going home.'

'I don't feel well, Carrie,' he whispered, clutching his stomach.

'Oh, dear. He's going to be sick,' Grace said weakly. 'I really have to go, dear.'

'Don't worry, I'll deal with this.' Phineas had come in from the terrace unnoticed. He lifted Max from the settle, looped the boy's arm around his shoulder and propelled him out through the open door.

'I can see you're in safe hands.' Grace kissed Caroline on the cheek. 'Coming, Freddie.'

Caroline turned to the children, who were spinning round like Dervishes. She clapped her hands. 'That's enough, you two. We're going home.'

'Max has puked over the railings,' Jimmy said, grinning.

'He's drunk,' Rose added triumphantly. 'He'll be sorry in the morning. That's what my pa says.'

Phineas helped a pale-faced Max into the room. 'He'll be fine,' he said cheerfully. 'Let's get him home. You as well, young lady,' he added, nodding to Rose. 'And you, young James, and if I hear that you've played Caroline up tonight you'll be in trouble.'

'Thank you, Phin. I can manage.' Caroline seized Jimmy by the hand and made a grab for Rose, who was still twirling madly. 'Calm down, or you'll be the next one taken ill.'

'My carriage is outside,' Phineas said calmly. 'I'll take you home.'

Caroline slipped her shawl around her shoulders. 'It's not very far to the Captain's House. The fresh air will do Max good.'

'It's not safe for you to walk along the wharf at this time of night. I'll see you to the door.'

Caroline was too tired to argue and Max was too tall for her to manage on her own. 'Thank you, Phin.'

'Can't we stay and listen to the fiddler?' Jimmy asked, tugging at Caroline's hand.

Phineas fixed him with a cold stare. 'If you play your sister up tonight you know what will happen.'

Jimmy stared at him suspiciously. 'What? I ain't afraid.'

'The old captain will be angry,' Phineas said in a low voice. 'You had better beware.'

'I'll be good,' Rose promised, crossing her heart. 'Can I sleep with you, Carrie?'

'Of course.' Caroline met Phineas' amused gaze with a grateful smile. 'Let's go home. Don't forget that we've got another wedding on Friday.'

Maria's wedding was much quieter by comparison. Theo had no family, having been brought up in an orphanage, and Mrs Colville had refused to attend. Cordelia's fiancé had invited the Bearwoods to his country estate for the grouse shoot, and Jacob and Falco were fully occupied getting the *Bendigo Queen* loaded and ready to sail. In the end it was just those closest to Maria who waited at the church for her arrival. Nanny Robbins and Mrs Morecroft sat side by side, chatting in low tones as if they had known each other for years, and Sadie, Laurence and Rose occupied the pew behind Esther, Raven, Grace and Freddie, while Caroline sat with her brothers on the groom's side. Theo had chosen Gilbert as his best man and they waited at the altar steps for Maria to enter the church on Phineas' arm.

Caroline held her breath as the organist struck up the Bridal Chorus, but she need not have worried. The playing was faultless and it was obvious that Mr Wilby's services were no longer needed. She glanced over her shoulder and her eyes filled with tears at the sight of Maria, looking ethereally beautiful in her white silk gown trimmed with Chantilly lace as she processed up the aisle. Caroline glanced at her mother, who was staring straight ahead, her hand clutching Raven's as if for support. Caroline could only imagine how her mother must be feeling at this moment, but Grace was obviously deeply moved. Her handkerchief fluttered in front of her face like a ghostly white butterfly and Freddie slipped his arm around her shoulders.

His part in the ceremony done, Phineas came to sit beside Caroline as if it were the most natural thing in the world. He gave her a sideways glance and an encouraging smile, and she experienced a sudden and almost overwhelming sense that all would be well, and an easing of the tension under which she had been labouring since Sadie announced the sale of her old home. The rest of the ceremony passed off without a hitch, although when the vicar asked if anyone objected to the marriage Caroline half expected Mrs Colville to make a dramatic appearance. Thankfully the moment passed and the couple were united as man and wife.

Outside the church Maria rushed over to Caroline and hugged her. 'Thank you for everything you've done for me, Carrie. If you hadn't come to work for Grandmama we might never have met, and I wouldn't know that I have a sister.'

'I wish I could stay in London,' Caroline said tearfully.

'You know that's not possible, Carrie.' Esther moved closer, taking Caroline's hand. 'We've been through all this, darling. You're my daughter and I love you, so naturally I want you to come with us. There's no question of you staying on your own in London, none at all.'

'Don't you think that's up to Caroline?' Phineas had come up behind them and they turned to stare at him.

Esther recoiled angrily. 'I'm sorry, Mr Colville, but what has this to do with you? It's family business.'

'And whether you like it or not I am connected

to your family, even if it's only in a roundabout way,' Phineas said evenly.

'What my late husband did before our marriage is no concern of mine.'

'Really, Mama,' Caroline protested, glancing anxiously at Maria. 'This isn't the time or place to bring this up.'

'I agree entirely,' Esther said firmly. She fixed Maria with an attempt at a smile. 'I do wish you well, Maria. I know you are the innocent party in all this, and I'm sorry if I've appeared insensitive to your feelings, but you must understand how I feel.'

Maria reached out to clasp Esther's hands. 'I do, Mrs Manning. And I'm truly sorry for any hurt you've suffered on my account.'

Esther glanced at Raven, who was standing a few paces away, deep in conversation with Barnaby. 'You'll excuse us if we don't attend your wedding breakfast, Maria, but Raven and I have an important appointment.'

'What is more important than this, Mama?' Caroline demanded crossly.

Esther turned to Raven, beckoning. 'We decided to get married quietly, because I'm officially still in mourning, but we wanted to do it here, in London, before we sail.'

'But this is Maria's day, Mama.'

'I know, which is why we didn't tell you before. Go with your sister, Carrie. I really don't mind.'

Caroline looked to Raven for confirmation and he nodded.

'It's best this way, Carrie. We don't want any fuss.' He proffered his arm to Esther. 'Are you ready, my love?'

She slipped her hand through the crook of his arm. 'I am.'

'You're getting married here? And you didn't think to tell me?'

'We thought it would save any embarrassment,' Esther said anxiously. 'I wish I hadn't said anything now, but you can see that this talk of splitting up our family has hurt me.'

Caroline threw up her hands. 'This is madness. I can't cope with this, Mama.' She walked away, heading blindly into the churchyard.

'Caroline, stop.'

She came to a halt, turning to Phineas with an angry frown. 'Did you know about any of this?'

'No. On my honour it was just as much a surprise to me as it has been for you.'

'I love my mother,' Caroline said slowly. 'But this was supposed to be Maria's day, and I don't want to go to Bendigo. My life is here, in London, or it would be if it hadn't been made impossible.'

Phineas took her hand in his. 'Your mother thinks she's doing the right thing, but you don't have to go with them if you don't want to.'

'I can't run the company on my own. I was stupid to think I could.'

494

'I've offered you a partnership.'

'But you sold out to Raven. He told me so.'

'I sold my share in the *Esther Manning* to him, it's true, but I've offered Sadie the asking price for the Captain's House, because I know you love it.'

'So what are you saying?' Caroline looked him in the eye and suddenly she was as breathless as if she had just run a mile.

'I've been trying to find a way of telling you this for weeks.' He raised her hand to his lips, holding her gaze with a tender smile. 'I want you to be my partner in everything, Carrie. I want you to stay here with me.'

'You want me to be your business partner?' she said warily.

'I love you, Carrie. I'm asking you to marry me.'

'Your grandmother would never agree.'

'My grandmother will have to get used to it.'

The ground seemed to be spinning beneath her feet. She could hear her mother calling to her and she was vaguely aware of the wedding party re-entering the church. Max and Jimmy were shouting her name, but nothing seemed real.

Phineas swept her into his arms, kissing her until she responded with equal passion.

'I knew it,' he whispered, covering her face with kisses. 'Say it, Carrie. Say that you love me.'

'I do,' she said dazedly. 'I suppose I knew it from the start.'

'We've wasted so much time, my darling girl. I'm

asking you again,' he released her and went down on one knee in the dusty churchyard. 'Will you do me the honour of becoming my wife?'

'Yes, I'll marry you, Phin.'

He rose to his feet and kissed her again. 'I think we'd better join the others. You don't want to miss your mother's wedding, do you?'

She clutched his arm, leaning against him. 'I suppose I could stop the proceedings and object to the wedding.'

'You wouldn't do that.'

'No, of course not, but it would serve my mother right for trying to rule my life. I belong here, with you.'

'That's what I wanted to hear. You'll never regret your decision, my darling. We'll build Colville Shipping together and you'll be able to visit your family whenever you wish. You'll be queen of the river and you're already queen of my heart.'

Read on for an exclusive extract of the
final book in the series

The Christmas Rose

Chapter One

Royal Victoria Dock, London, October 1882

Rose leaned over the railings, peering into the fog that had crept up on the steamship as it entered the Thames Estuary. It was even thicker when they arrived in Bow Creek, and as the vessel slid gracefully into the dock they were engulfed in a peasouper, making it impossible to distinguish the faces of the individuals waiting to greet the passengers.

'Is he there, love?'

Rose turned to give the small woman a weary smile. 'I can't see very far, Mrs Parker. But I'd know him anywhere, and I can't spot anyone who looks remotely like him.'

Adele Parker laid her gloved hand on Rose's arm. 'Don't worry, dear. I'm sure your young man is there somewhere.'

'Max promised to meet me.' Rose could not quite keep a note of desperation from her voice. 'We planned it all so carefully.'

'Then I'm sure he'll be here soon. It'll take a while for the crew to put the gangplank in place and unload the luggage.' Adele wrapped her shawl more tightly around her plump body. 'It's so cold and damp. We've been away for five years and I've almost forgotten what the English winter is like.'

'I was only nine when we left for Australia,' Rose said, sighing. 'But there's nothing to keep me in Bendigo now.'

Adele gave her a searching look. 'How old are you, Rose?'

'I'm eighteen, ma'am.'

'I do worry about you, dear. I sympathise with you and your young man, but you do know you can't marry without your parents' consent, don't you?'

'I'm an orphan. Ma died when I was very young and Pa was killed in a mining accident a year ago. He gave up the sea because he thought he could make more money in a gold mine. It was a bad move.'

'You didn't tell me that, you poor dear.' Adela gave her a hug. 'You're a brave girl, Rose. I wish you all the luck in the world.'

'Thank you.' Rose returned the embrace. Adele had shown her nothing but kindness during their time at sea, and, despite the difference in their ages, they had become good friends.

'We'll be staying with my mother-in-law, who lives in Elder Street, Spitalfields,' Adele said gently. 'I forget the number of the house but it has a black door with a lion's head knocker. Ma-in-law is very proud of that.'

Rose smiled vaguely. 'That sounds nice.'

'If you need anything just come and see me.' Adele craned her neck at the sound of the movement from a lower deck. 'The gangplank is in place. I must find Mr Parker.' She started off in the direction of the companionway, but she hesitated, glancing over her shoulder. 'We'll be catching the next train from Canning Town. You're more than welcome to travel with us if your young man doesn't put in an appearance.'

Rose was acutely conscious of the need to watch the pennies, but she managed a smile. 'Thank you, but Max will be here. He promised.' She strained her eyes as she peered into the thick curtain of fog, hoping to catch sight of the man for whom she had given up her home and her adopted family. A feeling of near-panic made her clutch the wet railing until her knuckles turned white. If Max, for whatever reason, could not meet her, she would be in a terrible fix. The possibility had not occurred to her during the voyage from the Australian port of Geelong to London. She had lived in a haze of romantic visions of what her life would be like as the wife of a dashing cavalry officer, but something as simple as a London particular was in danger of shattering her hopes and dreams.

Sadie, the woman who had become a second mother to Rose, had uttered dire warnings and these came flooding back to her now. Perhaps she ought to have listened, but she had ignored them and had allowed Max to purchase a berth for her on the *Bendigo Queen*. Sadie had been quick to notice the deepening affection between Rose and Max. He was five years Rose's senior and she had been slightly in awe of him when they first arrived in the mining town of Bendigo, and it was Jimmy, his younger brother, who had been her particular friend. Two years later Max had been sent back to England to attend Sandhurst Military Academy, and it was on his first trip home that they had met again. Rose closed her eyes, conjuring up a vision of Max, his gleaming blond hair waved back from a high forehead, his classic features, piercing blue eyes, and his newly acquired military bearing. It had been love at first sight when she had met him then, even though they had known each other since childhood, and, to her surprise, the feeling was mutual. What a handsome young man from a wealthy family had seen in a skinny green-eyed girl with wildly curling copper hair she had never been able to fathom, but Max loved her and she loved him. Unfortunately his mother and Raven Dorincourt, his aristocratic stepfather, disapproved, and Max was promptly packed off to England to finish his training, but his parents could not prevent them from corresponding. Rose had a bundle of Max's letters tied with pink ribbon, stowed carefully in her luggage. Reading them at night before she went to sleep had kept her going through the long days of their separation and during the voyage home to England.

'Rose, dear. We're leaving now. Are you coming with us?'

Adele's voice brought Rose sharply to her senses, and she was left facing a wall of thick pea-green fog and an uncertain future. There was nothing she could do other than to follow Mr and Mrs Parker down the companionway to the lower deck. Everyone was pushing and jostling for position as the passengers disembarked. The level of sound from the dock grew in intensity as people called out to each other, whistling and shouting to attract the attention of those who had come to meet and greet them.

Festus Parker disappeared into the crowd, telling his wife to stay where she was while he went to retrieve their baggage. Rose could only stand there, damp, cold and increasingly panic stricken as she searched the crowd for the young cavalry officer who had stolen her heart in such a dramatic way.

Adele tugged at her sleeve. 'Maybe he was delayed by the fog. Come with us, dear. We're going to stay in Elder Street until we get out next posting.'

'Thank you, but I'll wait. Max will be here – he promised.' Rose's voice caught on a barely suppressed sob, but she held back the tears of desperation that threatened to overwhelm her as she struggled against a wave of homesickness. Sadie would tell her to keep a stiff upper lip, whatever that meant, but Rose was beginning to wish she had never left the noisy, often chaotic house attached to the school in Bendigo.

Adele fumbled in her reticule and brought out a pencil and a religious tract. She tore it in half, pulling a face as she did so. 'I'm sure the Good Lord will forgive me, but this is the only piece of paper I have.' She wrote something and passed it to Rose. 'This is where we'll be for the foreseeable future. If you get into difficulties, you know where to find us.'

Rose put it in her pocket. 'Thank you, Mrs Parker. I won't forget your kindness to me during our voyage.'

'Nonsense, Rose. You've been a delight and you helped to alleviate the boredom of the long days at sea.' Adele moved aside as her husband emerged from the gloom, carrying a large valise and Rose's carpet bag.

'You travelled light, Rosie,' Festus said cheerfully. 'I wish my wife could limit herself to so little in the way of clothing.'

Adele beamed at him. 'It's my one weakness. I know it is pure vanity, and I should try to overcome my love of pretty gowns and lovely colours, but we are as the Good Lord made us.'

'I'm sure you make up for it in kindness, Mrs Parker.' Rose leaned over to kiss Adele's round cheek.

'You can still change your mind and come with us, Rose.'

'Thank you for your offer, but I will wait here for Max. He'll come, I know he will.'

Adele and her husband exchanged worried glances. 'Have you anywhere to stay in London?' Festus asked abruptly. 'Has your young man found suitable accommodation for you?'

'Oh, yes,' Rose said airily. 'We'll be lodging at the Captain's House in Wapping. I lived there for a while when I was a child.'

Festus nodded gravely. 'Do you know how to get there, should your friend be delayed by the fog?'

'Max gave me instructions, so you really need not worry. But I am grateful for your concern, really I am.' Rose stood her ground, despite the Parkers' continued questioning. She knew that their concern for her was genuine, but she trusted Max. She had given up everything to be with him, and she was certain that he would not let her down.

Discover more from
Dilly Court

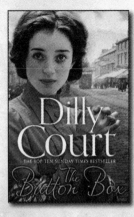

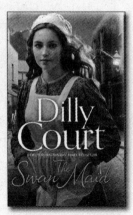

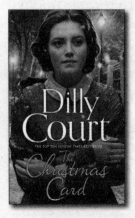

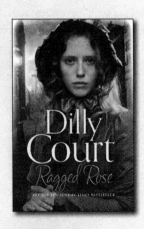

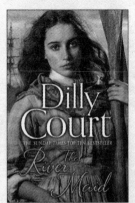